THE
BLACKBIRDS

Also by Eric Jerome Dickey

Naughtier Than Nice
One Night
A Wanted Woman
Decadence
An Accidental Affair
Tempted by Trouble
Resurrecting Midnight (Gideon series)
Dying for Revenge (Gideon series)
Pleasure
Waking with Enemies (Gideon series)
Sleeping with Strangers (Gideon series)
Chasing Destiny
Genevieve
Drive Me Crazy
Naughty or Nice
The Other Woman
Thieves' Paradise
Between Lovers
Liar's Game
Cheaters
Milk in My Coffee
Friends and Lovers
Sister, Sister

Anthologies
Voices from the Other Side: Dark Dreams II
Gumbo: A Celebration of African American Writing
Mothers & Sons
Got to Be Real
River Crossings: Voices of the Diaspora
Griots Beneath the Baobab: Tales from Los Angeles
Black Silk: A Collection of African American Erotica

Movie—Original Story
Cappuccino

Graphic Novels
Storm (six-issue miniseries, Marvel Entertainment)

ERIC JEROME DICKEY

THE BLACKBIRDS

DUTTON
— est. 1852 —

DUTTON
—• est. 1852 •—
An imprint of Penguin Random House LLC
375 Hudson Street
New York, New York 10014

Copyright © 2016 by Eric Jerome Dickey

LIBRARY OF CONGRESS CATALOGING-IN-PUBLICATION DATA
Names: Dickey, Eric Jerome, author.
Title: The blackbirds / Eric Jerome Dickey.
Description: First edition. | New York : Dutton, [2016]
Identifiers: LCCN 2015045477 | ISBN 9781101984109 (hardcover)
Subjects: LCSH: Female friendship—Fiction. | African American
women—Fiction. | Man-woman relationships—Fiction. | BISAC: FICTION /
Romance / Contemporary. | FICTION / Romance / Adult. | FICTION / Urban
Life. | GSAFD: Erotic fiction. | Love stories
Classification: LCC PS3554.I319 B58 2016 | DDC 813/.54—dc23 LC record available at
http://lccn.loc.gov/2015045477

Printed in the United States of America
1 3 5 7 9 10 8 6 4 2

BOOK DESIGN BY LEONARD TELESCA

For Koko and Erin

"You are terrifying and strange and beautiful. Something not everyone knows how to love."

—Warsan Shire, "For Women Who Are 'Difficult' to Love"

"Once you had put the pieces back together, even though you may look intact, you were never quite the same as you'd been before the fall."

—Jodi Picoult

"Those of us who color outside of the lines get called sluts. And that word is meant to keep us in line."

—Jaclyn Friedman

"Depression is not a side effect of cancer. Depression is a side effect of dying."

—John Green, *The Fault in Our Stars*

INDIGO'S BIRTHDAY MONTH

Chapter 1

The door to the airplane opened, and the four women were so terrified they were unable to cry out. The fear was tangible. Legs were weak. Palms sweated. Hands trembled.

They were ten thousand feet in the air.

A second later, Kwanzaa Browne took a deep breath and yelled into the wind.

Destiny Jones and Ericka Stockwell looked down at the earth and screamed.

Indigo Abdulrahaman had done this several times, and still she had been anxious and quiet on the two-hour ride north. Her palms had been sweaty all morning, same as Ericka's.

Kwanzaa shouted, "For the last time, *black people don't jump out of planes.*"

Ericka retorted, "Kwanzaa, I love you, but I will kick your rotund ass out of this plane."

Indigo snapped, "You're jumping, Kwanzaa. This is one of my birthday requests."

Destiny laughed another nervous laugh. "Must we argue about every damn thing?"

Destiny, Indigo, Ericka, and Kwanzaa were attached to their instructors with harnesses. They were moved toward the door, and one after another they rolled out, having paid to jump out of a perfectly good plane for no reason other than to do so for kicks, and were in free fall, accelerating toward earth, the ocean to the west, mountains here and there, the wind in their faces. They were flying, cheering, arms out like they were all Team Supergirl.

In that moment they were weightless, without problems, high above Santa Barbara.

The g-forces were incredible. Intense. Emotional.

They all released that same orgasmic sound at the same moment.

It was a unified screaming, a shrill they imagined was heard around the world.

When they were together they were in their second childhoods.

That was what Ericka loved the most, capturing what she had missed as a child. Everything she did, she did as if she would never get a chance to experience it again. As she fell she looked at the world. She noticed everything. She wanted to remember every sight, sound, smell, every noise, and all that she felt. This was life. She took nothing for granted. Nothing.

She had thirty-five things on her bucket list.

She planned to do them all before she died.

Chapter 2

Some weekends they were all channeling Beyoncé, on the roof of the Standard Hotel, imbibing and dancing like they didn't care, dresses short and heels high. Some weekends they were indulging in a few calories at the world-famous Hawkins House of Burgers in Watts, then down at Venice Beach bowling before Rollerblading to Santa Monica, maybe hiking the hills at Runyon Canyon. Most evenings, while Ericka was at her dining room table grading papers and doing lesson plans, Kwanzaa and Indigo were in the Crenshaw-Imperial public library studying until it closed. Destiny would come in from her job at FedEx and study until sunrise, nap, and then zoom to USC. A time or two, they were all broken-down Taylor Swifts, in someone's apartment in pajamas, hair every which-a-way, four bottles of wine from Everett Ridge Winery in Sonoma County on the table, bitching about men, or bitching about bitches, or giving their thoughts on thoughtless thots, drinking and doing shots, crying, hating the men they had loved and fucked, or had fucked with love, or laughing about the men they had stopped loving long after the men had already stopped loving them and were already fucking the fucking love out of someone else.

But there was more to them than conversations about men and love. Many days they had talked to each other and the topic or issue was not a man, so with flying colors they had passed the Bechdel test, that is unless the issue of oppression and blatant racism was considered a man.

When the need had arisen, wearing Guy Fawkes masks, they were with thousands of protestors, a multicultural protest that had kicked off at L.A. Live. There were BLACK LIVES MATTER signs, FUCK THE POLICE signs, people carrying upside-down American flags to symbolize that the country was in distress. They all held colorful motorcycle helmets in their hands as they marched arm in arm in the night through downtown Los Angeles toward Ninth and Flower, loud, boisterous, blocking traffic, while others in the demonstration carried banners that read STOP THE POLICE TERROR! MURDERS BY POLICE MUST BE STOPPED NOW! LAPD tried to surround the protesters by circling the crowd. Kwanzaa was terrified, but Destiny held her hand. Indigo was yelling in Yorùbá and Ericka cursed the system in English. Sirens blared. Helicopters shined down lights. Kwanzaa, Destiny, Ericka, and Indigo fled by demonstrators cuffed with zip ties, being thrown in police buses to be taken to the grown folks' Hoosegow. They ran toward their vehicles. On normal days there were at least two helicopters patrolling the sky from 8:30 A.M. until 4:30 A.M., looking for lawbreakers and people to criminalize, flying over corruption hot spots and disturbing communities with noise pollution, inspecting the infrastructure, and providing backup and eyes for officers who had boots on the ground. Every helicopter in the city was hanging over them at that moment, a thousand suns shining down, and that infamous Nightsun was maddening.

Destiny wasn't going to leave anyone behind to be taken to Hoosegow.

Kwanzaa became the passenger on Destiny's colorful yellow, white, red, and blue CBR. Ericka became the passenger on Indigo's motorcycle, hers too a CBR, only new and customized, painted bubble-gum pink with red rims to match her new hair color.

Two CBRs roared like lionesses.

Indigo sped away first, Ericka holding her waist. Destiny pulled away next, Kwanzaa her passenger. Kwanzaa had her face shield flipped up. Her middle fingers were flipped up as well.

Destiny's personalized tags on her motorcycle read: CUNXTU

See. You. Next. Tuesday.

Chapter 3

Of the four women, Indigo was the tallest. She was gorgeous, and what enhanced her loveliness were her confidence and an attitude born from two Nigerian parents telling her from her first breath how amazing she was, which coupled with an understanding of her true unsullied beauty. She was given the African-born truth before American society told her she was too dark-skinned to be searched for if she ever went missing. Straight Outta the Prestigious Hancock Park, Indigo was the first of her family born in the United States, therefore she had dual citizenship and dual accents. She claimed Nigeria more than she ever would America.

Straight Outta Windsor Hills, Ericka was a hair shorter than Indigo and the oldest in the crew. She was recovering from a divorce, a marriage to a man of the cloth that had been a marriage from hell, and she was in remission from cancer. She'd lost her once-wavy hair during chemo. It was growing back, but she kept it cut close on the sides and back, let it grow long on the top, had the hair dyed blonde and colored the tips of the top cancer-survivor pink. Ericka joked that she attracted European men who didn't like their women too white, and black men who didn't like their women too African. She was the woman brainwashed and biased men loved to have on their arms. She joked about shallowness, but in the heart of her heart she hated both biased mentalities.

Destiny Jones was Straight Outta View Park, the land of doctors, lawyers, entrepreneurs, and entertainers. She wore a thousand and one wavy sisterlocks, all bleached and cascading down her back. Destiny Jones had a face that looked the same now as it had when she was fifteen and attending private school in Bel Air and used her bleached dread-locks to conceal her facial features. She was the silent one in the crew, unless talking to her three girlfriends.

Kwanzaa was two inches over being five feet tall, but she packed seven feet of beauty into those sixty-two inches. Her complexion was smooth; Ghirardelli chocolate personified, with subtle orange under-tones, insinuating that her Middle Passage ancestry was amalgamated with the Trail of Tears. Two weeks ago she'd cut her hair in anger, was uncomfortable with having short hair, then immediately found hair that matched the texture of what she had mangled, and now she wore her top-shelf, custom handmade twenty-six-inch Brazilian hair with lace closure, flipping her mane every other second, as if a wind machine was always blowing in her mind.

Chapter 4

In the days before Indigo's birthday, despite having classes at UCLA, the L.A.-born Nigerian princess celebrated almost every night, including going to a free concert held in the parking lot down at Baldwin Hills Crenshaw Plaza. That was the mall-formerly-known-as-the-Black-mall. Now it was jokingly called North Mexico. Indigo had pulled Kwanzaa and Ericka in close, then snapped selfies with Deborah Cox, Jordin Sparks, and Chrisette Michele.

Indigo said, "If you are going to be African American, invite real Africans to the party. They should invite Jesse Jagz, Splash, Ruggedman, Mr. Incredible, and other Nigerian artists to perform here so the *African* Americans can learn how to add some artistry to their routines."

At the same time Kwanzaa and Ericka snapped, "Stop complaining."

A pride of men gawked at Indigo the longest, and if not the longest, then with the most intensity. She wore a fitted dress and, being five foot ten without the six-inch heels, drew enviable attention. Her body was the first impression, but even without the physical blessing, with her magnificent, undiluted complexion and figure, she was a showstopper. Men who dressed in sweats and sandals, as if they thought that was formal attire, stood before her stunned, leaving their badly dressed dates standing speechless so they could hurry over and try to upgrade, in trances, rambling about her exquisiteness. Indigo would share a word, be kind, but none of the men were on her radar. Indigo had dated Yaba the Laker, and now she dated a Nigerian NFL player. The former relationship had ended suddenly and badly, the latter wasn't going so well, but it was new and she had high hopes. Even beauty didn't assure life without heartbreak or struggle.

She couldn't take two steps without a man praising her. For each unsolicited compliment, she shrugged, proffered half a grin, waved as if it were no big deal, and told them she woke up like that. She loved to crank up the Nigerian accent and pronounce her full West African name—Indigo Bose Fumilayo Titilayo Titilola Mojisola Morenike Abdulrahaman. *Bose* meant "born on Sunday." *Fumilayo* meant "gives me joy." *Titilayo* was "forever joyful." *Titilola* signified that wealth is forever. *Mojisola* explained she was born into wealth. *Morenike* let the world know she was a child born to be spoiled. And Indigo children were children believed to be special children, children who were sensitive, intuitive, scholarly warriors with a life purpose greater than themselves.

Indigo Bose Fumilayo Titilayo Titilola Mojisola Morenike Abdulrahaman—an amazing name that used up a lot of ink, a name that could cramp your hand when trying to write it all at once, a name she was proud of and loved to articulate, then watch the stunned looks on Americans' faces. Whenever she said her name, wise men fell in love. Her name also signified she did not wear a designation that could be traced back to a family that had once been owned by white Christians. Her name let them know that her history wasn't rooted in American slavery and Jim Crow. Her heritage didn't go back to an area of Confederate flags. Her name said that, no matter how you felt about Africa, her family tree had not been compromised, and her bloodline had not been conquered. There were no chains in her direct ancestry.

When she fired up her Nigerian accent, she was seen as special.

They heard her history and recognized her influence.

Ericka, Destiny, Indigo, and Kwanzaa were all gorgeous in different ways. After the outdoor concert, men came toward the four of them and tried to decide whom to hit on first.

Dressed in skinny jeans, Ericka thought it was cute that the brothers thought she was ten years younger, barely in her twenties, near the same age as her three best friends.

Kwanzaa Browne was heartbroken, missing her ex, and didn't care about flirtations, but men were Columbusing for coochie and grinned like they wanted to discover hers. Her baby face, high cheekbones, and dimpled smile were heart stealers and attracted perverts who were fixated on her beauty like they wanted to hug her naked with their penises balls-deep inside her no-no.

In a country where the social construction called race outweighed class, political affiliations, and religion, Destiny Jones owned the hue of a sweet graham cracker. She was a lioness, a geek with the heart of a warrior. More than a handful of years ago, before being drugged, before being betrayed, before the sirens, before the controversial revenge, before the detour to the Hoosegow, before the bad diet and growth spurt, she would have been the most outgoing of the lot. Destiny carried her helmet but wore Wayfarers over her brown eyes as if those Ray-Bans were her mask. She needed to get away from the attention, from the eyes, from the aggressive men before her temper flared and it became ugly. She turned to Indigo, whose idea this was, but Indigo was frowning, busy trying to call her boyfriend Olamilekan on her cellular.

She had been trying to reach him all day, had called at least twice every hour.

One twentysomething brother wearing slim jeans, Chucks, and a University of Memphis tee complimented them all, said they had amazing skin, beautiful complexions.

He wanted to take a photo with the fine California girls and post it on Facebook.

Destiny Jones ignored the flirty man and kept walking, helmet in hand, her head down. Her body was toned, strong, with a small waist and a nice blessing that caught as much attention as her gorgeous face. She was a smooth size 10, but with her waist and shape, she looked like size 6 at the most. She wore a blue motorcycle jacket, the words DO UNTO OTHERS & MAKE THEM REMEMBER easy to read across its back. She adjusted her Wayfarer shades and walked on, her sensual sisterlocks both masking her face and bouncing like a cape with each anxious step.

Destiny Jones didn't take any photos. She didn't converse with strangers. She didn't allow people to touch her without approval, didn't give men attention no matter how handsome, no matter how hard they tried. She didn't trust men, and she definitely didn't trust women.

It would take a special man for her to let down her walls.

It would take a very special man.

Ericka, Kwanzaa, Destiny, and Indigo had sung the entire concert, then sang and danced and laughed their way inside the Baldwin Hills Crenshaw Plaza. It was impossible for the four of them to be next to a mall and not go inside in search of a sale. To broke college students and those living on a public school teacher's wages, a mall was a zoo with clothing, where they could look at the wild fashions or pet a few items if they chose. Kwanzaa had a few extra coins in her purse and wanted to check out the sale at Forever 21, grab something from the five-dollar-and-under rack. Destiny needed a few things from Walmart. Ericka wanted to browse through Pink and Victoria's Secret, then actually buy something on sale at Ross.

That was where the drama jumped off, without warning, but with cause.

Chapter 5

Indigo was the first to spot Marcus Jesús Delgado Muñoz Brixton.

Attorney Marcus Brixton was a double minority, an exotic, mixed-race man who stood just under six feet tall, a good-looking man who was slender, clean-shaven, and professional and stood out like a movie star on the law office billboards across Southern California. Some said he was a man who could win the confidence of two communities and eventually become mayor.

Indigo saw him as he went up the escalator. He was holding some woman's hand.

He wore slim jeans and a jacket, but Indigo didn't need to see his dark eyes to know it was him. It was the way Indigo reacted, or tried to hide her reaction, that caused Ericka to look.

Then Destiny jerked, turned, and looked.

And the last person the three of them wanted to look followed the course of the river.

Kwanzaa turned, saw her ex-fiancé leaving the food court and going up the escalator with another woman.

Marcus Brixton looked happy. He looked like nothing had ever gone wrong in his world.

The sudden breakup wound was still fresh, was an open wound, one that Kwanzaa had cried and drank alcohol over. She'd almost dropped out of university because she'd feared not being able to focus would ruin her GPA, and therefore her life. Kwanzaa lost her Jesus and dashed for the escalator, her trio of girlfriends flying behind her as she ran down her ex-fiancé, the man who was the reason she had cut her hair, wore a weave, and now had to slap herself upside the head when her head itched because she could no longer scratch her scalp.

Destiny ran behind her and snapped, "Let that trifling *blood claat* go on with his life. Go on with yours."

Ericka snapped back, "No, let her confront him."

Kwanzaa said, "Six years of my life. Six years and this is what I get as a reward?"

Destiny said, "Not in public. People will Facebook, tweet, or use Periscope and stream whatever you're doing live online and the world will see you at your worst, Kwanzaa."

Kwanzaa snapped, "Destiny, counsel me when your chakras are aligned."

Destiny slowed down, let them run ahead, always afraid of being recorded.

Kwanzaa ran in her heels and caught up with Brixton as he passed a row of kiosks, then slapped him in the back of the head. He jumped, surprised to see Kwanzaa. As they stood a few feet from the entrance to the Hair Architect, as the outrage drew a small crowd, Kwanzaa slapped the man again, cursed him in Spanish, told him what she thought of him for betraying her for a Chilean bitch and bringing a damned STD to her bed, and then not having the decency to take her to the doctor. The girl with Marcus was in shock, had no idea who Kwanzaa was. Marcus wanted Kwanzaa to lower her voice, to step somewhere they could talk in private. Before she could strike Marcus again, he had grabbed her hands, but let her go the way a man did when he knew he had much to lose both professionally and politically, and tried to moonwalk away.

Kwanzaa followed him, and Indigo and Ericka followed Kwanzaa.

"*Maldito desgraciado, pedazo de mierda. Desecho de la vida. Me engañaste me enfermaste ojalá te pudras en el infierno y te mueras con la puta esa con la que engañaste.*"

Brixton tried to get a word in, but Kwanzaa's fury was rapid and too damn powerful.

"*Se merecen el uno al otro coño y madre. Debería llamar a mi papá y decirle lo que me hiciste. Para que te de una pasada de coñasos por asqueroso.*"

Kwanzaa Browne slapped attorney Marcus Brixton again. The military brat who had never grown up in the hood imitated a *Housewife of Wherever* as she slapped one of the top lawyers in Southern California, then blasted him in Spanish, dared him to hit her back so she could call her dad and bonus dad and have them come and kick his half-black, half-Mexican ass so hard half of him would return to Botswana and the other half to the other side of Tijuana.

Some women applauded as others dragged their kids away as fast as they could.

The young woman with Brixton hurled a threat at Kwanzaa in Spanglish.

Indigo snapped, *"Sho fe ba mi ja."*

It was a Yorùbá phrase that basically meant, *"Boo Boo Kitty, you have messed with the wrong one."* Indigo told the girl she'd better stop, drop, and roll because she was messing with fire. The girl had second thoughts, especially when the girl saw Destiny standing there, motorcycle helmet clutched in hand like a weapon, shaking her head as if to say don't even think about it.

The girl with Marcus zipped her lip, kept the rest of her insults to herself, then took a dozen steps away and waited, did that as if to tell Marcus Brixton he was now in this battle alone.

Indigo and Ericka held Kwanzaa back, pulled her away. Marcus Brixton called Kwanzaa *loca* over and over. She called him a *diseased motherfucker* and told him every night she prayed for his crooked dick to fall off. The argument moved with them until they were in the Baldwin Hills Crenshaw Plaza Bridge, a portal that connected the second level of Macy's to the rest of the mall's second level, a glass see-through bridge overlooking the Shaw and MLK Boulevard.

Ericka and Indigo pulled Kwanzaa over to the side to calm her down.

Marcus hurried away, the girl with him struggling to match his pace, being left behind.

Ericka and Indigo held Kwanzaa back in a section that functioned as a waiting area for men who had grown tired of shopping with unruly children and inexhaustible women.

Kwanzaa laughed the laugh of the ridiculous, the angry laugh she had acquired recently, the laugh of a woman breaking down. She laughed like she wanted to break out the windows in Brixton's Maserati after she had keyed it and put sugar in the gas tank, and maybe put a dose of cyanide in his Froot Loops. Ericka and Indigo kept her from chasing Marcus Brixton out of the mall. Then Kwanzaa screamed and marched in circles, chained to her emotions and memories.

Destiny kept her Wayfarers on, kept her crinkly sisterlocks over most of her facial features. She bounced her helmet against her thigh as she walked behind her crew, staying behind them, even as she kept their pace. A teen girl wearing a T-shirt that announced NOTHING IS THE NEW BLACK was recording the incident like she was a wannabe snitch for *World Star*.

Destiny waited until the crowd had dispersed, waited until people had moved on with their irrelevant lives before she went to where her girls had reconvened. They were sitting on a leather sofa in the lounge area overlooking the pandemonium at the intersection of King and Crenshaw.

Destiny stood in the floor-to-ceiling glass window, still bouncing her helmet against her leg, and scowled down on the thoroughfare they simply called MLK, stared out at what used to be a West Coast version of Chocolate City without the intense political awareness.

She stared out just in time to be jarred. A well-known motorcyclist passed by, rocking her yellow Ducati. For a moment Destiny could hardly breathe. She wanted to scream at her past.

Ericka went to Destiny, put a hand on her shoulder. "You okay, Destiny?"

Destiny took a few deep breaths. "I'm okay, Ericka. Had a moment."

"What happened?"

"I told Kwanzaa not to act a damn fool. Did you see how many phones came out and started recording that madness? I don't need to be on social media ever again."

"We don't want Hulk angry. When Hulk angry, Hulk smash."

Destiny took a deep breath, then exhaled slowly. "It all gets to be a bit much."

"What?"

"Being afraid. School. Work. My mom's midlife crisis. My dad and his cancer. Being sick and tired of being sick and tired."

Ericka shifted, diverted her eyes. "How is Mr. Jones?"

"Dad is fine right now. I'm just worried. He will have to start radiation treatment soon. His PSA numbers are up and he has to get a prostate biopsy in a couple of weeks."

"But he's doing okay?"

"We should stop by there and get on Dad's nerves for a while."

Ericka paused. "All of us stopping by at the same time might be a bit much for Mr. Jones."

"Dad wouldn't mind. We're his girls. We should go eat him out of house and home."

"You are a lucky daughter. Mr. Jones is a great dad."

"We get hit by one thing after another in my family. Now it's fucking cancer."

"He will kick cancer in the ass. I know he will. He's a remarkable man."

"I know Dad used to take you to your chemo treatments when one of us couldn't."

"Mr. Jones would take me to Kaiser, wait on me, sit with me in the room while I got my treatment, tell me jokes, then take me to breakfast at CJ's after Kaiser pumped me with poison."

"I always used to wish your mother would take you to get your chemo treatment when one of us couldn't drive you."

"You know damn well that me and Mrs. Stockwell ain't friends like that."

"She's your mother. I had hoped that you two could work it out when you were sick."

"Our relationship was *worse* when I was sick. She kicked me when I was down. I was puking and she would say horrible things. Told me what I did when I was a teenager gave me cancer, said that cancer was God's punishment for being a problem child. I stayed alive because I refused to die before that bitch did. I refused to give her the satisfaction of outliving me."

"When you used to babysit me, Dad used to always say he wished you were his daughter too. I used to wish that too. I needed your guidance back then. If I had had a sister like you around me, I don't think I would have gone out into the world trying to make friends."

"Daughter? Wow. I'm sorry. Your dad saw me as his other daughter."

"My mother saw you as a daughter too."

"I never felt like Mrs. Jones cared too much for me."

"She liked you a lot. She hated it when you went away to Oklahoma."

"I was forced to go. Oklahoma was my Hoosegow. It was my prison."

"I doubt if they made you strip naked, bend over, squat, and cough when you got there."

"But it was still my Hoosegow. I was not received kindly or treated with dignity."

"You have no idea about the conditions in the girls' juvenile hall, have no clue what kids between the ages of eleven and seventeen have to go through at the hands of adults."

"Can't imagine an eleven-year-old locked up. Not even menstruating, and imprisoned?"

"They're not the normal eleven-year-olds. They have had interesting lives. Some are already hardened criminals. For some, gangs are their families. When you see them, you see how America has failed. America is more concerned with the black oil in the Middle East than its own citizens, and will invest more in incarceration than education. Where I was, a lot of people had been born in hell, had lived in hell, and for some, jail was better than their hell."

"No, I don't know the kind of evil you met, don't know the hell you lived in."

"They will put a fifteen-year-old in solitary confinement for a hundred days, give her a break twice a day, and offer no educational services for those one hundred days of solitude. When she's let out, she's in a cell the size of a mattress, with a window smaller than her hand."

"I know it was bad."

"They use isolation to break people, to try and kill their spirits. Keeping a teen in her own cell for twenty-three hours a day drives her a little mad. The only contact you have is when guards check on you four times an hour to make sure you haven't somehow found a way to hang yourself with a string of dental floss, and outside of that, you're lucky if they let you talk to a nurse, your attorney, maybe a priest, or one of the overseers. They call that bullshit *room confinement.* I think that was better than Oklahoma."

"I wished I could have been alone for a hundred days."

"You had your freedom. If not for my parents, especially my dad, I would have broken."

"I wish I had had your father. He lives and breathes to make sure you're okay."

"He was there for me every step of the way. Never bailed on me. Didn't have a breakdown and take a trip to London to get away from me and the problems I had caused."

"You hate your mother."

"I *love* my mother. Just hate that I had put more on her than she could bear. We're different as adults. She respects me. She took me to Paris last year and we had a ball."

"Wish me and my mother could be like that. Wish we could travel and laugh. Wouldn't have to be to Paris. If we could go to Long Beach and back without fighting, that would be nice."

"I do too. I really wish you and Mrs. Stockwell could find a happy medium."

"What she did to me, in the name of the Lord, was unforgivable."

"I know. I know."

Ericka repeated, "Fucking unforgivable."

"Calm down. You look like you're having flashbacks from your Hoosegow in Oklahoma. We can't have me freaking out, you tripping, and Kwanzaa having a meltdown at the same time."

"Catastrophic events like these have to be scheduled at least six hours apart."

Destiny laughed. "I'm worried about Kwan. Let's focus on her. It's her turn."

Ericka and Destiny went back to Kwanzaa. Destiny stopped by the gumball machines, bought four gumballs, gave one to each of her girls, and the bubble-blowing festival began.

Indigo said, "Let's exit stage left and break out of here before LAPD shows up and makes us the latest hashtags."

Chewing gum to maintain her cool, Kwanzaa said, "*Hashtag*, I'm not running."

"You just slapped the bejesus out of an attorney whose face is on signs all over L.A."

"*Hashtag*, I should have beaten the breaks off him."

"Private-school girl, you know your butt can't fight. Best you can do is give him a vicious cursing out in two languages, send him whimpering to a corner, and give him a time-out."

"He's down in my parents' zip code parading some can't-speak-Spanish skank around. And stop giving me the side-eye, Indigo. Don't act like you wouldn't have done the same thing."

"Where are we going now that you have ruined this part of my birthday month?"

"We're going *shopping*. Retail therapy at Victoria's Secret, Pink, T.J. Maxx, Walmart, and then drinks, drinks, drinks. Right, Indigo? It's all about you, so we do what you want to do."

On the down escalator, Indigo snapped, "Don't mess up the remainder of my birthday."

Kwanzaa retorted, "Go to hell. It's not your birthday yet. *Every* day is not your birthday."

Kwanzaa and Indigo exited the escalator walking fast, moving around the crowd, heels clicking, words flying back and forth, and arguing like the best of friends or the worst of enemies.

Ericka bumped into a few people, caught up, and asked, "Are we okay, Kwanzaa?"

Kwanzaa said, "All I need to do is hit Post and Beam, do a few shots, and I'll be cool."

Indigo asked, "Would that be penicillin or vodka shots?"

Kwanzaa cursed in Spanish, laughed a little, then cried in unrecognizable English.

Indigo said, "Here we go again. Must you continue to pout for that asshole? Every time you say his name I feel like I need to submerge my soul in calamine lotion."

Kwanzaa said, "I hate you, Indigo. I hope someone gives you a drink that makes you pass out and you wake up a slave, chained to some white man's wall in Alligator, Mississippi."

"When we get home we'll trace your slave name back to a plantation in Bumfuck, Mississippi, and send you there to pick cotton and sit under a tree and drink sarsaparilla. Don't forget to enter the plantation through the back door, if you're allowed to leave the fields at all."

"That was mean. So damn mean."

"In your history books, you'd be a field hand."

"You're not even a real African."

"*Weave-erella*, I have dual citizenship. What do you have, *African* American? I can trace my ancestry back ten generations of *free* Africans born in or around Nigeria, and they still practice their own religion. You can't trace yours back to an English-made slave ship used by Christians."

"Brixton always said you were nothing but a fake-ass African."

"Your rent just went up fifty dollars."

"Brixton never liked your uppity ass."

"And every time you say Brixton's name, another fifty."

"Brixton, Brixton, Brixton, Brixton, Brixton."

Chapter 6

It was almost dawn on Indigo Abdulrahaman's date of birth.

Indigo was born at 9:34 P.M., and despite partying most of the month, she planned to have fun from the crack of dawn up through the exact moment her mother had evicted her only child from her Nigerian-born womb at Cedars-Sinai Medical Center. Indigo wanted to start her birthday being physical, so she told Kwanzaa to make sure she had the day off from slinging caffeine at her part-time gig at Starbucks, had told Ericka there would not be a sixth-grade schoolteacher for twenty-four hours, and told Destiny Jones that she would have to skip her forty-eleven jobs, but any collegiate-level studying or grading of sixth-grade papers would be understood and forgiven. For this quartet of Afrocentric millennials, as they tried to find their place in the world, as they navigated the choppy waters of life and love, it was education and career first. Education and career were about one day being fiscally powerful; money was independence, and independence was power, and once empowered they would be able to make their own choices.

Always build each other up. No crabs, no barrel, never pull each other down.

They lived one gas station shy of Crenshaw and West Century, in the city of Inglewood where the negative-yet-embraced motto said the people were *always up to no good*. Most of the single-family stucco houses and apartments were built between the '40s and the '70s, and the average two-bedroom crib cost 400K. The average rental in the area was over twelve hundred dollars, but where they lived, Little Lagos, the building was outstanding, had better security, a pool, and palm trees, so the rent was a little above average. Most of the properties were renter occupied. Less than four percent of the locals had a degree from a four-year college. Over forty percent were born in some other part of the world. Almost fifty percent were Mexican, and over seventy percent spoke Spanish. It was a bustling area with a Home Depot, Costco, Target, Red Lobster, Chili's, and a gazillion more places to shop and buy artery-clogging food. It was a working-class strip mall zone.

The area was about as L.A. as L.A. could get.

Ericka rented the upstairs two-bedroom closest to Century Boulevard, so she spent many nights wearing earplugs to block out the sound of police and ambulance sirens, urban screams that sang the loudest after midnight. She also had issue with the late-night barking dogs and the early-morning crow of roosters coming from a few of the immigrant neighbors' backyards. Plus every car that passed seemed to be driven by the deaf because they all bumped music at Coachella level. Ericka lived above Kwanzaa, so Kwanzaa also had access to the same hullabaloo, but lately Kwanzaa had been making her own noise at night.

Indigo lived in the rear upstairs unit, away from the noise and above Destiny.

They had the same floor plans, kitchens over kitchens, and bedrooms over bedrooms.

Indigo was up dancing and playing Nigerian music, the songs "Johnny" by Yemi Alade and Lil Kesh jamming "Shoki" on repeat. She texted Olamilekan a third reminder to come to her party, then showered. She began knocking on the doors of Ericka's and Kwanzaa's apartments before 5 A.M. She told them to get up, use the bathroom, shower, and get dressed so they could go meet the sunrise. Indigo didn't see Destiny's colorful CBR in their stalls, and figured she was still working at FedEx near LAX. But the gate opened and Destiny cruised in on her motorcycle. The antisocial pessimist had been getting home three hours later a couple of nights a week.

Destiny made it upstairs wearing her FedEx uniform and lugging her USC backpack filled with a change of clothes and textbooks thicker than a porn star's cock. Indigo was waiting outside her door, dressed in yoga pants and a black tee that had a tree with the American flag as its leaves, the words AMERICAN GROWN WITH NIGERIAN ROOTS above its green and white roots.

"Destiny Jones, I know you're not about to go to bed, so don't even think about it."

Destiny yawned. "Good morning to you too, Indigo. I'm fine, and how are you?"

"Don't make me raise your rent. Shower and clean from where the Nile runs and the muddy Mississippi flows, slap cocoa butter on your elbows, knees, and please don't overlook the butt crack, then put on some fashionable workout clothes. Smell good and look cute."

She hugged Indigo, kissed her cheek. "Your music is loud, Indigo. It's too early for all that noise. Ericka and Kwanzaa cussed you out for being self-centered and inconsiderate yet?"

Indigo whispered, "Kwanzaa was up all night. That poor child was *restless* again."

Destiny lowered her voice, "You heard her?"

"She needs to get over Brixton so we can sleep."

"Has he been by here trying to see her? I will lose all respect for her if she's seeing him."

"If he had been by here, there would be a chalk outline where I left that ass's dead body."

Destiny dug in her pocket to get her keys, and something fell out.

It was a loose condom.

Indigo picked it up, waggled it, and asked, "What's going on, Miss Jones?"

Destiny took the condom from her hand, then winked. "Let me shower and get dressed."

"That's a regular-sized Trojan, not an extra-large Magnum."

"And?"

"I'm not stupid. I know what that means."

"What exactly?"

"It means you're creeping and sleeping with a white man."

Chapter 7

Before daybreak had touched the eighty-eight cities in Los Angeles County, they'd dressed in sports bras, T-shirts, colorful yoga pants, and collegiate hoodies, yawned and climbed on crotch rockets, then zoomed from Inglewood toward Culver City, doing over seventy in a forty-five zone. They slowed at Baldwin Hills Scenic Overlook, what the locals called the Culver City stairs. Workout warriors were there, parking, heading for the lopsided stone stairs in the mountain.

As soon as they parked, men took note.

Indigo said, "See? Aren't you glad we all look cute? We're women of a certain kind and we have to represent beauty, intellect, grace, and strength at all times."

Destiny said, "Whatever. I thought we were going to work out to keep the core strong and booty tight. I didn't know you were taking us *penis* shopping."

Ericka said, "African, Canadian, or European, Indigo loves sausages for breakfast."

Indigo said, "*Chineke mee.* No you did not say that, Ericka. *Otula.*"

Kwanzaa said, "Y'all are sad. All this education between us, all that's going on in the world, the destruction of humans in Yemen, Libya, Syria, Iraq, Afghanistan, and Mexico, and you choose to talk about *penis for breakfast.* I could've had a shallow conversation at work."

Indigo said, "The way the men are looking this way, I'm sure they're not talking about physics or social change or wondering if black lives matter. They're looking at us like we're four shades of delicious and are trying to figure out where they want to fall to their knees and eat first."

Backpack in hand, Destiny shook her head. "Well, your hole-in-the-wall might be open for new business, but the restaurant called Legs of Destiny is closed. I'll pass on new customers."

"And Coochie of Kwanzaa is not accepting another customer before her wedding night."

Ericka handed her helmet to Indigo. "Mine has *never* been open to the public."

Destiny said, "If Indigo was a place to eat she would be called Fresh N Easy."

Indigo laughed. "Always fresh, never easy."

Being silly, yawning, teasing each other, they locked their helmets to the CBRs, stretched a few moments, headed toward the snaking trail with the rest of the early risers, and became four queen warriors.

With Destiny Jones leading the charge up the 282 uneven steps made of recycled concrete carved into the rolling hills, they hiked at a smooth pace. They were four of at least one hundred people, the crowd growing, most of them strong-legged buppies, yuppies, and muppies.

The girls inhaled, cursed in three languages, muscles burning, yet begging for more.

Halfway up their third effort, they stopped where one of the dirt trails intersected with the rise of the harsh stairs. Ericka was drenched in sweat, moving like she was tired. They always worried about her energy level, even though she had been in remission over a year.

Indigo asked, "Miss opening at Starbucks this morning, Kwanzaa?"

Kwanzaa slapped the side of her own head two dozen times, tried to calm an itch, then pulled her expensive hair into a better ponytail. "The only thing I miss seeing is how the Latinas get all hot and bothered when Mr. Iced Coffee comes in the joint in the morning."

"You've mentioned him a time or two hundred. Is he really that fine?"

"It's like a crowd of women wait for him to show up, then just stare at him."

"You said the handsome man dresses nice?"

"Wears nice shoes, and head to toe, he's always decked out in Hugo Boss."

"He's either successful or a criminal."

"Or a successful criminal. He has some serious swag."

"What does he look like?"

"Tall, fit, broad shoulders."

"Sounds like Olamilekan. The body that man has is ridiculous, and he knows it."

"This one has long, wavy hair. Mixed with something, maybe swirled with everything."

"You talk to him? Is he single? Is the metrosexual man straight?"

"Joint's too busy to talk to anyone but customers experiencing caffeine withdrawal. The Latinas always talk about how hot he looks when he comes in. They break their necks to wait on him, so I rarely do. When he comes in, they start giggling, switch and whisper to each other in Spanish. *Guapo* this, *guapo* that. They all want him to go south of their border and put some special sauce on their tacos. I'm engaged . . . was . . . so I stayed out of it."

Ericka finally caught up and they resumed hiking the stairs. But she paused after a few steps, looked out at the land, and the areas that looked like patches of brown weeds. California was in a severe drought and most of the state had set irrigation and water restrictions.

She felt just as dry as the rest of the state. Last week she had felt stronger.

Kwanzaa asked, "How's your energy?"

Ericka nodded. "I'm fine. Don't wait on me. Meet you at the top."

"Why do you keep stopping if you're not tired?"

"Enjoying the view. I'm not in a hurry to get to the apex. I don't want to rush."

Indigo sent a text to Olamilekan, another reminder, then resumed taking the stairs in pace with Kwanzaa. Indigo wondered why Olamilekan hadn't been available all night.

She wished she had spent the night with him. Then she would be sure he would show up for her birthday party and not leave her humiliated in front of her parents, especially her mother.

Chapter 8

At the top of the Culver City stairs for the fourth and last time, they panted with their hands on waists, bent over as they sweated, caught their breath, then leaned against the metal railing on the concrete landing. They toasted the new sunrise with infused bottled water.

Destiny's cellular rang. The girls applauded, Kwanzaa and Ericka applauding the loudest.

Whoever's phone rang first, excluding Indigo on this day, had to pay for breakfast.

Still panting, Destiny answered, "Kismet Kellogg, how may I help? Yes, I stand by my work and will refund if you're not happy. What? Yeah, all sports channels. What? Yeah, hundreds of live channels. HBO, Cinemax, Showtime, everything plus Sky UK channels. What? UK means Great Britain. London. Porn channels? Yeah, lots of porn. Porn from all over the world. I wouldn't know. I don't watch porn. Another twenty-five to do in-home setup. We can meet tomorrow."

Destiny ended the too-early-in-the-morning call, took a deep breath, weariness in her eyes. Three jobs. School. Now her dad had cancer. Plus the weight of being Kismet Kellogg.

As if she had read the fears in Destiny's mind, Ericka asked, "Who is Kismet Kellogg?"

"Some people hear my real name and get real ugly. Especially women. They like to remind me I did some bad things, say the most disgusting things, try and slut-shame and ridicule, but forget people did horrible things to me. Been using a synonym for Destiny plus my Jamaican family name as my sobriquet. When I'm out alone it's easier to say I'm Kismet Kellogg."

Indigo smoothed her hands over her frohawk. "You're still hawking Amazon Fire Sticks?"

Destiny nodded. "Selling three or four upgraded with Kodi almost every day."

"How are you meeting these clients who know you as Kismet Kellogg?"

"Craigslist. That's the best way to make tax-free money."

Indigo asked, "Can the government trace the signal to my apartment and arrest me?"

"Indigo, it's not illegal. I wouldn't put anything criminal in your cribs."

"We're looking at movies and programs from all over the world for free."

"They sell them basically jailbroken, and knowing how to program them to get all TV and movies around the world for free is a loophole."

"Don't get me arrested over watching *Being Mary Jane* and *Chewing Gum*."

"Indigo, if it is an issue, it's their issue, the manufacturer's, not the consumer's."

"Just to let you know, if the police or feds come, I will snitch on you so fast."

"You claim you're Nigerian. You should be used to corruption."

Indigo became dramatic, splayed her fingers, and cursed Destiny in Yorùbá.

Destiny mimicked her landlord, threw the curse back at Indigo.

Ericka barked, "Squats. Let's keep the jam from jiggling like jelly in an earthquake."

Indigo groaned. "Let's get these over with so we can go eat some pancakes."

Kwanzaa said, "My birthday's next. We won't be hiking. Wow. It just hit me. This'll be my first birthday in six years without Brixton."

Destiny asked, "How are you holding up this week? Were you up crying last night?"

Kwanzaa paused. "Didn't cry. I studied, but most of the night I was up thinking, making a list, trying to be positive, writing down the plus side of being suddenly single again."

Indigo said, "There's a plus side to being single?"

"I can do what I want, when I want, and as long as I want."

Indigo said, "We don't care what you do, but when you're drinking, reminiscing, and playing Spanish porn in the middle of the night, you need to turn the volume down and close the windows. Not only do we hear you playing the fiddle at two in the morning, but also the Mexicans in the building behind us are in the backyard listening and masturbating. And that's the women."

Kwanzaa became snippy. "Why are you hating on me when I am down and out?"

Ericka said, "No one's hating on you. A person has the right to satisfy intellectual and emotional needs inside the privacy of their own apartment. But you don't hear Destiny moaning and speaking in tongues. You don't hear Indigo calling out her exes' names all through the night, although that would be more names than in the phone book. We hear you down there listening to your *bow chicka wow wow* and sounding like a dying cat in between their vulgarities and moans."

Indigo ranted, "And let's talk about you and your habits, Ericka. We smell you up there with the windows open smoking Purple Martian Kush from Afghanistan, or that Hindu Kush from Northern Pakistan like it's going out of style. You're sitting in the window blowing clouds from Inglewood to San Bernardino and we're all getting contact highs in the middle of the night."

"I had *cancer* and I have a medical card and I am *not doing anything illegal*. When I smoke some Kush the only thing you're going to hear is me munching on a bag of kale chips."

Indigo said, "Oh, please. I hear that humming coming through my walls and I know it's not an electric toothbrush. Weed makes you horny. I've smoked enough Kush to know. You're probably up there smoking and munching and using a sex toy to do some late-night fracking."

Ericka showed her the middle fingers. "Go fap your mud flaps."

"You could at least buy brownies or gummy bears or lollipops with a weed blend. And if you want to make it yourself, all you have to do is mix the Kush in the butter, and if you can't make decent brownies, bring me the Kush and I'll make them for you, you know that."

"I smoke because last time I had gummy bears and lollipops I accidently put a couple in the kids' bags on Halloween. I'm glad they didn't trace that back to me. I was so damn scared."

Echoes of their risibility moved across the summit and out into the City of Angels.

Then Kwanzaa sighed, and once again she was serious, in pain, still heartbroken.

Destiny said, "You need to get over Brixton, Kwanzaa."

"I know. It's not easy. I'm trying."

Indigo snapped, "Do better. Never cry over a man who ain't crying over you."

Kwanzaa said, "And Indigo, you are the expert at that, if nothing else."

"Don't make me accidentally-on-purpose shove you down these stairs."

Ericka said, "Kwanzaa, be glad you weren't married. Take my advice and date for decades. Dating only takes up part of the day. A marriage is twenty-four seven, three hundred and sixty-five, and has another level of responsibilities, predictable and unpredictable, plus emotional and financial obligations. When you're dating you can invest as little as possible and get the specific benefits you need. If it's just a date, you just go out. If it's sex, you can get the sex, then disappear until you feel like *clocking* in again. You can *clock* in, and *clock* out, as much as you want, just do it responsibly. Fuck marriage. Date."

Indigo said, "That trifling message is brought to you by the Preacher's Wife."

Ericka snapped, "Former preacher's wife. Never leave out the word *former.*"

Kwanzaa shook her head. "I don't want a damn Walk-of-Shame lifestyle. Half the girls who live in the dorms are doing the Walk of Shame every Saturday and Sunday morning."

Destiny asked Kwanzaa, "Have you heard from Brixton since the mall fiasco?"

Kwanzaa's nostrils flared. "Brixton has sent me a dozen text messages."

"And?"

"He apologized profusely and wants to meet at a restaurant so we can talk."

"Don't fall for it. He wants to separate you from the pack and devour you."

Indigo snapped, "Must all roads lead back to Brixton, Kwanzaa? Must they? Now your rent has gone up two hundred dollars. It will be three hundred if you say his blasted name again."

Destiny snapped back, "Indigo, as much as you talk about the footballer Olamilekan and Yaba the Laker, you need to raise your own damn rent. Brixton slept with his side chick until he ended up contaminated, then slept with Kwanzaa, and if not for the infection it would have gone on and on. If he had done that to me, you know I would not have been as nice as Kwan."

Ericka said, "Kwanzaa, it could've been worse. Take that as a sign to move on."

Kwanzaa said, "I could've been patient zero for some new incurable ish. And when you're the first person to get a new disease, they want to name the ish after you. They would've called the new STD the *Kwanzaas* just to mess up black folks' holiday season."

The girls laughed. Despite the grin and the light words, despite the joke and a moment of self-deprecating humor, tears rolled down Kwanzaa's cheeks, to her lips, to her chin and neck.

Kwanzaa said, "I guess liars and their games are part of my heritage. We are our parents' problems, victories, and history united by the blending of egg and sperm, brought to life by God."

Indigo said, "Heifer, don't even try to get deep and philosophical over Brixton."

Exhausted men filed up the stairs and stared at Ericka's, Indigo's, Kwanzaa's, and Destiny's bodies, ogling a tad bit too long. A few became entranced. Destiny became self-conscious of not only the eyes on her body, but also the eyes that lingered on her face. A sweaty Idris of a guy stared at her, smiled, nodded his head, and waited on reciprocation. She turned, walked away.

In the delicate and concerned tone of a den mother, Ericka asked, "You okay, Destiny?"

Destiny said, "I'm fine. Was just creeped out. One guy kept looking at me. He realized who I was. I could tell. When they left, he started whispering to his friend. He said my name."

Kwanzaa said, "More men have arrived. Looks like a few more eyes are on us."

Indigo said, "Because we're four bad-ass black bitches breaking the stereotype."

Destiny said, "Okay, Indigo, we need a better word than *bitches*."

Ericka agreed with a nod. "You're right. We have to do better, even when we're joking."

Destiny shook her head. "The *B*-word is just the *N*-word for women."

Indigo nodded. "We're too smart and *amazing* to use such a lowbrow term. I mean, unless we're listening to music, or describing other women whom we despise. Some bitches are bitches and there is no other word on reserve to call those bitches except *bitches*, unless we come up with a bitching word for those bitches, especially aggravating bitches who keep sending those bitching *Candy Crush* requests."

Kwanzaa Browne laughed. "What are we going to call ourselves when we powwow?"

Everyone shrugged.

Indigo said, "Pillow Queens?"

Everyone laughed and Destiny and Kwanzaa shook their heads.

Ericka wagged a finger. "You three might be passive, but that's not the way I roll."

Kwanzaa said, "The only thing I use a pillow for is to put under my butt or my belly so we can get the angle right. I turn a man into a pillow king. I had Brixton crying like a three-year-old."

Indigo hummed. "Black Pussycat Dolls?"

They laughed again.

Ericka ran her hands over her pink hair. She saw everyone was already doing squats. She joined in. Three minutes of squats later, they stopped, sweat dripping from them all.

Indigo said, "Ericka, did you know that you're missing an earring?"

Ericka nodded, touched her left ear. "I guess it loosened and fell off somewhere."

Destiny looked at the earring in Ericka's right ear. It was a sterling-silver post with a rose crystal ribbon, the symbol for cancer awareness, for fighting that unrelenting beast.

Indigo said, "We'll look around the apartments."

Kwanzaa said, "No one dumps the trash or vacuums until we find Ericka's earring."

Ericka shivered. "Vacuum cleaners."

Destiny said, "We know, Ericka. We know your phobias."

"Can't stand the sound. Brings back bad memories."

Kwanzaa said, "That's why I vacuum your apartment when you're not home."

Indigo said, "Dest and Kwan, check the bags on your vacuum, just in case."

Chapter 9

Next was birthday breakfast two miles away at CJ's Cafe. The mom-and-pop-style Latino-owned café on La Brea was packed, half of the customers speaking in Spanish.

Ericka said, "Twelve hours to go and it's your official moment of birth, Indigo."

Indigo said, "I want some buck naked before my birthday is over."

Kwanzaa said, "So, in other words, you want to celebrate coming out of your mother's vagina by letting someone come in yours."

"I hate you, Kwanzaa. And who names their child Kwanzaa? How ghetto is that?"

"Your name is Indigo. Why? Because you're so black you look blue."

Destiny said, "You two are so cute when you argue like warring nations."

Ericka bit into her toast, then asked, "Indigo, on the real, you and the footballer on or off?"

"Olamilekan wants to spend time with me. I'm number one in his heart. We know that."

Ericka said, "And? Are you going to see him tonight, or do you have a plan B named Yaba?"

Indigo hummed. "Depends on how the day goes. I'm thirsty, but I ain't crazy thirsty like Kwanzaa. Yaba is calling me over and over, so heartbroken that I'm serious with Olamilekan."

Destiny said, "We need to buy Indigo a Plan B for her birthday."

Indigo said, "Since all of you are so freaking interested in who's making it do what it do with me, it's time for another girl confession. Be real. Who was the last one at this table to have sex? It's been five excruciating weeks for me. So who's been on the baloney pony since then?"

Ericka said, "We don't say *sex*. We call it what it really is. Sacred energy exchange."

"It's sex. Keep the shit real. Who was the last one to get something that made them call out to both God and Jesus?"

Ericka said, "Indigo, his name was *Yeshua*, not Jesus. Yeshua to Jesus comes from mistranslations, mispronunciations when translated. The man spoke Hebrew, not English. Stupid people think he was American. They did an Ellis Island on his name, made over the name of the man many say is the son of El Shaddai; the son of He whom made Himself known to them by the name that was spelled *Y-H-W-H*, and that was done in Exodus, and the original pronunciation of that has been lost. God is Y-H-W-H. No one knows how to say those four consonants correctly. There were no vowels in Hebrew and they did an Ellis Island on that as well and made Y-H-W-H into *Yahweh*, then guessed the pronunciation based on what they could already pronounce."

Indigo asked, "What the hell does this have to do with sex?"

"If you called out to Jesus, he wouldn't turn around. It's like his name is Mike and you're calling him Jonathan, so he thinks you're moaning to somebody else."

Indigo snapped, "Smartass."

"Miss Smartass to you."

"No one asked for a scholarly lecture on my birthday. Just for that, I'm raising your rent."

"Go raise your own rent. That joke is so old."

"What difference does it make? The whole creation story was stolen from Africa. Now for the last time, who was the last one of us to get some? Stay focused."

Kwanzaa said, "Well, we know it wasn't Ericka or Destiny. Wasn't me. Had to be you."

All laughed except for Destiny, then they all turned to her to see what was going on.

Indigo said, "What about you, Destiny? You're carrying condoms for some reason."

Ericka said, "Destiny has rubbers?"

"The Trojan is carrying Trojans in her pocket. Tell us what's going on."

Destiny said, "Well, since you are my besties, and we do keep it real, unless one of you misfits got some since about two thirty, maybe three this morning, I think I might win that trophy."

Indigo said, "Get out of here. You met somebody and didn't tell us, or you had a one-off and didn't come and brag about it so we could call you a sneaky thot and a bloody whore?"

"I don't do one-offs. Slow down, girls. Since you feel the need to be all up in my business, let me tell the story from the start. Once upon a time, a few full moons ago, I went out clubbing one night, a night when all of y'all were busy doing whatever y'all do when y'all sneak away from Little Lagos. I met this guy. We had fun dancing, made out a bit, then exchanged numbers."

"Made out?"

"Yeah. We made out."

"You need to define what you mean by *made out*. For some folks, especially in the clubs, a blow job is making out. And anal isn't considered sex, it's just a way of asking *how ya doing*."

"You know, light kissing that became heavy kissing, light touching on top of the clothes. No oral sex and definitely no anal sex. I'm not as freaky as you, Ericka and Kwanzaa."

"You're lying. You kissed a guy *and* let him feel you up the night you met him?"

"I felt him up too."

"You jacked him off?"

"No. But we did a little grinding when he walked me to my motorcycle."

"Liar. You don't let people touch you and you don't touch people like that."

"That night I let down my wall and kissed for the thrill of being kissed, but drew the line at kissing and nice titty massage, didn't give up

Momma's pearl. It was hard because chills were going up and down my spine and the pearl was throbbing."

"You've slept with him, or are you still just petting and grinding?"

"About a month, two hundred kisses, and four hundred nipple licks later, I went on a double date with him and his best friend and his best friend's Asian girlfriend, and after a couple of glasses of wine, a lot of laughs, more dancing, and more grinding, I ended up half naked in his bed with a big, fluffy pillow under my booty. Damn. Why is everyone looking at me like I'm lying?"

"What does he do?"

"Mechanical engineer at Northrop in El Segundo."

"He's a geek like you?"

"A math- and sci-fi-loving geek like me."

"Did he have a pick-up line?"

"Don't they all?"

"What did he say?"

"He made me laugh."

"What did he say?"

Destiny imitated her male friend. "'Baby, you all that. Can I be your man? I got a Big Wheel parked out front, and we can roll down to Crenshaw and get a bean pie.'"

The girls applauded in slow motion, faces twisted, not impressed.

Destiny said, "I thought it was cute. He said *Big Wheel.* It was funny. He didn't say the standard stupid crap a brother usually says. He made me smile."

"What does he drive?"

"A Ram 3500. And the personalized plates say MYBGWL. My Big Wheel."

Ericka, Indigo, and Kwanzaa groaned in unison.

Indigo said, "Two nerds kissing. Sounds as romantic as romance on *Big Bang Theory.*"

Destiny beamed. "I'm a sapiosexual and *love* the Big Bang way he talks nerdy to me."

"Which is why I don't watch *Big Bang Theory.* I can't grasp what they're talking about."

Destiny laughed. "He's not all nerd. He loves hip-hop. He's a decent dancer. At work he dresses very conservatively, but he gets funky with it at night."

"Looks?"

"He's bald with a goatee."

"Complexion?"

"Brown."

"Light brown or dark brown?"

"Light brown skin, the complexion a cop would stop to harass but wouldn't do a full-blown Rodney King, at least not right away. He's a horrible speller and his grammar isn't perfect."

"Public school."

"Yeah. You can tell he went to public school and spent too much time doing hood dances, because he loves to party. He's not much of a cook, but he tries."

"Where is he from originally?"

"He grew up in the area. He was in public school while I was in private school, so we never ran in the same circles and never met each other anywhere that we remember."

"Sounds like a sexy geek who would never win at Scrabble."

"He would be a dominoes and spades kind of guy."

"How tall is he?"

"About five ten."

"Is he fit like you?"

"More or less. He's a normal guy, needs to work on the six-pack, but not fat."

"A fixer-upper."

"Since we met he's been spending more time in the gym."

"Well, at least he's trying."

"He loves my body, did I mention that?"

"No, you did not."

"He likes to be in the bed with me naked, watching *Star Trek* while he runs his fingers up and down my spine, across the curvature of what he desires to dress up and cosplay with."

"Corny."

"Whatever."

"How old is he?"

"Twenty-seven."

"Single or divorced?"

"Single, never been married."

"Ever been engaged?"

"Never been engaged."

"Kids?"

"No kids."

"Loves his mother?"

"Comes from a big family, loves his mom, but is not a momma's boy."

"Pedigree?"

"He's a second-gen college graduate in his family."

"Is the brother eligible to vote? Has he ever picked up trash on the side of the freeway?"

"No prison record. No felonies. Not a registered sex offender."

All eyes and grins stayed on Destiny and the embarrassed smile plastered on her face.

It had been a while since she had dated anyone. She had dated a junior at UCLA, a man who just wanted to sleep with Destiny because in his twisted mind she was an accidental porn star. He wanted to hook up with her at his parents' home in the Palisades, and after they had had drinks and made out, she almost did sleep with him, but she saw his iPhone across the room. It had buzzed with an alert. He had it aimed at the center of the bed, at Destiny, who was in her panties and bra. He was trying to record her, was trying to stream having sex with her live via the Periscope app. He had broadcast their foreplay live. It didn't end well for him. After Destiny had deleted all he had recorded from his phone, she had taken a knife and chased him through his home, caught him, beat him Hoosegow style, blackened both of his eyes, broken his nose, and was tempted to delete him. Word on the street was that he shall forever walk with a mild limp.

The guy before that was Eduardo Terrazas Gaxiola, a visual artist who had graduated from the Universidad Autonóma de Baja California. Destiny had been honest with him too, had told him her real name, which he didn't recognize, being from another country. On the third date, as they sat at Gladstones with the Pacific Ocean a few feet away, seagulls in the air, she felt it might go somewhere, and was ready to open her world up to him, was ready for him to meet her friends, her mother and her father. She told him what had happened. She never heard from him again. No texts returned. Befriended in his ignorance, then *defriended* in real life, like she had the bubonic plague.

Telling Indigo, Ericka, and Kwanzaa she had met someone was a big deal.

She had wanted to tell them. She had dropped the condom on purpose because she knew Indigo would find a way to bring it up when they were all together as a group.

Destiny said, "He grew up in Baldwin Hills and lives in Culver City."

Indigo asked, "Apartment, house, or condo?"

"Condo."

"You see him often?"

"He's taken me out a few times."

"Where? El Pollo Loco or McDonald's?"

"Neither. He took me to the Bazaar by José Andrés Beverly Hills, the Palm, Mastro's Steakhouse Beverly Hills, the Living Room at the Peninsula, the Ivy, Caffé Roma. Opaque."

"You went to Opaque? The restaurant where it's dark and the blind staff are waiters?"

"Yeah. You have to use your senses."

"Expensive?"

"About a C-note per person. No cell phones allowed. You can't even see your food or with whom you're dining, but you can feel their touch. Very interesting place. Sexy. I was comfortable."

"He's taking you to some nice spots. He's trying to impress you."

"Well, now you know I met somebody and I like him a lot."

"How often do you see him?"

"Some nights, especially Fridays, I stop by his condo after FedEx to get a good-night kiss. I try to stop by a couple of times a week. A woman has to secure and maintain her position."

Indigo asked, "You know ain't nothing open in L.A. after midnight but a woman's legs."

Destiny said, "That too. When I'm naked, he looks at me like I'm one of God's perfect creations and, yes, I've become a hopeless romantic with a dirty, perverted, curious mind."

"Corny."

"Stop hatin'. I confessed."

Indigo said, "No wonder you've been coming home right before sunrise so energetic."

Kwanzaa said, "She just giggled. Our Destiny does not do a girly giggle. Oh, my God. She's blushing. This is an imposter. Where is the real Destiny?"

Ericka asked, "When do we meet this amazing guy who has tamed the shrew?"

Indigo said, "We need to see him and his friends, the single, employed, and cute ones."

Destiny said, "I'm trying to see how it works out because, well, like I do strangers, I gave him my club name the night we met. He knows me as Kismet Kellogg, not as Destiny Jones."

Kwanzaa asked, "How serious is it between you and the mechanical engineer?"

"He gave me a key card to the gate and a door key to his condo last night."

Ericka said, "Get out. You can get in his crib and snoop around when he's not home?"

"And I have a toothbrush, a tongue brush, and a box of Honey Nut Cheerios over there."

Indigo said, "You're shacking up then. I hope he's charging you rent there too."

"Slow your roll. Don't put down a broom and expect me to jump over it just yet."

They laughed.

Kwanzaa asked, "Does he know what went down and how you handled it?"

Destiny twisted her lips. "Not yet. Like I said, he knows me as Kismet Kellogg. It's hard to tell how much of my past I should reveal, and when, or even if I should ever bring that incident up again."

Ericka nodded. "Don't blame yourself for what others did to you."

"I never imagined I would ever let a man touch me again after that."

Indigo ranted, "Fuck them all. Fuck the judge. Fuck the court system."

Ericka sighed. "They blamed the victim. It's the way they blame the rioters for the riots, but never acknowledge the conditions that led to the riots. People don't riot for the hell of it and you didn't do what you did for the fun of it. The courts did you wrong. The law reads the same to all, but is not distributed evenly and fairly. You had extenuating circumstances in your case."

Destiny said, "Ericka, let's not beat a dead horse. I need to put that behind me."

"The courts don't see black people as humans, only as animals. You're a brave woman, Destiny. I never would've had the guts. I would've rolled into a ball and died."

Indigo burbled, "If you had been a white woman, you would've been given the key to the city, taken to lunch by the governor, treated to Disneyland by a senator, picked up in Air Force One so you could shake the president's hand, dropped off in New York to sign a million-dollar book deal, then flown first-class back to L.A. for a bidding war to a movie about your life. So anyone who looks down their nose at you because you have brown skin, dick 'em with a dagger."

Kwanzaa took over the conversation. "So, you're seeing someone. You have a bae."

"Kwanzaa, with all you were going through, I didn't want to bring it up."

"I'm miserable and you didn't want to tap-dance in the place happy."

"Well, yeah."

"It would've been like blowing an air horn at a funeral."

They laughed.

Kwanzaa said, "Don't worry about me, Destiny. I want to know all about the guy. I can be unhappy for me and happy for you at the same time, because you know I'm good at multitasking."

Destiny smiled. "I'm really digging this guy. He's smart, handsome, and lots of fun to be around. Not looking for a husband or anything. I'm just enjoying myself. I'm finally dating. Feels good to kick it with a man and . . . and . . . being—*feeling*—like a normal woman feels for a change."

Ericka said, "You deserve some love. You had a six-year gap between . . ."

"It's okay for us to say it. I was raped. I was drugged, raped, and videotaped. I'm just glad they didn't have smartphones. Every bitch at the party would have recorded the crime."

"Didn't mean to— Wasn't trying to take you back down that ugly road. I was thinking about the last couple of guys you tried to date. Neither one of those were worth a cold cup of coffee."

Destiny said, "It had been a long time since I was awake and voluntarily had sex with a man. It's really exciting to know I have a guy I can go kick it with, talk with, watch sci-fi stuff on television with, and just have sex with, or make love with, or whatever we're doing."

Ericka said, "It's called fornicating. If he puts it inside of any hole, you're fornicating."

Kwanzaa smiled. "Glad you met someone new, Destiny. You're my favorite geek. Somebody needs to be happy. Keep it covered and hope he's not as trifling as Marcus Brixton."

Ericka added, "Or my ex-husband. You have no idea what preachers' wives go through. Too many see him as a second-tier deity and want to have a child of God. But this is about you."

Destiny said, "Really didn't expect it to last this long, but I've met his best friend, and we've had double dates. So not only have I lied to him, but I have also lied to his best friend and his friend's girlfriend, or jump off, or whatever she is."

Indigo asked, "Have you met his family?"

"No, not yet. I keep making up excuses to not meet them. I don't want to keep lying."

"Every lie takes you away from truth. You're digging a deep hole."

"I know. I have callused hands from digging. It's stressful, keeping the lie. Now I will have to call a group meeting and tell him and his best friend and his buddy's girl about . . . you know."

"What's his name? We need names to make sure we never bump heads or get played."

"Hakeem Mitchell. Graduated from Crenshaw High and went to Cal State Northridge."

"Hakeem? Is he Muslim?"

"Nah. Nondenominational."

Ericka groaned. "Oh, boy. And which church does Hakeem attend?"

"He's not at your ex-husband's church. He goes to Agape by the Fox Hills Mall. He asked me to go with him, but I can't. I take the helmet off and someone might recognize me."

Ericka nodded. "That's your fear. Public humiliation, in front of him and his family."

"I can imagine people coming over to me calling Destiny, or asking if I am '*that monster.*'"

Ericka agreed. "That would be a scary moment. Pretending to be Kismet, then outted as being her synonym, in the house of the Lord."

Destiny said, "Would be hard to lie on sacred grounds."

"Wasn't for my ex-husband. Wasn't for his flock of mistresses either."

Destiny hummed. "Would hate to turn my back for a second, then for someone to walk up and tell Hakeem my name and past, before I told him myself. Then everyone would start throwing holy water on me and hope I'd burn like the wicked witch in *The Wizard of Oz.*"

"She melted."

"Whatever."

"But they would want you to burn."

They laughed, all except Indigo.

Ericka said, "Glad you have a bit of sense of humor about it."

Indigo said, "You shouldn't have to hide the parts of you that you feel are broken because you think someone is incapable of loving you as is. No one is perfect. No one."

"I don't need a lecture right now, okay? People have made me feel unwanted, sad, depressed, and guilty. I'm in university. I'm late getting started, but I'm there, taking a full load. My dad is ill. I'm working hard day and night to pay my bills. And now I have found a moment of happiness. I need this right now. Don't ask me to be like you, Indigo. My life has never been like yours and it never will be. Let me be me. *This is me right now.* This is as strong as I am right now. Just be happy for me."

Indigo said, "Why didn't you just tell the man your real name? People are either going to accept you or not. End of damn story."

Destiny shook her head. "What I went through, it's not something that's easy to bring up. With most of these guys, you get more respect or empathy points if you say you had cancer."

Ericka shook her head. "Not always. People tend to think you're the walking dead."

"Oops, sorry. I didn't mean to trivialize what you went through. My dad has cancer now, and I just spoke too fast, without thinking, like I do most of the time."

Kwanzaa asked Destiny, "How is your dad doing?"

"He said that some nights it feels like he's in a house filled with fire and smoke and there are no windows, no doors. I can't imagine being that miserable, a prisoner inside of my body."

Ericka said, "Your body turns on itself. There is a civil war going on inside of you. You're trapped on the battlefield between disease and medicine, and there is no escape."

Kwanzaa said, "That sounds horrible. My grandparents died from cancer. My dad went through a lot."

Ericka said, "When you love someone, you go through what they go through. Having cancer showed me what my marriage was made of. Showed me even though we filed joint income taxes, I was in that marriage alone. He wanted no part of the disease or the suffering."

Destiny said, "Thanks for dropping off my dad's meds last week, if I didn't thank you."

Indigo said, "This is going to blow up in your face. *Ka-boom.* You hear me? *Ka-boom.*"

"Whatever." Destiny took a breath. "Give me your cell phones so I can become your female James Van Der Zee once again. All of y'all need to get on the same side."

Kwanzaa, Ericka, and Indigo slid Destiny their phones.

Kwanzaa said, "What about you, Ericka? I know you've been lying."

"Lying about what?"

"I don't believe you're celibate. I bet you're seeing one of the teachers at your job, or messing around with one of the parents. You're sneaky, and sneaky people are the freakiest. We just found out Baby Face Jones has been getting some almost every night, what about you?"

Destiny laughed. "What are you, the neighborhood vulva monitor? Get off our areolas. And I'm not having sex every damn night."

Indigo said, "Don't make my birthday sad and say you have a secret lover too, Ericka."

"Do you have to always be a hater and have to outdo everyone at everything, Indigo?"

"*Yes*. But I'm an achiever, not a hater. Everything I do should both inspire and motivate you. Watch me and learn to do better."

Destiny and Kwanzaa mocked Indigo's accent and sent playful boos her way.

Indigo chuckled and splayed her fingers at both of them. "*Ma ba mi soro.*"

An older guy, a man who was at least eighty and using a walker, stopped by to pay them a compliment, said it was like seeing Mariah Carey, Janet Jackson, Lupita Amondi Nyong'o, and Iman Mohamed Abdulmajid breaking bread at the same table. Indigo was impressed that the man could both remember and pronounce African names. He told them he had traveled around the world, but had never seen women as beautiful as the four of them. He said they were all fine as wine and he would like to take them for a ride on a private plane so he could sixty-nine them one by one. In harsh whispers, Destiny, Indigo, and Kwanzaa cursed the disrespectful old man out.

Kwanzaa cursed him in Spanish.

Destiny snapped, "*What de rasshole*. I'm young enough to be your great-granddaughter."

Indigo said things of equal disgust in Yorùbá.

Ericka added enough profanity to almost give the ancient freak a heart attack.

Chapter 10

They finished breakfast at CJ's, marched toward the parking lot venting and complaining about pathetic Bozo-the-Clown-looking octogenarians on walkers offering women oral sex.

They climbed on iron horses, revved engines, sped in the traffic on La Brea.

As Destiny and Indigo whipped their CBRs through traffic, Kwanzaa and Ericka their passengers, horns blew, the sounds of men flirting and fantasizing about taming a biker girl and making her just another pregnant woman driving in a four-wheel cage. Fifteen minutes later they were inside the Promenade at Howard Hughes Center at Happy Nails and Spa, all side by side in spa chairs, magazines in their laps as Vietnamese women gave them luxury spa manicures and pedicures before starting on their European facials.

Destiny said, "The magazine I'm reading says most women fantasize about a three-way."

Indigo said, "Then you need to stop reading that magazine."

Kwanzaa said, "I've fantasized about that."

"No, you haven't."

"Depends on the dudes. Or the dude and the girl. Depends."

"No, you wouldn't."

"Do you think I'm that boring?"

At the same time Ericka, Indigo, and Destiny said, "Yes."

Kwanzaa laughed. "It's on my bucket list."

Indigo said, "At the bottom. Under the bucket. And then you'd have to dig ten feet."

Ericka asked, "Since we're doing girl confessions, and I know my husband did at least one while we were married, which one of you sneaky freaks has actually done a three-way?"

No hands went up; they looked at each other, wondering, waiting, and anticipating.

Kwanzaa asked, "Okay, who has had a one-off?"

Ericka groaned.

Destiny said, "No, you did not have a one-off. You're my saint. You were a preacher's wife. You used to be my babysitter. I look up to you. Please, please, please, don't let me down."

Ericka groaned again. "I had a moment and gave a stranger five seconds of summer."

"When you were married?"

"Nah. Before I married. I was out of the country. Met an exotic man."

Kwanzaa, Indigo, and Destiny harassed Ericka until she started to talk.

Ericka told them the one-off had happened when she had gone to Buenos Aires when she was twenty-one, fresh out of university, right before she had met her ex-husband. She arrived there on a Monday, had eaten a steak empanada and gone to an Internet café in the affluent section of the city named Recoleta, an area that was as busy as Times Square, with miles of shopping. She was having trouble with the keyboards because they were configured for Spanish and South America. This local guy had come to help her, an Argentinian who was about twenty, a few inches taller than her, hazel eyes, soccer player legs, and Channing Tatum's abs. They walked through the Recoleta cemetery, saw Eva Perón's tomb, had lunch at McDonald's, browsed a bookstore, went to the movie theater, went to Floralis Genérica, then kept strolling down Libertador Avenue, passing embassies, and sight-seeing in the cultural center of the city.

Kwanzaa said, "Will you just get to the good part?"

Indigo said, "Let her tell her story."

Ericka told her girls that they ended up near the zoo, but didn't go inside. Ericka said that by then the jet lag had kicked in, so she told her new friend that she was tired, did that more with body language than actual words, and he escorted her back to her hotel. He held her hand the entire way. He was attracted to her, and she was attracted to him. It was strange being attracted to a stranger, a man she knew nothing about. She had never been with a non-American. The mystery was the attraction. She had never been with a man who wasn't categorically black. She was in a place she couldn't be judged. Back at her hotel room, they made out, then showered together. He went down on her, and she regretted all the years she had spent learning everything but Spanish as a second language. He didn't speak much English. And the middle school and high school Spanish she had learned sounded nothing like the Spanish he spoke. But they met in the middle and worked it out.

Ericka said, "Don't judge me. I was barely twenty-one. I was supposed to explore life and love. We spend most of our lives trying to figure out who we want to be when we grow up."

Indigo said, "Same day you met him you had a one-off?"

"Two hours nonstop, then a short layover, followed by another hour flight."

Destiny said, "That was slutty."

"Good and slutty. He started with the tongue, and ended with the tongue. His tongue wrote the sweetest essay, was as detailed as a dissertation."

Kwanzaa asked, "Why didn't you bring your *se habla español* marathon man back to California? I bet you and him could've made some real pretty babies. *Porteños* are mad sexy."

"It was what it was, nothing more. It was amazing. Was being wild and carefree."

Destiny asked, "You used condoms?"

"Of course. And was still nervous and had myself tested when I made it back home. I had wanted to go to a clinic there, but I was too ashamed to be an American getting tested for STDs."

Indigo asked, "You go down on him?"

"While he had a condom on. I did a little somethin'-somethin'."

Indigo said, "Smart girl."

"Now. I've confessed. Don't judge me. Let's move on to the next girl confession."

Indigo laughed. "This is fun. Finding out how freaky my friends really are sure is fun."

Ericka said, "This magazine says that at least one out of four women has had some sort of same-sex sexual experience. I know I haven't. Which one of you chicas have? 'Fess up."

Destiny, Kwanzaa, and Indigo shifted in discomfort, but no one answered.

Ericka repeated, "C'mon now. Nobody? Really? Not one of you had at least a girl kiss?"

They laughed as massage chairs hummed and kneaded backs and spines.

Indigo took a deep breath and said, "Dammit. That question, of all questions. Really? I mean freakin' really?"

Ericka leaned forward. "You're joking. Indigo, you? You're the one out of four?"

Destiny stared at Indigo's expression. "Oh, my God. She's dead serious."

Kwanzaa stopped blinking. "No way, Little Miss Africa. You were with a woman for real?"

Indigo sighed. "I hate this game. Dammit. Yes. I went somewhere over the rainbow."

Kwanzaa shifted. "Look at the hypocrite. This is about to get real interesting."

Destiny asked, "Why haven't you ever mentioned that you're bisexual before?"

Ericka wanted to know, "How many times?"

Indigo answered, "*Twice*. Not bisexual. Crept over the rainbow and hurried back home to Auntie Em. No place like home. Now will you nosey bimbos calm down and get your nails done?"

Destiny said, "We need a better word than *bimbos*. Bimbos are stupid bitches."

Kwanzaa asked, "Were you in Oz for two days, or two times, or for two orgasms? How was sharing key lime pies? Did it turn into a pie-eating contest? Don't get quiet now, birthday girl."

Indigo hummed. "Well, I tried to get all oral the first time."

Kwanzaa scrunched. "Yuck. Coochies are ugly."

Destiny laughed. "Mine isn't. Yours might be atrocious, but mine is awesome. Hakeem Mitchell told me mine looked and tasted so good it he wished he could give it five stars on Yelp."

Ericka asked Indigo, "You liked going down on her? What was that like for you?"

Indigo said, "It was a long time ago. She liked me, wanted me like that, and I guess I was being nosey and wanted to see what the hoopla was all about. I mean, all these parades and the two doctors on *Grey's Anatomy* made being with a girl look like it was so yummy. I see it on television all the time, they have women with women almost on every show nowadays. I mean, there are more gay people on television than black people, so it was in my brain and I guess I started to wonder if all that was worth marching for. She had a boyfriend and her child lived with the father. She's married now, matter of fact. I ran into her and her husband not long ago when I was shopping at Sprouts. We didn't say anything about it. Just said hi and bye and kept it moving. Her husband doesn't know, and as far as I know she doesn't go there anymore. She was gentle in everything she did, *until* the strap-on."

At the same time Ericka and Kwanzaa said, "Strap-on?"

Destiny said, "*Damn.* You took that to another level."

Rapid questions came from Destiny, Kwanzaa, and Ericka.

Indigo snapped, "Dammit, be quiet and let me tell the whole damn story. *Uninterrupted.* Geesh. It was her idea, but I didn't have any objections. She was attracted to me. She asked me out on a date and took me to the Lobster restaurant in Santa Monica. It was so damn strange letting a girl take me out, but I went. We went out to dinner one night and then went back to her house. She took the lead and did everything. She started touching my nipples and sucking them. I tried to fight it, but her touch was feeling good. It took twenty minutes of her touching and pulling my nipples before I reached over and started sucking her nipples. We ended up in the bathroom, in the shower. She made me stand with my legs spread open and she got down on her knees. The shower had six showerheads and she knew how to use those things very well.

Her wickedness. She sucked my breasts and put a showerhead down there, and that did it for me. I closed my eyes, and pretended a man was doing it, but her touch was different. A woman knows a woman better than a man, I can tell you that. Most guys I've dated have had beards or stubble. She was smooth. So, we did it that one time, and I thought that was that, but a week later she sent me a text and asked me if I was free for dinner again. She sent me a winky face. The winky face made me smile. So, we went out to the Lobster again, sat and talked normally, as if we had never been intimate, and after, I went over to her house again. The moment we got in the door, she was touching me, kissing me, on her knees. This time she had bought an African porn DVD, a strap-on, and liquor. I thought we were just going to touch each other like before, and she'd use her mouth, then we'd do that scissor thing again. I can't believe I'm telling you this. I could go to jail for this. My mother and father would beat me like I was in *Twelve Years a Slave*."

Indigo stopped talking, twisted her lips, shifted side to side, sighed, closed her eyes.

Ericka, Kwanzaa, and Destiny waited.

A second later, Indigo continued. "I guess being with a tall woman was her ultimate fantasy. She admired Nigerian women. It was her strong desire to be with a Nigerian woman. So, that night she wanted to role-play, wear a strap-on and imagine she was a guy, and she wanted to pretend she was a guy doing a sexy girl and get into some headboard banging, hair pulling, sweaty, sloppy, neighbors-writing-hate-notes kind of sex. I didn't like what she did."

Kwanzaa mumbled, "Jesus."

Destiny shushed Kwanzaa.

Ericka shushed Destiny, then said, "What did she do that you didn't like, Indigo?"

Indigo took a breath. "Okay. Well. She was doing it to me doggie-style, which was fine because that way I couldn't see her and imagined she was a man, despite her small hands on my waist, but she got aggressive and started twisting me and turning me and the positions got to be too much. It was a like a gym workout. She kept asking if the wood was good, so I started making all kinds of fake noises like it was the best fake penis I'd ever had. She kept asking me if I liked her big fat dick. She wanted me to give head to that thing. She had lost her mind. I was done. I was just in it for the tongue. Then I showered and left. We never discussed it. We ran into each other in Manhattan Beach a few times, even talked on the phone once or twice. Then a long time went by before I ran into her at Sprouts. We barely chatted. It's like it never happened."

Kwanzaa asked, "Someone we know?"

Indigo said, "No one present, if that's what you're asking indirectly, Kwanzaa."

"Just asking."

"What did she look like?"

"She looks like a mixture of Zadie Smith and Leona Lewis, to be honest."

Kwanzaa said, "Wow. I bet y'all could've made some pretty babies. People would have thought you were the dark-skinned nanny, but those babies would have had some good hair."

The girls laughed.

Ericka asked, "How did that even happen?"

Indigo said, "We met at the Barnes and Noble in Manhattan Beach, by chance. I used to hang out there. She heard my accent, and then I heard hers, and we both talked about our countries, and Africa in general, how we wished all the nations were united, and Africa would rule the world. So, we talked literature, politics, and we talked Africa."

"She's Nigerian too?"

"She's African, and that is all I will say. I will not name her country. She is brilliant. She knew things I have yet to learn, and as we sat in the coffee shop, she seduced me with her intelligence. I could tell then she was being more than the normal friendly. It was cute. It scared me too. She was so much like the woman I want to be when I am older. Her wanting me, I think that turned me on. A woman excited me. I'm so over that."

Kwanzaa and Ericka stared at her, stunned by the admission.

Ericka asked, "Are you telling the truth, or is this one of your jokes?"

Destiny said, "That rodeo show Indigo described sounds about right, Ericka."

Kwanzaa groaned. "You too? Is that also included in your catalog of depravity?"

Ericka asked, "Destiny, child, are we running at fifty percent on that pop quiz?"

"Did you see me waving my hand in the air? No, you did not. Indigo is the one of four."

"Then how would you know what *sounds* right?"

"I can tell you what I saw in Hoosegow, and that's that a lot of pretty girls were up in there, and a lot converted. I watched other girls seduce girls, and that was some weirdness for me. I saw girls impress other girls, get them to talking, get them laughing, then they are making out like it's no big deal. They have so much Bambi-sexuality up in those joints its crazy."

Ericka said, "Leave Bambi out of this, Destiny."

Kwanzaa said, "Don't spoil my childhood memories, but what is Bambi-sexuality?"

Destiny sighed. "Bambi-sexuality is when they kiss and feel each other up, but don't go all the way. They use each other to practice some parts of foreplay. But sometimes the heat is too much and it goes to the next level. Some were making scissors. I'd see girls who had been turned out, when their girl was set free, become the one who was trying to turn a new girl into a scissor lover."

Kwanzaa raised a brow. "What are scissors? You said scissors and Indigo said scissors. What does that mean?"

Ericka said, "Jesus, Kwanzaa. Even I know what that is."

Destiny said, "Google it, hit Images, and be prepared to see a new world."

Indigo said, "Before we go on, let me be clear and set the record straight. I am not *converted*. Taking a weekend vacation to London won't make you British. I'm not British."

Destiny teased, "Sure you're not a hasbian?"

"What is a hasbian?"

"A has-been lesbian."

"One can be a has-been?"

Destiny said, "You learn about another world in Hoosegow. It's not charm school."

"Well, I didn't learn about that world in Oklahoma," said Ericka. "All I learned was the Bible and weed."

"I believe you, Indigo. You are two-timer with one girl. I don't think you're a LUG."

Indigo asked, "What the hell is a LUG?"

"Lesbian until graduation."

"Don't insult me with your foolishness."

Destiny laughed hard. "It's cool if you are. How you roll is how you roll."

"What I did will never happen again."

Ericka laughed so hard she cried. "Lesbian until graduation. Will she get a degree?"

"*I dropped out,*" Indigo said, then pointed at Destiny. "You sure know a lot about the lifestyle of women who like women. This person you're seeing, the one no one has seen yet, is a man, to be clear, right?"

Destiny laughed. "Might be fun for you and lobster girl, and I am not knocking what you did, you like what you like, but that's not for me. I like beef, not seafood."

Ericka tried to calm down. "I can't imagine Indigo like that, with a woman acting like she was a man. What's the point of being with a woman acting like a man, when there are men?"

"I'm right here. Have some respect."

Destiny said, "I get hit on all the time, especially since I started rocking on two wheels. The power of the CBR. My derriere is always in the air. Guys holla, but a lot of girls come at me too. Married women are the worst. They are aggressive. They pull up next to me at red lights and flirt the hardest, have that *hotel, motel, Holiday Inn* look in their eyes. They'd cheat on their man and go down on me in a minute. They think *CBR* means '*coochie be ready*' for them to play with or something."

Kwanzaa had her phone in hand, was looking at videos, then raised her voice. "*This is scissoring?* You did this? This is what girls do with other girls? I thought girls were just going downtown and finger banging and calling it a damn day. This crap ain't real. If I can't do doggie or reverse cowgirl, what's the point of even getting in bed with somebody?"

Indigo said, "Jesus, lower your voice, idiot. Stop trying to scissor-shame me."

Destiny said, "That's probably why the second time the girl didn't want the dry humping and brought the toy. I guess a woman can do doggie and reverse cowgirl with a strap-on."

Kwanzaa announced, "Indigo-the-Nigerian has another dual citizenship."

"I *visited* Britain. *I did not change citizenships.* I would never change citizenships."

Kwanzaa laughed. "My, oh my. Are we feeling defensive?"

Indigo hissed, then snapped, "I was with *one* girl—"

At the same time Ericka and Kwanzaa said, "*Two times.*"

Then Ericka howled. "Indigo's *CBR* stands for '*coochie been retrained.*'"

Kwanzaa howled too, "*CBR* stands for '*coochies bumping repeatedly.*'"

Indigo laughed. "I am *hetero.* I was curious and infatuated. I tried something different. I have to get all of this out of my system while I am single, unmarried, and childless, because I will soon be in law school, and then I will be a lawyer who engages in either the business industry or entertainment law. Family and a Nigerian man will be in my life, taking up time. Yaba the Laker didn't work out for me, but I have moved on with no regrets. Maybe Olamilekan will be ready soon, and maybe he will be ready today to make a serious commitment."

Ericka asked, "So is Yaba the Laker out of the picture for good?"

"He calls. He wants to see me. But Olamilekan is more handsome, is sexier, is an intelligent man who makes me laugh, a man who is focused and ambitious. I want Olamilekan, but he has to be a man who respects women, a devoted man, loving and caring, God-fearing and wants to settle down. I want my clichéd soul mate, but until that man stops hiding from me, until a ring is on this finger, I'm not going to rest and use this real estate as a bloody paperweight."

Destiny winked. "Sounds like she got you real good, Indigo. Woman was like a man."

Indigo snapped, "Did you not hear a word in that moving speech I just gave? I told you that in *confidence*. I'd better not see it pop up in Linda Ikeji, Uche Eze Pedro, or Emeh Achanga's blog. If any African blogger confronts me about this, if I receive one phone call from one relative overseas and this is the subject matter, I will deny every word, then contact my mother and sue each of you individually for defamation of character. *Don't cross me*."

Kwanzaa said, "The woman did you like she was a man. Woman was like a man."

In her soprano voice, Kwanzaa sang the lyrics *Woman like a man*, from Damian Rice's CD. Kwanzaa and Ericka joined in and added their mezzo-sopranos to the teasing. Soon Destiny lent her remarkable contralto singing voice to the dancing bright tones the others had created. Indigo added darker and richer tones as the others sang a smooth harmony with the strong lead voices. They ended the jam session and laughed, ceased the teasing chant. Then the others asked Indigo to repeat her wicked story again, slower, with more detail.

Chapter 11

Still teasing Indigo, soon they were on the escalator heading down to the lower-level parking garage, colorful helmets in hands. The motorcycles had been left in spaces at the far end.

Destiny said, "Okay, which one of us has been with the oldest guy? Let's judge that one by both the age of the man *and* by age difference in years between the woman and the man."

Kwanzaa said, "Two categories. A doubleheader. Cool."

"Let me see some hands in the air."

Ericka groaned again, six eyes going to her as she was prepared to raise a hand, maybe both hands, add herself to at least one of the other lists, but a car screeched down the ramp. The sharp noise and loud music startled them and all attention shot toward the fast-driving fool.

It was a brother in his twenties. He was handling a convertible Mercedes.

Indigo's frown turned upside down and she said, "What have we here?"

The brother had light-brown skin, a rich complexion that had hints of oranges underneath. His hair was close to being shaved on both sides, longer on top, in a short and stylish *bro*hawk. He rocked a beard, full and dark. The brother pulled up four spaces from them, top down.

The song "Blackbird" by Nina Simone played on his system.

The ceiling in the garage was low, the acoustics amazing. It sounded like Nina Simone was alive, feet away, and having a concert. The brother sat there, eyes closed, in a zone, listening to the song as it reverberated throughout the garage as if he were at Carnegie Hall.

He was a handsome man, very Will Smith meets Blair Underwood, only half their age.

The music from his sound system was mesmerizing. Without a thought they began humming. Then Indigo sang the first line. Ericka joined in on the second line. Kwanzaa changed the duet to a trio. Destiny made it a quartet. They sang the song together, softly at first, with feeling. Their singing grew louder, and with heart and soul, they gave away their blues.

They became a choir singing out their pain to the sweetest rhythm.

Their voices echoed in the emptiness of the promenade's garage.

When the song ended, when their quartet was done, the driver applauded.

Then as the brother turned off his radio and started raising the top on his car, there was more resounding applause. Men, women, parents, and children who were walking in the garage had stopped in their tracks to listen to them sing. Not until then did the friends realize their voices had echoed in the hollowness. As people passed by, everyone called them Blackbirds.

The brother eased out of his car and came toward them, a pleasant smile on his face.

Indigo said, "If he's not wearing a wedding band, isn't gay, is articulate, has at least one degree, has subject-verb agreement, and doesn't stutter, I call dibs."

Ericka said, "What about Olamilekan?"

"My backup might need a backup, so back up off of this one."

Kwanzaa said, "He's too short for you."

Indigo said, "To be fair, I can only judge a man by length and girth."

Destiny said, "You're going to mess around and catch the Kwanzaas."

Ericka and Indigo laughed.

Kwanzaa showed her middle fingers and said, "That is so not even close to being funny."

He stood at the average height for a man, but being lean and toned made him seem taller, though not as tall as Indigo's ex before the footballer. The brother wore gray Morehouse sweat pants, colorful Reeboks, and a black fitted T-shirt that had the neologism NEGROPHOBIA across the chest in white letters, that term inside of a red circle, a slash across its center. He wore an Apple watch, carried an Apple phone, and had a big apple smile for the apple bottoms.

Destiny did a double take, and lost her awareness of where she was in relation to the rest of the world. She was pulled back to another regretful day, into another part of her past, into another compartment, the era of her teenage life. He was someone she never wanted to see again. Destiny walked away when he came closer, turned her back to the conversation, made herself busy with her hoodie and helmet, felt her palms sweating, began taking short breaths.

He said, "You ladies sounded amazing. I was going to say y'all look like four fine-ass Bond girls. But the way y'all killed that Nina Simone song, forget Bond girls, I'm calling y'all the Blackbirds. I'd better send a tweet and tell the Supremes, En Vogue, 702, SWV, and Destiny's Child you beautiful Blackbirds could harmonize and resurrect the girl groups."

Indigo said, "We'll be Bond girls if they let Idris be James Bond."

"Then the world would end because 007 would never want to get out of bed."

"You think we'd *let* him get out of bed if 007 looked like Idris?"

They laughed, all but Destiny Jones. She was in a state of mild panic.

He told Indigo, "Love your accent. Where are you from?"

"My parents are from Nigeria, and no Nigerian 419 scam jokes, please."

"What's your name?"

"Indigo Bose Fumilayo Titilayo Titilola Mojisola Morenike Abdulrahaman."

There was a pause. He said, "Bet you can't say that ten times real fast."

She did.

Everyone laughed. Everyone except Destiny.

He asked, "All of you are from West Africa with names longer than the alphabet?"

"I am the only Nigerian. My friends are Americans. They have slave names."

Kwanzaa said, "Here we go again."

Ericka said, "Indigo, you know it was your people who sold us down the river."

He laughed, asked Indigo, "Your parents are from Nigeria, but where are you from?"

"I'm Nigerian. That answers your question, does it not?"

"Where were you born?"

He had derailed the little game Indigo always played. It was a thing she always did, implied she was also born in Nigeria. She would be quick to point out that the United States was one of the few places on the planet where illegals and noncitizens could come from anywhere in the world on Sunday, have a child on Monday, and the child was considered a citizen. Other countries would stitch the mother up and send her back to her country, unless the father was a citizen, as most of the world was still patriarchal. No matter where a Nigerian had their children, those children were still Nigerian. So Indigo wasn't lying. She was Nigerian.

She said, "I'm Nigerian. African, baby. That's all you need to know. Stop swimming in my Kool-Aid. You're wearing Morehouse, but I don't hear an ATL accent. Please explain."

Kwanzaa asked, "Yeah. Who are you, man from Morehouse who talks to strangers?"

He said, "I was born here in L.A. I was born at Daniel Freeman before they tore it down."

"Would be hard to be born there after they tore it down."

"I stand corrected."

"I was born at Daniel Freeman too. Before they tore it down."

They playfully threw up the letter *W*, representing West Coast, not gangbangers.

The brother introduced himself. He told them his name was Dubois.

"You're not dropping the final *G* on your words. I actually understand you. People from Atlanta call College Park 'Collie Park.' Say things like *skraight* instead of *straight*." He had just graduated from

Morehouse, and now was back home to start work on his master's at Pepperdine.

He said, "I also have this other hobby I do on the side from time to time."

Indigo said, "Don't tell us you're a male stripper. Every brother wants to be Magic Mike."

Kwanzaa said, "I have a few quarters to put in your G-string if you are."

They laughed again. He jogged to his car with the stride of a long-distance runner, and hurried back, handing Kwanzaa and Indigo a red, black, and green flyer.

He did standup comedy too, said he had been getting on stage since he was fifteen, told them he was doing a show soon to help raise money for the families of black men killed by the police.

He said, "We're doing a show called *Red, Black, and Bruised*. We're going to tear down a few Confederate flags and hit the black experience in America, going to get on stage and talk about the hypocrisy, rip on decades of abuse and atrocities, but it's straight standup."

"Can you make what we go through in America as black people a gut buster? Can you make us laugh about slavery, Jim Crow, police brutality, mass incarceration, and bad hairstyles?"

"I could've made Harriet Tubman laugh from the plantation to freedom, then back to the planation to free some more people. I could've made Rosa Parks laugh on the bus, and made Martin Luther King Jr. crack up as he wrote a letter from a hot jail cell over in Birmingham."

The girls told Dubois that it was Indigo's birthday, and that they'd gone hiking that morning. He said he had hit the pavement at sunrise with his mother and her running group, had run five miles, then had worked out again, hitting the heavy bag and getting in the ring for three rounds at Crenshaw Boxing Gym. Now he was heading to Johnny Rockets to get a burger.

He said, "It's your birthday for real, pretty girl born in L.A. with parents from Africa?"

Indigo smiled. "Sure is, man who was born at the black hospital, went to Morehouse, is built like a male stripper, wears no wedding ring, runs, is going to grad school soon, and plays hood-rat loud music as he drives a nice car."

"My Nubian queen, on your special day, I will have to sing 'Happy Birthday' to you."

He sang, and he could sing. He sang the traditional happy birthday song, his tenor voice rocking it between one octave below middle to one octave above middle, then switched it up and did the funky version, the Stevie Wonder classic, had Ericka, Kwanzaa, and Indigo smiling. But when he changed up and sang 'Happy Birthday' with an African accent, did African dances, did them well, and at the same time became a human beatbox and imitated instruments, Indigo became ecstatic. He became drums, African talking drums, flute, and piccolo. His silliness and being on point had Indigo jumping up and down, clapping, and laughing, especially when he pulled her over and made her dance with him. Indigo showed him how to do it right, moved like Tiwa Savage and Yemi Alade. Soon Dubois had started a party, had Indigo, Ericka, and Kwanzaa singing and dancing, and the African dancing switched into them doing the whip, the Nae Nae, and the Superman. All the girls joined the impromptu birthday fun, all except Destiny Jones.

When Dubois was done he asked Destiny, "You okay over there, my sister?"

Destiny had hoped the brother would come and go without paying her any attention. But he had noticed her. Jaw tight, memory strong, she exhaled, faced him, unsmiling, pulled her hair back from her face into a loose ponytail, let her entire face be seen, and then took a hard breath before she looked him straight in his eyes. Her jaw was tight. Heartbeat strong, galloping. She sucked her teeth.

"Hey, Dubois."

He stared at her features, at her mean expression, his mouth open as his eyes moved over the topography of her appearance, evaluated her, all the while muted and surprised.

He said, "DJ? You have to be kidding me. DJ, is that you?"

Nostrils flared, Destiny Jones nodded. "Hey, stranger."

"I'm serious. DJ, that's you for real?"

She nodded again. "Yeah. It's been years."

"You're looking awesome."

"Thanks for the hyperbole."

"I mean it, and not in a disrespectful way. Your hair, the color, the way your locks are crinkly, they look very Afrocentric. You were on the creamy crack last time I saw you, that or a press-and-curl. You're taller than I remember, and I guess the best way to put it is, well, fuller in the right places, not trying to sexualize you, just revere the change, and damn, you are fit. I mean, you always had a nice body. Your arms are solid. Your core is tight. Amazing transformation."

"I had a final growth spurt when I was almost sixteen. And I went away to Hoosegow, and the place I stayed wasn't a gluten-free or farm-raised environment, so thanks to the food with fat, steroids, antibiotics, and other poisonous additives, I put on a few pounds. And thanks to the rustic gym they had, and so many girls who worked out all day, I'm no longer flabby. I'm toned."

"You were never flabby. Not at all. Always had a baby face and a woman's body."

"Yeah. I know."

Silence settled between them. She didn't hide her past. He knew. She knew he knew. Destiny twisted her lips, uncomfortable in her skin as she looked into his light-brown eyes.

Dubois said, "Wow. Sorry I keep looking at you like this, but . . . wow."

"Yeah, my thighs are thick and I have a heart-shaped butt like a video vixen."

"That's not what I meant. You've been on my mind off and on."

"Since when?"

"Since the last time I saw you."

"You mean, when I stopped by your mother's house in Baldwin Hills?"

"Yeah."

"What were those off and on thoughts, exactly?"

"Had wondered how you were doing."

"I guess you lost my number a few years ago."

"Okay, I deserve that."

Destiny posted a false smile. "I'm fine. Thanks for asking. Thanks for caring."

"I should have called you, or at least gone to see your mom or dad."

"Thanks for checking on me."

"I'm serious, how are you? How have you been? How are your parents?"

"Does it matter to you?"

"We're friends."

"We *were* friends. My real friends stuck by me when life got rough."

Destiny glanced left to right, realizing that Ericka, Kwanzaa, and Indigo had moved in closer, and all were touching her. She said she was fine, then faced Dubois again.

She said, "So, you're fresh out of Morehouse, heading off to grad school at Pepperdine, and doing standup now, like your father did. I'm sure he's smiling down from heaven right now."

"My mom's not crazy about me doing it, but I guess that part of my dad is in my blood. I used to do spots at Uptown Comedy Club in ATL. Was the club MC when I was eighteen. I wish I had been old enough to be considered to play my dad when they made the movie."

"Well, I guess you're carrying the baton and the brand for the Leonard Dubois name."

Ericka said, "Hold on. Your father is the comedian Leonard Dubois?"

"Yes. I'm Leonard Dubois Jr. I was born after he passed."

"Jesus. Your mother is a nurse at a doctor's office near Fox Hills Mall?"

"She was a nurse."

"Oh, my God. Did you lose your mom too?"

He smiled. "Mom's fine. She was a nurse then, but she's a doctor now."

"She's a doctor now? Wow. Nurse Debra Mitchell is a doctor."

"Dr. Debra Dubois. She married my dad."

"That's amazing. I am so happy for her."

"She took over the same office when Dr. Faith retired. I saw Dr.

Faith yesterday. She's helping Mom with her manuscript. She's writing her memoirs, the story of her life growing up, about people who have had an impact on her life, and about her and my dad. Mom also does volunteer work with a nonprofit for battered women and children and victims of sex trafficking. She wants to sell her memoirs at some point, then let the proceeds go to help other women."

"I met your mom and your dad when I was . . . I guess that was before you were born."

"You look like you're under twenty. Thought you were in high school when I pulled up."

"I'm not, but thanks. She was Debra Mitchell then. She was compassionate, like the sister I always wanted. I almost went into nursing because of her."

"What's your name, so I can tell Mom I ran into you?"

"Ericka Stockwell. I doubt if she would remember me from over two decades ago."

"Wow. Are you serious?"

"What was that 'wow' all about?"

"She mentions you in her manuscript. I proof her pages."

"And you're sure she said Ericka Stockwell?"

"I'm sure. I've read the chapters where she talks about meeting you and your mother."

Ericka said, "Your mother is writing chapters about me and my mother?"

Silence moved between them.

In that awkwardness, Indigo told him they were celebrating her birthday with a California-causual get-together later on, sort of a Friday-evening happy-hour-pool-party-rug-rats-friendly affair, then invited him and any good-looking friends to stop by if he could find the time between driving around L.A. in a drop-top and breaking out in song when he saw beautiful women.

Dubois said, "It was a pleasure meeting you gorgeous, effervescent, and passionate sisters. Indigo, I hope you have a fantastic birthday with the rest of the Blackbirds."

Indigo gave him her number and address, enamored by his charisma, and said she hoped she'd see him and a few of his friends later.

Ericka, Kwanzaa, and Destiny said nothing.

After looking back twice, he disappeared up the ramp.

Destiny cursed, ran her hand through her bleached sisterlocks, tugged hard, screamed.

Ericka asked, "What was that?"

"Nothing, nothing, nothing, nothing, nothing."

"Don't do that."

"I lost my virginity and he lost my number."

"The plot thickens."

"I think that's how it went back then. Not even one phone call after it was done."

Ericka whispered, "Hard to escape things from the past. The past never leaves."

Destiny nodded. "Someone always shows up to remind you of the bullshit you want to forget."

Ericka asked, "Why only one time with Dubois, Destiny?"

"Because it hurt like hell."

"Why didn't you call him?"

"Because I left cherry stains on white sheets. It was humiliating. And the guy should call. I mean, he can call every day until he gets some no-no, but can't make one call after? Messy sheets or not, that's unforgivable."

"You didn't put a towel down for your first time?"

"Well, it's not like I had read an instruction book."

For a moment, they gazed up the ramp where Dubois had vanished.

Destiny pulled her helmet on, face shield up, and said, "Dubois called us Blackbirds."

Indigo said, "Everyone who heard us sing in this echo chamber called us Blackbirds."

Ericka asked, "Can we be Blackbirds? That wouldn't be like being a crow, would it?"

Kwanzaa said, "Blackbirds sounds like an urban sequel to a classic Hitchcock movie."

Destiny said, "Sounds better than calling each other *W*-words, *N*-words, and *C*-words. The way we talk to and about each other nowadays, MLK has probably rolled over in his grave so many times that if he were buried vertically, he would've drilled his way from ATL to Madagascar."

Indigo asked, "Are you sure we don't want to call ourselves Pillow Queens?"

At the same time Destiny, Kwanzaa, and Ericka laughed and said, "*Hell no.*"

Kwanzaa said, "Or we could go by our initials. Destiny. Indigo. Kwanzaa. Ericka."

Destiny frowned. "DIKE? Really, Kwanzaa? I mean really?"

Again they fell out laughing.

When Ericka calmed down, she said, "Blackbirds."

Kwanzaa nodded. "Blackbirds."

Indigo gave two thumbs up. "Blackbirds."

Destiny said, "Then it's settled. We're the Blackbirds."

Chapter 12

By early afternoon a jumper in the theme of a princess castle had been put up in the back of the fourplex. Indigo said it was for the kids when they came, but she was the first one to crawl inside. Destiny followed her. Not to be outdone, Kwanzaa climbed in and so did Ericka.

They became five-year-olds once again, jumping, bouncing, and squealing.

The kids in the neighborhood peeped over the wall, hoping to be invited over.

The jumper was for Indigo. She was still a child at heart.

The deejay arrived, a former rapper named Butter Pecan. She set up her equipment away from the pool. Music played as the Blackbirds, all in bikinis and vibrant half sarongs, arranged tables and chairs by the swimming pool. There were two large cakes from Hansen's Cakes on Fairfax in the unofficial Ethiopian district.

The caterer set up long tables with Nigerian food: shuku shuku, fruit salad, chicken skewers, coconut shrimp, rice, Nigerian pancakes, peanut soup, egusi soup, and meat pie.

Ericka, Kwanzaa, and Indigo gave Destiny their cell phones, then they gathered by the pool. Destiny took photos of them, again her three friends in their classic *Charlie's Angels* poses.

The caterer came over and offered to take a picture of all four of them.

Destiny said, "I'm fine being behind the camera."

Balloons were all over the building, and presents were put on another table near the pool area. About twenty people were over to swim and celebrate, just as many more on the way. Rush hour had commenced, but most had been en route and were ahead of traffic.

Indigo's straight-outta-Nigeria parents arrived neatly dressed.

Her father was Nagode Allah Abdulrahaman, his cognomen a very familiar Nigerian surname with the Hausa tribe. His family had moved to the north, but he had left Nigeria decades ago, made his way through London, then to America.

Indigo's father had grown up in the Nigerian northern state of Borno, in far-out arid lands like Ngala, Gwoza, Damboa, and Chibok. He was the ninth of twelve children.

Indigo's beautiful mother, Chimamandanata, was born in Nigeria's southern state, in Akwa Ibom, surrounded by Cross River, Rivers and Abia States, near the Atlantic, on land known to have oil reserves that were hit hard by Shell Oil activities, her birthland a more tropical area with forests in the remote areas. She was the fifth of nine children.

Indigo's father had worked hard and found the dream that had eluded most Americans. Her father was an astute businessman who lived on his mobile phone, always working a deal, his custom-made slacks and custom shoes handmade in South America speaking of his success.

He was not the stereotypical African seen in movies made by people who had never been to Africa, not the African on late-night television in front of organizations begging for American donations for underprivileged and malnourished children, kids who would never see a dime of that charity and were having their misery exploited the same way Haiti had been exploited and was yet to see any real money from the billions raised due to humanitarian efforts to help its people after earthquakes and hurricanes.

Mrs. Abdulrahaman was an attorney who had attended Obafemi Awolowo University, OAU, before coming to America and training in law once again. Every immigrant who came to America started over. Women who were lawyers from Brazil were in America cleaning homes to get by. Chimamandanata was one of the fortunate ones, one who was not afraid to work hard today for a better tomorrow. She specialized in construction, environmental, and real estate law. She was smartly dressed, a Nigerian fashion queen, always well put-together, very chic in her tan Capri pants and lively, sleeveless top. Malaysian hair cascaded down her back, not a stitch showing. She always wore high heels, the sexiest shoes known to man, today her choice being Christian Louboutin daffodil-yellow leather pumps. With the shoes and freshly done hair, it was obvious she had no intention of swimming or getting wet.

Destiny, Kwanzaa, and Ericka greeted Indigo's family, gave them hugs. Destiny's dad arrived next, a birthday present for Indigo in hand.

Indigo and Kwanzaa were happy to see Mr. Jones. They ran to him, sandals flapping against their feet, gave him daughterly hugs, and asked how he was doing. Destiny walked to her dad too, then playfully-yet-territorially eased the others out of the way so she could hug her old man and kiss his cheeks.

Destiny catered to her dad, even though he objected to the preferential treatment. Kwanzaa did the same with her father and bonus mom the moment they showed up. Her true mother and bonus dad wouldn't be here. She could invite only one set of parents to any gathering in order to avoid conflict.

While Indigo entertained her parents and let her mother and father playfully fight to be the one who spoiled her the most, she noticed that Ericka was in high spirits but avoiding Mr. Jones. Mr. Jones talked to everyone else, was energetic and jovial once again, but didn't give Ericka any eye contact. Ericka was usually the first of the newly crowned Blackbirds to run and give Mr. Jones a hug. She had known him since she was a child, when she used to babysit Destiny for him and his ex-wife.

Indigo shook it off, saw Kwanzaa was texting someone, and went to make sure she wasn't sending messages to Marcus Brixton because he was not invited to the family affair, but Kwanzaa hadn't invited any man to the party.

"I was hoping you invited some rich Nigerian men who knew how to be monogamous," Kwanzaa said.

"And I was hoping you, Destiny, and Ericka had invited some hot American men who understood the value of a woman and had vowed on their ancestors' graves to be loyal as well."

"Butter Pecan might be your type."

"Don't make me curse you."

"Did you really bump uglies with a girl twice and let her use a strap-on and play giddyap horsie in your no-no?"

"Fool, why don't you have the deejay announce that in front of my very religious parents and watch me get verbally beaten and disinherited from all that I am entitled to when I marry?"

"Lower my rent or I will have Butter Pecan make that announcement."

"One girl. Two times. Two years ago. Let it go. Never mention that again. *Never*."

"Calm down. I was joking."

"Don't joke with me. My parents are *Nigerian*. Not American. Not from Rwanda. Not from Chad. *Nigerian*. They better not hear a whisper of what I have told you. Where they are from, homosexuality is a crime. Do you hear me? There is legislation and it is illegal for straight family members, or anyone, to be supportive. They send straight people to jail if they encourage things like I did only twice with one African girl. My only dual citizenship is American and Nigerian."

"Okay, okay, okay. Calm down. But it's nice to know I can blackmail you if I need to."

"So hush your face before you disgrace me."

"I might let it go and never mention it again, if you tell me one thing."

"What, what is it you want to know so I can have a peaceful birthday?"

"Did you use the strap-on on her too?"

"Kwanzaa, you're disgusting."

"Did you?"

"You're the most disgusting individual I know."

"Did you?"

"I despise you."

"Did you?"

"*I did use the bloody thing*. She wanted me to use the bloody thing on her. Satisfied?"

"Did you like being the one in charge? Did you woman-like-a-man her like she did you? You played giddyap in her no-no, too?"

With her right hand, Indigo touched her own forehead, then the lower middle of her chest, then her left shoulder, and finally her right shoulder. Kwanzaa mocked her and did the same.

Kwanzaa said, "Destiny sure knew a lot about the lesbian terminology and lifestyle."

"Much more than I ever will know. That is not part of my world. *I am not British.*"

"I'm done talking about your shenanigans. But it was fun teasing you. You're sensitive."

"Good, now let's talk about someone else while they can't hear us."

"Sounds like Destiny has been seeing old boy for a while. She is as sneaky as Ericka."

Indigo asked, "Is Ericka sneaking, creeping, and freaking with somebody too?"

"She had a mild bruise on her neck last week. Last Saturday morning. I saw it when we were Rollerblading from Manhattan Beach to the Santa Monica Pier. You didn't see it?"

"Did she? How did I miss that?"

"Her yellow ass covered it with makeup. Somebody sucked her neck bone."

Indigo and Kwanzaa made thinking faces, hummed at the same time.

Indigo asked, "On another note, don't leave me hanging, Kwanzaa."

"Regarding what, Chatty Cathy?"

"Well, tell me something about Hugo Boss."

"I thought that conversation was over when we were climbing the stairs."

"What does he drive?"

"No idea."

"How can you not know?"

"Indigo, I do my job and let the Latinas get all giggly and rush to help the guy."

"Kwanzaa, this is Los Angeles and it's all about what he's rocking."

"Should be about character, not about possessions."

"Nobody wants to date the bus stop man, not even the bus stop woman."

"That's shallow, yet pretty accurate. L.A. is a culture of ever-growing egotistical values."

"Brixton is an attorney. Would you have dated him if he were the garbage man?"

"I wasn't with the man because of his job. *You* date men based on their occupation."

"I keep it real. A relationship is nothing to be played with. If you see yourself as garbage man material, go for it. I just need to know what Mr. Iced Coffee is driving so I can evaluate him. If a man in L.A. has no car, he either has no ambition or too many DUIs. Smart women must consider these things, or else we are setting ourselves up to fail. I want us to be winners."

"If a man has no character, in my world, it doesn't matter how deep his pockets are."

"Well, at least tell me if what matters most hangs to the left or to the right?"

"Are you mad? I didn't look between the man's legs. That's your forte."

"Liar. We watch crotches the way men watch breasts, and we text each other pictures of naked men damn near every day, so quit lying."

"What difference would that make?"

"I need you to forget Brixton. Man-shop. You're not engaged to that man-slut anymore."

"Hmm, I think saying *man-slut* is as redundant as saying *man-whore*."

"Flirt with the man in Hugo Boss. Or flirt with the garbage man next Tuesday. Up to you."

"I don't flirt. That is not in my skill set."

"You don't have to show a man your nipples. You can flirt and be cool with it. If he orders a Grande, give him a Venti and wink. Nobody will even notice. If he's that damn fine, flirt."

"With all the questions, I thought you were interested in the Hugo Boss guy."

"He sounds intriguing. But boo, you know men are like smog; they are all over L.A."

"And they are all over you."

"Don't hate me because I have both a vertical advantage and horizontal skills."

"I'm not hard up to the point I need to flirt with a customer at my stupid job."

"You hate being alone. You are not built to be alone. That's your fault."

"I hate you as much as you despise me."

"You love me as much as I love you and we both hate the truth."

"Why tell the truth when lying feels so much better?"

"Exactly."

Chapter 13

Indigo and Kwanzaa went to the crowd, made sure everyone was comfortable. Already, Indigo's father had started a political conversation. Indigo playfully put her hands over her dad's mouth and reminded him it was a birthday party, not a gathering at the United Nations. Chimamandanata hurried over, laughing, and joined her daughter, putting her hands over her husband's mouth too.

Indigo's parents were constantly touching each other, always kissing and engaging in PDA. If ever there was a power couple, that flirtatious, naughty, handholding couple was one.

When Indigo and her parents were together, their accents were full Nigerian, and the attitude that came with it, the histrionics, the hissing, the exaggerated sighing, the addition of Yorùbá phrases and words to emphasize a point. They emphasized their culture without shame to separate themselves from the black American. Indigo always practiced her mother and father's tongue so when she returned to Nigeria she wouldn't be teased for sounding like an American woman. If she returned home and sounded too American, even as they stamped her Nigerian passport, they would poke fun at her, and her close family would criticize her parents for making a perfectly good Nigerian child into an American brat, and never let up once they started the pejoratives and jokes. They teased her for eating American food the same way Americans would tease her for eating oxtails, pepper stew, and goat. Everyone's family had so many layers, so many challenges, and so many stories.

Even Indigo's parents were seeing other people when they met each other. They had had an affair, and then abandoned their lovers to be with each other. The path to love wasn't a smooth road. Love would show up while you were busy with another love, leaving you to decide.

Indigo looked away from her parents and noticed Ericka glance toward Mr. Jones, whom she was still avoiding as if his cancer were contagious, and touch her ear where her prized earring was missing, but it didn't stick to Indigo's mind. She was too busy wondering if Olamilekan Babangida was going to come to the celebration.

Or if she would be humiliated in front of her friends and family.

Indigo called Olamilekan's cellular. No answer. Two seconds later her cellular rang back. It was Olamilekan's number. Indigo answered. A girl was on the other end.

In the accent of Accra, maybe Nairobi, a girl who barely sounded twenty and had just as many pounds of attitude asked, "Did you just call this number for Lekan and for what purpose?"

"Who are you and why did you dare call my number if I do not know you?"

"Who are you and why did you just call this number for Lekan?"

"May I speak with *Olamilekan?* His name is *Olamilekan.*"

"Who the hell is this?"

"Did my number, beautiful photo, and name not show on his caller ID, stupid girl?"

"Who are you calling stupid?"

"You know who this is. Put Olamilekan on *his* phone. This is *his* girlfriend."

"I am his girlfriend. Be glad that you are not near me. I would beat you senseless."

"If you want to meet me right now, tell me where you are, and I will come to you."

"Bitch, never call this number again, *stupid girl.*"

Indigo cursed the girl in Yorùbá, and as the girl spat profanities at her, Indigo hung up.

She smiled at guests, gave hugs, maintained a big smile, her phone buzzing over and over in her hand. The stupid girl was showing the wrong woman how stupid a stupid girl could be.

Chapter 14

Ten minutes later Olamilekan sent Indigo a text. She went upstairs to her apartment, closed the door, went in the bathroom, slammed the door, and then responded.

Who dafuq was the stupid bitch who answered your phone?

I lost my phone, so someone found it and was probably playing a trick.

You are lying to me.

I'm serious. I lost my phone. I had to go to the Apple store to get a new one.

So you bought a new phone that fast?

What's the issue?

Some goat called me from your phone and said she was your girlfriend, Olamilekan.

You are my girlfriend, so that is not possible. Were you having a bad dream?

I told you that I want more. I need more than to be a time-to-time girlfriend.

Eventually I want the same.

What does eventually mean?

I want you to be my wife one day.

When will you take the proper steps with my family?

You are young with many ambitions and we both need to be patient.

I can be very patient with a ring on my finger.

That will happen.

When will that be? Perhaps today?

Indigo, please, do not pressure me with another ultimatum.

When they are the same age, a woman is more mature, but not as young as a man.

I understand how nature works. I know about your biological clock.

Let's remain focused on this issue. Some girl called me from your phone.

I lost my phone. How many times must I say that?

I will not let you make a fool out of me, Olamilekan.

I love you, Indigo, and you know I love you. Have I not told you that many times?

Who was the girl who called me from your phone? I need her name and address. I need to go meet her properly.

How many times do I have to tell you I lost my phone and just purchased a new one?

Explain to me how dafuq you were able to lose a phone and purchase a new one in ten minutes?

Let's not spend all our time arguing on your birthday.

I do not need this nonsense from you. I dealt with this foolishness with Yaba and you promised that you were nothing like him, yet some goat is answering your damn phone.

I miss you so much, Indigo. I have not seen you in what feels like forever.

Miss you too, Olamilekan. I miss you the way I am starting to miss hearing the truth.

What do you miss the most about me? What do you miss the most about my tongue?

You know how I feel about you, Olamilekan. You know this day is very important to me.

I will try to come to your party.

You said you were coming. There was no contemplation. It was definite.

Something has come up.

What has come up since yesterday? What is more important than this day?

You know I have many obligations.

Is that girl there with you? Are you unable to get free from her, is that the issue?

There is no girl. I only have other obligations.

And being available on my birthday should be one of those obligations.

Sponsors want to meet. We are talking millions of dollars in endorsements.

I am sure they all have girlfriends and boyfriends and family and children. They are human beings and understand humanity. If I do not see you today, lose my number.

I will see what I can do.

Is this because of that bitch? Did she
check your phone, read our text messages
like a book, and now she knows about me,
about my birthday, and now you have to
change your agenda? How did she get your
phone? I demand to know who she is so I
can meet her.

Don't be paranoid.

Who is she? Her accent is African, but not
Nigerian.

I have no idea what you're talking about
because there is no other girl.

I am faithful to you, Olamilekan. I am
faithful by choice. My mind can change.

What about your relationship with Yaba?
Has your mind already changed?

Yaba and I are done and you know we were
done before I engaged with you.

He messages you often. You still
communicate with him on social media.

As a friend. I have nothing to hide. I let
you read the messages. I do not hide my
phone when I come to see you. I leave it
on the table face up, not upside down. My
phone is never locked and never hidden.
I don't freak out when you reach for my

phone. If Yaba messages me, it is during business hours and never during booty call hours.

So you can have friends of the opposite sex, but I cannot?

Yaba has never answered my phone. Who answered your phone, Olamilekan?

I do not want to argue with you again regarding this matter.

What time shall I expect you to arrive?

Let me see what I can do.

I have many guests waiting for you to arrive. They expect to see you here. I don't have time to argue, but all I ask is that you honor your promise and don't let me down on my birthday. My father is here and I told him you were coming. If you do not come, I will never hear the end of it from him or my mother.

Indigo, I will try.

What if I make it special for you? Is that what it will take, Olamilekan?

How would that happen if your parents are there and you have so many guests?

I always make it special for you, do I not?

You do.

Do you not enjoy the things we do when we are alone?

It has been too long.

Come to my party.

And if I come?

Then maybe you will come.

Chapter 15

Phone gripped in hand, Indigo lowered her head, wiped away tears.

She wondered if she was vulnerable because she was optimistic.

Or if she was optimistic because she was vulnerable.

She wondered if men were opportunistic because women were vulnerable.

Or if women were vulnerable because men were opportunistic.

Indigo heard her living room door open, and her mother's voice call for her.

She answered, "I'm in the bathroom. I'm coming. Give me a second."

"Do you feel okay?"

"I feel fine." She flushed the toilet. "I feel great. I've never felt better."

Her mother turned the handle on the bathroom door, eased the door open.

Standing in the mirror, busying herself with her eyelashes, Indigo avoided eye contact with her mother and repeated, "I'm fine. Just touching up my face a little."

"No, you're not okay. Lie to others, lie to your father, but never to your mother."

"Mother."

"So what is going on with you and Olamilekan Babangida?"

Indigo swallowed, took a breath, tried to smile. "Something came up."

"It's your birthday."

"Mom. He will try to make it. He's a busy man. Money never sleeps, you know how it goes. He sent the jumping tent, and he paid for all of the Nigerian food as well as the deejay."

"That is not the same as him being here."

"He will do his best to come."

"Olamilekan Babangida touches you like you are his wife, and you touch him like he is your husband, but I do not see a ring on your finger as of yet. And there should not be one, not without a proper introduction and approval. Is there some legal arrangement of which I have not been made aware? Don't dare do like Western girls and show up engaged to a man who has not been presented to the family in the proper way. Women here meet a man in a club on Friday, then go away for the rest of the weekend and come back home married. Marriage has no value here; it's just something to do when Americans are drunk. Marriage is a sober decision."

"He and I are not eloping. There has not been a secret marriage."

"I know who he is, and so does your father, but Olamilekan's father or an uncle still needs to arrange a formal meeting so there can be a proper introduction between two families."

"His family is not in America."

"Even if they have to fly here from Lagos to do so, that is how it should be done."

"Why do the old still feel like they have to plan the lives of the young?"

"Because the young are foolish and will sacrifice culture for thirty pieces of silver."

"Leave it alone today. Let's just say we're dating and feeling each other out."

"Dating is not for fun. Dating should have a purpose. It should have a direction."

"Are we there yet? How long will this guilt trip last?"

"We have a few exits to go before this conversation ends. Keep your seat belt on."

"This is a lecture, not a conversation. And could you speed up, please?"

"I am at the proper speed limit for this talk. The things that you do with your American friends, the clubbing, the partying, the drinking, we know that is the American way, but all of that is indecent for a Nigerian wife. Do those things now so you can be done with those things. And if a Nigerian man is looking for a wife and sees that is your current behavior, then he will not see you as a wife. Nigerian men come to this country and allow American women and American ways to be their getaway. These things are your getaway as well. The friends you have now, they are your getaway friends. One day you will mature beyond them and you will move on from them all."

"Mom, stop it. I have a headache and loud words keep coming out of your mouth. I can see each word in bold, capitalized, italicized, and you're using a font larger than our house."

"I can tell you things, but you must listen; and those things I teach, you must practice. You will marry an African man, and he will love and lavish things on you in ways you have never dreamed. Your world will be like my world. That's why of all the women in the world, your father came back to Nigeria for me. He flew back to Nigeria to bring me to England. After he had had many trial-and-errors with the white London girls and the black American girls who lived in London, women who were enthralled by African men, he came back home and I became his wife, not them."

"We are getting to know each other. I have known him two years, but it has only been three months since we decided to take this to another level, to become an official couple."

"A man knows if he loves a woman in three months, if not three days, but what he desires in three hours, if that is all he desires, he should never get from you in three hundred years."

They sat still a moment. They sat as mother and daughter, the music outside not resonating, only the emotions within.

Indigo asked, "How did I get so lucky to have you for my mother?"

"The same way I am so lucky to have you for my child."

"I forgot to ask you how you are doing."

"I am fine."

"No, you're not. You have dark rings around your eyes."

"Did I not just say that I am fine?"

"How is my father?"

"Today is your birthday. We focus on you. You are the princess."

"What's going on, Mother?"

"Let's not be rude and leave your guests waiting. Be the perfect host."

Then they put on smiles, prepared to go back outside.

Chapter 16

In the midst of their exhilaration and afternoon calm, as birds both in the sky and in the alleyways sang, at a moment when there were no high-speed chases, no sirens, and no ghetto birds hovering overhead, the world stopped rotating. Ericka's mother, Mrs. Stockwell, arrived.

Indigo was coming back down the stairs, her mother walking in front of her, when she saw Mrs. Stockwell's Lexus ease by the gate, blocking a lane, in search of street parking.

Indigo hurried over to the jumper and told Ericka, "Get ready to rumble. Your egg donor has arrived. I'm surprised she accepted the invite."

Ericka stopped jumping and darkness descended on her sun-filled heart.

"Why in the hell did you invite her? You know I don't want to be around her."

"Try and make amends. You haven't seen her but once since you had cancer."

"You *know* what she said. We are way past that 'amends' bullshit and you know that."

"She's your mother, Ericka."

"I didn't get to choose from whose birth canal I would arrive. I would've chosen Oprah."

"Get out of the jumper and greet your mother."

As far back as Ericka could remember, her Oklahoma-born mother had always worn long Mildred Pierce–style dresses, only lately she had worn the dresses fitted, hugging her curves. She was trying to be sexy.

She was in need of attention. Women had midlife crises, felt their youth fading, same as men. A woman changed her style of dressing and wore a new perfume when she had had a second awakening, or was desperately clinging to that which was fading, that which time and gravity either eroded or devalued. She wore three-inch heels and kept a designer purse on her shoulder. In the mild breeze gently touching the arid afternoon, as waves murmured against the beaches eight miles away, the Queen arrived in the light of the sun.

She was a very attractive, religious, and self-righteous redbone. The color-struck world in which she lived always colored her red or yellow, never brown, and hardly referred to her as being black. She usually wore her salt-and-light-brown hair pulled back into a bun so tight she looked Asian, but she had dyed her hair, had colored it light brown with blonde highlights, so it had a much younger woman's flavor, and today Mrs. Stockwell had worn it down, let her vanity flow across her soft shoulders. Her face was relaxed, her features less extreme, her eyebrows perfectly done. She'd taken on the look of a Hollywood starlet past her prime but still trying to be in the game. Ericka's mother had lost forty pounds since Ericka saw her last, looked fifteen years younger, once again an hourglass of a woman with big breasts, slim waist, and wide hips.

Mrs. Stockwell held a Bible in her right hand, a birthday card in the other. Ericka saw her mother pause and shoot a familiar look of disgust toward her and the other Blackbirds in bikinis. Ericka's mother focused on her, yielded a stare so harsh that in order not to start a knock-down drag-out fight on Indigo's birthday, Ericka went back to her apartment, nostrils flaring, and put on jeans and a blue EAT.SLEEP.READ. tee. When Ericka came back to the pool area, she found her mother sitting underneath palm trees, next to the folding table where the Blackbirds had left their cell phones. She was ending a conversation and putting one of the phones down. It was Destiny's.

Livid, Ericka asked, "What the hell are you doing talking on my friend's phone?"

"It kept vibrating, and that was irritating, so I answered in case there was an emergency of some sort."

"You don't just answer someone's freakin' phone. Why would you do that?"

"*Because it kept ringing.* It was the wrong number. I was being considerate."

Ericka looked at the caller ID. Saw the name HAKEEM MITCHELL.

Ericka said, "So damn nosey. I've caught you on my phone creeping my messages."

"Did you not hear me say the blasted phone kept ringing and irritated me?"

"Answering someone's phone is like wearing their underwear. Don't ever do that again. You pick up their phones and put your germs and bad energy all over their lives."

She wiped down each phone, and when it buzzed, she looked at Kwanzaa's phone, read her older messages.

Buenos tardes, Marcus.

Buenos tardes, Kwanzaa.

Yes, Marcus? Is there a reason you keep calling and texting?

I love you.

Love you, too.

Do you miss me?

Yes, I miss you.

Marcus Brixton had just sent her another text, wanting Kwanzaa to come see him tonight, wanting to have a late dinner, drink wine, and reconcile. He said he missed her and begged for forgiveness. Ericka deleted the text that Kwanzaa hadn't read yet, but left the older ones alone.

She made a mental note to sneak into Kwanzaa's phone and block Marcus's number.

Indigo's phone had many texts, people from all over the globe sending birthday greetings.

She read the exchange Indigo had just had with Olamilekan and her heart dropped.

Mrs. Stockwell said, "You're just as inquisitive regarding someone's intimate affairs."

"They don't mind if I read their messages. We're friends, but we are like sisters."

"You have befriended Destiny Jones. Of all the people in the world."

"Is there an issue? Or did the church stop preaching about the art of forgiveness?"

"She's still just as fast now as she was when she ended up in jail for attempted murder."

"You might want to tuck your tail, Satan. Your evil is showing."

"That is her past. That is who she is. I am only stating the facts."

"I'm sure if they put up a stripper's pole, you'd have flashbacks. Just because the things you did when you were young weren't recorded and shared, don't act like you didn't do them."

Ericka gathered all the phones and put them near the other Blackbirds.

When she came back, her mother said, "This is ugly music."

"It's Nigerian."

"It's still ugly."

"Mrs. Stockwell, if you don't like the music, go home and play old-timey gospel."

"If it gets any louder, the police will come, and you know how they respond to black people at pool parties. I am too old to be thrown on the ground in front of the world."

"This is Indigo's celebration. We told all the neighbors we were going to be loud for a couple of hours this afternoon, the same way they came by and let us know they were going to blow the roof off the block last weekend. Besides, can you hear how noisy the area is already?"

"And this is where you choose to live."

"I live where I know you will never come visit, at least not after the sun goes down."

"Well, I'm glad you put on something appropriate. That's how you dress day to day?"

"I changed to get that embarrassing expression of disgust off your face."

"That thing you had on is not what I would call a proper bikini. This is not a beach in some foreign country that has no values. It was barely a patch over your business and was barely supporting your breasts."

"Well my burka is still at the dry cleaners."

"I come in here, in the middle of the day, in this area filled with pedophiles and thieves—"

"Knock it off, and please give that cantankerous personality back to Donald Trump."

"—and you're outside all but naked. *You know how men are.* No man will ever respect a woman who parades around showing everything God gave her. Why are you outside naked?"

Ericka spoke in a harsh whisper. "It's a pool party, not a Pentecostal revival meeting."

"People in L.A. don't have pool parties to get in the water. The pool is for show."

"I had on a goddamn bikini outside of my damn apartment at our damn pool."

Her mother smiled. "Don't disrespect me, Ericka. And don't disrespect God."

"Disrespect? Let's not even go there, with the damage you've done to my life."

"I've done nothing but my best to protect you."

"Is that your spin on banishing me, on extraditing me to Oklahoma like I was a fugitive?"

"I sent you away to learn ballet, tap, jazz, and to be in an engineering program."

"Stop. Don't go there, Mrs. Stockwell. Enough with the lies."

"You are an underachiever and you have sold yourself short. You were born with certain advantages over your friends. You are as beautiful as a biracial woman."

"Wow. A bigoted, backhanded compliment that actually sounded like a sweet melody drenched in agave as it left your twisted lips. The earth must be about to fall into the sun."

"I did not create the rules of the society in which we live. You need to play the role of a biracial woman in this country, because no one in the world respects black women."

"I'm not biracial. *You are*. Your estranged husband, Mr. Stockwell, might be. I'm not."

"You don't have nappy hair. You can pass the paper bag test."

"Well, guess who's coming to dinner? You're bringing the ignorance from the '60s back."

"You're educated, working beneath your dual degrees as an urban schoolteacher, something no sane person would do. You could at least have become a teacher at the performing arts school downtown, if you have to be a teacher. You could be so much more. I wanted you to be everything I never could be. You are over thirty and living in an apartment building in South Central, in a zoned business district, near where they have warnings about gangs promising to kill one hundred people in one hundred days. You're acting like you're a tragic mulatto in a race film and expecting some rich man to come and rescue you like you're a half-bred Cinderella."

"The way Mr. Stockwell rescued you, right?"

"I raised you to be smart, an achiever, to be more than you've become."

"*I'm not you*, and that is all that matters to me."

"I sacrificed all I had, and did it in vain."

"I am so tired of your attitude, Mrs. Stockwell. I'm so tired of you complaining about everything all the goddamn time. You don't like my life, well guess what? I'm just like you. We both pick bad men so we're both lonely bitches."

"Don't talk to me like that."

"I talk to you the way you talked to me when no one could hear how evil you were."

"You talk to me the way my mother used to talk to me."

"And you treat me the same evil way she treated you."

"My mother used to slap me across my mouth, or beat me with a two-by-four, hit me with a shoe, beat me with an extension cord for taking that tone or talking back."

"I wish you would try. I swear to the God you get on your knees to pray to the same way you used to get on your knees to suck the men you used to sneak over at night."

"I should slap you across your filthy mouth, then baptize you in that pool."

"Hit me. Just draw your hand back like you used to. I will drag you through Koreatown, Harvard Heights, Jefferson Park, and through Mid-City, will fight you up and down Olympic Boulevard, Gramercy Place, all the way to the Santa Monica Freeway before I sit down and write a blog and let the world know what kind of wicked mother raised me, you cock-sucking bitch."

Mrs. Stockwell sucked her teeth. "You will go to hell for talking to me that way."

"You judge me, and were an expert at giving blow jobs when you were eleven."

"*I was forced to do things.* There is a *difference.*"

"*So was I.* You killed my child, *your* grandchild."

"Well, I sure as hell wasn't going to raise another child, you ungrateful bitch."

"There she is."

"What the hell would I look like, having a child who has a child, and raising both?"

"There is the real Mrs. Stockwell no one has ever seen."

"I was cursed with you."

"And you haven't exactly been a blessing in my life."

"You are my only child, and my only regret is that I had one problem child too many."

Ericka asked, "Is that supposed to hurt my feelings?"

"You have no feelings."

"Quite the opposite. If I felt nothing, that would be a blessing."

Mrs. Stockwell said, "Mr. Stockwell is a whore who has no feelings. He stays married to me so he can tell the women he sleeps with he can't get married."

"If that is his game, he could have stayed single and put on a two-dollar ring and pretended to have a wife somewhere. He didn't have to get married to be a player."

"Mr. Stockwell did have to get married if he wanted to lie in my bed."

"Well, nice to see how that worked out for you. Great strategy, Mrs. Stockwell."

Mrs. Stockwell whispered, "He has treated me this way from the day we married."

"That was thirty-some years ago. Get over it. I'm sure he's forgotten about you by now."

"I was twenty-one when I met him at church."

"Let me grab my violin."

"I used to be fun. I was fun to be around. And I was smart. I was sexy. I was beautiful. Men were mesmerized. I could've been a movie star. I was finer than Jayne Kennedy."

Ericka didn't disagree. By *Cosmopolitan* standards, her mother was much prettier than Ericka would ever be. Back in the day when Mrs. Betty Stockwell was still Caledonia Koepling, when not many knew her middle name and people called her CK or Cee-Cee or Yellow Gal, she had been a young woman who wore short skirts every day, was always in high heels and something that showed how proud she was of her cleavage, and spent Thursday through Sunday nights sipping on Long Island iced teas at the Speakeasy on Sunset, Mingles on Airport Boulevard, or Gammons by LAX. From the moment she was legal and old enough to let a man buy her a drink she was all dolled up in the latest fashion and getting her groove on at the Red Onion on Wilshire, Bit 'N Apple in L.A., Curries in Long Beach, Little J's downtown, or the Golden Tail in El Segundo. Caledonia always participated in some sort of Miss Big Legs, Miss Sexy Booty, Miss Brick House, Bad Mama Jama, or Miss Super Freak contest. The woman had also been on *Soul Train* a few times, always put up front because she could dance, could shake her yellow ass, and was the winner at the aforementioned contests based on physical attributes almost every time. She was an underground star until she discovered the Lord. She described that point of her life as a weak period, as the period that would go unrecorded, as went part of Jesus' life. For her it was the era when alcohol and sex were used to salve her emotional ills, but only heated uncontrollable desires. She regretted those days the way Janet Jackson regretted performing with Justin Timberlake. Caledonia found God when she had heard a sermon at West Angeles, had looked deep within herself and broke down in tears, and rebuked her Thursday-through-Saturday-night experiences, rebuked everyone who had clapped for her to win a Miss Big Legs, Miss Sexy Booty, Miss Brick House, Bad Mama Jama, or Miss Super Freak contest, rebuked bohemianism, burned sage for months, and declared herself a born-again virgin. She read the Bible cover to cover, was baptized again to wash away all her recently acquired California sins, and rebuked the men who had caused those sins. She stopped using her first name, and began using her middle name. Caledonia Koepling became Betty Koepling. With newfound chastity and conservative skirts that stopped below her knees, she had found herself a husband, all done in that order. On the strength of her figure, calves, and prayers to God, the Good Book in hand as she sat in Bible study on a Wednesday night, she had snatched up a green-eyed, gorgeous man who could pass for the second coming of Smokey Robinson, and become Betty Stockwell.

Ericka said, "You were a regular Jayne Kennedy, and I guess you found your own Leon Isaac. I guess you asked God for a man and my father was the man God felt you deserved."

"What I thought was God's voice was but the charismatic singing of the devil."

"The devil does impersonations. That's good to know."

"The man who fathered you married me with no intentions of ever being faithful. He married me to get me in bed with him; that was the only reason. We weren't married three months and he had already had at least two affairs. I was married ninety days and ready to divorce him, but I was pregnant. He didn't want a baby with a dark-skinned woman, but he loved to be with them day and night. I was his pregnant trophy, in a marriage tainted by your father's fetishes and infidelities, fighting women in the street, and arguing with women on the phone in the middle of night. There were too many women. That wasn't marriage. I lived in a war zone."

"There have always been mistresses trying to upgrade to being a missus."

"We got into a fight in church on Easter Sunday because one of his little mud ducks had the nerve to spit on me. You were in my arms and that crazy woman tried to spit on you, too, but I turned you away. That was it. I had to do fine by myself. Looking back, I was happy before I got married. Could have had any man I wanted when I was twenty-one, and I chose the wrong one. God punished me for that. He punished me with him, and then He punished me again with you."

"And God punished me with you. Only a child of the devil would do what you did."

Ericka wiped her eyes.

Mrs. Stockwell wiped her own eyes.

"Since we're going down Memory Lane, guess who I saw today, Mommy Dearest?"

"Who did you see, Problem Child?"

"I saw Debra Mitchell's son. Her son is an adult, graduate of Morehouse."

"Who is Debra Mitchell?"

"She worked for Dr. Faith, the lady who was your doctor when I was thirteen."

"Nurse Mitchell? The nurse who involved herself in our family matter?"

"She's a doctor now. Dr. Debra Dubois. I guess she's doing well."

"Well, good for her. I hope she's a better doctor than she was a nurse."

"Dr. Dubois is writing her memoirs. She mentions me in the pages."

"Why would she dare mention you in her biography?"

"From what I understand, she has written a few things regarding you, too."

"What, is she trying to get sued? Does she not know who I am, what I can do to people?"

"We know how litigious you are. You sue everyone for everything. From child support to any injustice you think has been put upon you, you file a lawsuit. You sue neighbors for trees hanging in your yard. You were Marcus Brixton's best friend. Kwanzaa's ex loved to see you coming, because it meant money."

"I exercise my legal rights to the fullest extent of the law."

"You are an entitled snob. And you know whatever Mrs. Dubois has to say about you and me will not be nice. She knows what you did to me. You hit me with your Bible while we were in the doctor's office. She knows the real you. She saw you without the Christian mask."

Again, Mrs. Stockwell's nostrils flared. "Doctor-patient confidentiality."

Ericka whispered, "I should go see her. I need to know what she's written."

"What purpose would going to see her and reliving that period in your life serve?"

"She didn't like you. I don't like you. So I can add to whatever she has said."

"I will sue you too."

"You won't."

"Fucking test me and see how quickly you fail that test."

"That's the Mrs. Stockwell I know."

"I am tired of this shit, Ericka. I am tired of you blaming me for your sins."

Ericka clenched her teeth. "One day you should apologize for what you did to me."

"I didn't impregnate you. I didn't steal money to buy pregnancy tests."

"I should have kept running."

"You never revealed who impregnated you."

"I never should have come back."

"I wish you had kept running and become someone else's problem. I wish they had found you dead in a ditch, or not had found you at all. I would have been free from you."

"I know you wish the same things I wish about you."

"You have brought me nothing but grief."

"You have told me that more times than I can remember."

"You did what was wrong. I did what was right for you."

Ericka's voice shook. "No, you did what was right to maintain your image, including sending me away. You sent me to a house of abuse, and you did that to punish me."

"What I did *for* you, it's the same thing those fast little girls' mommas who live in Newport Beach or in the Palisades do *for* them. All those trust fund babies have left a few secrets in the toilet. I went against my beliefs to save you from sin."

"You can find a million reasons to justify what you did."

"You needed to go to Oklahoma to save your soul. You were out of control."

"You put me on a table, turned on the vacuum, and did what you had to do to remove your shame."

"You required me to make a hard decision."

"You have never *once* said you were sorry. You didn't shed *one* goddamn tear."

"If I feel as if it is needed, when I feel I have done wrong, I'll ask God for forgiveness, not you. You put me in a horrible position, forced me to make a horrible decision, and you blame me."

"Your attitude about everything is why I couldn't wait to get out of that house of horrors. You talked down to me. You said I'd never get married, said no man would want me."

"But you did marry."

"I did marry."

"Just to prove me wrong."

"I married a man who told me he loved me and wanted to marry me."

"It didn't last."

"I was married longer than you were married."

"You became a preacher's wife."

"I was somebody important for a while, and that ate at your heart every damn day."

"I heard your church wedding was nice."

"It was nice because you weren't invited to come piss in the punch."

"Not being able to see my only child, my only daughter on her wedding day, that hurt. I will never forgive you for that. That hurt me in ways you will never be able to understand."

"So does a forced abortion. I will never forgive you for that."

"It will never hurt as much as birthing an ungrateful child."

"Then I wish you'd taken a hanger and ended your misery as soon as it started. When I had issues trying to get pregnant, I had to sit in the doctor's office with my self-righteous husband and admit I'd had a secret abortion. He blamed that for my inability to get pregnant. He told me if I could not give him a child, then it was pointless being with me, said that God had punished me for my sin by making me barren. He never saw me the same after that revelation. After that, he saw the sophisticated woman he married as a well-dressed hood rat. Then came the cancer. He'd already pulled away from me emotionally, had affairs, had so many women I called them his copulating choir and conjugal congregation, and then cancer confirmed I was a bad choice. He stood in the pulpit and asked his congregation to pray for me, but behind closed doors he rejoiced in my suffering. I was worth more to him dead than alive."

"You married a minister who saw you were not worthy of the Kingdom of God."

"I married a European man who is the leader at a nondenominational church."

"Well, you're divorced now. Glad I didn't waste my money."

"Always negative. No wonder Mr. Stockwell knocked you up and slept with other women. Who would want to be laid up with a frigid, evil bitch like you in the middle of the damn night?"

"You really want to hurt my feelings."

"As much as you want to hurt mine."

"You're going to have to try harder, *Miss* Stockwell. A divorced woman has to try harder."

"Same to you, *Mrs.* Stockwell. Same to you. A woman who hasn't seen her husband in two decades, a woman who had a man's child but never had the man, she has nothing on me."

"With the amoral things you've done, how the fuck do you face yourself?"

"How the fuck do you?"

They took a breath, then sat back and watched the others enjoy themselves.

Chapter 17

Destiny, Kwanzaa, Indigo, and all the parents and stepparents were eating, sipping wine and West Coast IPA beer, interacting wonderfully. Ericka knew that she and her mother would never be able to resolve the irreconcilable event from two decades ago.

Mrs. Stockwell said, "Destiny is another one who was very belligerent and rebellious."

"She's amazing. She's a survivor. I wish I had her strength, her nerves."

"She went out into the streets and got what girls get who are disobedient to their parents."

"Are you saying she deserved to get drugged and raped?"

"God has His way of showing children what happens when you disobey your parents."

Ericka laughed. "Right, the floods, my cancer, and Destiny being raped are all in the plan. So I deserved what you did to me because I didn't follow your rules? Or better yet, the abuse you suffered, having your uncle's cock forced in your mouth for a few years of your life was God's lesson to you? Tell me how that fits into some grand plan for the universe."

Mrs. Stockwell was visibly shaken, her right hand trembling.

Ericka's nose flared, her middle fingers tapping against her legs at a rapid pace.

Destiny began playing dominoes with Kwanzaa and their families. Indigo and her people were all laughing and talking, enjoying each other's company. "Teach Me How to Dougie" came on and everyone rocked it and soon the other three Blackbirds led the charge as they all went into dancing the whip, Nae Nae, and Stanky Legg.

Then someone was at the gate, and when it was opened, Indigo's present from her parents was driven inside. It was a new, four-door Jeep Rubicon. Indigo jumped up and down screaming. Indigo's new Rubicon was pulled into the back, parked near her CBR and BMW.

Mrs. Stockwell said, "An apartment building. A BMW. A motorcycle. And now this? Indigo's parents have spoiled her rotten."

"That's what you do when you love your child, Mrs. Stockwell. When a man loves his child, the mother doesn't have to beg and sue for support, then go to court over and over to get the payout raised, and the mother of that child wants her child to have the best. She would buy more things for her child than she bought for herself. She wouldn't pimp her child for child support."

"You wanted for nothing."

"I wanted for everything that was not material. I wanted what couldn't be bought."

They gathered around the cake and sang Stevie Wonder's birthday song. While they were singing, a West African man who was regarded by some as a god appeared. His name was Olamilekan Babangida. It was Indigo's on-again off-again boyfriend–booty-call–almost-fiancé. He walked through the wrought-iron gate and up the incline, smiling, with a large box in his hands.

The West African was six foot two, very Adewale Akinnuoye-Agbaje–like, a Mandingo of a man wearing designer jeans and a tank top, the veins in his arms strong, his muscles aplenty. He was the type of man women responded to the way most men responded to Beyoncé.

Ericka waved at him, said, "Hey, Olamilekan. Glad you showed up for the party."

He missed the loathing and sarcasm in her tone, waved, and kept going toward Indigo.

Mrs. Stockwell asked, "Who is he?"

"Indigo's boyfriend."

"He's handsome."

"Do you expect Indigo to have anything less than the best on her arm?"

He was born in Nigeria, but was raised in America. He spent some summers in Lagos, some holidays in the Hamptons. He was the perfect balance of two nations. A Princeton graduate. A polyglot. A man who made women squirm in their imagination each time he smiled.

Mrs. Stockwell said, "But he sure is black. Indigo is just as dark. They need to mix with people lighter than them if they want their children to have a chance in this country."

"On that racist note, would you like something to drink before you leave?"

"I was going to stay awhile longer and break bread with Indigo's parents."

"No you're not. You don't have to go home, but you are not staying here."

"Indigo invited me."

"Now you're *uninvited by me*."

"Because I told the truth?"

"This is a happy occasion and we're going to keep it that way. So smile, be your usual phony self, tell Indigo happy birthday, then leave so I can enjoy the rest of my day."

"A glass of water will be fine. No sugary drinks. I'm trying to lose ten more pounds."

"With that diet, are you sure you want to eat a piece of cake, Mrs. Stockwell?"

"I've been avoiding sugar, but I'll cheat today. Cut me a corner piece, if you can."

"A small slice from the middle is what you'll get. Be glad I'm getting you a full cup of water. I'll try to not spill it on you. Would hate for you to start melting in front of all my friends."

Ericka rushed to get her mother a cup of water and a slice of cake.

Mrs. Abdulrahaman was talking to Mr. Jones, but her eyes were on Mrs. Stockwell.

Beyond curt pleasantries, Mrs. Stockwell and Mrs. Abdulrahaman had nothing to say to each other. The cultural difference was too wide.

Mrs. Abdulrahaman told Mr. Jones, "There is a cancer support group at Faithful Central. It's for anyone with any kind of cancer. They meet on Saturday mornings. You should go."

"I will check it out. Thanks. Maybe I'll see if Destiny can go with me."

"If you need, I will make time to go with you. My husband would not mind."

Seeing Mrs. Abdulrahaman so close and chatty with Mr. Jones left a negative tingle moving up and down Ericka's spine, a tingle she had never felt when she was married and women flirted with her sanctified husband, the tingle that was the dangerous fire of jealousy.

She couldn't imagine Mr. Jones being intimate with Mrs. Abdulrahaman.

Yet the image did play in her mind, and it played in HD.

She imagined Mrs. Abdulrahaman bent over a sofa, and Mr. Jones going to town. Mr. Jones was a blessed, intense lover, good enough to make a woman go mad. Ericka shook that image out of her mind. She felt foolish, and turned away to give hugs and hellos to Kwanzaa's dad and bonus mom, chatted them up for a couple of minutes so as to not be rude.

When Ericka turned around again, she saw that her mother had left her seat.

Mrs. Stockwell had adjusted her boobs, fixed her dress, then gone to chin-wag with Indigo's dad. Ericka maintained her sweet smile as she took slow steps toward her mother. As she moved closer she heard Indigo's father saying, "—is called the Buharian Culture Organization. There is a lot of anger in the country and the people are in the streets screaming that enough is enough. Young Nigerians are standing up and protesting corruption."

"Is the corruption really that bad? I read about the former oil minister—"

"Diezani Alison-Madueke. They say she was in bed with Kola Aluko and he was her money launderer. He's hiding in a Swiss estate, from what I hear. Alison-Madueke was arrested."

"Yes, her. I read about her arrest. Shell Oil companies. Money laundering. Bribes. I mean, is it any worse than corruption here, or do they have your country under the microscope?"

"Police, political parties, the educational system, public officials, the media, even the religious bodies, they are all corrupt. Many say that Goodluck was bad luck for Nigeria."

"I have to admit, I haven't done my research, but continue."

"I am not afraid to say an orange is a fruit. The kerosene subsidy scandal, the police pension fund fraud, the Stella Oduah car purchase scandal, the campaign telling the government to kill corruption, not Nigerians. They have destroyed the economy, caused more poverty, and caused industries to collapse. You can see where the money is going because the officials now have flashy cars and homes all over the world, as their own communities are failing."

Ericka interrupted, "Don't forget your appointment on the other side of town."

Indigo's father said, "We hate you have to leave so soon. I haven't had a chance to have a full conversation with you regarding important business matters."

"Maybe some other time."

"Don't become a stranger. There are global concerns we should discuss."

"I would love to hear your international view on many matters."

"You sure are looking lovely as usual, Mrs. Stockwell."

"Why thank you. And you are always so fashionable."

"What is your secret, Mrs. Stockwell? How do you keep a figure like a teenager?"

"Yoga, walking, drinking plenty of water, and eating salads."

Ericka interrupted, "Mom. If you don't leave right now, you will be late for church."

"Of course, my always thoughtful and considerate child. So much like her grandmother."

"I don't need you near Indigo's father. I'm sure his wife wouldn't appreciate all the flirting at her daughter's party."

Mrs. Stockwell said, "No one is flirting. I congratulated him on his successful journey from basically having nothing to being such an astute businessman both here and abroad."

Indigo's father said, "I was just paying your *beautiful* mother a compliment."

"Save the compliments for your *beautiful* wife, not my *Half*-rican American mother."

"I compliment my wife all day and all night."

"And continue to do so. It will keep your marriage stronger. And Mrs. Stockwell, why don't you be a churchwoman and go hug, kiss, and congratulate Mrs. Abdulrahaman on all she has achieved while being a wife and a mother. Go observe a healthy mother-daughter relationship."

"I'm sure she has a better daughter than the one I have, Miss Stockwell."

"I guess we both want what other people have, Mrs. Stockwell."

"What is the meaning of this, Ericka?" Indigo's father laughed a hearty, Nigerian-born laugh. "There is no need for you to be rude at my daughter's party. I am only being sociable with your mother. Kwanzaa's father is friendly to her and makes jokes. So does Destiny's father."

Ericka smiled. "Do me a favor, and I say this respectfully, but go attend to your wife and daughter. And as for you, Mrs. Stockwell, I will see you to your car."

When Mrs. Stockwell left, Ericka returned to her apartment and showered, scrubbed her skin like she was removing nuclear contamination. She put on a different, more provocative bikini, jumped in the pool, and swam a few laps before she eased out and sat underneath the lush palm trees, her temper now cooled.

When she came out of the pool she noticed that Olamilekan was already gone. The West African superstar had made a twenty-minute appearance and moved on.

Ericka sat at the edge of the crowd of joyous people, then realized she had positioned herself where Mr. Jones could see her wishes and desires, but she didn't gaze in his direction. Not at first. Soon they made eye contact. She remembered, and she knew he remembered. She saw it in his eyes. It felt like she was laying down her heart. She wanted him to come to her now, take her hand, dance with her, kiss her in front of everyone, tell them he felt for her the same way she felt for him. A girl could dream. She wondered if he had felt the love she felt when he had been inside her, when he had made love to her and put her up, up, and away, ten miles beyond cloud nine. She stared. Those gray eyes. So damn mesmerizing. She swallowed. Felt her nipples rise. Heat rose down below. Mr. Jones shifted in his seat, nodded at her. That simple nod made her feel sexy. That nod said he thought she was beautiful. That nod said he was thinking about when he had squeezed her ass, grabbed her hips, and pushed himself deep inside her. He had made a sound like he was dying. She had made a sound like a woman who had finally come alive. She imagined Mr. Jones. She imagined his six feet of solidness on top of her, between her legs. She imagined him moving inside her. He was a DILF. A bona fide DILF. Her hips moved to the Nigerian music being played, the heat down below making her rock, made her do a sensual Baikoko dance. Her hips rolled like the singer Shakira, evolved into a slow wine, moved her waist like she was a West Indian girl. He gazed. She danced. A chill went down her spine. Ericka finger waved at Mr. Jones, and then turned her head away, unable to breathe. He had gazed at her and his energy had set her afire. Despite her body being filled with angst due to her mother, she tingled and her hips moved. Ericka closed her eyes, hoping Mr. Jones was still watching her dance, hoped he too was remembering being inside her.

Chapter 18

Destiny saw Ericka was alone, stealing her role as the antisocial pessimist, so she headed Ericka's way with two pieces of cake. Ericka adjusted her top, took the plate with the largest piece, dug in with a fork, and began stress eating.

Destiny asked, "You okay over here? Mrs. Stockwell and you, guess there was no reconciliation, no truce, and no olive branch. Would be great if you could make peace some way."

"Stop it."

"It's stopped. Moving on."

"Olamilekan didn't stay long."

"A man with many women can't stay in a spot too long."

"You ain't never lied."

"Indigo's dad is a sports fan and is probably glad his daughter has him as a part-time whatever. Her mother gave him the cold shoulder. She's not happy with Indigo seeing a Nigerian man who acts too American, and too American means she thinks he's uncouth."

Ericka asked, "What did he buy Indigo?"

"Hot clothing. Sexy shoes."

"Damn. New ride. New clothes. I wanna be African. Can I get a dual citizenship?"

"She's going to look real hot going out tonight."

Ericka shrugged. "I think she expected an engagement ring."

"I know she did."

"She cool?"

"She acts like it isn't a big deal, and that means she's sort of pissed off."

"She needs to stay where she is, in Singleville. Marriage Land is overrated."

"Yeah, well hide your bitterness and put your angry on the shelf. It's a party."

"No, that's based on the text argument she had right before Olamilekan showed up."

"What did I miss?"

Ericka told Destiny.

Destiny shook her head.

Ericka said, "I'm surprised Indigo didn't sneak her bae upstairs for a quickie."

"I think she did."

"You're lying."

"He carried her box up to her apartment so she could hang her stuff up."

Ericka asked, "How long were they in there without adult supervision?"

Destiny shrugged. "Maybe ten minutes."

"Door was closed?"

"It was. And I don't think her windows are open."

"I didn't hear them."

Destiny shrugged. "Maybe she talked to the mic."

"Or they did it in the bathroom."

"If he was hitting it, the building would have shaken."

"Yeah, we've heard them trying to tear down the walls more than once."

"I've only heard them once. Thank God for earplugs."

"You work late and I think you missed the nights when it was crazy on that end. A few nights it was Kwanzaa with Brixton *and* Indigo with Olamilekan at the same time. Before that, when she was with Yaba, they both happened to entertain their men the same night."

"I'm missing all the fun. *Not.*"

"You're out having your own fun on the other side of town." Ericka chuckled and changed the subject. "So, *Kismet*, tell me about this guy you've been seeing."

"I told you all I wanted you and the rest of the crew, the *Blackbirds*, to know."

"Destiny, I want the details. Don't bullshit me."

Destiny blushed. "He's special, but typical. Why are men so typical?"

"How so?"

"The questions."

"Oh, yeah. That. The insecurities that arise when a man's emotions get involved."

"Why do they want to know the details about every penis you've met before them?"

"My ex-husband was the worst. He wanted to know who was the biggest, where I did it, if I did oral, how I did it, why I did it, and all but made me put my hand on a Bible when I answered."

"Is this what dating is like? Question after question about every penis your body has enveloped in some fashion?"

"This is what dating is like. At some point men take you into a small room that has no window, turn up the heat, and put a bright light in your face as they dig inside of your brain."

Destiny asked, "And why do they always want to know if you've had a damn orgasm?"

"They are worried about their performance, their stats, not you, not your orgasm."

"Just when I thought they cared."

Ericka sighed. "It's irritating."

"Well, it's hard to focus on coming when a man keeps asking if you have come. It's like a kid asking over and over, 'Are we there yet?' I would think it would be obvious by the smile or frown on my face after we're done if I arrived at my destination, or if he needs to keep driving."

Ericka said, "They will keep asking you over and over, so just say you did for his ego."

"And why do they keep trying to slip a finger in your butt?"

"I like it."

"You probably like everything."

"Use a lot of lube. You might open up and find a brand-new heaven."

"For real? Are you telling me that that is what I should add to the repertoire?"

"Not saying not to do it, or to do it, but if you do do it, make sure you do it properly."

"And what's the obsession with having a woman swallow?"

"You don't?"

"You do?"

"I was married."

"It's gross."

"Why do you say that?"

"Because when a man comes, it looks like his dick has a cold and mucus is coming out."

"You're wrong for that. It's very personal. For me it is. It's an act of love."

"If God wanted women to swallow come, he would have made it look like ice cream. Or taste like chocolate. As dark as Hakeem's dick is, seems like chocolate should come out."

"He's dark?"

"He's not dark, but his dick looks like it should be on a darker man's body."

"That cracks you up. All you have to do is make sure he's eating a lot of sweet stuff and keeping away from acidic foods and asparagus. Especially asparagus."

"That intrigues me. Why is a man's dick so much darker than the rest of him?"

"Add that to the mysteries of the universe."

"Anyway. Want you to swallow. Want to become booty bandits. Men are unique."

"All look for something to do to you that no one else has done, or some position you haven't done, or some location, so they can make their mark on the territory in some way."

"Yeah, that's true. Hakeem is trying to find the roads untraveled."

Ericka nodded. "Men always want you to do the freaky things they see freaky girls do in porn."

"But they don't want to do the freaky things the freaky guys do to get the freaky girls to do those things."

"The only thing that's different between men is the credit score and condom size."

Destiny smiled. "Even with all that, Hakeem is different where it counts."

"Where it counts? Are we talking credit score, condom size, or, egads, love?"

"Butterflies. Tingles. Can't wait to see him. Think about him all day and night."

"OMG. Are you in love, Destiny Jones?"

"I can be, could be, and want to be in love with him. Hakeem could be my destiny."

Ericka laughed. "He's Destiny's *destiny*."

Destiny laughed harder. "Or Destiny is his destiny."

"Cute and corny. Your IQ is too high to be that corny. You're a bona fide Mensa."

"I know, I know. I am such a geek. Corny stuff makes me laugh."

"Being corny is the first sign of falling in love."

"Yeah, I'm getting corny, getting all girly, so I am, *egads*, in love with him."

"And there we have it."

"Is that a bad thing? Am I going too fast? Is this going too fast?"

Ericka smiled. "It's not the speed of the music, it's all about the right dance partner."

"The song feels beautiful and the music is at an unrushed tempo that feels right to me."

Ericka asked, "When are you going to tell him your real name, *Kismet Kellogg*?"

"Let me escape reality and enjoy being Kismet Kellogg with him a little longer."

"Is he attentive in bed? Is he a good lover?"

"I don't kiss and tell."

"It's not like I'm asking if you suck and swallow."

"My hand didn't go up when that girl confession regarding ingesting protein came up last weekend."

"Oh, right."

"But yours did. Kwanzaa raised both hands."

"Well, I was married and Kwanzaa had been with her guy for six years."

"And Indigo? Her hand went halfway up."

"I guess she's trying to get that taste of lobster out of her mouth."

"I guess that's no big deal for you freaks."

"Eventually it will happen. If you stay with a dude, it will happen. You'll like it, too."

"Maybe I should get it over with, but then again I don't want to create a new level of oral expectation. If I do it once, then he might expect me to be sucking on him all of the time."

"Anyway. So is the guy boss in bed?"

Destiny laughed. "He was horrible the first time."

"Like that first time with Dubois?"

"Nothing will ever be that bad. Or that messy. That was a wasted two minutes."

"Most first-time sex is pretty bad and is to the point."

"It's never like in novels. Damn romance novels messed me up. They all lied."

"What went wrong with Hakeem?"

"It didn't really happen. He didn't get it up. It was soft and squishy and he kept trying to push it in and it just wouldn't go. I felt sorry for him and gave him a second chance."

"I hate it when that happens. It improved?"

"I gave him a hand job and nothing happened. It was like overcooked spaghetti in my hand. Then it would start to get hard, and before I could get it in, he'd go soft again. For a moment I thought he was impotent or something. Wondered if I was even physically attractive to him. He almost got hard three times. I felt bad for him, but it pissed me off after the third time."

"You had to be miserable."

"I was so horny I wanted to scream. And his best friend and his jump off were over."

"What does that mean?"

"We had gone on a double date. They stayed over and were busy in the living room."

"The living room?"

"Yeah. The second bedroom functions as an office-slash-library. They use that bathroom, but do the do in the living room on the sofa. Or on the floor. Or in the dining area."

"Who are they?"

"Eddie is a personal trainer. Nancy is a cute little Asian girl. They stay over a lot."

"Eddie's black, white, Asian, or something else?"

"He's a brother."

"What kind of Asian is Nancy?"

"Nancy is Chinese and Japanese on her mother's side, Korean on her father's side."

"Okay. Now the picture is clear. Continue."

"I could hear them in the living room going at it for an hour and a half."

"You're joking."

"Nancy screams. Eddie moans. With all the cussing, it was like a pornographic rap concert. Never heard a Buddhist say Jesus' name so much in my life."

"For an hour and a half?"

"And I was sitting there frustrated and trying not to hurt Hakeem's feelings."

"How did that turn out? You're still seeing him, so something went right."

"I told him if he couldn't get it up, he needed to man up and go down, or I was leaving."

"So he hooked you up."

"I had to give him a few directions."

"Directions? Did he need GPS to find his way south?"

"I pushed the top of his head and held his ears."

"Okay."

"He applied too much pressure and I felt his teeth. And he was sucking and making this sound that made me think he was down there making a cappuccino or something."

"That's not good."

"We really need to start slicing a slit in a mango and teaching men how to eat a woman out. If you leave teeth marks, you've done a bad job. Suck, don't chew me like a pork chop. Then we had a little talk about him not being able to keep an erection for *three* condoms in a row."

"He's young enough to have a flagpole all night. What was the issue?"

"Get this. He said I intimidated him. He has a degree, is making paper, but I work three jobs, I'm confident and independent, ride a motorcycle, my dad's an engineer and my mom is an attorney. I am articulate and from time to time unintentionally use words he doesn't comprehend, and all of that added up and gave him erectile dysfunction. He was worried about being good enough for me. He worried about impressing me. He was scared to have sex with me. Crazy, huh? Can you believe that? I guess he was used to low-rent chicken heads and girls he had to play the role of Captain Save a Ho with, until he met me. He told me I was a real woman."

"I take it that things have gotten better between you in the bedroom, or wherever you do it."

"Better, but still has a lot of room for improvement."

"Why didn't you tell us earlier, during our pre-Blackbirds era?"

"Don't we all like to pretend our relationships are a little better than they really are?"

"Yeah. It took a lot of chemo for me to admit my marriage had become a farce."

Destiny laughed.

Ericka asked, "What's funny?"

Destiny confessed, "I was with Hakeem before I hurried home to go hiking the stairs."

"That's funny?"

"No, but let me tell you the funny part."

Destiny said she had almost laughed at Hakeem when they were having sex. He was standing at the edge of the bed, had her legs around his neck. He pulled her up and down, like he was working a jackhammer, and as he moved her down and up, he had on a baseball cap, and when she looked up in between her *oooohs* and *ahhhs*, when she looked to see the need to orgasm etched in his face, the bouncing, the way her legs were around his neck, and especially that damn baseball cap, he had looked like he was a jockey riding a horse at Hollywood Park.

Ericka laughed. "Baseball cap? Did he at least take his socks and boots off?"

"I was waiting for him to yell for me to *giddyap*. Or say, *Hi-ho, Silver.*"

"A man should never say *ho* while he's having sex. Not even if he's with one."

"Good point. Even a ho wants to be treated like a lady."

"So, now that it's up and working properly, does your jockey know how to ride?"

"It's not like that hour-and-a-half session his friend Eddie puts down on Nancy."

"Hold up, Destiny. Y'all not swapping partners, are you?"

"Hearing Eddie banging Nancy in the next room does put fantasies of Eddie in my head. I hear him and it makes me wonder what it would be like to have a bedroom bully for a few nights."

"The penis is boasting, the vagina is boasting, the meeting point is on the bed. When the two organs meet in a sexspree, one will bow for the other. You're making bruh bow down."

"For once, I'm winning when I wish I were losing."

"You might be with the wrong friend."

"Eddie is twenty, dropped out of community college, and lives with his grandmother. He smiles but doesn't talk around me. I guess I intimidate him too. I've caught him looking at my ass more than once. He doesn't leer, but he has looked at my bottom one time too many."

"He's fantasizing."

"Of course."

"You're with the right guy, but you might be with the wrong body."

"Eddie is a bodybuilder. He's a gym rat. He's not working and not looking for a job."

"So, being in bed with Hakeem, I'm confused. Good or bad?"

"It isn't like making love next to a lake on a purple blanket, but Hakeem can get the job done. Once he gets it to stay hard, I get on top to make it happen. I saw a woman on *Masters of Sex* and she had a problem with her lover, and that was what the doctor told her to do, to get on top and take control, let him get used to being where it's warm. Still, I need to open up."

"How so?"

"He keeps asking me to do some freaky things. When I'm totally comfortable, maybe I will. Will be nice to have somebody to get into some real kinky things with. I want to get one of those naughty nun outfits and play make-believe. Or dress up like Nyota Uhura from *Star Trek* and let him put on a Spider-Man costume and cosplay in the bedroom."

"Your voice is trembling. You're scared. Nothing scares you, and you're scared."

"If I didn't like him, it wouldn't matter. He likes my mind, breasts, booty, and body; I know that for sure. I'm still trying to figure out what real love is. Is it a mushy feeling? Is it someone being in your corner, no matter what? I know I like him and maybe I am sort of recklessly in love with him, at least a little bit, because I loaned him some money to buy a new mattress."

"You loaned him money?"

"He had to pay his property taxes, car note, mortgage payment, and his homeowners' association dues had a special assessment attached, so he was short on the money to get a new mattress while it was still on sale. It's a nice pillow top. He's going to pay me back within three months."

"Never loan anyone more money than you can stand to lose."

"I know. I'd never loan my rent money to anyone. I'm fiscally responsible."

"How much are you out of pocket?"

"Five hundred."

"Jesus."

"Hakeem had taken me to all those dinners. He'd dropped a lot of coins."

"So what? That's what a man does when he's courting a woman. He doesn't get a rebate. A woman isn't supposed to give a man her money *and* give him sex. Have you gone mad?"

"Don't tell Kwanzaa and Indigo. And we need these rules posted on a wall somewhere."

"You gave him cash? Did he sign something acknowledging the loan?"

"Used my credit card. Put his mattress on my Visa."

"Will he pay back the interest as well?"

"Hadn't thought about that."

"He has to pay you back the interest too, else you're paying part of his obligation."

"As long as he pays what he owes, I'm cool."

"And that includes the interest. Otherwise you will be paying to loan him money. It doesn't work that way. He should be obligated for every dime."

"I will remind him."

"Don't get screwed, then screwed on a personal loan. And do not do any more personal loans. When you two are at least engaged, if it gets to that, then it's cool. No ring, no loans. And even when you have a ring, keep the paper trail for the loan, in case the marriage does not come to fruition. I'm telling you the things Kwanzaa wishes she had done. She loaned Brixton money too. No, she's not going to admit it, and you better not repeat it. He got in her hole, then left her in the hole. She paid for this and that over six years, and will not recover one thin dime."

"Ericka, I will make a point of mentioning that to Hakeem, and will follow your advice."

Ericka exhaled. "He knows you as Kismet. How do you see it going when you tell him the truth?"

"He's really into me. He sends texts throughout the day."

"And at some point you have to tell him your real name. And if the relationship gets serious, he will need to know your real history, because it will come up at some point. Not everything dead stays buried. Certain things need to be revealed before things get too serious."

"It won't be easy, but I will tell him what happened to me, and that which I did in return. I don't want to come off sounding like a victim. I was victimized, but I stood up for myself."

"And then? You think he's going to be cool with it?"

"In my mind, I see him take my hand, be understanding, start to cry if I start to cry. I see him holding me and telling me that what matters is who I am now, not what happened then."

Ericka nodded. "That would be beautiful. To be loved unconditionally would be beautiful."

Destiny wiped tears away from her eyes. "Then part of this nightmare will be over."

"I want you to get married, have kids I can terrorize, have a chance at normalcy."

"We can all be normal in our own, unique, nonconforming ways."

Ericka shook her head. "It's too late for me. I have to accept that."

"Your mother, don't let her mess up your life. Maybe you can adopt."

"I wouldn't adopt a kid knowing my mother would demand to be part of the kid's world."

"She's been on her own all of her life."

"So have I. So have I. Even when I was married, I was still on my own."

"My mom and dad are great separately, but horrible together. I used to want them back together, but now I see that is not the way it should be."

"I'd take that over what I have. Your dad is an awesome man, Destiny."

"Too bad our parents aren't like Indigo's parents."

"Rich?"

"No, I mean all over each other like they are still high school sweethearts. Look at her dad. Dancing with her mom, laughing, kissing her like they are the only people in the world."

"Yeah, I guess that is too bad. Would make things easier for all of us."

"Right now, I wish everyone was happy enough to sing every word they said."

"Because you're happy. You want the world to feel your natural high, be happy by osmosis."

"Yeah. I guess so. Had never thought about that. Songs sound better and colors seem brighter these days, and the smog and humidity from that storm in Mexico aren't bothering me."

"From these eyes, everything is in black and white. My mother left my soul uneasy."

"I'm sorry. Indigo was just trying to do what she thought was the right thing."

"Mrs. Stockwell makes me want to put a bullet through my right temple, but not until after I have put one in hers."

"Don't ever joke like that."

"She made me kill my baby."

"I'm sorry you had to go through that, Ericka. I really am."

"And my child would be an adult. Having birthday parties."

"Look at me."

"No."

"Look at me, dammit."

"What do you want?"

"Wipe your eyes."

"Okay."

"Wipe them again."

"Okay."

"Put on a smile."

"Okay."

"A bigger smile."

"Okay."

"Not that big."

"Okay."

"We're going to be okay, Ericka."

"Okay."

"Don't go back down Memory Lane."

"Some devils carry Bibles and quote scripture."

"Stop it."

"Okay."

Silence rested between them for a moment.

Ericka said, "I would have been a great mother."

"Ericka?"

"I'm done."

Ericka wiped tears from her eyes. Without looking, Destiny reached for Ericka's hand. Ericka gave it to her. They held on to each other. They kept each other from falling.

Just then they spotted another handsome man coming up the driveway.

The young man was twenty-four, built like LeBron James, and seven feet tall.

Ericka said, "Indigo's basketball player. Yaba the Laker is in the house."

"Good thing he didn't bump heads with Olamilekan."

Indigo hurried to him gave him a hug. In his large hands was another sizeable present.

Ericka asked, "Wonder if he will take it upstairs and lock the door for ten minutes."

"If he does carry it up there, I'll bet it's a hand job as a thank-you."

"I'll bet he's a two-hander."

"Two hands and two feet. You could probably climb his cock like a coconut tree."

"You could probably put your phone on the end and use it for a sel-fie stick."

"And we'd look like we were in the next room."

They cackled, laughing, joking, teasing, not serious about Indigo's sexual habits.

Not long after, another handsome brother made an appearance.

It was Leonard Dubois Jr.

He brought Indigo a gift card, was introduced to everyone there, but was very excited to meet Yaba the Laker, especially since he happened to be wearing Idowu Yaba's Lakers jersey, the real deal, not a knock-off. They got along swimmingly, became new best friends as they chatted with Indigo.

Destiny avoided her first-time lover, wished the man she was seeing now was there, wished Hakeem Mitchell was with her the way Yaba the Laker was with Indigo.

Yaba got in the pool with Indigo and they played around awhile. Many times Dubois looked at Destiny, and Destiny looked at him. He stared at Destiny almost as many times as Ericka stared at Mr. Jones, as many times as Mr. Jones glanced toward Ericka.

Yaba the Laker followed Indigo up the stairs to her apartment, his present in his hands.

Chimamandanata watched her daughter, lips tight, arms folded, shaking her head.

Chapter 19

At 9:34 P.M. they were in short skirts and high heels, drinks in hand, braless breasts doing jumping jacks as they bounced and sang "Happy Birthday" to Indigo during a Badu concert. Ten minutes later Ericka, Kwanzaa, and Indigo had once again given Destiny their cell phones, then posed in their classic *Charlie's Angels* position. She had taken photos for them all evening.

Someone offered to take a picture of the Blackbirds.

Destiny said, "I'm fine being behind the camera. I'm the official group photographer."

Indigo's phone began blowing up. Her father called from his phone. Her mother called from her phone. Her mother was home, but her father wasn't. He had stepped out to run an errand. Relatives called from Nigeria. And Olamilekan Babangida called. His call was twenty minutes off, but still that call made Indigo's night. She spoke to him for twenty seconds, if that, and then the called dropped. Indigo tried to call him back, but there was no answer.

She yelled, "The reception is bad in here."

Kwanzaa yelled back, "My service is great. My phone has more bars than a jail cell."

"Let me use your phone."

She did that to see if he was screening his calls.

Indigo tried Olamilekan again and again and again.

Each time the call went to voice mail.

She took a half dozen selfies, her cleavage popping, and sent them to

Olamilekan. She wanted him to see her dressed in the *sexylicious* outfit and shoes he had given her. This was what he was missing. The same photos she had sent to Olamilekan, she also sent to Yaba the Laker. Two seconds later, Idowu Yaba called, and that call expanded Indigo's joy.

If you can't be with the one you love, love the one you're with.

While she talked to Idowu Yaba, her phone beeped; it was Olamilekan's number.

Indigo didn't answer. Then Kwanzaa's phone rang, again Olamilekan's number.

Indigo told Kwanzaa to answer, and if it was a woman to curse her out in Spanish and hang up. But if it was Olamilekan, tell him that Indigo was disappointed and now she was on another call with someone who cared enough to remember to call at the proper time, and she was occupied and would call him back whenever she was once again available. Indigo continued her conversation with Yaba the Laker. She laughed, spoke in a strong Nigerian dialect, and hoped her words burned Olamilekan's ears. She wished Yaba had arrived at her party earlier, before Olamilekan. She needed Mr. Babangida to see and understand she had many options.

That had actually been her plan, but it hadn't worked out that way.

Chapter 20

At two in the morning, they were just getting back from the Badu performance. They had ridden in Indigo's new Rubicon. They had taken the doors and the roof off the Jeep, and Destiny had driven while Indigo wore a birthday tiara and became the singing front-seat passenger. When they made it back home, they were all dog tired but energized.

Indigo showered, changed, and without informing the Blackbirds of her after-party plans, had left again within minutes. When she heard the security gate *clack-clack-whirr* open, Ericka went to her window. She wasn't concerned. The gate across the driveway only opened either by remote or when someone was being buzzed in, the same for the gate at the walkway.

Indigo was leaving in the Rubicon. Had to be a birthday booty call.

Ericka went to her kitchen table. Many pamphlets on cancers were next to her laptop. Websites for herbalists who offered miracle diets, supplements, and cures were there as well.

For a moment her body felt off, had a wave of exhaustion, and she felt afraid.

She went to her bedroom, to her closet, and reached into the back, pulled out her Remington 870 Express Shotgun, the shotgun she had named Hemingway.

Ericka looked at Hemingway for a moment, then she put her shotgun back in its hiding place. That would be her last resort. But she hoped it would never come to that. She hoped she never had to pull the trigger on that shotgun. She convinced herself that she would if she had to.

The wave of weakness went away as fast as it had come.

So did her fear.

She told herself that she was fine, that she was just tired from working and keeping up with three younger women who had endless energy. She paused to count the number of hours she had slept each night, and realized she had slept only around thirty hours in the last seven days. They had had fun and time had zoomed by, each day more exciting than the one before. Last week, they had partied at the BET Experience. Indigo's parents had gifted her and the Blackbirds with a $4,000 Diamond Package: orchestra seating, red-carpet experience, only VIP for Indigo.

Ericka yawned and stretched, tired and running on fumes but unable to close her eyes.

She convinced herself all she needed was a good night's sleep.

She was fine. The invisible demon that had lived inside her had been defeated.

She was in remission and it was time to move away from the fear.

She went back to the kitchen table, collected all the pamphlets, put them in the trash.

Soon she would do the same with the shotgun.

Ericka sipped infused water flavored with strawberry, lemon, and basil. She reorganized books featuring places she wanted to travel. Eritrea. Russia. Iceland. Canada. Japan. Egypt. Rwanda. Oman. Morocco. Ecuador. Denmark. Italy. Croatia. Kenya. Ethiopia. Yemen.

She wanted to visit all those places. She told herself that one day she would.

Not long after, Destiny's colorful CBR revved to life and the wrought-iron gate whirred open. Since the garages were in the back, they had to drive by the front doors of the apartments to come and go, and none of them could leave or arrive without being heard by the others.

Ericka assumed Destiny had become Kismet Kellogg and was creeping to see her mystery man in Culver City. She was long overdue and Ericka was happy for her.

Five minutes passed.

She assumed that Kwanzaa had weakened and called Marcus Brixton because her car started up, the gate whirred once again, and that Blackbird sped out onto Crenshaw Boulevard.

The Blackbirds were gone and that made her feel so damn alone.

Ericka picked up her phone, first with the intention of searching for Dr. Debra Dubois, but instead she looked at recent text messages from her ex-husband, invitations to reconcile.

She was tempted to call him even though it was late.

Out of loneliness. Out of anger.

But as she was about to text her ex, the security gate whirred open.

It was Kwanzaa, back ten minutes after she had left.

Ericka sent her a text and asked what that was all about.

She responded that it was a tampon run.

Ericka Stockwell stayed home, looking out the window, Mr. Jones on her mind.

She thought about Destiny's father. She always thought about Destiny's father.

Mr. Jones. Mr. Keith Jones. *Keith.*

Ex-husband of Mrs. Carmen Jones.

She thought about how he had felt inside her.

How he had given her a full-body orgasm.

She had spoken in tongues, lost control in a wonderful way.

She had almost raised her hand when Destiny asked about older men, but the Blackbirds would have asked questions and she never would have been able to face Destiny.

As Ericka thought about that night, she became aroused; she quivered.

She thought about the oversize sofa in his town home. That was where she really wanted to be, next to him, with him, underneath him, on that sofa. She wanted to feel that again.

But that intimacy never should've happened and couldn't happen again. It was too weird. The tool that had been used to create Destiny had been inside her. It had become awkward to have Destiny as a friend, and that memory, that unexpected moment, as the secret of all secrets.

Ericka remembered how her Bible-thumping mother would always chant scriptures at night, trying to pray away the flaming demons that exacerbated her womanly desires.

After Ericka had been pregnant, her mother forced her to get on her knees in order to *pray away the sinful urges that should not be acted upon outside the blessed institution of marriage.*

Her mother had made her chant scriptures and pray for healing together.

Ericka gazed at the worn Bible on her dresser, wished it would speak to her.

If it would not speak, she spoke, hoping it would at least listen.

She apologized for the things she had said to her mother.

She had only one request, and it had been the same prayer for as long as she could remember. She begged she didn't become her mother. She would kill herself. She wondered what had happened to that smiling, fun-seeking Caledonia Koepling to make her become the hateful Betty Stockwell she was today. Ericka wondered if that was her own fate as well.

Ericka thought more about Mr. Jones.

She thought about that night, on his sofa, smoking medicinal weed, kissing.

Then losing control.

She remembered the shock she felt when he slid inside her.

She had been so wet, so open, so ready.

Still there had been a sweet sting. There had been more to him than she had imagined.

Mr. Jones had been sultry, rumbling, back-arching thunder, a storm unleashed. Ericka's dress was up around her waist, panties pulled to the side, Mr. Jones's pants unzipped and at his waist, the way people were when sex was sudden, unexpected, unplanned, out of control. He had entered her and made skin slap. She had straddled him and he had given her rugged strokes.

He had never seen this side of her.

She had never witnessed that side of him.

He created a tempest inside her.

She saw dancing lights behind her closed eyes when she had moved against him. He was a hurricane. Her moans were elongated flames in the air as orgasms came in powerful waves. He had withdrawn, gone down on his knees, and blessed her sex with his tongue. That night had brought her two years of celibacy to an unexpected end. She came, trembling, cheeks tight, legs straining, her face etched with desperation and pain, her hand clamped on her sin eater's head, praising his tongue, dampening his mouth, writing her name on his face.

She came wanting love.

Then they had rested on the sofa, cuddled, smoking weed as the aura waned. After two years of celibacy, she was surprised she hadn't blacked out from feeling so good. To be fair, after a few minutes had passed, without a conversation, without cleaning him, she stroked him, fellated with passion, tasted him, tasted herself on him, made him jerk, curse, and call God.

He shot an inordinate amount of semen a good five feet in the air while lying on his back. He was a fountain. She didn't know a man could skeet like that, had never seen her ex-husband skeet more than a few inches. After Mr. Jones had cleaned up, after she had gone to the bathroom and washed herself, after resting another two hours, the third time, she rode him, felt him when he grew, felt his explosion, felt him fill her up, then river out of her again, and she wanted it to go on until time ran out of time.

Ericka had been with Destiny's father.

Destiny never noticed the guilt in her eyes.

Ericka couldn't get Mr. Jones off her mind or out of her heart.

She stripped down to her panties and bra, took photos of the curve of her bottom from a side angle, of her breasts from the same angle, of her areolas, then added them to a text to Mr. Jones. Asked him if he had company, and if not, if he wanted company for a couple of hours. Told him she missed him. Wanted to be with him again. Then was too scared to press SEND. Too scared to put her feelings and desires out there.

Her nipples were stiff. The itch was strong. The celibacy clock had been reset.

She crawled into bed, Mr. Jones on her mind, touched herself awhile.

Fantasized. Climaxed. Panting, recovering, she saw that the window was open, wondered who had heard.

She closed the window. Turned the ceiling fan on high. Fantasized again. Reached heaven again. Remained restless. She ate slices of a mango, then broke out her stash of Kush.

As Nina Simone played on Pandora, Ericka smoked a little White Widow, took four puffs, and fantasized about being on that sofa and climaxed again and again and again.

Once she started, she could touch herself for hours.

She showered, the water turned cold. Then she snacked on a bag of low-calorie baked potato chips. She lay back, crunching, chewing, swallowing, crunching, chewing, swallowing, floating, floating, floating. She wanted to puff until her room had a cloud of marijuana covering her home the way smog blanketed the city, but she didn't, not tonight. She flipped her pillow from the warm side to the cool over and over.

She was a restless Blackbird who wanted to fly away from all she knew.

Chapter 21

Tingles from her orgasm subsiding, Destiny caught her breath.

Music by Kendrick Lamar jammed from the living room but wasn't louder than the unrighteous copulating on the other side of the door. Eddie and Nancy had outlasted her and Hakeem. They always did, and Destiny was very aroused, was only getting warmed up.

Destiny pulled her locks away from her neck. Leg trembling, she heard Nancy moan like she was coming over and over. She sounded like she was in the next room losing her mind. Destiny took a frustrated breath, flared her nostrils, and opened her envious eyes.

She said, "Hakeem, wake up."

He shifted, rubbed her bottom, and yawned. "I'm awake, Kismet. Barely awake."

Her voice was rusty, like a Blues singer. His was postorgasmic, in his refractory stage. Her stage was the opposite. She had had an orgasm but she needed the healing to continue in order to be effective.

But she knew Hakeem's rhythm, knew it would be a while before he could go again.

She had to keep him awake, because once he slept, the fun was done.

She whispered, "Hakeem, baby, you were really hard that time."

"Yeah. I was a brick."

"You put it down. That round was profound. You were deeper than Dostoyevsky."

"Dostoyevsky? Did I just get literary on you?"

"What was it to you?"

"I was a beast like a Klingon. I felt like I was Dr. Spock going through pon farr."

"You found an angle and it was a crime the way you gave me that sweet punishment."

She hoped there would be a sequel, maybe a trilogy before the night was over.

It sounded like Eddie was putting down a miniseries. Two seasons. Dramatic moans and whimpers came from the other side of the door, mixed in with Kendrick Lamar jamming "King Kunta" on repeat, the tenth time she'd heard that song since she was in bed with Hakeem.

Destiny's clothing rested on an armless chair near the foot of the bed. She glanced at her jeans and biker's gear. DO UNTO OTHERS stared at her.

Here she was not Destiny. Here she was Kismet Kellogg.

Here was where she felt guilt because here she told her greatest lie.

She wouldn't want Hakeem to lie to her about who he was.

"King Kunta" ended, then started again.

Destiny asked Hakeem, "What does a mechanical engineer at Northrup do, exactly?"

"I research, design, develop, manufacture, and test tools, engines, machines, and other mechanical devices. I'm in one of the broadest engineering disciplines. It's cool for right now."

"May I ask you another serious question?"

"Sure, Kismet."

"You always flirt and kiss girls at clubs, then engineer your way into a sister's pants, and manufacture orgasms by eating out said girl the first time you hook up? That's your MO?"

He yawned. "How did I end up getting lucky enough to be with you, Kismet?"

She grinned. "You caught my eye. You caught my eye and my guard went down."

"I walked in the place, and you stood out. My eyes went right to you. Your locks. That tight T-shirt. Tight jeans and heels, confident and dancing by yourself like the music had taken you to another place, another time, another universe."

"And you walked over and asked me if I wanted to ride your Big Wheel."

"You laughed. And when you smiled, damn, your smile was so damn sexy."

"Making a woman laugh is like a flame to ice. Makes an ice queen melt."

"Had never seen a woman with a smile as nice as yours."

"You seemed surprised when we started talking."

"You're artistic and eloquent. You don't seem like a girl who would be so smart."

"Thanks. I think. Assumed stupid until proven intelligent is every black woman's crime."

"That's not what I meant."

"It's cool. I'm used to being taken for granted based on epidermis, race, and gender."

"What I meant to say is that you're amazing. You just look so free-spirited, and you know a lot of the free-spirited aren't really motivated to do much. I'm not good with words like you are."

"Erykah Badu was the deejay."

"You were standing over to the side jamming your ass off, moving like Missy Elliott."

"That was my return to hip-hop that night. Badu pulled me back in, had me fired up."

"You had given it up?"

"I used to love hip-hop and wanted to be a singing rapper so I could pen rebellious songs and get on stage, be like Nina Simone singing 'Mississippi Goddam' and 'Strange Fruit.'"

"Really?"

"I fell in love with rap and hip-hop and wanted to run away with both of them."

"Hip-hop and rap. You say that like you're talking about two dudes."

"Not fun loving someone who has no love for you. That's a reformatory in and of itself."

"What do you mean?"

"One night it showed me its true face, its real feelings, and betrayed me. I snuck away from home. I went to a private affair to partake in hip-hop and rap one night. Took it my young soul. And it laughed behind my back and deceived me. It smiled in my face and did me wrong. It's left a damaged nerve. An open wound across a chasm no sutures can close. But I went to see Badu, let her be my doctor, let her help me get my love for the music back in my blood."

"What happened in your life that made rap and hip-hop seem that bad?"

"I thought that I was finding my true self. I went to become one with rap and hip-hop, only to find out they were just as fake. It was a bunch of crabs in the barrel and backstabbing assholes. Women were two-faced, betrayed women, and the men were just as bad."

"What happened, Kismet?"

She almost told him.

She almost stopped being Kismet and became her true self, the infamous Destiny Jones.

Then the music stopped playing.

Without "King Kunta" jamming, Destiny heard Nancy and Eddie moaning and groaning in the next room, the sounds extreme, like a break-in and a murder were in progress.

Hakeem said, "Eddie and Nancy are going at it hard again."

"They never stop."

"That's their thing."

"Do they ever do anything else, like have a conversation, or play a board game?"

"Nope."

"What did you say her parents do?"

"Her mother is an archeologist; her father is a bigwig at Jet Propulsion Laboratory."

"All that intelligence, so much potential, and she's attracted to Eddie?"

Hakeem closed his eyes. Destiny channel-surfed until she found a rerun of *The Big Bang Theory*, then turned up the volume, but it didn't compete with the reality of the big banging Eddie was giving Nancy. Aroused, shivers went up and down Destiny's spine.

Destiny growled, sat up, cursed toward the door. "They are killing each other in there."

"She needs another pillow over her head."

"That or a plastic bag."

"Damn, she gets loud."

Destiny asked, "Why is Eddie saying 'chug, chug, chug'?"

"He's about to finish and that means for her to get ready to swallow."

The sexual sounds in the front of the condo wound down, moans and catlike whines, calls to God and Jesus and requests to have it given to her harder, harder, harder, stopped.

Destiny turned the volume back down, whispered, "Wow. That sounded so ridiculous."

"So, are you mad or jealous?"

"I want us to be alone."

"You're mad."

"All I want to hear is our sounds and this bed rocking."

"And you're jealous."

"Of what? Of not being able to be with my man and walk around his house naked?"

"Of Nancy and how she's so freaky and uninhibited."

"I don't care what she does."

"Eddie says she loves the hell out of anal."

"Are you gay?"

"Of course not."

"Then stop asking if you can do me in my booty. When I want back-door sex, when it interests me, you will be informed. And I was joking about the gay thing, so don't get an attitude, okay?"

"For my birthday at least? Let me take a peek in the basement for my birthday."

"You plan on making a salad?"

"I just might toss one, if that's what it takes to loosen it up and get you ready."

She laughed. "In that case, let me think about it. Never had my salad tossed."

"Really? We need to add that to the list."

"That intrigues me. You'd do that?"

"For you I would, if you're fresh out of the shower and don't stop to potty."

"Maybe we should do the whole thing in the shower."

"Just the tip. Just the tip of the tip. Just the tippity tip of the tip."

She laughed harder. "Will you stop it?"

She leaned over and kissed him for few seconds.

She wanted more stage time, like Eddie gave Nancy.

More stage time might inspire other orifices to open.

Maybe.

She wasn't sure.

She had a flashback. Hoosegow. Getting her salad tossed for the first time.

Destiny put the television on mute.

The condo was quiet now. No Kendrick Lamar. No Nancy wailing like she was both in heaven and in hell. No Eddie grunting like he was a Neanderthal about to bust a big fat nut.

Destiny went to the door, cracked it open, and felt a rush of the heat Eddie and Nancy had created. Their kinetic energy had raised the temperature at least fifteen degrees. Destiny peeped out only to find Eddie and Nancy weren't done. They were next to the sofa bed, on the floor. Eddie was on his back, pillow underneath his head, feet planted on the carpet with his knees bent. Nancy was on top of Eddie, on her back, her head resting on his bent knees, her back against Eddie's six-pack, legs wide, her sex presented to his face for oral stimulation and gratification. Nancy was biting a pillow to muffle the sounds from receiving superstar oral sex. Her body was rejoicing. Nancy was all of five feet tall. Legs like a soccer player. Full breasts. Her face was sheened in sweat, and her blonde-and-purple hair was unruly, had a just-sexed-into-a-frenzy wildness. Nancy sat up, held on to the edge of the sofa to balance her body, and continued to bless Eddie's face with her sex. She was still chewing the pillow, huffing and puffing as she came. Eddie held her hips, pulled her, gave her tongue, made her grind on his face, on his tongue, on his chin, on anything hard, and she was mutilating the pillow to muffle her orgasmic cries. That girl was on fire, desperate to set free the orgasm that controlled her. Destiny had seen that in Hoosegow many times, only with two girls. Nancy fell away, panting. Eddie crawled to her, put his cock in her mouth. They were winding down. Either Eddie had never come, or he was ready to come again before he quit. He came and made Nancy come again. Eddie looked toward the bedroom. Destiny made eye contact with him.

Eddie smiled at Destiny's nakedness, nodded with approval of what he saw as he slid his cock in and out of Nancy's mouth, as he tested her gag reflex with his half-hard appendage.

Destiny closed the door, again tingling, her clit throbbing, and went back to the bed.

Destiny squirmed, wanted her nipples sucked. Wanted a tongue inside her.

She heard Eddie. Nancy was sucking him and driving him crazy.

Destiny nudged Hakeem. He didn't respond. She touched herself for a moment.

She touched herself and made her pussy hum, made herself come imagining Hakeem was eating her out the way Eddie had eaten out Nancy, in that superstar sex position.

Destiny sipped the last drops of her bottled water, waited ten more minutes, gave Eddie and Nancy time to get cleaned up and cuddled up. Destiny pulled on Hakeem's yellow Reverse-Flash T-shirt, left the bedroom, and tiptoed through the wafting scent of cologne, perfume, and orgasm. The condo was one keg away from smelling like a two-man frat house.

Nancy and Eddie were nude, cuddled up on the sofa bed in the living room.

Nancy's pink overnight bag was at the foot of the sofa.

She brought her bag only when she planned to spend the night, which meant she had lied to her parents and told them she was staying at one of her girlfriends' houses tonight.

Nancy and Eddie were over so much Hakeem should charge them rent.

That was Nancy's routine, pack her pink bag, cook Eddie a four-course meal, have sex like sex was going out of style, then leave L.A. and speed back to her Orange County life after a night of debauchery. Nancy and Eddie were in the living room because the second bedroom was an office. Still Destiny wished they would at least buy an air mattress, or just go rent a room at the Snooty Fox or Deano's Motel. Both seemed like places where degenerates went to be degenerates with other degenerates. But Eddie and Nancy were Hakeem's friends. They had been grandfathered into Destiny's relationship with Hakeem. They had been there first.

Nancy raised her head and said, "Hey, Kismet."

Destiny did a curt wave. "Pardon the intrusion. Going to get water. Want some?"

"I'm so dehydrated and too weak to move. Thanks."

"Eddie, you want water too? You should be thirsty. Sounded like a donnybrook out here."

He didn't respond, but the anaconda bobbed twice, which Destiny took to mean no. Destiny went to the kitchen, tasted the baked chicken Nancy had cooked. It was delicious. Same for the herbed bulgur, lentil salad, and steamed veggies. Destiny ate a little protein, then grabbed two bottles of water, handed Nancy one.

Nancy opened hers, took several desperate gulps, wiped her mouth, burped, then said, "Kismet, I searched for your mother all day yesterday."

"What do you mean?"

"A family friend needs a good attorney and I looked up Henrietta Kellogg online, but couldn't find her. I put her name in Google, searched Facebook, and looked for her on LinkedIn. Henrietta Kellogg. That's what you said your mother's name is, right? Can you give me her info?"

Destiny diverted her eyes. "She's not taking any cases right now."

"The family friend is a CEO of a company and got himself in some serious trouble."

"My mom's not available."

Nancy rolled over on her back, pulled her knees to her chest, stretching. "Oh. Okay. This case would bring in a lot of revenue and I wanted to give her first right of refusal, since you and I are new best friends."

Destiny said, "Eddie sure has a big one."

"What?"

"His magic stick. It's a big one. Looks like it could jump up and bite you."

"It's harmless now. I sucked all the venom out."

"A girl has to do what a girl has to do."

"I heard you in there riding the Big Wheel. Eddie says you sound sexy when you moan."

"I'll make a point of keeping down the noise."

Staring at Destiny, Nancy held up her fingers, made a square director's lens, said, "Kismet, your face looks familiar. Wow. I just realized that when I look at you straight on like this, and block out your hair and just look at you from your forehead to your chin, you look familiar."

Doing her best to be kind and suppress irritation, Destiny turned the ceiling fan on.

Eddie jerked awake, pushed up on his elbows. He took a sharp breath, then stood up, still naked, and staggered toward the bathroom. Nancy stood up, also nude and unashamed, and went to the kitchen. Eddie had paused at the doorframe. While Nancy was getting Eddie a beer, Eddie smiled at Destiny. Nancy smiled at Destiny. Both smiles felt like an invitation to an impromptu party.

Eddie disappeared into the bathroom that was inside of Hakeem's office. He left the bathroom door open, began to urinate, and it sounded like he was a racehorse.

Nancy opened two beers, opened them, put them on the end table, on coasters.

Destiny asked, "For you and Eddie?"

"For Eddie."

"That's his secret? That's how he is able to go all night long?"

"He takes a pill that make him stay hard for about a week at a time."

"Viagra?"

"Nah. He buys some pill at the Chevron across the street. Some red herbal pill."

"Does he have any extras?"

"We only had one. Cost almost fifteen dollars. He picked it out and I paid for it."

"You're getting your money's worth."

Nancy said, "You can stay out here with us if you want to let Hakeem sleep."

"And what would I do out here?"

"Take a break."

"No thanks. I'm sure Hakeem wouldn't appreciate me keeping his friend company."

"I meant we could play Scrabble."

Destiny yawned. "With our intelligence and vocabulary, we'd embarrass Eddie. We would embarrass Hakeem too. It would be the private school girls slaughtering the LAUSD boys."

"Or some drinking game."

Destiny shook her head. "I'm done drinking for the month."

"I think Hakeem has a Monopoly game too. Want to play one game?"

"Nah. Maybe some other time. When Hakeem is awake and I'm not half past delirious."

"If he wakes up, we can play spades."

"What's going on with you?"

"I need a break from Eddie, if you know what I mean."

"Oh. Thought you were having the time of your life out here."

"Sometimes I wish he would let me watch *The Real Housewives of Atlanta* for a while."

"Well, be careful what you wish for."

"I'm going to be sore."

"You bought the pill. The rocks come with the farm."

"And the rock stays hard and Eddie keeps farming me all night long."

"You've got a good thing. Enjoy it."

Nancy yawned. "Yeah. Guess I shouldn't be jealous of you and Hakeem."

"I will be careful what I wish for too."

Destiny went back to the bedroom, and pulled the door closed behind her.

Hakeem sat up on the bed, yawning. Destiny sipped the water, and then handed it to him.

He said, "I heard you and Nancy talking."

"She kept looking at my body. *Awkward.*"

"Uh-oh. Do you like hers?"

"Don't even think about it."

"Me and Eddie could get some popcorn and watch."

"If anything, I'll get popcorn and watch you and Eddie do protein shots."

"That's gross."

"So now you know how I feel when you said me and Nancy. *That's* gross."

Hakeem laughed and squeezed her bottom. Destiny laughed too.

She said, "Nancy is smart, yet naïve. Educated, yet ignorant."

"You don't like her?"

"I like her. I like her because she reminds me of me years ago, but I wasn't in some random guy's condo on the floor getting screwed six ways to Sunday three or four days a week. I wasn't having sex, but I was naïve. I was too trusting. She has book sense, can kill a differential equations exam, but Eddie has street smarts, and book smarts will never be better than street smarts after five P.M. Eddie has finagled himself into her drawers."

"She's been sheltered. She went to an all-girls Christian school until she started university, and finally has herself a taste of freedom."

"I can tell. Her parents have protected her, and now she's exploring."

"Everything about L.A. is new to her."

Destiny said, "Eddie is new to her. She's impressed by what I find unimpressive."

"She finds black men very exotic. She told me that. Getting attention from Eddie, a man built the way he is, and I'm just keeping it real because the girls at the gym be all over Eddie. I guess him giving her so much time, well, that would be like a brother getting attention from Scarlett Johansson. He'd have to try and swirl. She's getting her swirl on, so to speak."

"Seeing a black man, she's just being a rebel. It will wear off."

"Bet she's never had dick like that."

"Not many women get dick like that."

"You like my dick?"

"When it's hard and inside me."

"You want me to put it back inside you?"

"I never asked you to take it out."

"So you want it back in?"

"I always want you to put it back in me."

"Never would have thought you were this sexual."

"I never would have thought I was this sexual either."

"I do this to you?"

"Guess I am having an awakening."

She wished Hakeem would lick up and down her spine, suck her toes, get on his back, and pull her to his face, wake up the Jamaican in her blood, make her dance until she came, make her go dance hall as she sent up moans that rivaled every orgasmic utterance Nancy had ever made. As Destiny lay on her belly moving her butt side to side with her restless thoughts, she watched Hakeem stare at her eyes. She tried not to smile. She felt so damn happy.

She wanted him back inside. She wanted him to give her what Eddie gave, what Nancy was complaining about. But Destiny didn't want to come across as just another Nancy.

Intellect over lust. She told herself to think of this as extended foreplay.

She moved her ass, made soft sounds, licked her lips, bit her lips like that lady in that popular sex novel, gave the proper cues to be taken, but she would endure the flames and wait.

Hakeem said, "Wish I had met you when I was still in high school."

"Me too. I really do. I'll bet we could've had fun kicking it here and there."

"You have pictures of yourself on your phone from back then?"

She hesitated. "No. There are no pictures on my phone. I told you that a dozen times."

"Why won't you let me take at least one selfie of us together for my Facebook page?"

"No. Stop asking."

"My uncle Stephan and aunt Chante keep asking what you look like."

"Hopefully one day I will meet them in person. In the meantime, feel free to sketch my image from memory. Be creative. Use adjectives to paint the picture of me how you see me."

"Something is off. I can't figure it out. Are you married?"

"No, I'm not married."

"Nancy thinks you're married."

"She's wrong."

"I want to see where you live and meet your friends and family, is that too much to ask?"

"No. No, it isn't. It's reasonable."

"Well?"

"Right now this is all you need to know, Hakeem. This right here. Come *Eddie* me."

"*Eddie* you? Oh, he's a verb now?"

"*Eddie* me. Do to me what Eddie does to Nancy and make me moan like that."

Hakeem put the water down, moved his body next to hers. Destiny rubbed up against him. He reciprocated. Then they were kissing, touching, making out under the covers until Hakeem once again became aroused. He moved away from her. He rolled on another condom.

He was hard, but not hard enough.

Destiny asked, "What's wrong?"

"Just give me a second."

"Nancy says Eddie takes some sort of pill."

"I don't need a pill. I just need to get back in Vulcan mode and groove like it's pon farr."

She was about to tell him they didn't have to go on, but he pushed, opened her. She felt him finally get sufficient girth, length, and firmness. He crept inside, and then fell inside her. She hummed, put her nails in his skin, and marked him as he sucked on her neck, as he marked her.

Then they were kissing, stroking, rolling, in sync, in rhythm, heat rising with moans.

He said, "I'm in love with you, Kismet."

"You know I'm in love with you."

"Since when?"

"Since the night I met you. I felt this connection. You have my heart."

He moaned, then asked, "So, Kismet, are we officially a couple?"

"Do you want to be a couple? Just tell me what this is we're doing."

"I gave you a key. I thought we already were a couple, Kismet."

She moaned. "So did I. I assumed we were a couple a while ago, after all the nice dinners, but you never said and I didn't want to assume, and was kind of afraid to ask."

"If you think we are, and I think we are, I guess that means that we are."

"We are a couple. Wow. I'm officially and not assumedly in a relationship."

"Can we do it bareback? I stay hard, get much harder when I ride bareback."

"I want to feel you too, but I don't want to make any mistakes."

"Can I take the condom off this time?"

"I'm not trying to be your baby momma, Hakeem."

She heard Nancy moaning again. Eddie was back at it, back in it.

Destiny asked, "Can't she blow Eddie and let Eddie blow her back out somewhere else?"

"Eddie's my boy. We go way back. It's just until he gets his own spot."

"Doesn't she have a place to take Eddie? She pays for everything else, why not a room?"

"She said if her folks saw the hotel charge on her credit card, they'd have a fit."

"Then tell her to rent an SUV and park by the airport or down by the beach."

"Eddie called earlier. I thought I'd be gone. I told him he could use the living room."

"Oh, I didn't know he had made a reservation. Should I make one for us to be alone?"

"Kismet, I had already promised. Didn't know you were coming by. You just showed up."

"I just showed up? You texted me all day long and said you wanted to see me, and now you say I just showed up? I'm tired, but I made sure I put in some time with you."

"No, I'm happy to see you. I'm always happy to see you, you know that."

"And you were going to be in bed while they go at it half the night?"

"I would've gone out. New spot called the Club is the business."

"But you didn't leave."

"Had a long day. Was too tired to go out. And they were already here. Nancy cooked. She always buys groceries and cooks for Eddie. Eddie says he's hungry and she buys a bag of food, turns the kitchen into a restaurant, and feeds him like a king."

"I'm calling bullshit on that one. She feeds him like he's at a homeless shelter."

"She cooked, made his plate, and then she was nice and made me a plate. I sat down with them and ate, then came and got in bed, started streaming classic *Star Trek*."

"They were going at it like chipmunks on cocaine when I got here."

"I know. They were going at it froggy-style as I closed my bedroom door."

"They start to sound obnoxious."

"They sound loving. Nancy loves Eddie. She's not ashamed of how she feels about him. She will do anything to make Eddie happy. That's what I hear. I hear people in love."

"Eddie does do a pretty thorough job; at least it sounds that way."

"Your nipples are like bullets. Does listening to Eddie make your nipples hard? Are you fantasizing about Eddie?"

"You turn me on, Hakeem. Other men do nothing for me. I'm a loyal woman."

"You're mysterious."

"But I am loyal. This is yours. All I need is in this room. You're all the man I need."

"I feel the same about you, Kismet Kellogg."

"You have no idea how special you are to me."

"You really love me?"

"I'd be your ride-or-die, no matter if you're right or wrong."

Destiny turned him over, put him on his back, took him back inside, rocked the boat, made the headboard *bup-bup-bup* against the wall, showed him ride-or-die, made moans evolve from guttural sounds to lip-biting expletives, to louder uncontrollable excited utterances and passionate confessions. Destiny felt his energy when he told her that he loved her.

He moved with her, tried to match her groove, failed.

So she told him to stop moving, to be still and let her get him where he needed to go.

She closed her eyes, heard Vybz Kartel singing for her to ride it like a bicycle, heard the lyrics in her mind, and did a sweet whine, and showed Hakeem her femininity and versatility.

Hakeem told her he loved her, said it over and over, praised her mind with words as clear as moans, praised her ambitions, said he loved making love to her, told her he wanted her to be a part of his life, not only at night, but during the daytime as well, wanted this to become something real. She rode and trembled and he moaned without end and poured his heart out.

On the road to nirvana, she shuddered, told him, "You'd better not come yet."

"Okay, okay."

"Don't be weak. This is your castle. Be the king."

"I'm the king. *I'm the muh-fuckin' king.*"

"*Eddie* me like a king *eddies* a muh muh muh muh-*fuckin'* queen."

Destiny didn't slow or relent her command when Hakeem tried to push her over, turn her so he could get on top, so he could take the dominant position.

She showed him how a jockey was supposed to ride.

Destiny stayed on top of Hakeem, and in the broken light, she saw his face, saw that look that said he was astounded. He gazed up and stared at her when she started to shudder, saw the ugliness that was so beautiful when her sisterlocks had come loose and framed her lust.

She moved up and down with her eyes closed.

She growled, moaned, and made the headboard attack the wall.

It sounded like he was on top of her giving it to her good.

She wanted Nancy to think that she was getting it from Hakeem as good as Nancy was getting it from Eddie. Female ego. Destiny leaned forward, held Hakeem's hands, rode him as if he were her bitch and she were stroking him, *a woman like a man*, as if she were taking him.

She moved round and round, up and down, varied her rhythm, rocked him steady. She set free her passion, was set on fire by love, by hope, by her emotions.

She showed him that she was delicate, but at times did not want him to be delicate with her; showed him how she needed and wanted to be handled in bed. Slow, then with intensity. She wanted a long ride, not necessarily a marathon—she had too many obligations, too many things to do—but at least half of one from time to time. It would ease the stress in her life.

Destiny was on top of Hakeem, felt him lose some firmness, felt him become too flexible, and that frustrated her at a crucial moment. She needed the wood in order to keep feeling good.

She growled, "Don't go soft on me."

"Okay."

"Keep it hard."

She sat up, rode him, closed her eyes, moved with the fire, scratched her itch, rose and fell. She danced. She danced the Dutty Wine, Pon de River, Row the Boat. She moaned and felt him inside her making her dance the Pepper Seed, Butterfly, and Bogle.

Destiny was loud. It was her turn to be loud. She didn't care who heard them. She wanted them to hear her. She was just as much woman as Nancy.

She could make her man feel as good as Nancy made Eddie feel.

Destiny rode Hakeem and he groaned and moaned for Jesus to save his soul.

He softened up again.

"Keep it hard, baby. Keep it hard a little longer. Just a little longer."

Again Hakeem tried to turn her over, tried to flip her, maybe so he could take her doggie-style. Destiny leaned forward, held his hands down, rode him as if she were taking his virginity, sometimes subtle, most of the time with force. Hakeem called out, told Kismet he loved her.

"I'm coming, Hakeem. Shit, I'm coming. I'm coming so hard."

"Me too, baby. Me too."

"Push it. Push it. Give it to me, like that, like that, like that."

Destiny danced, danced, moaned, and danced. Wayup, Gully Creep, and the Shampoo. She felt Hakeem do his best to keep up, but his best felt like he was under her dancing the Charleston, the Hustle, and the Electric Slide. Again she told him to stop moving.

She barked at him, told him to relax.

She had this.

She didn't need his help, only his erection.

She had moves a dance-hall queen would need three years to learn.

The headboard banged and banged and banged.

Hakeem's toes curled and he became the grunting Neanderthal.

When Destiny slowed, as sweat dripped from her and she stopped doing the Butterfly, as Hakeem panted and wheezed and softened inside her, when she fell away from him and finally caught her breath, there was silence. For the first time ever, they'd outlasted Eddie and Nancy.

Destiny felt like she had won the gold and a key to the city.

She hoped she had disturbed Nancy and Eddie as much as they had disturbed her.

Destiny felt as if she were being watched, looked toward the door.

The door wasn't closed all the way. It had been closed. Now it was cracked.

She saw Nancy watching her and Hakeem.

She saw Asian eyes blink rapidly, then back away.

Destiny smiled, hoped the nosey bitch learned how a real woman moved her ass.

Chapter 22

After Destiny and Hakeem had cleaned themselves, they cuddled.

In a moment of restlessness, Hakeem asked, "Kismet? You sleeping?"

"Wide awake."

"Can I ask you a question?"

"Sure."

"Are you ever submissive?"

"What do you mean by that?"

"You always have to be in control."

"No, I don't."

"I wanted to get on top. You always have to have it the way you want it."

"I come better when I'm on top. I'm confused. I thought a man wanted a woman who knew how to work her ass and work his ass. I just came so hard on top. I guess I do lose control. When I'm like that and you're hard and I get at that angle, you rub my spot and that sends my head through the roof. I thought a man like you would want to make his woman come like that."

"I like you on top. Maybe it's the way you do it, the way you take control and Eddie me."

"The way I *Eddie* you? Are you saying I'm making you feel like Nancy?"

"I'm not sure what I'm saying."

"Are you worried your boy and Nancy heard you moaning and think you're weak?"

"You're pretty aggressive at times. It's like a different you."

"You want me to Nancy you. You want me to Nancy you the way Nancy *Nancies* Eddie."

"She's become a verb too. Okay. What's the definition of Nancy as a verb?"

"You want me to cook, swallow, do anal, do the things Nancy does for Eddie."

"It's not that. I don't want to be *Nancied*, just want to feel like I'm the man in this relationship. You hide me from your friends; you do shit a dude does when he's playing a chick. You come by late at night and are hard to reach in the daytime. I don't know where you live."

"Have I done anything right?"

"You've done everything right."

"Then what's the issue?"

"It's just I'm in love with you, Kismet, so things matter. I'm down with a woman being equal, but some of the ego needs to get checked at the bedroom door."

"I work three jobs, hustle fire sticks, go to USC, and have a sick father, Hakeem."

"Don't take it the wrong way, Kismet. I just want both of us to get what we need."

"Okay. I'll work on a few things. I'm not trying to make you be less of a man, and I'm not trying to be a bedroom bully, but you think I'm stopping you from being one. I'll work on being more acquiescent. I'll Nancy you, only take control when you ask me to, at your request."

"That's not what I mean."

"No, you want submissive. I will pop a Valium and give you submissive."

"I don't want you to become a mannequin."

"I'm not a pillow queen. Sex feels good to me. I have to move. I can't control it."

"That's for sure."

"And I'm just getting to know my body. Despite how I move, sex is new to me. I was so aroused. I guess I've entered pon farr."

"You did go Vulcan on a bro. That was feral sex. The way you made the headboard tap out *War and Peace* in Morse code, damn, boo. That was freakin' awesome. Lord have mercy. Never had a woman ride me like that. Never."

"I'm confused. Do you like making love with me or not?"

"Kismet, I'm just trying to speak up, keep the communication open."

"Maybe this isn't working for you. Is that what you're trying to say?"

"I love it. You have bomb-ass wife pussy, Kismet. You have bomb-ass wife pussy."

"Thanks for telling me how much you love my nonsubmissive poon-tang. Thanks for reducing all that I am to the act of sex, my importance as a being to one orifice."

"I didn't mean to hurt your feelings."

"I make love to you, Hakeem. I don't come here for booty-call sex."

"I love you too, Kismet. That's what's most important. Sex is the bonus. What we do before we get in bed matters most. The way we dance and laugh, the way we enjoy one another's company is gold."

"I guess I have some things to work on. That's all. I haven't been with as many guys as you have been with girls, and I have no idea what to do in a relationship, so I need the feedback."

"Let me know when we can set up a meet-and-greet here for our families."

"And we're going to have to find a word other than *pussy*. I hate that word. It reduces my existence. I want to make sure you see me as more than a hole surrounded by a sexy woman."

"Maybe it would be better if you moved in with me. It's been on my mind. That's why I gave you a key. Hoped you'd move in at some point. I don't mean like right now, but eventually."

"Are you joking?"

"I'd get to see you more and you wouldn't have to leave to go home to change."

Destiny paused, anxious. "I'd need a ring before I moved in with you, Hakeem."

"We'll talk about that too."

"Are you serious?"

"I'm on a tight budget, but maybe we can go look around at the jewelry shops downtown."

"Wow."

"We should price some rings. Not buy, just see your size and what you like."

"You are serious. So, are you . . . Do you want to take this to the next level?"

"I want you here with me every night, not just once or twice a week. This ass is perfect. This is a sweet mountain. I want to be able to climb the mountain at dusk, then again in the middle of the night, and once more at sunrise. I want to wake up and have breakfast with you."

"You want me here so you will have access to sex?"

"I want to know you."

"Well, I want access to sex."

"Better for a woman to say that than a man. I say it, then I am a chauvinistic pig."

"I want more sex, and I want to raise the bar."

"I don't understand you. I don't understand women."

"I know you want more than sex, Hakeem. You take me places, love taking me to dinner. You love dancing with me. I'm just not as available for the things we should be doing to keep this from just becoming me stopping by for a couple of hours. You're right. If I were here, then I would be here when I'm not working, would study at home when I could, would be here between jobs. Would be here for breakfast when you went to work. I could shower and get in bed with you after I left FedEx, or stay up and study. Would be here doing our laundry on weekends."

"You like doing laundry?"

"I study while I do laundry, so, yeah. I would do our laundry together."

"We could have quickies."

"A lot of quickies."

"We need to have that kind of quality time. Eddie and Nancy get to kick it a lot."

"Eddie will have to Eddie Nancy and Nancy will have to Nancy Eddie elsewhere."

"You're territorial."

"I can't live in a frat house. I've already lived in a place that had no privacy."

"The dorms?"

"Yeah, you could say I lived on campus in the dorms for a while. I don't need to hear people getting busy and chugging in the next room. I don't want to tiptoe around come stains to get water. I don't need people looking at me while they are naked, hoping that turns me on."

"Eddie did something?"

"Nancy looks at me in a peculiar way."

"She admires your body, your build, that Africa you carry."

"She stares too long. And I know Eddie sneaks a peep. I need them out when I move in."

"When would you move in, if we could make that happen?"

"After my birthday. Let's see where we are after my birthday."

"Momma wants the house to herself."

"If I do move in, if we get that sorted, Eddie and Nancy's presence is nonnegotiable."

"So, you don't ever want them to kick it here?"

"I'm not coming between you and your buddy, but they will have to get their freak on elsewhere. Okay, time to time they can be here, but not every day, not every weekend."

"Understood. We'll see how this goes."

"I don't understand them. It's like looking at two stereotypes."

"What do you mean?"

"What does she see in him? I would ask what he sees in her, but she has a vagina, and for a lot of men that's all they need a woman to have. I mean, she's a smart girl, and a smart girl like her, even if she wants a brother, she could get one just as fit and three times as educated."

"Maybe she likes Eddie because she feels that much smarter around him."

"She's too smart for Eddie."

"Maybe Nancy has found something in Eddie that was missing in herself. And Eddie has found the type of girl who normally isn't at-tracted to a guy like him. She's smart, but he shows her some basic things that she's never been exposed to. It works for them, Kismet. Maybe both of them just like fucking, and that's enough to sustain their relationship. Maybe Nancy wants to have sex, but not with someone she would ever have to claim in public. If she goes back to the Asian boys, she doesn't have to ever mention the black guy she hooked up with. Same for Eddie."

"I don't get it. Why let a man put his dick in you if it means nothing at all?"

"Don't hurt your brain trying to understand people by your personal standards."

"I'm serious about them not being on the other side of that door moaning and chugging and slapping booties and whoo-hooing and booty loving all night long when I move in."

"We can have the doors wide open then. Just you and me. I want what you want."

Destiny took a deep breath, smiled. "This is a surprise, Hakeem."

"I like to have my life organized, not in limbo. I need you here. I want to wake up with you. I want to start my day with you and end my day with you. That's what I want, Kismet."

Destiny whispered, "I can be submissive. I can learn to Nancy my man."

"Anal?"

"At some point. A couple of my friends do it; seem to like it a lot. We will see."

"Chug?"

"You will have to put in the miles in order to earn those upgrades to premium class."

"Bareback?"

"After I get on the pill, we can have the discussion again. That is not a promise."

"Anything you need me to do to make this relationship better for you?"

"Dancing, movies, workouts, theater, concerts, dinners, skydiving, and beach volleyball."

"You want to have fun."

"Yeah, I want someone I can have fun with. I want to enjoy my life."

He yawned. "I'll Eddie you better. I know you want it like Nancy gets it."

"And I know you want it like Eddie gets to get it when he's getting it from Nancy."

"Just work with me."

Destiny yawned. "Okay. Work with me too. I am new at this. Haven't read the handbook."

"Love you, Kismet."

Hearing her sobriquet stopped her, pulled her out of the fantasy.

Hakeem yawned again, then whispered. "Who are you, Kismet? Who are you?"

"I'm the woman who loves you, Hakeem Mitchell. And because of that, I am afraid. We're talking about living together. We're making comments about ring shopping. This is scary. Babe, I need to tell you something. I need to tell you now, so I need you to listen to me. Don't hate me."

He didn't reply.

She whispered, "Hakeem?"

His breathing had become heavy. Hakeem was off to dreamland.

She said, "My name isn't Kismet. My real name is Destiny. Destiny Jones."

Chapter 23

Ten minutes later, as Hakeem snored, Destiny sat up on the edge of the bed, on the new mattress, on the mattress she had loaned Hakeem the money to buy, on the mattress she had christened with Hakeem and broken in. She was frustrated, wanted to cry. The things she had done along the way, the way she had made time for him, when the moment came, she hoped the jury would take those things into consideration. She wished she existed on the other side of this lie. She pulled on her clothing—her motorcycle boots, her leather DO UNTO OTHERS jacket, and felt overwhelmingly troubled. She had wanted to tell Hakeem then, after intimacy, when emotions were the strongest, when emotions were also the weakest. If he had been awake, he would have seen her troubled face. The lie of being Kismet had made what could be beautiful become uncomfortable. He loved Kismet Kellogg. She whispered his name, shook his arm.

He was in his twelfth dream.

Sounds of rugged intimacy started again, resounding from feet away in the living room. Destiny cursed. It never ended. Nancy once again was being Eddied like getting Eddied was going out of style.

Destiny needed to leave. It was time for Kismet to creep out the door and allow Destiny to yawn back to life. Three jobs, USC, studying, her dad, her mom, the Blackbirds, Kwanzaa's upcoming birthday, her own needs, too many obligations danced in her brain.

Now Destiny had committed to a relationship using half-truths and a false name.

Hakeem wanted to meet her friends and family. That meant he wanted to see her world, see if she really fit into his life. That meant he wanted to introduce her to the rest of his world.

It was too much—inevitable, but too much. Stress rose and erased all calm brought by orgasm. She pulled her sisterlocks into a low ponytail, then put her black stocking cap on top of her crown. She stepped out of the bedroom, helmet in hand, leather gloves tucked inside the helmet, and tiptoed through the sweet profanity and soft moans coming from Nancy and Eddie.

Eddie was Eddying Nancy real good, had her humming and coming and making strained faces, then the man who spoke softly and carried a big dick looked up. Destiny had hoped Kendrick Lamar's explicit rap would cover her exit, the same way it had covered her entrance.

Eddie panted, took a breath, smiled, and said, "Kismet."

"Sorry to disturb you again. I'm on the way out."

Eddie caught his breath and said, "Hang around for a few hours. We were going to breakfast in the morning. Nancy is driving down to El Segundo to the Point so we can eat at True Food Kitchen."

"Nancy, Eddie, enjoy your morning. I'm out."

Nancy said, "You do look real familiar, Kismet. I swear I've seen you before."

Eddie said, "She's been yapping about that all evening. Been saying it for weeks."

"I think she used to be a child actress. I know I've seen her on television. Or in a movie."

"Damn, Nancy. I love when you move your sweet little ass like that."

"Twerking it for you, baby. Twerking it just for you."

"Don't stop the twerk. Twerk it until it hurts."

"All the way in, Eddie. Push that anaconda all the way in."

"Like that, baby? You like it when I do that?"

"You're going to make me come like Kismet was coming for Hakeem."

Eddie continued Eddying Nancy. As he screwed Nancy, he threw down the lyrics, rapped along with Kendrick Lamar, word for word.

This disgusting lifestyle would change when Destiny moved in.

This would change.

Destiny averted her eyes, tripped over Nancy's trembling legs, stumbled over Eddie's aggressive thrusts, said good night, heard moaned responses, then she left Hakeem's condo.

As she walked away, she heard Eddie call out to Nancy, *"Chug, chug, chug, chug, chug."*

At the same time, Destiny's phone buzzed. She read the text message.

Destiny cursed, ran down the stairs, sprinting to her motorcycle.

Chapter 24

Indigo was in Olamilekan's bed, naked, aroused, tipsy from celebrating, wanted him inside, but she stiffened, tightened her thighs, and stopped Olamilekan before he could put it in.

That sound. That irritating sound. That ringtone of love intruded.

She snapped, *"Get off of me."*

"What's the problem?"

"Are you deaf? Can you not hear? *Get off me.*"

He complied.

She rolled away from him, sucking her teeth, enraged.

He asked, "What is the problem, Indigo? Why did you stop?"

"Are you deaf? Your phone is ringing and ringing and ringing and that is driving me mad."

"Let me put it on silent."

"That is not the issue, Olamilekan. Why is the witch calling you at this hour? What could she possibly want from you?"

"Who are you talking about?"

"The girl who thinks she is your girlfriend is calling your cell phone, is calling your house phone, is blowing up all of your phones. *Talk to her.* Tell her to never call you again."

Olamilekan didn't comply.

Indigo stood and stormed into the bathroom, slammed the door behind her.

She sent text messages to the Blackbirds.

Then the doorbell rang. The doorbell rang as the house phone rang.

The stupid girl had arrived to challenge her. That meant war. Indigo grabbed a white satin robe and headed toward the staircase. Still naked, Olamilekan tried to stop her, but Indigo fought past him, left the second-floor master suite, argued with Olamilekan as she battled him down the marble staircase. He kept standing in front of her, and she kept fighting, stair by stair, to get down to the main level. Once she did, phone still ringing, doorbell still ringing, she fought to get past the spacious living room with the fireplace. Indigo couldn't get by him. The estate was huge, had many doors, many entrances and exits, so she took off running in another direction, and he chased her past the great room, almost caught her, then Indigo raced through the dining area, ducked and dodged Olamilekan and made it past the remodeled kitchen, sprinted past tall beamed ceilings, past his office, ignored the way the lights glistened against the water in the Olympic-size swimming pool. Olamilekan caught her, lifted her up, said he would not let her go until she calmed down. She promised to get back to her right mind, promised to be sensible on her birthday, promised to go back upstairs and let Olamilekan handle whatever misunderstanding had arisen. When Olamilekan loosened his grip, Indigo kicked him between his legs, kicked him with her toes, not the instep, and hurt her foot. Indigo cursed him for grabbing her in such an animalistic manner, and as he crumpled, Indigo limped toward the door, her housecoat open, sweat on her brow, pain in her right foot. Olamilekan tried to crawl toward her, tried to reach out and grab her ankle, tried to stop her from making it to the goal line.

She hobbled toward Olamilekan's front door the best she could, then leaned against the wall, taking a breath, texting the Blackbirds that some real shit was about to go down in Bel Air. Indigo was the fastest thumb-texter in the West. Took her all of five angry seconds to send her group message. Phone in hand, even as she was texting, she hopped on her left foot; made it from furniture to wall to furniture.

Olamilekan made it up to his knees.

Indigo shoved her phone in her robe's pocket, had to hurry before he caught her again. She put her foot down, and kept going, limping to where Olamilekan had taken off his Timberland boots when he entered the estate.

Olamilekan made a sound like he was in agony.

Indigo hoped she had left Olamilekan with his nuts begging for morphine.

The NFL superstar was still down on his knees, in a panic, barking, forbidding Indigo to unlock his front door and let evil inside his home. But it was too late. Indigo opened the door, the large double doors made of imported wood and glass, a door that cost more than a car.

Her heart was full of anger and her hands were not empty.

Indigo faced a stunning South African woman who was as beautiful as Candice Swanepoel and Charlize Theron combined. For a man as rich and famous as Olamilekan, Indigo had expected nothing less than a top model like the one she was facing. The woman cut Indigo up and down with her eyes and commanded her to go and get Olamilekan as if she were talking to a servant. Indigo held one of Olamilekan's large Timberlands in each hand, her fingers with a firm grip on the shoelaces of each massive boot. The woman asked Indigo if she was the bitch who had called her boyfriend's phone. Without so much as one word, Indigo snarled, swung hard, and smacked the beautiful girl in the mouth with a boot. And as lips burst and teeth cracked, as the stunning, stunned girl wobbled and fell to the pavement, as Olamilekan screamed, the real fight began.

Chapter 25

While two idiots in Beverly Hills were drag racing the streets, causing a scene and freaking out the moneyed denizens, Ericka and Kwanzaa zoomed toward a $10 million home in Bel Air, where another disruption had transpired. For the emergency, they relied on GPS to direct them to a 1.26-acre property on Stradella Road, an area with 180-degree views of the city and lined with dream estates. The headlights on Ericka's roadster revealed a suntanned girl who looked like she could have been a winner on *America's Next Top Model* running barefoot and naked down the pristine streets from a property at the back nine of Bel-Air Country Club. The top model saw Ericka's roadster and headed for them, flailing her arms and calling out for help. But when Miss Top Model realized it was two black women, and one looked like a miniature version of the one she had just met at Olamilekan's door, at least based on her complexion in the night, she backed away, started running again, but this time the wounded gazelle ran faster. Behind the beautiful girl was a trail of hair, extensions that were blowing in the breeze like tumbleweeds, or *tumbleweave*. Tumbleweave blew along with ginger hair that had been ripped from the top model's head. Behind the girl were the echoes of threats and curses, more of the former than the latter.

The trail of uprooted hair led back to a line of ripped and scattered clothing, high-end, fashion-forward, Rodeo Drive wear. Each piece of clothing cost more than a Walmart worker earned in two months. It all had been torn from Miss Top Model's body in a short-lived fight, one that had left a boot print on the left side of her face. That same trail of mangled high fashion led back to where Indigo had stopped chasing the girl who had insulted her one time too many. The pristine area had 7,691 residences built on less than seven square miles, and if Indigo had not been winded, if she had been wearing her Nikes, she would have chased that witch past every estate until she caught her, beat her again, then dragged her naked body back to Olamilekan, dropped the coward at his feet, and told him to choose, and to choose wisely. Indigo marched back toward Olamilekan's estate, his huge six-inch Timberland boots on her bare feet, the shoestrings untied, creating a blister with each step. The loose laces flopped across her shins. She was dressed only in a silk bathrobe, the kind made for seduction, not the night air. In her hands was a thong that had belonged to the top model, the fit South African woman she had chased for a quarter of a mile.

If Miss Top Model's hair had been real, if it had not disconnected the way a gas hose at a gas station would separate if a vehicle drove away while the hose was still in the tank, Indigo would still be beating Miss Top Model toward common sense.

That fuchsia Victoria's Secret thong that had flossed the butt crack and covered the pussy smell of Miss Top Model's bottom now belonged to the victor, was Indigo's trophy.

Indigo stood in front of Olamilekan's estate, stood where she could see the glimmer of coins settled at the bottom of the fountain. She ignored the pain in her right toes, pain that was exacerbated by running in oversized boots, pain that was slowly fading. She marched back inside her quondam lover's castle, marched in like a queen, a battle queen who was sweating, breathing hard, and yet snapping her fingers and doing a Naomi Campbell strut.

Olamilekan wore joggers, nothing else, the side of his face sporting a new boot print too.

The pain in his testicles had subsided enough for him to take baby steps.

He looked at Indigo and saw Miss Top Model's thong in her dark and lovely hands.

Indigo waved that eye-patch-for-a-vagina in the air like it was her gold medal, then threw the coochie cover in Olamilekan's face, told him to smell it, to sniff the material and know how a coward smells, to lick the string and know what a coward tastes like, if he didn't already know.

As Olamilekan opened his mouth to speak, Indigo took off a Timberland, threw it at his head, caught him in the nose. She rained curses on him. She took the other boot off and threw it at his penis. He caught it like it was a football. The ripped high-fashion clothing scattered on the ground and in the grass were all that remained of Miss Top Model.

Indigo looked behind her and saw that Ericka and Kwanzaa had arrived in a hurry.

Nothing had to be said. They knew their Blackbird too well.

They knew it was too late, but they hadn't known how too late this too late was.

Ericka got out of the car and gathered the clothing, tried to make sense of the shreds that were left, came to the conclusion that what she thought was a wide belt was a very short skirt, and the thing she thought was a bra was what was left of a blouse that was meant to cover as little as possible. Walk of Shame booty-call attire by Me So Horny and Fuck Me Now.

Kwanzaa found two battle-scarred Jimmy Choo shoes within forty yards of the estate's front door, designer shoes that now had scratched leather and broken heels, like their wearer had been caught and dragged twenty yards, kicking against the concrete and screaming about sudden hair loss. Kwanzaa handed Ericka the beat-up Choos, then collected the chic purse that was on the ground at the front door and its belongings, picked up the cell phone that had a broken screen, and handed everything to Ericka. Ericka added the shoes, purse, and other items to the pieces of mangled wardrobe she'd already tossed on the passenger seat of her red roadster.

Kwanzaa said, "Hold on. Give me that girl's phone."

Ericka handed it to her.

Kwanzaa dropped the phone, stomped on it four times, made sure it was deceased, then picked it up, walked past a fire-red Ferrari parked like someone had pulled up at the estate in a hurry, and from there, she threw the phone's carcass. The destroyed Samsung landed in the pond in front of the estate, sank to the bottom, disturbed the rest of hundreds of koi fish.

Ericka said, "Really, Kwanzaa? I mean really? Was that necessary?"

Kwanzaa said, "I am not giving that skank her phone so she can call 9-1-1, a lot of recessive genes with badges show up, and this time tomorrow we're all found mysteriously hanging in a jail cell like we had a secret death pact. We can't win because our skin is our sin. That nonfat ersatz can make one call, and we will feel like we've been transported back in time and are trying to do that first crossing of that bridge in Alabama during the civil rights movement. Tell me I am lying."

Ericka nodded. "Yes, that was necessary. I don't need to see inside of Hoosegow. Still, I'm not going to leave whoever she is out there in the dark naked. She's still a woman."

"When you find her, tell her that calling the po-po won't be a good move. Don't threaten her. Smile, be nice, listen, then tell her to think twice before she opens Pandora's box. Ask her if this is the kind of moment she wants to be broadcast on TMZ and *World Star*."

"What are we going to do if she doesn't see it our way?"

"Tell the thot we are all best friends with *the* Destiny Jones."

Kwanzaa stayed with Indigo, became David guarding Goliath's rage.

Ericka left, sped through the streets where the Fresh Prince had once lived to catch Miss Top Model who had dared to confront Indigo, the girl who had been beaten until she was naked. Ericka found her hiding behind bushes, broken down, busted, suffering from an ass kicking that was sure to leave her with some form of PTSD. Ericka had a first-aid kit in her trunk. It was part of the earthquake preparedness kit all Los Angelenos were supposed to have in their vehicles. She dressed the girl, gave her water, put Band-Aids and gauze on her wounds, then headed back to the mansion.

Chapter 26

Kwanzaa tried to calm Indigo as Indigo shouted at Olamilekan.

"Am I not good enough for you, Olamilekan? *Alailpoplo*, answer me. *Ode oshi*. Is a Nigerian not good enough for you? Is that the type of girl you want? Is she what you want? Every time you put your dick in a woman like that, you not only disrespect your Nigerian mother, but you disrespect Nigeria, you disrespect Africa, and I don't care if the girl is from Africa. You have disrespected me for the last time. Before I touch you again I will sleep with George Zimmerman. Before you ever speak my name again, you may as well go to the Holy Land and support apartheid and racism against Africans from Eritrea and Sudan. Go there and I hope they force you to get circumcised again and violate your rights as a human every day, as you have violated my rights as a woman. Don't sit there looking like a sad puppy. This is your doing, Olamilekan."

"She means nothing to me, Indigo. I did not even try and help her."

"Do I look stupid? Like I was born two hours ago? Your words do not possess even a modicum of the truth, and have no respect for my intelligence. I am not a stupid, crazy person."

"I did not invite that woman to my home. The woman is a stalker. She is stalking me."

"Do you love her? She cried out that she loved you, Olamilekan. At least that is what I think she said. I was too busy giving her a makeover to stop and ask her to repeat herself."

"You have my heart, Indigo, and you know that."

"That woman tries to dress sexy, but she is not. Dressing raunchy is not dressing sexy. She comes to your door dressed like she is an escort. And you deal with her?"

"That woman knows you have my heart."

"But what do I mean to you, Olamilekan? What do I mean to you? You have lied to me over and over. And now this? This is an insult. This is a travesty. Imbecile, this is an outrage."

"Indigo, calm down. Did I not pay for everything at your birthday party today?"

"*Whole ass. You are cow manure. Castrated pig, castrated dog, you and that imbecilic goat, you and that witch ruined my birthday. I hope nothing good ever happens to your* muda *or your* fada. *I hope you marry that unfinished lab result and have a baby that looks like a zonkey.*"

Minutes later, a CBR sped to the location.

It was Destiny. Ericka quickly followed her.

Ericka said, "The girl left her car here, but is too scared to come back and get it."

Indigo snapped, "I wish she would come back. I am not tired and I am not done."

Indigo dared Olamilekan to even consider helping that girl.

She said, "If you leave me to follow her, never speak my name again. *Never.*"

Olamilekan limped to his five-car garage, stood in front of his five luxury vehicles and three motorcycles. He chose his Mercedes. He eased inside, then went to go find the girl, to make sure she was okay, to make sure she wouldn't call the police. That was not the kind of Tiger Woods–style publicity he wanted. Indigo cursed him and threw rocks as he drove by her.

Olamilekan had left Indigo and gone after the other woman.

And he had done it on Indigo's birthday.

Ericka, Kwanzaa, and Destiny put their hands on Indigo, tried to absorb the negativity, but it was overwhelming, too powerful. It felt like Indigo could explode and destroy the world.

Touching her had been like putting their hands on the sun.

Indigo went back inside the estate to get her clothing, turning over any and everything she could as she walked through elegance. She pulled clothing from Olamilekan's closet, took designer shoes and suits, threw the pile in the bathtub, and then opened a bottle of bleach. She left the water running, made it all swim toward new colors. She screamed, and as that fire inside her burned uncontrollably, she turned over whatever she had missed during the initial rampage. She went to the girl's car, carved the word *coward* into the paint a dozen times, then kicked off the side mirrors, behaved like she was doing a remake of a Jazmine Sullivan video. Tense, terrified, the Blackbirds stayed out of the path of the hurricane.

Chapter 27

Soon Indigo was dressed in a negligee and a pair of her new birthday pumps, the sexy clothing she had worn to go booty-call Olamilekan. She pulled her trench coat back on.

She snapped at the Blackbirds. "Not a goddamn word. Not a word. Not one word."

She was back in her Rubicon, inhaling the new-Jeep smell, speeding back toward Inglewood. Destiny sped up, got Indigo's attention, and then signaled for her to slow the hell down. She did slow down and let everyone else get in the front. She fell back behind Destiny, called Yaba and told him what Olamilekan had just done, called him because she needed to vent, ranted as they trailed Ericka and Kwanzaa back to their complex known as Little Lagos.

She asked Yaba, "Am I a horrible person? Will every man I meet do this to me?"

"I love you, Indigo."

"And you did the same thing."

"Forgive me."

"I've forgiven you, but I will never forget. No one forgets the sting of a scorpion."

"Take me back into your heart."

"We are just friends now, Yaba. I'm not trying to be any more than that."

"Give me one more chance."

"So my heart can be broken again?"

"I would never break your heart again."

"You never should have broken it the first time."

Yaba asked her to calm down, apologized for how his relationship with her had ended.

She asked, "Should I just give up? Should I join a convent and become a nun?"

Indigo parked her Rubicon between her CBR and her convertible BMW, turned off the engine, ended her call in the middle of Yaba's trying to comfort her. She hung up on him, then sat in her Jeep crying, angry, embarrassed, again the broken-down Taylor Swift. The Beyoncé in her had been crushed.

The Blackbirds came to her and she eased out of her Jeep and slammed the door. As they had done before, Ericka, Destiny, and Kwanzaa each put a hand on Indigo and they stood still for a moment.

Indigo thanked them, gave each a hug, gave each a kiss, then walked away, the Blackbirds following her clacking heels as she took slow steps past the pool and moved toward their building.

Indigo didn't say anything else until they were all inside her well-appointed apartment, seated, watching her, concerned.

Indigo vented as she yanked off her negligee and pulled on UCLA sweats.

"I am ashamed of myself. What I did was a very disgraceful act. That was worse than Nigerian and Ghanaian students fighting over the origin of Jollof rice and the world knows you should use fat-grain rice. I used my fists. And a boot. An intelligent Nigerian woman should display class and integrity, not trashiness, no matter the situation. I am too smart to behave this way. I am about organizing, public advocacy, civil disobedience when it is called for, and for social change that will benefit all of mankind, not about lowering my standards and fighting some *thot* in the middle of the night. *Not even on my birthday*. Olamilekan is not worth what I flush away in a toilet. I should have walked away and let her have him. My emotions got the best of me when she disrespected me. *On my birthday*. They pulled me down to their *ghetto* level. Olamilekan told me that he was through with the girl, that she came tonight because he had ended whatever they had, and swore on his grandfather's grave all he told me was true."

At the same time, Destiny, Ericka, and Kwanzaa snapped, "He's lying."

Indigo said, "Stupidity took over me. I am trying to lift myself up, but Olamilekan has not only ruined my birthday, which is *unforgivable*, but has caused me to degenerate my morals. Nigeria would not be proud of me tonight. My mother and father must never know."

Indigo's cellular rang. Olamilekan's ringtone. She rejected the call.

Bright lights flashed at the gates, the horn blowing over and over.

Olamilekan had followed Indigo home and was at the gate.

Chapter 28

Olamilekan called out in the night, told Indigo he loved her and would do anything. He begged to be let inside.

Indigo yelled for him to get away from her property and go have sex with stupid women.

As he stood at the gate, he recited the poem "Candle" by Vee Bdosa, proclaimed how he would live for Indigo until the day he died. He stripped away his clothing down to his black boxers, adding that he was not only baring his soul, but he was coming to her as he was born. He was being so damn dramatic, like he was the brokenhearted star in a Nollywood film.

He said he would stand naked if he had to.

He yelled he would go on a hunger strike to get her back into his life.

He screamed he would pray and fast.

He stood at the gate calling Indigo's name, begging for forgiveness.

Indigo sent the other Blackbirds back to their apartments.

Then she picked up a steak knife and stormed to the gate to yell at Olamilekan.

"I want the truth, Olamilekan. May thunder fire you if you keep lying to me. If you are not sincere, go away. I want the truth or I will cut it from you, use it to make a pot of stew and rice, will use your tongue to make soup for fufu, and feed it to you as you lay in the streets bleeding."

After a half hour of arguing and pleading, Indigo opened the gate. Olamilekan stood shivering in his underwear until Indigo told him to put his clothes back on. He tried to touch Indigo, but she wouldn't let

him. Now Destiny and Ericka were in Kwanzaa's apartment, below Indigo's unit, the lights off, each Blackbird peeping out the window, each
adding negative commentary.

Kwanzaa said, "She gave in too soon. I was hoping we'd see him get
naked."

Indigo and Olamilekan stood outside and argued, the conversation
passionate, loud, emotional. Soon she let him touch her. He touched her
hand, held on to her pinky finger like she was a balloon he was trying to
keep from floating away. Then he held two fingers and she kept her arms
extended to keep him away. After a couple of moments Indigo lowered
her arm, and Olamilekan touched her chin. He touched her chin and she
slapped his hand away. But then she let him get closer. Closer. She didn't
strike him. Soon he hugged her. Soon he kissed her cheek.

Ericka said, "No, no, no, no, no."

Soon Indigo's arms were around Olamilekan's neck. He touched her
face again, put his hands on her waist, and soon his hands were on her
ass. He tried to kiss her and she kept turning her face away. He persisted. He held Indigo's face, her head tilted to the side, and eased his
tongue in her mouth. She reciprocated, put her tongue in his mouth.

Ericka, Kwanzaa, and Destiny were all in the window, appalled, each
saying some version of the word *no* over and over.

Lights still off so they could see without being seen, they watched
Indigo take his hand, her head lowered because she knew the Blackbirds
were watching her in what was not her finest hour. Olamilekan followed
her up the stairs, his weight heavy, his footsteps strong. The argument
continued, but the argument stayed outside Indigo's apartment.

Kwanzaa cracked the door so they could try to hear what was going on.

Not long after, the door to Indigo's apartment opened.

That same door closed.

There were no dejected footsteps coming down the stairs.

Indigo had taken Olamilekan inside her crib.

Footsteps moved from the living room to the bedroom at an unsure
pace.

There was silence.

No argument.

Destiny said, "They're kissing. I bet she's letting him kiss her on the mouth, when she needs to bend over and let him kiss her black ass until his lips go numb and fall off."

Ericka scrunched her face. "I bet he's going down on her. That's how they get you back."

Kwanzaa said, "Brothers won't go down on the regular, but will eat you out to apologize."

There was a long, slow, sinking squeak, like a man's weight on a woman. It could have been the weight of a tall woman when she reluctantly straddled a man she loved and hated.

Next a dozen creaks filled the air, each creak more intense than the one before. Then steady, slow, rhythmic squeaks, continual movement.

Ericka and Destiny at her side, Kwanzaa opened her bedroom window, the window directly under Indigo's bedroom window. They heard Indigo and Olamilekan making up.

Kwanzaa said, "What the hell? She had us up in the middle of the night, driving across the damn state, and this is what she does? I should go up there and beat on the door."

Ericka yawned. "I am too tired to deal with this mess. Just let it remain their issue."

"To hell with that. I'm not going to sip tea like Kermit. This is our business as Blackbirds."

Destiny said, "Sit your short ass down, Kwanzaa."

Music came on upstairs. Tiwa Savage singing "Get Low." That meant that Indigo's inner Beyoncé, Rihanna, and Lady Gaga were about to be unchained. It meant Africa was rising.

One by one, Ericka, Destiny, and Kwanzaa shook their heads.

Destiny said, "That's how it was with my mom and dad. Argue, fight, get emotional, then end up in bed. Some people get off on the drama, then need to get off because of the drama. Indigo and Olamilekan are like that."

Ericka said, "Really? Your dad . . . Mr. and Mrs. Jones were like Indigo and Olamilekan?"

"There were no other women, just drama, fighting, perpetual conflict, and mistaking ten minutes of sex for resolution."

Ericka shook her head. "Oh. Okay. When I'm angry, sex is the last thing I want."

Kwanzaa said, "My mom and bonus dad are the same way, at least they used to be. They'd fight and I guess my bonus dad would bone my mom until she was limp like a rag doll. I heard my dad and bonus mom were the same way when I was a little girl. Par for the course. Marcus and me used to fight, then end up having the *best* sex ever. Okay, let's change the subject. I don't need to remember certain things when I don't have access to a man, or some well-educated woman who wants to take me to the Lobster before making me a pair of scissors."

Destiny said, "Yeah, Dad did the same thing with my mom. Turned her into a rag doll."

Ericka whispered, "Wow. Maybe I should change my attitude about angry sex."

Destiny said, "Indigo is our Chimamanda, not a *Fake Housewife of Atlanta*. I don't understand why she would even talk to him after tonight, let alone let him inside the gate."

Kwanzaa said, "She's let that cheating low-down dog inside more gates than one."

Ericka spoke up. "We all get the love we think we deserve. If that jerk, that *goat*, is the best she thinks she can do, if that's as good as she sees her life, if what's going on tonight is what she thinks she can handle, if this behavior and conflict is really what excites her, and she must love it because she keeps doing this cha-cha with Olamilekan over and over, then it's not for us to judge, not up to us to decide her life for her, even if we know she deserves better."

Destiny said, "Ericka, lower your voice. Don't wake up the whole damn neighborhood."

Kwanzaa talked louder, "Nelson Mandela is turning over in his grave and so is Steve Biko. This is so wrong. She's up there getting the grace of God put in her after he's cheated, and I'm supposed to shut up? I'm going to break in her apartment and drag Olamilekan out to the street, beat Mr. NFL naked, kick his butt like we're at a Mike Epps comedy show, beat him like Rodney King, and hold Olamilekan's nasty drawers over my head. And yeah, I hope that cheating, low-down asshole can hear me, piece of shit. You're a *mitch*. A goddamn *mitch*."

Destiny said, "Kwanzaa, don't."

"We should've chipped in and bought her a damn chastity belt for her birthday."

Destiny shook her head. "Let her deal with it. Everybody come to my crib and crash. You can't hear them as much in my unit. Grab a pillow and follow me home. I'm done. I need some sleep."

Kwanzaa yelled, "I hope she is using a condom. I hope she's making him use a condom covered with a Hefty bag and she's wearing a female condom inside a Glad bag. She just chased his bald-and-bloodied side chick off his estate. *Protect yourself, Indigo.* If our Blackbird lets the wrong dick inside, her coochie will have more problems than that old Vista operating system."

Destiny said, "Well, at least he chose a black woman. And no offense to your yellow ass, Ericka, but he chose a dark-skinned black woman at that, over a *Playboy* centerfold with big tits."

"I'm offended."

Kwanzaa said, "When a sister wins, well, I guess Indigo had a good birthday after all."

Destiny said, "I hope Olamilekan went home before he came across the freeways."

Ericka asked, "Why?"

"Indigo left the bathtub filled with bleached clothing and the hot water running."

Ericka huffed. "In that case, I hope he didn't go home before he came here."

Kwanzaa nodded. "That's what his ass gets. She should have done a Left Eye and set the place on fire, and I would have prayed the fool didn't have any insurance on that castle."

Cool winds blew across the desert as songbird Tiwa Savage sang, but it became a duet between Nigerian singers when Indigo's cellular rang over and over. As her phone rang, the creaks and moans came to an abrupt halt. Olamilekan said something unkind. Indigo retorted. They had harsh words. Then Indigo's landline rang. The bed creaked like someone was getting up, and feet marched across the room. Heavy steps. Had to be Olamilekan. Roosters crowed. Dogs barked, and at the apartment buildings in the vicinity, lights came on, laborers starting their day. Upstairs, Indigo's cellular rang again. And again. It wasn't one of the Blackbirds calling. The ringtone was a Nigerian love song.

Kwanzaa looked at the time on her phone. "Shit. It's almost five in the morning, I'm dog tired, and now it's almost time for me to get dressed for work. I have to open at Starbucks."

They heard Indigo's revived anger. They heard her resuscitated resentment.

The Blackbirds went to the window and listened.

Indigo cursed Olamilekan for answering her phone. Olamilekan shouted insults in Yorùbá as Indigo yelled vulgarities. Olamilekan shouted Yaba's name as if his rival were standing at Indigo's front door. Ericka, Kwanzaa, and Destiny hurried toward the next round of the fight.

They went to Indigo's front door, and stood there, heard more of the argument.

Kwanzaa said, "Holy catch-a-mota-check. Isn't that Yaba's ride outside the gate?"

They looked toward Crenshaw Boulevard.

Yaba was parked behind Olamilekan's car.

Chapter 29

A moment ago, Yaba the Laker had called while Indigo was in the throes of passion, had called during the hours of restlessness, jump-offs, and booty calls, had called while he was parked outside the gate. He was in his Range Rover, had seen Olamilekan's luxury car.

Now Olamilekan was the one upset; he was the one with Indigo's cell phone yelling at his rival and making threats because now he had found out that Yaba the Laker had been to the birthday party, and that Indigo had swam with him. Yaba blew his horn over and over.

Indigo snapped, "At least no one is at my door in the middle of the night."

"What is that *mumu*, that idiot, that imbecilic imbecile man doing here at this hour?"

"Because I called Yaba and told him what you had done to me on my birthday."

"Why would you call Yaba? You are still seeing him. You are his lover. I know you are."

"May God set you ablaze. I am not his lover. Yaba and I are friends. He does not get in my bed and I don't care who is in his, not anymore. No man has touched me since you."

"Is he better in bed? Does he make you moan the way I make you moan?"

"I moan when I have cramps. I moan when I stub my toe. I moan when I am constipated, and I moan when I take a shit. So what, I moan? Every moan is not a good moan. I moan with you. Maybe I moaned better with Yaba. Maybe he made me moan from my heart and not from boredom.

Don't think you have done something special. Now move, move so I can go see what Yaba wants. He is my friend. At least he feels my pain and apologizes for breaking my heart. *You have no shame.* You lie and believe your own pathetic fabrications as if they are the truth. Move out of my way. Move away from me, Olamilekan. Move or I will kick you in your pathetic dick harder than I did before."

"Are you really going to him?"

"I am going to him the same way you went after that South African whore."

"If you go out there and go to his car, if you go to Yaba, you will never see me again."

"I know you will leave. The problem is you come back. You will be back tomorrow. Or I will run back to you. Maybe one of us needs to leave and not answer when the other calls."

"Is that what you want? Tell me never to call you and your wish will come true."

"No. *Tell me what you want from me.* I can't keep doing this, Olamilekan. I love you with all of my heart, more than I ever loved Yaba, but I can't keep doing this over and over."

"After all I have done for you on your birthday, this is the gratitude you have?"

"Did you not hear a word I just said? Are you deaf? Get your head out of your ass."

"Yaba is here because he senses you are weak and wants to take advantage of you."

"The same as you always do? You are afraid Yaba is a real man and loves me more."

"Did he come to have sex with you on your birthday?"

"My birthday was yesterday, and *you missed most of it.* You failed to call me at my moment, but Yaba did not fail to call me and wish me happy birthday. He cared. You didn't."

"Did you have sex with Yaba when he was here yesterday? Is he back for more?"

"I did not have to have sex with Yaba yesterday for him to know I'm sweet like tangerine. He knew before you. This was his, but not any longer. Because he cheated. Now answer me this, Olamilekan. Did you have sex with the South African woman who answered your phone?"

"No woman answered my phone. I lost my phone. You see I have a new phone."

"You will give one of those girls, one of your groupies, the belly, but it will not be me."

"There is no other woman. You are the woman I want to marry, and you know that."

"When will you ask? You say words. You make promises. But there is not a ring sparkling on my finger. Until there is, you have no say as to who comes to my gate, and for whom I open my gate is not your concern. You will not continue to lie and drag me to the middle of nowhere."

"You attacked someone at my door, and she is now in the emergency room. I will have to pay to repair her car."

"Not because she was at your door, but because she called me out."

"Do you think I have no intention of marrying you?"

"You look me in my face and tell lie after lie like Pinocchio. Your nose should look like an erect penis on your face. I'm sure the South African model would love to sit on that as well."

She cursed him and said mean things in Yorùbá, and Olamilekan did the same. Kwanzaa had to do a one-minute shower and dress quickly without drying off any more than the hot spots to not be late. Yaba had gotten out of his car, was standing on Crenshaw near the busiest intersection in the area, and the star Laker player had been spotted by fans, and now traffic was slowing down. People were running to him from bus stops to get an autograph or beg him to take a selfie. It was hard to be a giant in a land of Lilliputians and not be noticed. He ignored his admirers, was concerned only with getting Indigo's attention. Kwanzaa had seen it all as she hurried to her car, now dressed in all black and carrying her Starbucks apron. As she drove out the gate, Kwanzaa slowed down her hoopty and said a few hard and hostile words to Yaba. Yaba was still out of his car, and when the gate opened he was about to go inside. Kwanzaa threw her car in park, jumped out, blocked his path, and begged him to not cause a scene, to not be here when Olamilekan came out because there would be a fight, and he was drawing a crowd, so there would be witnesses, and there would be press, and the police would be here soon if he kept holding up traffic, and that could get ugly real fast, and he needed to think about his career, about his brand, about his endorsements, about how it would look in the online papers and all over social media with two Nigerians brawling in Inglewood, and if they had a fight they would be called animals, the NFL would get involved, the NBA would get involved, both of them could lose their contracts and end up on *Dancing with the Stars* trying to make a comeback, and for those reasons he should go back to the Palisades, back to his luxurious life, and not add more drama to where Indigo lived. She told him Indigo wasn't coming outside because she was with her boyfriend, reminded Yaba he had had his chance, that Indigo was his woman, but he crept out to be with an Ethiopian girl. Kwanzaa told Yaba that his heartbreak was of his own design. Indigo had moved on and he needed to do the same. She told him that if he was worried, to just check on her later in the week. Miserable and lovesick, Yaba the Laker walked around fans who were trying to get a photo of the giant. Today Yaba was not Yaba the Laker, he was just a man trying to earn back the love of a girl he lost. His currency no longer held any value in Little Lagos. Yaba spat on Olamilekan's ride, spat on the Nigerian prince of Bel Air's chariot over and over.

Yaba said, "I should piss all over his car door."

Kwanzaa said, "Only if you want that on YouTube before you can shake the snake dry."

Yaba looked at the people holding up their smartphones, barked at them, told them to stop recording him, to go mind their own business, to leave him alone, then galumphed back to his own luxury ride, eased his seven feet of jealousy and broken ego inside, then sat there holding the steering wheel, staring at the apartment where the woman he wanted back lived, and called again. His call was sent to voicemail. On the verge of breaking down and crying, Yaba revved his engine, ready to screech away. But Yaba backed up, rammed into the back of Olamilekan's car, then clipped the rear of that hot ride as he pulled away. Horns blew as he almost ran a handful of cars off the road. Fans turned ugly, cursed him, cursed Africa, and said they would never support his black ass again, hoped the Nigerian *nigga-nigga-nigga* was traded to Utah or Milwaukee, yelled that he would never be in the Lakers record books like Magic, Kareem, or Kobe. As cheers turned to jeers, Yaba beat his steering wheel and joined in the morning road rage as he raced down Crenshaw toward the onramp for the 105 freeway.

Kwanzaa sped down Crenshaw too, in the opposite direction, in a hurry to clock in and push caffeine and sugar to the addicted, but none would be as addicted to coffee as Yaba and Olamilekan were to Indigo's sweetness. Yaba was finally gone, but by ringing Indigo's phone at this hour, by parking outside the gate so his car could be seen, by blowing his horn to make his presence known, by calling again and again, Indigo's ex-bae had done irreparable damage.

Chapter 30

Ericka and Destiny banged on Indigo's door until they were let in the apartment, then both did their best to separate Indigo and Olamilekan. Indigo was in her panties and Olamilekan was still nude. She had thrown his clothing out the bedroom window and his things were in the Mexicans' backyard, their fleet of dogs chewing at everything. Indigo once again had Olamilekan's Timberlands in each hand, and would swing when he came close to her. His nakedness was the only reason he hadn't gone outside to confront Yaba. One man would never confront another man with his fluffed coconut tree and balls exposed to the world. That was an unwritten rule.

As two of the Blackbirds tried to calm the fire, Indigo and Olamilekan called it quits.

She swore to God she was done with him. He swore that he was done with her.

When Olamilekan returned home to the bleached clothes and flood that had been left behind, he called, screamed, threatened to sue for the damages Indigo had caused to his estate. The breakup lasted two days, until sixteen dozen roses and diamond earrings appeared at Indigo's door. But for those two days, she had spent time with Yaba, had cried on his shoulder, had let him console her, had kissed him many times, then dumped him again, went back to Olamilekan the way an addict returned to her dealer.

KWANZAA'S BIRTHDAY

Chapter 31

Kwanzaa Browne jerked awake, nude and sweaty, underneath an unmoving ceiling fan, in a strange bed in a strange loft after having bareback sex with a stranger, a handsome man she had seen occasionally during her mornings as a barista at Starbucks in Inglewood.

The stranger, the man who was one in five million, was next to her, as naked as she.

She eased the sheets back and looked at the blessing between his legs.

It had not been a dream.

Chapter 32

Hours ago, on the eve of her birthday, Kwanzaa was out by herself, taking herself on a quick pre-birthday date, *mastur-dating* being the proper term, at the latest and greatest spot called the Club. It was a high-end hot spot, one you could get into only if the bouncer liked how you looked, because Hollywood was about as postracial as its casting, and one day might be as liberal as its casting couch. Bloggers had called it the West Coast version of Studio 54. It was built for the young and the restless.

End to end, the club was decorated with long, flowing drapes and had sensual sitting areas decorated with soft cushions for the rhythmically deficient wallflowers. There were plenty of looky-loos, those who came to the trendy and overpriced hot spot to experience ear-deafening house music and the ultimate comfort while they sipped on overpriced drinks, did lines in the bathroom, pretended to be as important as the decision-making women and men in the venue.

L.A. wasn't a party-all-night town. Clubs started to close around 1:30 A.M., as soon as last call was announced, so most of the revelers were already in full swing by 10 P.M. Some who wanted to be famous were giving what they hoped would be career-advancing blow jobs, on their knees underneath the Italian tables. The front windows offered views of the nighttime traffic and normal debauchery on Sunset; there was a glowing pool in the back that offered a view of stars, but only a few could be seen through layer upon layer of toxic smog.

Kwanzaa was actually away from the Blackbirds in case Marcus Brixton called, since she knew her friends would go off on her for even thinking about being in his company. While she bounced to the beat, in between sending and receiving text messages, she looked into the crowd and recognized someone.

As she sipped a cosmo, she saw the tall, golden, and handsome stranger who frequented Starbucks, the man who always wore Hugo Boss and always ordered an iced coffee. Tonight he wore a fashionable black suit paired with a striped shirt and a solid red necktie.

Kwanzaa knew he'd never seen her out of her Starbucks uniform, had never seen her in makeup, had never seen her with her Brazilian hair whipped to perfection by the Dominicans on La Brea. He had never seen her in princess mode, but he recognized her. Since her face was made up in colorful dramatic tones, her eyes in blues and hints of gold, her lips seductive red, her fingernails hot pink, and since she was in high heels and a very short dress and looked nothing like a conservative college student or a boring barista, she assumed the man in Hugo Boss recognized her because of her fashionably colored hair, despite its wicked style.

They made eye contact, held it as the music bumped, and then he moved by celebrities, wannabe celebrities, and used-to-be celebrities, squeezed through the crowd, eased toward her.

It took her a moment to realize that he was not just coming her way, but to her.

Her heart raced. She hadn't expected that reaction, that nervousness to envelop her.

She had responded to him the way all the Latinas at her job responded to him. Maybe when she was engaged, her ring had protected her from his energy, from the possibility of his life-force mixing with hers, of there being some synergistic response if they ever interacted.

When he was close, he proffered a gentle gesture that asked her to dance.

It was house music. People just danced. Most didn't need a partner. Many were in their own zone. He had broken protocol. He said nothing, just made a confident gesture. Him coming to her with that silent sureness, direct eye contact, and soft grin had put a thousand butterflies in her belly, made her reach to touch her engagement ring, but it wasn't there.

It wasn't there.

Music bumping, Hugo Boss extended his hand and Kwanzaa capitulated, gave him her fingers. As they touched, as she felt the power crackle in his flesh, no words were exchanged.

He led her through the dancing crowd. She hid her fear. She hid her excitement. She hadn't told anyone, but part of her always smiled when the man in Hugo Boss entered Starbucks. Her coworkers became horny when he peacocked in the door, all wanting to serve him more than an iced coffee, and now he had picked Kwanzaa from the bunch, asked her to dance. The Latinas at her job wouldn't believe this, would all drown in envy. Her birthday eve was wonderful, perfect with this high-energy, cosmo-infused moment.

They found a spot near two femme guys dancing, both celebrities who played masculine roles on television. On the other side of them were two girls half drunk and coked up, arguing over another girl. Hugo Boss started his groove. Masculine. Suave. Kwanzaa started out slowly, warmed up, felt the music in her blood, turned it up, and danced with him for fifteen minutes, long enough to start to feel the heat in her twenty-two-dollars-and-ninety-cents-before-sales-tax LBD—Little Blue Dress—from Forever 21, and feel the pain in her six-inch FMPs—Fuck Me Pumps—she had bought for fifteen dollars, marked down seventy percent at DSW.

New heels made a woman learn how to be cute and dance without much movement of the feet. Heat rose and there was barely a place to stand. It was impossible to squeeze through the crowd without making her body parts molest the body parts of more strangers. In the loud, overpacked room, she stayed in her cozy spot, let the stranger slide his strong arms around her, figured if someone was going to press against her ass and touch her tits, it might as well be one person and not every hungry, swollen penis in the arena. She felt his strength, the dominance that was both intimidating and comforting. It didn't feel lewd, didn't feel like an aggressive come-on. But she knew it *was* a come-on; it was almost her birthday, and she wasn't born yesterday.

When Kwanzaa finished her drink, Hugo Boss took her glass, swam upstream, and came back with a fresh cosmo. She guessed that he sensed she was committed to alcohol and bad decisions. He observed her, not in portrait mode, not only her face, but in landscape mode. He examined the topography beyond her expression, focused on as much of her as possible. She did the same with him, drank him in, liked what was presented, then returned to enjoying the pounding music. She sipped. He didn't talk. She didn't mind not talking.

The less men talked, the fewer lies a woman had to hear.

The fewer lies a woman heard, the more she liked a man.

He had said nothing. The meticulous man in Hugo Boss remained perfect.

It was strange how seeing this man over and over, knowing what he ordered, made him feel so familiar. She had seen his self-assured walk, had been in his presence separated by a counter. Those minor interactions made this stranger seem like less of a stranger.

She had met thousands of people in her life who never really meant anything to her, and still, in her heart, she wanted to find the one who would change her life forever, in a positive way.

Marcus Brixton was supposed to be the man who brought her happiness.

She wanted to *unthink* Marcus Brixton, if there were such a thing as *unthinking*.

She assumed that unthinking was more powerful than forgetting. Forgetting could be temporary, reversed by a song, a picture, or just a sudden thought. Unthinking was a complete reset, a CONTROL-ALT-DELETE on unwanted memories. She wanted that Marcus Brixton sector of her mind scrubbed, with nothing left but space for new memories, then be able to use McAfee to keep a single thought of Marcus Brixton from ever popping up anywhere in her brain again.

Maybe a new lover was just as good as a memory scrubbing and McAfee.

The tall man in the Hugo Boss smiled at the not-so-tall woman wearing Forever 21.

His body language told her that he was impressed and thought she was gorgeous tonight.

Still, no words were spoken. No lies were told. The illusion of perfection remained. She couldn't be in the grueling process of unloving one man and have the energy to smile at another with decent intentions. Her heart and morals had never worked that way. She was all or none.

She fanned herself, hot. Hugo Boss took her hand, led Forever 21 through the crowd, and took her outside near the pool. Cool air moved across skin and felt like heaven.

As they stood and bounced a bit to the rapid beat, he removed his necktie, eased it off and put it in his inner coat pocket. Kwanzaa realized women were watching the strange man in the Hugo Boss, watching him as if seeing him take off his necktie had aroused them all, as if they wanted him to keep undressing. Men nodded his way, gave secret handshakes of the mind, some transmitted conversation. Kwanzaa and the stranger maintained the groove. She saw men buying the svelte ingénues drinks in hope of recruiting candidates for the next sunrise's Walk of Shame.

This was a normal night; this was how the sexual exchanges, the infidelities began.

Her ex had said the Chilean girl had meant nothing, that sex with her had meant nothing. And that was worse. If he could have sex with a woman and it meant nothing, he could have sex with any woman, at any time, because it wasn't about emotion, only about space and opportunity.

That stupidity from the man she had wanted to eventually marry. That bullshit from the man she had loved. If not for the present his cheating had left behind, if not for the contamination, if not for the discharge that had sent her to her doctor, Kwanzaa never would have known she'd been poisoned. That played in her mind now, as she danced against the cool breeze.

She needed more alcohol. The damn memory refused to be drowned. The fire from the hate wouldn't diminish, so she might as well add some firewater to keep the flames burning.

She raised her empty glass to Hugo Boss, and he nodded, took her hand, led her back inside, and she stood to the side as he bought her another drink.

She sort of wished the other Blackbirds were with her. But then again, they would all have been drink-stopping and cock-blocking and girl-preaching by now, especially Destiny.

Destiny didn't want any woman to experience what she had experienced.

And Indigo would be throwing out a thousand phrases in Yorùbá.

Ericka would be in some sort of overprotective mommy mode.

Back on the dance floor, back in the middle of the heat and energy and controlled madness, Kwanzaa Browne sipped her way into Tipsyville, and soon drank her sensibilities toward the border of Throbbing Clit and Bad Judgment. It didn't help that the house music in the Club boomed with the power of a vibrator. The powerful beat resonated and felt like a prelude to sexual intercourse. The rapid, thumping, booming, reverberating bass was an invisible stimulator causing thumping, booming, reverberating clit-tickling foreplay.

The man in the Hugo Boss was tall and muscular. In a packed room where most of the intoxicated revelers yelled into their phones, squinted to read messages, posted the irrelevancy of their lives on social media, or texted messages to people standing next to them, she had let a stranger caress her from behind, ass against unknown genitals, not exactly doggie style, but it still brought that impersonal sexual position to mind.

She felt the girth of his blessing against her bubble, against the thin material of her discounted dress. His impressive bump touched her and a chill of need navigated her spine. That contact, combined with the beat that had become an invisible vibrator, sent a series of tingles dancing across her thighs. She eased away from his girth enough for the contact, the pressure to be removed. She exhaled slowly, those chills now heated. Kwanzaa shifted from heel to heel, became a brown cat on a hot tin roof. She sipped, enjoyed the music, kept time, danced like it was 1999.

Kwanzaa enjoyed the sensation of floating higher, but soon frowned. She wondered where Marcus Brixton was, if he'd remember her birthday moment was in a few hours, if he had set an alert in his phone, if he cared enough to text, or had the audacity to call. With that, she was about to tell the stranger thank you, leave, and go home, knowing en route she would end up drunk dialing, then somehow finding herself at Marcus's front door. She had almost done that on Indigo's birthday. She had left to go see Marcus, but had changed her mind, was too tipsy, and turned around, went back home, then, too ashamed to say she had been weak, lied to Ericka and said she had made a tampon run. Tonight she would visit Marcus Brixton. She didn't know if she'd end up fighting or fucking, or fighting then fucking, or fucking before fighting, but she would bang at his door, and no matter which path she chose it would not be pretty. By the time the sun came up again, she'd have regret.

But then the guest deejay broke the pattern of the house beat and soca music came on, the music of the Caribbean, and the room erupted like it was the fete of all fetes. As the stranger dry-humped from behind, she planted her feet, backed it up, and rolled against him. They danced like they were having public sex. She danced, hummed, sang, sweated, and enjoyed the music.

Attire by Hugo Boss danced its grind on couture by Forever 21. Kwanzaa tried to figure on which side of his pants rested his virility. Felt like it was across both sides. He did his smooth dirty dance against her backside, massaged her butt with his fluffed blessing. She reciprocated with moves like she was the kind of girl who gave wickedness as good as she took wickedness.

She sipped the last of another cosmo. Memories gagged, fought for air, were drowning.

Again Hugo Boss took her empty glass and came back with a fresh cosmo.

She thanked him wordlessly, with a grin and nod, then worked on the new drink as they resumed dancing. She was tempted to do a Fantasia, kick off her shoes, and bend over until it was six thirty. Having a fresh drink in her hand, she bent over only so far. She channeled Patra, Fay-Ann Lyons, and Alison Hinds. The way Kwanzaa moved her body, her trio of besties would have slapped the drink out of her hand and pulled her off the dance floor kicking and screaming.

Frustration had to go somewhere, had to be sweated out.

Kwanzaa raised her hands as she danced. Sang. Made her hair move side to side. She sipped. Rocked her ass against the stranger. The thump of the beat, the bump in his pants, the way he moved as she moved, it intensified her growing arousal. Soon she leaned back into him, closed her eyes, took a deep breath. She inhaled him. His aroma was magnetic. His scent was lush herbaceous notes dancing with elegant woods and rosemary. She looked at his lips. She imagined the softness of his lips against the softness of hers as curious tongues crossed borders into unknown lands. His nose was broad, but small, just like hers. His hair was long and natural, not like hers, but like hers had been once upon a time. She envied his mane, its power, its sensuality, its length, and hated she had ever butchered hers to the point of humiliation.

The stranger leaned in closer and it looked like he wanted to kiss her neckline, but instead put his mouth close to her ear, so close she could feel the tickle, the vibrations from his direct words. In a kind and intelligent voice he asked if she wanted to go to his place so they could be alone. It felt as if his full lips had grazed her ear as his provocative words moved to her brain and her breath caught in her throat.

Articulate, confident, maybe arrogant, with a voice that echoed intelligence, maybe postgraduate work. She swept the beautiful hair from her face, scoffed, considered shutting this down before it became a problem. He had gone too far. It was just dirty dancing. She wasn't bartering for drinks. Men would make all women whores, even a barista, if possible.

Kwanzaa was going to go find a spot and dance by herself, but again she stared at the non-talkative, tall, and well-built guy in Hugo Boss. He smelled so damn good. She focused on the handsome mane. His hair was long, pulled back from his face, into a heroic ponytail. She reached and made his mane fall loose. He didn't protest. It cascaded across his shoulders. Samson. Hercules. Maybe the blood of the Chippewa Indians. Over the loud music, she heard a collective sigh, a longing from the three-sheets-to-the-wind and sober women who had a clear view, and men who loved to be with men.

Kwanzaa trembled as tingles erupted and created a magnificent fire.

Letting his powerful mane down had an effect on her, made her lick her lips, then desire for all lips to be licked. Tonight when she had left home she had convinced herself that she had put barbed wire across her sex. But that barbed wire had been loosened by cosmos and was being tugged away by Hugo Boss, breath by breath.

A man so desirable was enough to turn queens into educated fools, make a churchgoing woman lose her religion from dusk to dawn.

The room was filled with one-nighters. Go home, have sex, be done before sunrise. She wondered if this was the type of existence she was destined to lead, one of those who led a dual, vampire-like lifestyle after the sun had set on Sunset. Nighttime was when they left their pedestrian lives to feed their nocturnal desires, then returned back to their metaphorical coffins to sleep a few moments, or drink energy drinks, before the sun yawned and they headed to work with the rest of the walking dead.

But her engagement had ended. It was time to move on, even if that meant moving into deeper, darker, uncharted waters.

She touched the stranger's magnificent hair again, then extended her exquisite fingernails to the metrosexual man who wore Hugo Boss. Without a word, communicating through affirmative body language, she capitulated to his request. She was a grown woman and knew what grown men desired, and she craved the same salaciousness to quench her neglected carnality. She was tired of making love to herself, imagining a man she needed to forget. What Hugo Boss offered, she wanted as part of her celebration, a present to herself. She would be his and he would be hers for a few moments.

She wondered if this was the way it had been with Marcus Brixton and the Chilean *thot*. She wondered if the Chilean *thot* had felt this way when she went to enjoy someone else's man.

Chapter 33

Kwanzaa retrieved her car from valet parking, then pulled to the side and waited while Hugo Boss reclaimed his car. She thought about her parents. The way they behaved now, the way they presented themselves to their children, was not the way they had behaved when they were her age or younger. In their youth, nights like this, what she was doing now, this had been her parents' behavior as well. Clubs. Drinks. The search for companionship, if they had no companion to get them through the night, that was what Friday and Saturday was all about, especially for the college student. She had heard the tales, and had heard her mother in the middle of girl-talk with her friends, so she knew that her mother never had been a saint. Her mother had been just as restless. She had been because that was the design of a woman. That was why many of her friends had rushed to get married, or already had a baby, if not babies. That was why women were unfaithful. That was why there were so many women lined up on Sunset to get into the same places where music throbbed like randy clits. The need for sex, because the body needed what the body needed, and man was better than a hand, and a boy was better than a toy.

This was why she had needed Marcus. To avoid nights like this.

Now she had elected a stranger to be her lover.

Countless frat parties were going on, but she wasn't a frat party girl. Too many frat boys handed out Cosby-tinis and became gangbangers. She didn't want to go through what Destiny had gone through. She couldn't even imagine the horror of waking up after that assault.

If this went wrong, at least his credit card number was on file at Starbucks.

If she needed to find him after tonight, she knew she could.

Without knowing where they were going, she trailed the stranger down Sunset Boulevard, the traffic as thick as oatmeal that had been in the microwave an hour too long. Two lanes of brake lights. Two lanes of headlights. A movie was being filmed, so there were looky-loos. Every person who had a convertible had their top down so they could look like they were the shit.

She followed Hugo Boss through miles of vanity and narcissism, past billboards advertising the latest and hottest television programs, vasectomies, lingerie, lawyers, automobiles, phones, and horrible movies. Then she saw a billboard and slowed down. She saw Marcus Brixton on a billboard, the token Blaxican at a prestigious law firm that was a magnet for minorities.

He hadn't called her. He hadn't saved her from herself. She cursed him in Spanish, damned him in English, gave him the middle finger as she turned on La Cienega, then shadowed Hugo Boss south, away from Hollywood, away from billboards featuring Brixton.

There was something about Hugo Boss. He didn't have porcelain skin, golden eyes, or supernatural gifts, but he was both irresistible and enigmatic.

And other than inviting her to go have sex with him, he hadn't said a word.

But tonight wasn't a night for words.

Daylight was for talking.

Nighttime was about action.

When they were caught at a red light at Cadillac Avenue, across from Kaiser, she took a photo of his silver four-door Elantra. Its license plate's frame announced it had been purchased at Hooman Hyundai of Los Angeles. She contemplated sending a group text to Destiny, Ericka, and Indigo, was going to include the photo of the guy's car and tell the Blackbirds if they didn't hear from her within three hours to send the picture to the LAPD, and to hurry and clear out that bedroom drawer in her apartment where she kept her battery-operated stress-relieving tools she'd never want her mother and stepfather or her father and stepmother to see. No one would inherit those. She had a bottom drawer filled with things that only a woman would understand, but not things a girl wanted her parents to find. Kwanzaa had her finger on SEND, but she didn't want the Blackbirds to know she was finally being slutty. But she was being only as slutty as the good-looking, Hugo Boss–wearing, Starbucks iced coffee–drinking man she followed.

This was her birthday. This was her present. Ericka had Argentina. Indigo had had her two-time girl thing. Even Destiny had a steady boyfriend.

This would be Kwanzaa's story to tell, some wickedness to brag about.

She would have someone to talk about other than Marcus.

As she followed Hugo Boss down the 10 westbound, she hoped he had protection.

She could be done with this iced coffee–drinking customer from Starbucks, could be wayward and celebratory in less time than it takes Domino's to deliver a pizza, rush back home, get showered, change into the amazing outfit she was dying to have on tonight, and spend time laughing and sipping wine with the Blackbirds. She would have fun, live outside the box, and get Marcus Brixton out of her mind.

At least for a few minutes.

She would reel herself back as soon as her initiation into the One-Off Crew was done.

She would go back to being the conservative college student, the barista at Starbucks.

It would be odd seeing Hugo Boss, Mr. Iced Coffee, after whatever happened tonight.

She would have him tonight, would have the man all the Latinas lusted after.

And tomorrow she would request to be put in a different Starbucks, just so she never had to see this stranger again.

Chapter 34

On the eve of Kwanzaa's birthday, as I tossed and turned and wondered how and when to tell Hakeem Mitchell that my name wasn't Kismet Kellogg and my real name was Destiny Jones, lies were exposed and my world went to hell.

In the morning, after Kwanzaa had left home, I tied colorful balloons to the rail in front of her door. Kwanzaa had left her crib just before five. She was working what she called the Severe Withdrawal shift at Starbucks. The first cantankerous customers who hurried in for overpriced coffee were addicts who used snarls for words, and most couldn't wait to get online and give the young baristas at her branch bad ratings. They would be outside the doors, or sitting on the patio, frowning, waiting, feenin', checking the time every other second, pulling on the door to make sure Starbucks wasn't open yet. Since Kwanzaa wasn't going to work on her birthday, Ericka, Indigo, and I zoomed by to sing an early happy birthday to her at six thirty in the morning. We wanted to both surprise and embarrass her. Then I zoomed up over to Crenshaw and headed east on Exposition so I could catch my morning classes at USC.

When the classes were done, I studied about two hours before I white-lined my way to job number one. I was already dog tired, was just as cranky and bad-tempered as the first customers, and I had many miles to go before I slept, because I had to be up to celebrate Kwanzaa's birthday moment. I wasn't going to let her down.

The night before, I had spent a few hours updating fourteen Amazon Fire Sticks and doing the same on boxes for six Amazon Fire TVs, all I had bought online at Gizmodo. I sent out individual text messages to my customers from Kismet Kellogg, told them to hit the ATMs and have legal tender in hand because the devices had been upgraded. I reassured them that it was legal and they could get rid of cable and save at least two hundred a month, plus cancel Hulu and Netflix and pocket those coins as well, and for less than one month's cable bill, have absolutely-positively-free-with-no-strings-attached access to over four thousand channels worldwide, every sport, and porn sites from all around the world so they could see that the same things they do in America they do in the rest of the world as well, only with an accent.

One teenage customer, a magnet-school Westside boy, said, "I'm short on cash."

"Your issue, not mine."

He offered two hundred in premium Kush for the eighty-dollar Fire Stick.

I asked, "Are you a police officer or working with any part or aspect of law enforcement?"

The guy laughed, said he wasn't, and then asked me the same thing. We shook hands, then he ran to his momma's car to get the Kush, stole it from her stash. His problem, not mine.

I delivered all I had to sell within thirty minutes by having customers meet me in the parking lot at Home Depot on Slauson and Fairfax. That done, tax-free money lining my pocket, I sped toward Baldwin Hills and Dad's trilevel town home, where he had the AC on and was jamming Marvin Gaye's "I Want You."

I entered the house dancing, singing with Marvin, being silly, doing a cha-cha with my old man, and that cha-cha changed to us Chicago Steppin'. When the song ended, I realized I'd left the steroids and other meds that I had bought on my last run across the border into Tijuana in my apartment on the kitchen table.

My dad said, "It's no biggie about the extra steroids, baby girl."

"It is to me, because I need to know this is handled, Old Man Keith Jones."

"Old?"

"*Keith*, you're kicking fifty. Just because you've turned hipster and wear slim jeans, 1000 Mile boots, fitted T-shirts, and cool fedoras, just because you look like you're thirty-going-on-twenty-nine, doesn't mean you're thirty-going-on-anything. You are still old. You're dinosaur old. You're so old you were sitting next to Abe Lincoln that night he went to the theater. Jesus' babysitter used to babysit you too. You're older than the seventh day. You're older than racism. You actually heard the Big Bang. Should I keep on going, Old Man Keith Jones?"

He massaged his pepper-with-a-teaspoon-of-salt goatee. *"Destiny Jones,* my one and only child, *ain't ya heard?* Ain't nothing old in my house but money and your lame jokes."

"Dad. No. Don't ever talk like that. You are so not cool."

"If there's anyone cooler than me, they must be naked in Iceland."

"You're older than MTV, BET, and almost older than TV."

"I'm the same number of years in front of you now as I was the day you were born."

"Dad, you're older than the Internet, cable, and push-button phones. When you were a child, clothes hadn't been invented and you used two cans and a string to make a phone call."

"No, we didn't. We clacked dinosaur bones together to send messages."

"Right. You invented Morse code and Samuel Morse stole your idea and got the credit."

"You're getting old now."

"Never."

"Soon you'll be out of USC and starting your own family."

"Afraid not. After undergrad comes master's, then PhD."

"You'll never be smarter than me. You know that, right?"

"Anyway, Poppa Poppa bo bappa. Now let's be serious. You look okay, but I really need you to tell me how we're doing in this fight with cancer. I want you to be comfortable at all times."

"I am fine at the moment. I only take the steroids when it gets bad."

"What level of discomfort are you at now?"

"About level three. If it gets to be about a five, I take the meds."

"I have more for you just in case."

"I'm good for now."

"No, you're not. I'll ask one of the Blackbirds to drop the package off like last time."

"No, I can wait another day."

"I will have it dropped off. I'll text the Blackbirds and they will make it happen."

"On to important issues. You bring the books I wanted?"

"I did. But one more thing first."

I reached into my pocket, took out the two hundred dollars' worth of Kush I had traded a Fire Stick for. I tossed it to him, told him not to ask any questions so I wouldn't have to lie. Then I opened my backpack and took out copies of *33 A.D.*, *61 A.D.*, and *79 A.D.*, a vampire trilogy by David McAfee. My old man smiled like it was his birthday instead of Kwanzaa's.

He said, "You picked up all three?"

"Sure did. Bought copies for Kwanzaa's birthday too."

Dad said, "Best vampire series on the market."

"Kwanzaa said it's better than *Twilight*, and she is a hardcore *Twilight* fan."

"Vampires that sparkle, go to school, dress like a Gap commercial, and date are not vampires. This is the real deal."

"Dude was over a hundred, dating a girl in high school, and no one called him a perv."

"Yeah. I guess he would be seen as a perv attracted to a young woman."

"She was under eighteen and he was over one hundred. That's gross."

"I guess that would be like George Burns dating Kim Kardashian."

"Outside of that being a street by the Beverly Center, I have no idea who George Burns is."

"I'm telling my age."

"You sure are, old man."

"I will start these as soon as I finish reading the biography on Phan Châu Trinh."

"The Vietnamese Martin Luther King Jr."

"You could call him that, but he had some Garvey and Malcolm X in his philosophies too. No one leader's plan has ever been the right plan, but it takes a combination of ideologies, and those have to, at times, remain flexible. Trying what we did in the '60s will no longer work."

"Dad, don't start. Please, don't start. Don't make me slit my wrists. You know I will."

He laughed.

I borrowed one of his fedoras, pulled it on.

He laced up his 1000 Mile boots and grabbed another stylish fedora.

We climbed into his SUV. He didn't look ill, but he was weak. Cancer lived within his body and hadn't revealed itself fully outside. He looked normal to most, but I knew the truth.

I tried to be the best daughter because I had the best dad ever.

I refused to lose him to any disease.

On the corner of La Brea and Rodeo Road, across from Target, was a large billboard hovering over the epicenter of the black and brown community, an area that existed on the edges of Culver City and its other social strata. The billboard had the image of a brown-skinned boy, the hue that had become the symbol of all things wrong in the United States of America. A line was drawn down the middle of his face, depicting two lives, two choices. On the left side his skin was darker, as if that were both a reality and rigid metaphor, and announced the cost of incarceration was sixty-three thousand dollars. On the right side, the other half of his brown skin looked more white than brown, and it said that the cost of education was ninety-one hundred dollars. When a person of color stood before the court, no matter how she had been wronged, America loved to choose the left side.

My father saw me staring at the billboard.

He said, "All of these areas, Blair Hills, Windsor Hills, View Park, Baldwin Hill, all of them have the name of white developers. We are living where the Europeans tried to build their own world, had laws that kept the black man out, then were angered and left when the black man was allowed to have land. We're all living where the white man had built Whiteville after Whiteville, and I bet every white developer would want his name erased, or moved to some other area."

"I know. You've said that one thousand kazillion billion trillion times."

"And now this area, every avenue that touches MLK or Crenshaw, is part of the prison-to-pipeline system. That billboard, the prison side is profitable to the rich man, and the rich man uses the prison system as his way of controlling the population of the black man by no longer having him available to the black woman, or no longer having the black woman available to the black man. The government invented AIDS to control the black population and that backfired, the same way it back-fired when they tried to kill the Native Americans by giving them smallpox-infected blankets. They are the coconspirators that have al-lowed prisons to be built and the court to fill them with modern-day slaves. They didn't see you, Destiny. They didn't hear your case or your cries. The racist system just saw another victim for the system. That's why they tried to try you as an adult, but failed. They wanted you to lose every chance you had to make it in this world. They wanted to use you as an example. Education is not profitable for those who build the in-dustrial prison complexes. That's what we were fighting. The black man has had to have laws made to allow him to do what the white man is naturally able to do. And when we do what they do and they hate it, they make laws that make it illegal for us to have the same right. Laws are not for the rich, because they commit the same wrongs and never see a day in jail, but to control the poor."

"Dad. Please. Not now. I can't do a conspiracy theory right now."

"It's not a theory. The government gave black men syphilis. Evil gets pretty evil. Slavery. Black Codes. Jim Crow. Now prisons."

"Not now, Dad."

"You okay?"

"Will be. I have no other choice but to be okay."

In a flash, I remembered when it felt like I had no freedom, when it seemed like I'd never have freedom again, being barked at like an ani-mal, being told when to go to bed, when to get up.

My dad put his hand on mine. His fatherly touch pulled me back to freedom.

I put my eyes back on the road, took three deep breaths, tried to leave Hoosegow in the back of my mind.

"Dad, I love you."

Without hesitation he responded, "I love you too. I love you more than anything."

"I know."

"Then that's what matters."

"I know."

"That's what gets us to the other side of every problem."

"Including this one."

"Including this one."

No matter the universe, my dad loved me and I loved him.

That would never change.

Chapter 35

Indigo headed toward Hollywood Hills. The prominent area where Indigo white-lined traffic and sped to on her CBR was known as Mount Olympus. It was higher than the stench from the homeless encampments that had spread all over L.A. Indigo had finished her classes at university and zoomed to an exclusive area developed between Hollywood Boulevard, Laurel Canyon Boulevard, Willow Glen Road, and Nichols Canyon Road.

She was headed to her parents' home to video-chat with her relatives in Nigeria, the ones who didn't care about the eight-hour time difference. It would be late there, but only early afternoon in Los Angeles.

Indigo's parents owned a three-million-dollar estate, which they had moved to when Indigo was sixteen, after living in Hancock Park. It was a property that had an unrestricted view of hills and mountains. It was a magnificent home of marble and glass located on Mannix Drive, a narrow snaking road in the hills, away from high traffic, in an area of people unknown to the public, but more powerful than the A-list celebrities on the silver screen. Inside, ceremonial Igbo pots, royal Bini masks, and a picture of President Obama, former president Goodluck Jonathan, Indigo, her parents, and Michelle Obama were on display next to novels by Nigerian writers Chinua Achebe, Wole Soyinka, Femi Osofisan, Ben Okri, and Folasade Coker.

There was enough to show they were proud of their homeland, enough to let their Nigerian friends know where their hearts lived, but not enough to scare their American friends.

The formal kitchen table was filled with newspapers: *Daily Nigerian, Nigerian Inquirer,* and *Nigerian Tribune.* Dressed in colorful sports attire from Lululemon, Indigo's mother asked Indigo to find a short video for them to watch before the call.

Her mother asked, "What are the titles of the latest Nollywood movies on YouTube?"

Indigo coughed, then motioned at the MacBook. "Trust me, you don't want to know. There are a lot of wonderful Nollywood movies, but these free ones are not what you want. Maybe we should just watch an old episode of *Meet the Adebanjos.*"

"I am really curious. What are the titles of what is being offered to the world for free?"

"The first ones that came up are *Cyber Sex 2, Holy Lesbians, Pastor Got Me Pregnant.*"

Her mother frowned, rolled her eyes, and then hissed. *"Blasphemy."*

Indigo continued, *"The Mistress, Rich Spoilt Lesbian,* and *Lesbian Fantasies."*

"These actors should be incarcerated. This puts those ideas in people's head. Would you have looked in the sky and thought of jumping from a mile up if you had never seen someone jump out of a plane? All involved should be marched through Lagos naked. You should not ever start watching this sort of thing. You should never allow these things to poison your mind."

"Mother, calm down. They are only movies."

"And to make it worse, those movie titles are abominable. Who would call a movie those titles? They sound like the disgusting and disrespectful too-too book titles I saw when I stumbled across the *African* American section of a bookstore when we were in Chicago for a conference, and that was the last time I made that mistake."

"Mom. Calm down."

"There are no gay people allowed in Nigeria and there should not be any gay movies. Just the idea of wanting to film such a thing is an abomination. Chinelo Okparanta has written what she wants to write, but President Goodluck Jonathan has spoken."

"Muhammadu Buhari is the new president."

"Still, I agree with former president Goodluck. I listen to him, not to a book that should be burned. If I could send Boko after those abominations, I would. That's how strongly I feel."

"I know the law in Nigeria, Mother. It is a life-or-death matter. I know. But Chinelo Okparanta's book is dope. It's a great novel. We need to understand what's going on. I read that and Chigozie Obioma's *The Fishermen* after my birthday, when I finally had a break."

"I need you to understand traditional Nigerian ways, not the vile ways of the West. We live in the West, but we are not servants of the West. We understand their ideologies, but we will not embrace them; we will not be indoctrinated and become their servants, like other blacks here who spend day and night trying to impress the designers and maintainers of Western philosophy."

"I understand the difference. You have repeated your views like a national anthem."

"Lilly Singh. Let's watch a few of her outlandish videos. The way she mocks her parents makes me laugh so hard. But if you ever make videos mocking me and your father in that way, I will beat you from here to Lagos and your father will beat you from Lagos back to this house."

"You've never beat me and neither has my father."

"I still have hands, so don't think I won't."

After they had watched a few videos and laughed until their bellies hurt, to balance the comical with the serious, Chimamandanata put on her glasses, searched YouTube, and found a documentary on one of Nigeria's lost sons. The entertainer had Nigerian roots, but had never been to Nigeria, and was leaving America and discovering his fatherland for the first time.

Indigo's mother went on a rant, said that nothing about the young man was Nigerian.

She said, "This disconnect is what I did not want to happen to you, Indigo. I did not want you to become an adult like this young man and be a stranger in your homeland. To be a grown man and have no association to your true culture is offensive. And when you have children, you will make sure they know their heritage as well. They will know all of their kinsfolk."

"I know. You have told me that a million times."

"That boy goes to Nigeria, tattoos all over his precious body, dressed like he lives in the bush, horrible posture, and seems irate when people tell him so. I do not care how long the flight was, he should have exited the plane looking respectable, not like a thug walking through Walmart at two in the morning. Look at how he is dressed. He looks worse than the coconut vendors on Acapulco's beach. He dresses like a clown. Unprofessional. Man or woman, underwear should *never* be seen in public."

"Mom, he's a hip-hop superstar."

"Then he should be able to afford clothes that fit and a belt, or a pair of suspenders."

"Showing your drawers is a fashion statement."

"He just *dribbled* a soccer ball."

"Yeah. That was blasphemy. I can't defend that. Not even going to try."

"I have made sure you are not one of *them*. Too many leave as Africans, come to America, embrace negativity, then call themselves *niggas*, use that word as if it were the flag to their own narrow-minded country. They arrive and lose their cultural GPS, discard their self-esteem; they lose their pride. *Pride*. That is what I have given you from birth."

"And I appreciate all you have done, every sacrifice you have ever made."

"Inhale. What do you smell? You smell food. You smell me preparing dinner. I worked all morning, was in court, and since I have conquered the world, I am home early, and I am making dinner. And in the morning I will rise and make breakfast. Why? Because I am a good wife. A California wife will not go into the kitchen and prepare her husband's meal for him every day. She buys fast food, which is the same as poisoning her family, or she will call ahead and order, stop at some place and pick up prepared food. Or even worse, she will hire someone to cook her husband's meal, and if they have babies they will use that same woman to take care of their children while the wife runs away from her obligations to spend the day at yoga, and that is why their husbands will leave them for the woman their wives have hired to cook and take care of their child. What is her purpose if some other woman is in her home cooking, cleaning, and nurturing?"

"Mother, now you know we know many Nigerians who have maids, cooks, and nannies."

"I never had a nanny and I have never allowed any woman to cook for my husband."

"I know. You're amazing. You are a woman who goes after what she wants."

"I am proactive and pursue what I deserve, not what I want. There is a difference, Indigo."

"Back home, you left the boy you were seeing and stole my father from his girlfriend."

"Ask any woman who thinks I am a fool. Ask your father how I am when riled."

"Mother?"

"What is the question? That is the tone you have when you have a serious question."

"This tone you have is unsettling. Has there been some issue with my father recently?"

"Nothing of any true concern. Your father is handsome and a man of means, so some foolish woman is always trying to test us, some *asewo* is always trying to test our marriage and commitment."

"Did something else happen I am not aware of?"

"Nothing you need to be concerned with, my daughter."

"Has it been confirmed?"

"I only have my suspicions."

"Please elaborate."

"He is working more, working late, and every so often he takes a last-minute business trip and goes away for a day, maybe two days."

"He makes many business trips. A man in his position has to make many decisions."

"But lately, I guess something has changed. He never gives me his itinerary, or the hotel information, only says to call him on his mobile. And if I call late, either there is no answer, or he answers and is curt, says he is tired and sleeping. Sometimes I call and there is no answer, but he will text me in return. As a wife, should I not know where my husband is at all times?"

"Since when?"

"Not too long. Only a few months."

"Buy a new phone. Buy a phone like my father has and I will use a program that will create the same information on the new phone. I will tell him I need to use his phone, and I will go in the bathroom, and within ten minutes you will have a phone that has all of his contacts."

"Is it possible to do such a thing?"

"Yes. I did it to Yaba and he never knew, and that was how I found out about the Ethiopian. I read their text messages. I read their emails. I saw truth beyond the lies. Your phone will receive all of my father's emails and calls. You will know everything he does, and he will not have a clue because my father is not tech savvy. If you suspect there is an issue, that's what I will do for you. And if you do not want the phone, I will do it anyway, and I will monitor him myself."

"Indigo."

"There is no other option. It is done. Consider it done."

"Indigo."

"What?"

"Do not take that tone with me."

"Yes, my sweet mother. What is your question? I know your tone of inquisition as well."

"Where is Olamilekan Babangida and why hasn't he come to state his intentions? Does your boyfriend think he is that special, or perhaps he thinks that since he plays American football he is better than other Africans? Wealth does not come before values, and never before God."

Indigo hissed her disapproval of the recurring topic. "We're back to that. You would rather look out of the window at *my* life than look into the mirror and thoroughly examine your own."

"You take precedence. You have always taken precedence in my life."

"I know that. And you take precedence in mine as well, Mother."

"Giving a man your body too soon only ensures a bad deal for a woman. When a man has had a woman there is no room for negotiations. When a man knows other men have had relations with a woman, there is no room for compromises. Having conjugal visits with a man as if he were your husband only ensures he will never feel the need to become your husband. Despite your intellect, despite your strength, despite your beauty, he will not see you as a wife."

"Mother, times have changed. These are not the days of Jane Austen."

"Jane Austen? Spoken like a child who grew up in the West."

"Even in Nigeria times have changed."

"Men never change, and *Olamilekan* is the issue. I did not like the way the boy touched you at your birthday party."

"What are you talking about?"

"Don't act like I am half blind and stupid. I remember all I see."

"I am serious. What did I miss? Did he touch me in an inappropriate manner?"

"*Yes*. He touched your waist and his hand moved across your *bottom*. In front of your father and me, in front of your friends, in front of our friends, he lingered on your bottom."

"His hand probably dropped from my waist and you assumed he was trying to grab my bottom. He would never do that. He's Americanized, but his core values are Nigerian."

"He behaved so familiarly with you. Are you being intimate with him?"

"I am still a virgin. I will be purer than Caesar's wife until I am sold for a whale's tooth."

"That is your answer?"

"And after I am married and have three children, it will still be my answer."

"Were you intimate with Yaba?"

"Of course not. We held hands, but only when we crossed the street."

"Your father liked him. Your father was impressed."

"Enough with my personal life. You have suspicions regarding my father."

"I do. But do not speak a word to your father. Let's not anger him."

Indigo said, "I will buy a duplicate phone to track my father's messages and movements."

"No, you will not. We will not disrespect him. I would hate it if he did that to me."

"Fine. I will do nothing. I will be passive. Do not come to me crying the next time."

"Do not have your father's ways, Indigo."

"What do you mean by that, Mother?"

"You had two boyfriends at your party. And everyone saw. Everyone whispered."

"That's not what is going on, Mother."

"But as your mother, I do not like to see so many men my daughter has dated in one gathering. People talk and rumors are spread regarding your character. It makes you look bad, Indigo. It makes American people think you are some sex-craved West African stereotype."

"Who are they to judge me?"

"I know. No one wags their finger at themselves."

"I didn't think Olamilekan was coming. I told you he said he was not available, and then he showed up after we had had an argument, and I had no idea he would bring so many gifts."

"An argument on your birthday regarding what?"

"Do not ask another question."

"Idowu Yaba brought gifts for you like you were a queen."

"So did Olamilekan."

Her mother smiled. "Your father likes Yaba the best. He hates that you broke up with him."

"My father wants free tickets for the rest of his life, especially tickets during playoffs."

"That is not a nice thing to say regarding your father's character. I like Yaba the best too."

"Because you would love to wreck my insides giving birth to tall grandbabies."

"Is that all you think you are to us? Do you think your father and I are that shallow?"

"I am a girl child. You and my father would sell me for a goat."

"You are almost as beautiful as you are intelligent. You are worth two goats."

"You're a two-goat woman yourself."

"Three goats, four camels, and six chickens. I have degrees and speak six languages."

"I'm cuter and I am younger and I can do more squats than you can."

"I'm the better dancer."

"You were a dancer, so you should be."

"And you will never be as beautiful as I am. Concede to the truth."

"Whatever. Guess I'm just a two-goat girl in your eyes."

"Does Olamilekan want to marry? If not, does Yaba want to make you his bride?"

"Mother. Take the batteries out of this aggravating conversation, please."

"You need to make the plan to start having babies soon, Indigo."

"Are we going to have this same discussion again? Unless you plan on being a surrogate at this point, we really should table this issue, as for me it is truly a nonissue at this point."

"Family is never a nonissue. Family is the only issue that should never end."

"Look. I am waving a snot rag in surrender. You win. You win. You win."

"But you say you are dating Olamilekan, and not Yaba, yet you spent more time on your birthday with Yaba than you did Olamilekan. You are wearing the watch that Yaba gave you as a gift. And you are using the iPhone Yaba gave you as well. Yet you claim Olamilekan as your boyfriend. It did not feel like a relationship when I saw you with him. I saw lust and disrespect."

"Yaba and I parted ways. I moved on. I am trying to figure it out with Olamilekan."

"Will Olamilekan Babangida marry you at some point? Other than touching you on your personal areas each time he passes by you, *and in front of your father,* what is his intention?"

"I have no idea."

"If Olamilekan does not mention marriage, if family is not part of his discussion, then that is all you need to know, Indigo. Maybe he thinks you are too American for him, or maybe he has become too Western for you. It's time to move on and find a suitable husband."

Indigo coughed. "Why won't you stop talking? So many words are exiting your face."

"You should let me choose your husband."

"When the British invade Vatican City and set fire to Monaco, you can choose."

"I have told two wonderful Nigerian men, professional men, about my wonderful daughter. Alamieeyeseigha is a doctor here at Cedar Sinai and Chukwumereije is a barrister in London."

"Now I know what this conversation is about."

"I am looking out for your best interests."

"You don't get to choose the egg fertilizer, Mother. That is illegal."

"Oh, I may not be able to legally choose whom you marry and create my grandbabies with, but I get to choose who inherits what your father and I have built. Choose badly, inherit the wind."

Indigo coughed a few times, found tissues, blew her nose, washed her hands, and said, "On to business. It's Kwanzaa's birthday tonight, so I will need to get some rest."

"I should make a call to Dr. Alamieyeseigha and have him prescribe something proper."

"Not today. When I leave here I'm going to exercise and try and sweat it out."

"You need to be in bed taking the proper medication and resting, not exercising."

"I promise I will rest tomorrow. But today I have to help cook Kwanzaa's dinner."

"Sit. Let me put makeup on your face and wrap your head. I will wear gold and azure, plus an embellished kaftan, gold neckpiece and matching bracelet, and pair it with a gold head tie. I will look humble, but classy. I will be as gorgeous as the first lady of Lagos State, Mrs. Bolanle Patience Ambode, and you will be as beautiful as Genevieve Nnaji. It is time to call home and I will not let them think that I am abusing you and not taking care of my daughter."

"Mom, we're just calling relatives. You are not President Muhammadu Buhari addressing leaders at the United Nations Assembly in New York. And I don't need to look all Nollywood."

"To our relatives, we are just as important. We will not look like Western paupers."

Indigo initiated Skype to call their relatives abroad. Her mother always used the television to Skype, and the relatives had a view of the immaculate home. A dozen relatives had gathered for the call, and some had driven two hours in horrible traffic just to be able to see that view. Indigo had pulled it together. She and her mother looked like fashion models.

When the Skype session was done and Indigo was preparing to leave, her mother came up behind her. Her mother hugged her, sighed, then handed Indigo a black credit card.

Indigo asked, "What is the meaning of this?"

"My secret credit card. The one I use so your father will not see the bill."

"I know what it is. Why did you give this card to me?"

"Buy the extra phone like his, Indigo. And program the phone to mirror your father's information. I want to have access to his text messages and email. I need to know the truth."

"May I buy two, Mother?"

"What is going on?"

"Mother, with Olamilekan, there was a girl. A South African insulted me."

"Was there a confrontation?"

"I taught her to not disrespect me."

"Be careful with your choices. Men are not worthy of half the battles we have."

Indigo said, "If you are a girl who won't, they will find a girl who will."

"For any woman, other women have always been an issue. They will do what you will not do. But if you feel as if you need to understand Olamilekan better, buy the second phone."

"Now, say it out loud. You have to say it out loud."

Her mother hesitated. "I think your father is having another affair."

"We will find out what is going on. We will not allow him to embarrass this family."

"Almost a decade ago, he bought me this large home as an apology."

"I know."

"He begged me to not take you and go back to Lagos."

"I know."

"He fell on his knees, promised to be a better husband and father."

"He did that in front of both of us."

"Men pursue you, marry you, then suddenly they feel trapped and have to act out."

"Why is that, Mother? Why is that?"

"They become boys and try to continue to collect toys. There are two kinds of men. Those who cheat and get caught, and those who don't get caught."

"There are no absolutes. Not all men are cheaters."

"I think men see cheating as a bonus, as some earned reward. Maybe being loving, calm, and gentle becomes boring, but they never realize their wives are versatile. If you are a wife who won't do particular things, they will go on the Internet to find a girl who will."

"Between Viagra and that damn Ashley Madison, we don't stand a chance."

"Marriage, children, work, maybe a man feels trapped, but he acts foolish and refuses to be honest about who he is, refuses to give you your freedom, does not know how to let go of what he is destroying. I stayed because he made promises, and I wanted to keep the life I have, the job I love, my dignity, my friends, my accumulated wealth and my home, your home, our home. But you are a woman now. I will leave him if I have to."

"Mom, don't get ahead of yourself on this issue."

"I have to continue being a good example for you, even with this . . . this . . . this . . ."

"Is this why you have been looking for a second home in Lagos? You said you wanted to have a family home for us there. Is this why you are looking at property on Banana Island?"

"This is why. But if needed, I will move to the Seventh Arrondissement in Paris, or if you're not leaving as well, then maybe to La Jolla. If I did not have you, the first time I would have left on a plane, flown to Tokyo, and moved into either the Shibuya or Roppongi neighborhoods. I have stayed to maintain family. Women always stay to fix that which men foolishly destroy in search of that which they already have at home. No, there is no proof, but I sense something. Each time he goes away, he brings me back expensive gifts, as if he is apologizing for that which I do not know. I hope for the best, and prepare for the worst. He needs to understand how serious I am this time. A woman makes idle threats and a man laughs a thousand times."

"Do as you have trained me, wait until there is evidence to prove your case. Be an attorney. You keep being the good mother, the good wife, and don't let him know you suspect a thing."

"If he has not honored his word, if she knows he is married and has done this willingly, we will hold her panties high over our head, then I will deal with my husband in my own way."

Indigo coughed a dozen times, then shushed her mother. They hugged, held each other for a long time. Indigo trembled as her mother shuddered, unable to hold back tears.

"Heed my words, my daughter."

"Yes, Mother. I am listening to you as if you are the Ghost of Christmas Yet-to-Come."

"My child. Never let a man use you only to cure his insomnia, because then you will become the one with the restless nights. No deceiver can deceive a person two times. If he succeeds in doing so, it is not that he is so wise, but it is due to the foolishness of the deceived. Do not be foolish, Indigo. Do not be foolish."

"Stop talking, Mother."

"And if you start a relationship fighting for a man, you will always be fighting for him."

"I know. I know."

"A wife may have to face degrading situations that are brought to her door. At times she may feel like she has no option, as if there is no alternative, but you are not married and there is no need for you to do the same."

"Please. Mother. I am already feeling despondent regarding Olamilekan."

"You are better than me, Indigo. You are better than me in every way. You are the woman I admire and adore. Don't let a man kiss you and turn a princess into a frog."

Chapter 36

I drove my dad to Kaiser's Sunset facility, sat in the oncology waiting area with him, textbook in hand in case I found time to study. Today we were the wisecracking hipster and his jovial daughter in skinny jeans, Chucks, fedora, Wayfarers, and a black T-shirt.

I looked at the people fighting some form of the same battle, some for the second or third time. Everyone was in the middle of personal warfare. Dad knew most of them, considered them his fellow soldiers. They wore T-shirts with slogans. LIVE TO WIN. YOU ARE NOT ALONE. FUCK CANCER. One bald girl around my age had on a shirt with a scowling bulldog across the front. CANCER MAY HAVE STARTED THE FIGHT, BUT I WILL FINISH IT. I wondered if this was my destiny as well.

Once they had regular appointments, patients befriended others scheduled around the same time. People who ordinarily wouldn't have said two words to each other on the streets, didn't matter if they attended a church, synagogue, or mosque, were like family in the oncology waiting room. There was no talk of bombings on the Gaza strip, inhumane treatment of minorities around the world, or whether lives of all colors and backgrounds mattered.

It's a shame people need a common enemy to open their eyes to friendships.

The common enemy here was the clock on the wall. Here everyone looked up at the clock, or at their phones, like they could hear it ticking, counting down one second at a time.

Dad's radiation treatment lasted eight minutes total, but with the prep they had to do, it took as long as forty minutes for him to be done. Doing homework made the time fly.

Afterward, I drove my hipster dad back home, battled traffic as he closed his eyes.

Back at the townhome, I crashed on the sofa. Needed to close my eyes for a minute.

I yawned, then said, "I'm starvin' like Marvin. What's here in this boring house to eat?"

"Ribs, chicken, brisket, sausage, and Memphis-style spaghetti and slaw."

"When did you cook all that delicious-yet-fattening food?"

"Yesterday. I was here, watching TV, and got bored. Knew you'd want some."

"This is why I keep gaining weight. I will have to eat and run to the next job."

"You're working too much."

"Working is in my Jamaican blood. You have to thank my mom for that."

He called to me from the kitchen. "You've talked to Carmen?"

"Me and my prodigal mother talked yesterday. She's kicking it in New York. Her friend Lola Mack is on Broadway. She went to the opening. She'll be back home in a few days."

I looked up at his walls. There were images of me in every phase of my life, from infancy until I was a teen. I stared at the shrine, looked at my photos, and remembered when I was that child, that little girl, and closed my eyes for a moment, needing to shake off the fatigue.

I dreamed I was sitting in a chair, facing the little girl I used to be. She was scared of me. She ran away. I chased her, calling her name, yelling my name, our name.

Minutes later, Dad shook me awake. Our plates were on the table. I grabbed my backpack, yawned, took a seat, opened my backpack, and took out work for advanced chemistry and differential equations. That was how we stayed bonded. This was my father and me, as we had always been, even before that night that ruined our world. I was a daddy's girl to the bone.

I sent the Blackbirds a group message, asked them to drop his medicine off sometime this evening, and I wanted it done today, even if Kwanzaa had to do it on the eve of her birthday. She was going to listen to music later and then meet the rest of the Blackbirds back at the fourplex. My dad would be up late, so if someone had to drop it off late, it was no problem.

My dad was their second dad, as Indigo's father and Kwanzaa's true dad were my second dads.

After we ate, we sat on the sofa together, dad and daughter streaming *Jonathan Strange and Mr. Norrell*. When Dad got up to go use the restroom, I yawned and sent Hakeem a stream of girly emoticons, hearts, sunshine, teddy bears, smiley faces with the tongue out, regular smiles, the in-love emoticon, and a devil emoticon that meant horny. The smiley face with the tongue out meant I missed his tongue being in a very special place. Most of all, I missed him.

He didn't respond. That was a first. My man was busy being a mechanical engineer.

I smiled. *My man.* He was my man. I was in a relationship. We were a couple.

We were also the fear that set fire to my soul. He was hooked on Kismet Kellogg.

I sent Hakeem a message.

> Thinking about you and I'm feeling naughty, like I need you inside of me. Also thinking about giving you fellatio until you explode. I might let you come on my face. Maybe in my mouth. I could try to be your quaffing queen.
>
> So.
>
> Drink a lot of mango juice and eat a lot of sweet stuff, but no asparagus or anything acidic. Maybe I will try to swallow, see

what that's all about. Others girls do it.
Some girls say there is no point of sucking
if a girl's not going to swallow.

It's on my mind right now.

Or maybe we could try anal. I want to take
this to the next level. I love you boo.
Imagining us living together, sharing the
same space, and being a real couple. I
want to cook for you. I do cook, believe
it or not, just not every day. You have
me smiling. I miss you. Want you inside
me. I'm getting excited, wet, nipples are
aching while I am typing this. So, blow job
to completion or anal. If we did one, ONE,
which would you prefer first? Pick up more
condoms too. Condoms prevent minivans. I'm
so tired I'm rambling. Gonna nap awhile,
then study. Books before boys because boys
bring babies.

There was no immediate response as usual. I guessed my *mu-fukin'*
king was busy.

Two shakes of a leg later, I felt uneasy, read over the message I had
sent, read how explicit it was, and wished I could untext that sexual
text. Some things should be said face-to-face. That message had been
from Kismet. That had been Kismet sending a naughty message,
sending words that showed she had bonded, words meant to excite
her man.

That was not from Destiny. Destiny would never send a message like
that.

I put my phone away. Being two people was becoming too much.

I wanted to tell my dad about Hakeem.

I wanted to tell my dad I had met someone.

I wanted to tell him what I had done, about Kismet, and ask for his advice.

He'd like Hakeem. I knew he would.

And I knew Hakeem would like my dad.

I needed us at the same table, breaking bread, telling stories, and laughing.

Dad pulled a chair into the dining area, then came back with his hair clippers and several razors, as well as shaving cream. He grabbed towels, turned on hot water, motioned toward it all.

I said, "Serious?"

"If you're serious, I'm serious."

The TV was on. We started watching *Sliding Doors*, a film starring Gwyneth Paltrow before anyone in the public knew her well enough to not like her. It was a sci-fi rom-com number about choices, about fate. Walking through one door, or not walking through one door, changed everything. I wished I had never crept out of my bedroom window that night.

I said, "Dad, do you think there really are many universes?"

"I think there are. Based on scientific experiments, and what little we know about the universe in which we live, there could be many universes, some a duplicate of this one."

"So, do you think there could be many versions of us?"

"An infinite number of us."

"Do you think we make all the same choices?"

"No, I don't. We'd have different brainwashing. We make choices, or walk through different doors, have different paths, meet different people. In one universe I might be president."

"President Jones."

"In another your mother might be the ruler of America."

"Queen Henrietta Kellogg aka Carmen Jones."

"In another we could be homeless, or I could have died from some disease during childhood. In one universe the black man could have enslaved the white man. In another the idea of slavery never took root. In another the dinosaurs are still alive and man is all but extinct."

"In another the Native Americans and Arawak rule."

"In another it's an altruistic society, not capitalistic. Still another has no word for murder, because there is no murder."

"And no word for cancer, because that is not an issue."

"In one, Hitler could be the ruler."

"Godwin's Law, Dad. Godwin's Law."

"Sorry, but that was only as an example, not as a comparison. In one universe the twenty-five thousand blacks that had been taken to the Rhine could have risen up and defeated Hitler's madness."

"I've never heard about black folks being over there during that era."

"Without the presence of truth, only propaganda remains."

"I would hope the rest of the universe would have kinder denizens across the board."

"Maybe in some universe, there are better people than the ones here on this planet."

"In one universe, it's a perfect world and nothing bad ever happened to me."

"One universe is our utopia where nothing bad ever happened to us as a family."

"In one universe you and Mom are happily married."

"I suppose so. And in one we never met and never married."

"And you might have more than one child in a different part of the multiverse."

"I suppose so. All the combinations and permutations are possible."

"I would love to see that version of me, the one who didn't go through this, the one who didn't put her parents through what I put you through, the one who loves to take pictures, the ones boys want to be seen with. I'll bet that Destiny is happy and has no idea she's happy."

"You can be happy too, Destiny."

"I want to, but I need you to be happy too."

"Don't worry about me."

"Then don't worry about me."

"Stop it."

"You stop it."

"I'm happy when you're happy."

"And I'm happy when you're happy."

Probably triggered by our conversation talking about multiple universes and endless possibilities, Dad fired up the television and used the app on his Fire Stick to find a movie called *Rheinland*, a film about being black in Germany in the year 1937, when the Nazis ruled. While it played, I used the clippers and cut his hair as short as I could, then put hot towels on his head before I lathered his crown. I shaved my old man's head until it was smooth as a baby's butt.

When I was done and we were cleaning up the mess, I said, "Wow."

"Do I look funny?"

"You look pretty good, Dad. No gray here and there. You look younger."

Soon I kicked back on the sofa again, and saw something shiny sticking up between the cushions. Dad always rested on the sofa and coins would fall out of his pockets. I dug between the pillows and what I pulled out wasn't money. It was an earring, a sterling-silver post earring with a rose crystal ribbon, the symbol for cancer awareness, for fighting that unrelenting beast.

It was the earring Ericka had been looking for the last few weeks.

I said, "I just found one of Ericka's favorite earrings between the pillows of your sofa."

"Really? Wonder how that ended up there."

"She dropped off the medicine last time."

"She sat on the sofa when she stopped by."

"Must've come off when she was here."

"If you found it there, then I guess it did."

"She stay long, or just dropped off the package?"

He ran his hands over his baldness and shrugged. "Not too long. She was in and out."

Dad didn't make eye contact when I asked him about Ericka.

I asked, "Are you dating anybody?"

"Nope. You seeing someone, Destiny?"

"Nope. Destiny is not seeing anyone."

"I understand how it was for Ericka when she was ill. People want perfection."

"But I don't want you to be alone."

"I'll be fine."

I dropped Ericka's earring in my pocket, then found oils and massaged my dad's scalp.

He said, "You're a lot happier these days. You're smiling more, laughing a lot."

"I know."

"Bow chica wow wow."

I laughed. "We are not having that conversation."

Chapter 37

At 8:00 P.M., in Destiny Jones mode, I arrived at FedEx in El Segundo.

I was scheduled to work until midnight. That was how I spent most Friday nights, driving tugs and loading containers filled with packages onto planes. I felt safer having an excuse not to be out in public, at a club, any place I might be recognized, or confronted, or ridiculed.

I almost only hung out when I was with the Blackbirds. I felt safe with my girls.

Not everyone reacted to me the way Leonard Dubois Jr. had, and even now I wasn't sure what to make of the way he had responded to our sudden reunion. People were two-faced.

My cellular was inside my leather jacket, so when it vibrated I felt it against my chest. It was a message from Hakeem. I became that giggly version of me, a part of me I had no idea still existed. With him I felt like who I would have been if not for that one night in my life. My smile was broad because I imagined us hooking up later tonight, after I had met with the Blackbirds for our ritualistic birthday celebration to raise our glasses to Kwanzaa.

The smile I owned was repossessed as soon as I read his message.

His text had two words, and seeing those words terrified me.

His text was in all caps, screaming, and it read: DESTINY JONES?

The world stopped.

My heartbeat sped up, loudened, rested between my ears.

The next message included two photos. One image was of me, as a teen, and one of me now. He had disregarded my wishes and photographed me while I slept. It was an image of me from my face to my breasts, an areola showing. It shocked me that he had done that. That pissed me off. I felt violated all over again. I forgot how to breathe. My brain expanded, squeezed against my skull.

> YOU CREPT A PHOTO OF ME WHILE I WAS NAKED
> AND SLEEPING ON TOP OF THE COVERS?
>
> ARE YOU DESTINY JONES?
>
> I NEED YOU TO DELETE THAT PHOTO AND ANY
> OTHER PHOTO OF ME YOU TOOK.
>
> ARE YOU DESTINY JONES?
>
> WHY WOULD YOU DO WHAT I UNEQUIVOCALLY TOLD
> YOU NOT TO DO?
>
> ARE YOU DESTINY JONES? YES OR NO.

I had known that his finding out was as inevitable as rain in Seattle.

I thought of all the things I could say, thought of pointless lies I could tell.

Chest rising and falling, agony in my eyes, I typed back one word.

> YES.

Then I waited for his next message. There was no next message.

I dialed his number twenty times in a row, each time it rang and went to voicemail.

> WHY WON'T YOU ANSWER? DON'T DO THIS. YOU
> KNOW HOW I FEEL ABOUT BEING PHOTOGRAPHED.
> YOU TOOK A PHOTO OF ME NAKED. I CAN SEE MY
> BREASTS AND MY FACE.

I waited on another reply.

WILL YOU PLEASE DELETE THAT PHOTO AND ANY
OTHER YOU MAY HAVE TAKEN?

It was a reply that would not come.

I couldn't send any more texts. My words could be put on social media.

I'd just sent the man a text and told him I would swallow his seeds. I told him I would do anal. All of that could be taken out of the context of the relationship. No black woman could ever do half of what a famous Kardashian had done and be respected. It was hard enough to be private in a public world, was impossible to keep most of your business to yourself.

I called Hakeem over and over. My anger went straight to voicemail each time.

A larger fear erupted.

Once again, I was damaged goods.

Fear rose as tears fell.

Chapter 38

That night, an hour after leaving the Club on Sunset Boulevard, Kwanzaa had followed the man who wore Hugo Boss into the heart of Southern California, beyond its miles of shopping alleys, beyond the Staples Center and the Lakers, beyond the nightlife at L.A. Live, to the gentrified Arts District off Fourth Street in Downtown L.A. She was on the numbered streets. It was a zip code where career homeless, discarded veterans, and mentally ill lived rent-free, but now most of the vagrants in certain areas had been removed, pushed a few blocks this way or a half mile that way to make room for tattooed hipsters who craved to live within a thousand steps of a Trader Joe's, Coffee Bean, and dozens of restaurants that served gluten-free meals.

During the day, with all the kids taking acting, dancing, and singing classes in the area, despite homeless encampments being on every vein leading into downtown, most of the areas looked hipster-family friendly. At night it looked like the corner of Ted Bundy and Jeffrey Dahmer.

Kwanzaa Browne parked on the street. She saw movement in the shadows as Hugo Boss parked and came to her car. She got out with his assistance, still looking toward the shadows, knowing this part of L.A. was close to the bridge that led to Boyle Heights and Latin gangs. Still no words as she adjusted her dress and nervously followed him. He didn't hold her hand. She just followed him, stayed a step behind him, let him be her shield from trouble.

People came out of the shadows. Women. The women hurried toward them from four locations, heels clacking like tap dancers. She counted eight women. They all stopped in front of him. High heels, beautiful short dresses, beautiful long dresses, business suits, tight jeans, white shorts, and one sporting a hijab. All looked like librarians, engineers, dancers, politicians, fashion activists, models, or attorneys. They appeared to be professional women between the ages of barely legal to the age of cougars, all in search of a good time at midnight. The Friday-night collective had waited, and now was surprised to see he wasn't alone. None turned away. In silence, they offered themselves to him. He shook his head and reached for Kwanzaa. She gave him her hand, trembling as her eyes moved from woman to woman. It was like seeing delegates from Great Britain, Canada, France, Germany, Italy, Japan, Russia, and the United States.

Their expressions begged to be chosen.

Kwanzaa had assumed the women were prostitutes.

They weren't.

She realized they were women Hugo Boss had been with before.

He shook his head.

The international lot of women turned away, anger in the way their hips moved, disappointment and envy in the way their heels clicked against the street. The scents from their perfume followed.

They reluctantly went to their cars.

Kwanzaa didn't understand. The moment had been tense, but esoteric, something only Hugo Boss and the gaggle of women comprehended. Hugo Boss stood for a moment, and as the scents from eight perfumes faded, inhaled the staleness of the nipple-hardening night. He looked left and right, unfettered, as if this type of attention was normal in his life. No one else waited in the darkness of the converted warehouses.

The octet, the G8 of women, was gone, and already that moment felt like a dream. Eight women were a lot of red flags, but Kwanzaa didn't question his policy. If eight women were in a queue, what he was putting down had to be good. It had to be spectacular. It had to be Magic Mountain, Disneyland, and Pornhub rolled into one. No one wanted to eat at the restaurant that had the empty parking lot. And this metaphorical parking lot had been filled with repeat customers. Repeat customers were the foundation of all businesses. When loving was good, everybody wanted a repeat.

But Hugo Boss had chosen Forever 21, had sent the other women to sulk in their tears.

Kwanzaa loved the idea of being the chosen one by the most handsome of the handsome. She wished Marcus Brixton and that contaminated Chilean bitch could see her now.

Tipsy, moving like she was in a dream, she followed Hugo Boss to the wrought-iron door of a three-level brick warehouse. He had led her to a private entrance. The stranger who would soon be her lover used a key, entered, disabled an alarm, and then turned on the recessed lights.

Chapter 39

After Indigo left her parents' home, she sped by AT&T to purchase two telephones. With much on her mind, feeling her mother's angst, she white-lined traffic to her father's office in Sherman Oaks on Ventura Boulevard.

She told him she was in the area, talked to him for ten minutes, then lied and said she had left her cellular at the family house when she was with her mother and asked to use his. She walked away, went to the ladies' room, called her mother, told her that Operation Creep Dad's Information was in progress, and fifteen minutes later she gave her father his phone back. Too much on her mind, she kissed her dad good-bye, took to the freeways. She hated lying to her father, but she hated for her mother to be in pain. She was afraid of what she would find on her father's phone. Stressed, she really needed to work out to clear her head.

Coughing, nose stuffy, she was finally en route to the Culver City stairs.

Indigo cruised by Cameo Woods apartments and saw a Honda pulled over, slanting to one side. The car's emergency lights were flashing and a sister was standing next to the car, her face a ball of fear, anger, and fret. Indigo didn't know if she was from America, the islands, Dominica, Haiti, Central or South America, or from the heart of the Motherland, but the girl was her sister no matter where she was born. Indigo slowed down, downshifted. She saw the girl was about twenty, hair in a tree-size Afro that bounced with the dry breeze, tall, dark, and sexy.

The coffee-hued mademoiselle stood with her arms folded, jaw tight, face etched in anger. The car's front tire was flatter than the middle of Texas. Indigo wouldn't want one of her Blackbirds stuck on the side of the road. Wouldn't want her mother stranded. Would appreciate if someone stopped to help her dad. She made a U, then passed the girl as the girl gazed at her, nodded at the girl, didn't see anyone else in her car, saw nothing suspicious, then made a U again. Indigo pulled up behind the girl's car, stopped two car lengths back, and put her CBR's emergency lights on, so traffic would see them ahead of time.

Indigo removed her bikers' gloves, undid her chinstrap, and removed her pink helmet. Her red hair was braided toward her neck, and there was a stocking cap on her braids to keep the helmet from pulling the roots. As her boots crunched across grit in the road, she pulled the stocking cap off, then tugged tissues out of her pocket, blew her nose for the hundredth time since yesterday, became a litterbug and tossed the sullied tissues. She felt ill, like she had the flu, but she'd never let being sick slow her down. She planned on sweating the virus out of her body.

Sinuses still stuffed, Indigo asked, "You okay? Someone coming to help?"

The girl wore stacked Jones Katami jewelry, handmade bracelets made of natural stone beads, vintage charms, and other random objects to create uniqueness.

With unhidden frustration the girl said, "I have a damn flat."

"Obviously. Have you called Triple-A?"

"I don't have Triple-A."

"What are your plans?"

"I don't know what to do. Can I drive it like this until I get to Venice Beach?"

"That is not advisable. Your tire is mangled. How far have you driven with it like that?"

"It got real bad when I was on the other side of La Brea."

"That's a little over a mile. Couldn't you tell you were already down to the rim? The tire is destroyed."

"Started to smell like the car was on fire, and the car wouldn't go more than a couple miles an hour after a while, so I gave up and stopped, got out, and hoped I was cute enough to get some man to stop and help me out. Glad I have on nice clothes and had just done my face."

"You look nice. Everything head to toe is on fleek."

"Thanks. You look pretty hot on that motorcycle."

Indigo coughed. "Do you have a spare tire and a jack?"

"I don't know. Where would those be?"

"Open your trunk. That is where they usually play hide-n-seek."

"You've learned how to change a flat?"

"Had no choice. My father wouldn't let me drive a car until I knew how to change a flat, change the oil, put air in the tires, put in antifreeze, change the battery, the whole shooting match."

"That's evil."

"Well, those skills have come in handy more times than I can remember."

Indigo coughed again, and checked the doughnut, made sure it was usable and not busted. She loosened the lug nuts, jacked up the car, took off the lug nuts, pulled the flat off and rolled it to the side, put the anorexic spare on, screwed on the lug nuts, let the car back down, tightened the lug nuts, and had the flat sitting in the trunk of the girl's car in ten minutes.

The girl grabbed her purse from the car and asked, "How much do I owe you?"

"Nothing. Pay it forward."

"You're coughing like you need a little help getting well. What's your name?"

"Indigo Abdulrahaman."

"Wow. That's an amazing name. Pardon me if I don't try and repeat the last part. I'm Rickie Sue Walker. Indigo, are you sure there is no way I can thank you for saving me?"

"Actually, do you have any tissues? This bug is worsening."

The girl reached in her car, pulled out coarse napkins from El Pollo Loco.

Indigo stepped to the side and blew her nose again. It felt like her brain was stuffed with cotton. Indigo pushed her tongue against the roof of her mouth, then pressed a finger between her eyebrows. Did that for twenty seconds and hoped that would help clear her stuffed nose. Didn't work. Coughing, Indigo headed back to her motorcycle. Rickie Sue followed, jogged after her, calling Indigo's name. Indigo stopped at her CBR, turned, faced the girl's telling smile.

"Indigo, I could make chicken soup and rub Vicks on the bottom of your feet."

"I was just paying it forward, not in search of a Florence Nightingale."

"Sit in my car with me and chat awhile. Let's get to know each other."

"*Ori e o pe*. Unless you have a *penis* . . . Look, you are a woman, and I am a woman, and my preference is Nigerian *men*, therefore there is *nothing* you can do for me. You offend me."

Without a good-bye, Indigo shook her head and sped away. But she turned around, pulled back up to the girl's car. The girl was inside. She let the window down, her face now nervous.

Face shield flipped up, Indigo killed her engine, then said, "I am *not* a bloody lesbian."

"I understand. Didn't mean to offend. Your accent and sexiness caught me off guard."

"I just wanted to be clear that I only stopped to *help* you, not hit on you."

They stared at each other, the CBR resting, rumbling between Indigo's thighs.

Rickie whispered, "Where is your bae, Indigo? Girl as fine as you has to have a bae."

"Probably somewhere being disrespectful with someone not quite as sexy."

"Your man should be nursing you back to health."

"I'm really getting tired of his nonsense."

Rickie Sue bit her bottom lip. "I make a real good chicken soup."

Indigo coughed a half dozen times, then looked toward the Culver City Stairs.

Rickie Sue whispered, "Homemade soup. And anything else you need to feel better."

Chapter 40

"Dr. Debra Dubois."

"Good morning."

"Hi. You might not remember me. My name is Ericka Stockwell."

"Ericka Stockwell? My Lord, is it really you all grown up?"

At eleven in the morning on Kwanzaa's birthday eve, when Ericka walked into her office, Dr. Dubois stood slowly. It had been over twenty years since she had seen Ericka Stockwell, had been more than two decades since Ericka had been in the halls of this OB/GYN clinic with her mother.

Dr. Dubois evaluated Ericka, saw the woman the child had become, exhaled like she was relieved, like two decades of worry could finally be put to rest, and Dr. Dubois's bottom lip trembled as her eyes filled with tears. Ericka pulled her lips in, hadn't expected to feel such a surge of heat in her throat, hadn't expected her emotions to become a ball of fire because she had hardened herself to that time in her life, but all of the toughness went away, fell like the walls of Jericho, and she took shallow breaths, began to suffocate in a room filled with fresh air.

Her chest heaved like a baby crying after a spanking, and she was unable to speak another word. She tried to shake off the heat, but failed at hardening herself again. Seconds after walking back into her past, she was embarrassed. She gave in and the tears began to pour. Hot tears streamed across her reddened face. She cried. Just like that Ericka was no longer the woman she was today, she was back in time, back before the divorce, before the cancer, before the marriage, before college, be-

fore she had been shipped off to Oklahoma. She was the frightened
thirteen-year-old girl who was living in one of the worst eras of her life.

Dr. Dubois wiped her eyes, then hurried to Ericka, arms open, pulled
her close to her bosom, and hugged her like they were long-lost sisters.
Emotions ran in both directions.

Dr. Dubois's voice cracked as she said, "My God. You've grown up."

"Yes, ma'am."

"Look at this. I forgot how tall you were. You were taller than me
then, and you are even taller now. I'm amazed."

"Yes, ma'am."

"I've worried about you, Ericka Stockwell."

"I'm fine, Miss Mitchell. I mean, Dr. Dubois."

"I have worried about you for so many years."

"I'm fine."

"I'm so glad we've found each other again."

"Me too, Miss Mitchell. I mean, Dr. Dubois."

"Young lady, twenty years ago, didn't I tell you to call me Debra?"

"Yeah, back when I was . . . here . . . and I was . . . when I was a child."

"You're an adult now, Ericka."

"Sometimes I'm not so sure about that."

"We are both adults. Please, call me Debra."

Through a stuffy nose, Ericka laughed, then cried more and said,
"Me too, Debra. I'm glad we have found each other again. I have missed
you. I have missed you so much."

Chapter 41

Tissues in hand, Ericka wiped away tears as she sat facing Debra. Debra did the same, dabbed her eyes with Kleenex. Ericka congratulated Debra on becoming a doctor. Ericka saw some photos of Debra on the walls. She had run more than a few marathons.

Ericka complimented Debra on how young, beautiful, and fit she looked.

Debra said, "Love your short hair. That is so funky."

"It's not short by choice. I had to get in the ring and have a fight with cancer."

"No. Cancer? How are you?"

"I'm in remission now. Fifth-round knockout, but it might be sneaky and demand a rematch. I'm feeling good, feeling stronger than ever. Going to have another PET scan soon."

"Stay on top of that, please?"

"I don't think I can go through this again, so the PET scan better come back clear."

"What does that mean?"

"I'm not good at suffering. I don't want to die a slow, painful, nasty death."

"Stay strong."

Ericka didn't say anything.

After a short pause, Debra asked, "Married? Children?"

"Was married for a couple of years. No children."

"Oh. I didn't know."

"No, I didn't have the baby."

Debra said, "You vanished back then. I had no idea how things turned out."

Ericka told her that she had lived in Oklahoma with relatives, but left out the parts about being forced to go, didn't bring up the obvious reason why, just said that while she was gone her parents had legally separated.

She lived in Oklahoma from the age of fourteen to the age of sixteen and when she was sent back she had lived with her mother for only a year. She had studied hard, earned a full ride, and used that room and board to get out of her mother's house. Education was the tool she used to escape, and scholarship had earned her her freedom. She worked hard during the year, and stayed with friends during the short breaks. She went to summer school each year so she would have a place to live on campus. Ericka told Debra that she hadn't spent a night in her mother's home since she had gone to university, but she did occasionally talk to her mother, which was a lie. She didn't want to say she had talked to her mother only a couple of times in several years.

It was a soft lie. A church lie, the kind told on Sunday mornings so people wouldn't think badly of you, the kind of lie meant to shorten certain types of conversations.

"Is Mrs. Stockwell okay?"

"She's Mrs. Stockwell. Let's leave that as that. You haven't seen her since . . . then?"

"She stopped coming to Faith's clinic after . . . after. She had her records sent to another OB/GYN somewhere near the Beverly Center, maybe on Robertson, from what I remember."

"My father wanted her to cut ties with this clinic. She did whatever he said."

"Yes, she did."

"He was the man of the house, even if he was never in the house."

"The controversy that came and went in forty-eight hours was too much for him."

"He was disappointed and angry, to put it mildly. He's never been a nice man."

Debra nodded, took a breath. "So, L.J. told you I'm writing a book."

"Dubois did."

"My bad. Dubois. Jesus, that boy of mine. I call him L. J. Leonard Junior."

"Morehouse grad. You've done well."

"And soon he's off to grad school. His dad would be so proud of him."

"I introduced myself, and when I said my name, he reacted like he already knew about me."

"He's been helping me organize my journey in writing."

"So, he said that my mother and I are included in your project."

Debra went to her desk and took out a manila envelope. She handed it to Ericka.

Debra said, "These are only the chapters that include you and your mother. Chapters sixteen, nineteen, twenty-two, and twenty-six. Every page is based on my decades-old journals. I have written about every day of my life. I wrote about those days you were here with your mother in detail. It was really heavy on my mind. My agent informed me that a publisher might be interested in my story. Same for a producer. Years ago, Hollywood did a pretty decent film based on my late husband's life, and now they are interested in his world as seen through my eyes, through my words. Long story short, you were there, and you made an impact on both of us."

"This scares me. I can't imagine anything nice being said about that part of my life."

Debra told Ericka, "I was contemplating changing the names before my son ran into you. For legal reasons. This is the original version, just as I typed it from my notes. It's choppy, needs to be cleaned up, but this is straight from my journal, only with a little more structure, thanks to my son."

"It's about me?"

"It's about my relationship with my son's father, was doing this for him initially, to help him see his father through my eyes, and meeting you was a powerful part of his and my relationship."

"So part of my journey is part of your journey?"

"You were part of the story, of my journey, of my life when I met the man who would be my future husband. While I was in crisis with you, while you were in crisis, he was there for me."

"Should I read these chapters pertaining to me here, or in the lobby?"

"No, I would prefer you read them in the privacy of your own home."

"I can take this with me?"

"Yes. I made that copy for you. In case you did come by."

"Understood. I have to tell you, I don't know what to make of this."

"It's as personal for me as it is for you."

"It's more than personal. It's the unseen scar on my soul."

"Are you okay, Ericka?"

"I am afraid to see my life written down on paper from your perspective."

"Ericka, I'm afraid to see *my* life written from my own perspective. I wasn't born an adult. I have done many things, and there are parts of my life I never wanted to discuss. I read the words in my journals, see my past, see the way I have felt about things over the years, see how I have changed, how I have evolved in some areas and have devolved in others, and it scares me."

"This sounds so personal."

"It is."

"Are you sure you want to share this with me?"

"I trust you."

"You haven't seen me in two decades. I've changed from who I was then."

"I used to wish you were my relative so I could have taken care of you."

"It means a lot to hear you say that. I had wished you were my big sister."

"I worried about you so many days, and dreamed about you so many nights."

"I'm fine."

"You've grown up to be a beautiful woman. You've survived cancer."

"You know how that goes. It's a battle in progress. I have to get through the next seven years to know what the real deal is. Seven is the magical number. Until then, I'm still in the ring."

"You're a survivor. You will beat this the same as you have beaten everything else. You have always been a survivor."

Ericka joked, "I survived marriage, too; let's not leave that battle out."

"I've survived being a widow."

"I am so sorry to hear that. I can't begin to imagine what you've endured."

"I will rest a little bit better knowing that you are doing okay, Ericka, even if it's only on the outside. We never really know what's going on inside a person. I've had to smile and laugh on so many days when all I wanted to do was stay in bed and cry until I couldn't cry anymore."

"I've had too many of those days. And twice as many of those nights."

"If you ever need anyone to talk to, I can put you in contact with Dr. Shelby Williams."

"A shrink?"

"A therapist."

"Will let you know if I need to talk to a therapist again. It's been a while. Maybe I should."

Debra told Ericka that she needed to get to her patients now, then instructed Ericka to take the printed pages with her. She handed Ericka two cards, one with her cell number.

Ericka assumed the second card was for her to call Dr. Shelby Williams for therapy, but it was Dr. Debra Dubois's son's cell number.

Debra said, "My son would like to get back in touch with one of your friends."

"Indigo?"

"No, your other friend, Destiny Jones. I have done my due diligence, so now he can stop asking me every day if you've contacted me regarding my memoirs. He's working my nerves."

"You know her story?"

"Of course I do. I would love to have a conversation with her too, at some point. I would love for her to come to a meeting with me and tell her story to others as a cautionary tale."

"She wouldn't be comfortable with that. A lot of people don't like her."

"Everyone didn't like Jesus, so some people aren't going to like me, you, or Destiny."

"Some people don't like you? Are you serious? What's not to like about you?"

"Sometimes it feels like I have more haters than Rihanna and Nicki Minaj combined."

Ericka laughed. "I will pass it on. Again I have to tell you that being in public is not her thing. But I'll tell her your son is looking for her so she can be a speaker. Since both of us have been called upon to be your son's emissaries, I will also do my due diligence."

"No, he's looking for her for other reasons. I would like her to be a speaker."

"Oh, okay." Ericka chuckled. "Now I understand."

"Ever since he ran into her again, all he talks about is Destiny Jones."

They were quiet for a moment. Ericka looked at the wall, saw a photo of Debra and her deceased husband. She hadn't seen that at first. Debra was younger, so beautiful.

Debra looked up at the photo and said, "It's been years, and I still miss my husband."

"I'm sorry, Debra."

"It was the best time of my life. The *best* time. It also taught me that life is short. Life is short and you have to live it. When you find love, you have to open your arms to love, you have to grab love, hold on to love, and never let it go. I had the love of my life. No regrets. No regrets."

"I want that. The love of my life. I want the love of my life and no regrets."

"Before it's all over and done, that's what we all want."

Chapter 42

After walking inside the converted warehouse with the man who wore Hugo Boss, Kwanzaa was introduced to a colorful space with musical instruments decorating the high brick walls, a dimly lit area that smelled like lavender. There was a lot of space and the temperature was cool, but much warmer than the night air in the city. A Harley motorcycle was on the other side of the room, and there was a vintage car that looked like it was being restored. In that area there were posters of classic comic book covers on the walls. Spider-Man in *Amazing Fantasy*. The Hulk versus Wolverine. A gigantic Superman when comics cost a dime. Thor. Avengers. Captain America. Her first thought was that her true dad would love this man cave. Her bonus dad would find it too avant-garde. One wall was a mural, colorful, the image of a black two-headed snake. The two-headed snake was mesmerizing, almost seductive.

As music from Pandora played in the background on a sixty-five-inch flat screen anchored to a wall, her high heels clacked toward the open area that functioned as a living room. Chairs. A sofa. Lots of space, not much furniture. He was a minimalist in words and possessions.

Without a word being spoken, Hugo Boss took her hand, pulled her to him, and she was in his arms. The kisses started softly, gently, in a measured manner. He was sweet, had chewed a lot of gum between the Club and arriving in this area. He tasted like Juicy Fruit. She loved Juicy Fruit. The tongue exchange became ravenous, turned so intense she felt like they were trying to consume each other. When the hardcore petting started, as she kissed him, she rubbed him, felt his rising erection with one hand, then *touched his firm erection with her other hand,* and her eyes opened wide with a combination of *What the bloody hell* and *Oh my God* etched on her face. He was calm. He moved her hands away from what each held, gazed into her stunned confusion. He pulled his long hair back, and nodded. Still no words. He stood up, clicked on the light, unzipped his pants, undid his belt, eased his pants to his knees. She saw he was wearing a black man-Spanx-meets-extreme-jock-strap number. He pulled down his special underwear.

And there they were.

He showed her that which she had felt as they had danced was not an illusion. Be it gift or curse, his expression said it was for her to decide. Speechless, she entered a world of unreality. She gawked, took a deep breath. It could not be real. But it was real.

He had to have been the baddest and most-talked-about boy in the locker room.

Every girl at his school would had to have had a moment alone with him, for tactile reasons, even if they didn't allow him to gain entry to one of their orifices of pleasure.

Orifices of pleasure. She thought that and smiled inside at her own corniness.

He had to be the king of ding-a-lings.

Again she smiled inside.

He was more than twice the man Marcus Brixton was.

She inhaled though her nostrils, felt a rush of heat, the kind that came from fight or flight. She was astonished, shocked, overwhelmed. She stared without blinking. She stood to leave, stood and adjusted her Forever 21 dress. He pulled the pants to his Hugo Boss back up, began moving his erect equipment from her view. She stared at the way the front of his dark pants bulged. She was poised to leave, to leave running if she had to, but something wedged itself in between the desire to flee and the desire she'd had at the Club. She was owned by something more powerful than sexual desire; she was owned by her own curiosity. What she had seen, it could not be real. She reached for his pants. She undid his zipper. She freed his equipment. She stared. She raised her left and right hands. She stroked him with her left hand, and at the same time stroked him with her right. Mesmerized. Seduced. In awe.

This was real. She paused, eyes locked on all he offered, then she managed to lift her eyes, break her trance and gaze at the wall, first at the images from comic books, then briefly at the two-headed snake staring down on her. Kwanzaa stroked him with her left hand, then with her right. He touched her face, lifted her chin, and she changed her focus, looked into his eyes, but only for a moment. Her eyes went back to his equipment, went back to inspecting all he had to offer. She shuddered. She had no idea that this was medically possible, but she had the impossible before her eyes. A rush of fear danced with curiosity and flooded her thoughts and imagination.

This was different.

It was too much.

Her thoughts moved back and forth, ticktocking in her mind.

She had a chance to experience what few would ever be able to experience in their lifetime. But she was still undecided. This was not her character.

This wicked way was not how her parents and bonus parents had raised her.

This was not going to happen.

Sex with a stranger made like this was definitely not going to happen.

Chapter 43

Kwanzaa wore only her skin. She was sweaty, bent over a steel industrial desk, getting it doggie-style. Hugo Boss stood with one foot on the floor and the other on the edge of the desk, in a very yoga-ish position. He entered her at an amazing angle, with athleticism. She held on to the edge of the desk, trembled, trapped, her feet not touching the floor, aroused, on fire, legs moving in a swimmer's motion. She swam toward the shores of orgasm, toes tight, swimming and being stroked, feeling him fill her up, then abandon her, pull all the way out, only to forcefully fill her up again. Each time she felt the difference between left and right, the alternating intrusion spectacular.

This was how he had amazed them all.

He did it over and over. Over and over. Over and over.

She wondered how many women he had had in that spot, that sexual position that seemed to have been performed many times. She was amazed, mouth open wide, spasms coming in waves. He was flexible. His repetition was as impressive as it was strong. He kept that groove until he grunted, held her hips like he was falling, became desperate, and with her sounds, with her actions, the way she moved back into him, with her body, she begged him to come. She moved into him and commanded him to orgasm, her groans echoing in the converted warehouse and begging him to get his nut. It felt good. It felt so damn good. Orgasm embraced her, wrapped its arms around her, heated her, made her want to moan and cry. It felt like she had vanished from life, had been sent to some warm, tingly place far, far away. Soon she felt Hugo Boss slowing down. She was still chock-full of penis, but he had lessened his grip, slowed his stroke, and was catching his breath, eyes opened, floating down toward sanity.

She panted, realized he hadn't pulled out.

He had finished inside her.

She had been reckless.

It pulled her from the act of madness and propelled her into a moment of fear and concern.

But in two ragged breaths she said to hell with it, what was done was done.

Besides, where he had come, that was not the route to the egg.

She waited for him to slow down and withdraw himself from being inside her. She was surprised when he did the opposite, pulled out, shifted, reinserted, and started back again, the sensation feeling like she was with a second man, one equally as powerful as the first, but with a little less length and a little more girth. But it was all him. He resumed his stroke from a slightly different angle, and that surprised her. She worked with him, determined to not embarrass herself and let this man outperform her. *Damn* his uniqueness. But, *damn*, his uniqueness. First-time sex was always about performance. She knocked things from the metal desk, and as notepads, bottled water, remote controls, pens, coasters, and books crashed to the wooden floor, she extended her arms and pushed against the brick wall, got her wind, inhaled, exhaled, took it all, grinded against him until he had to put his foot down to restore his balance. That small victory made her grind harder. She growled and became aggressive, followed his erection wherever it went. He couldn't handle her groove. He slowed down, picked her up by her waist, and soon they were on the bed, him between her legs, one of her ankles on his neck, almost in a cheerleader's split. He had her where she couldn't challenge him with her moves. It was fine by her. Let him do all the work. Let her rejoice in this miracle of a man. She took deep drowning breaths, on the way to coming again, coming as good as she had while she was bent over the desk, every part of her alive and once again shaking. He grew inside her, grew and gave her madness until she felt him come. The spurt hit her insides and she shook. It felt like a river had been released, the pressure amazing, and with that she came again. As flush moved across her breasts, as sweat sculpted her tricolored hair into some original and obscenely tousled mess, she shifted her hips and felt him fill her up with his orgasm. Her adrenaline was high and what should have been pain was sheer pleasure. She set free her high-pitched sounds, put her nails in his flesh as he worked to get his sin out of his soul, growling his manly growl, a growl she could hardly hear because she was in her own special place. Forever passed before he slowed down, before her hips stopped dancing, before his urgency dwindled, before her jerky dance calmed. A moment later it was them panting and wiping sweat from each other's faces, staring into each other's eyes.

Strangers.

Kwanzaa had felt his energy gush inside her. She felt the alcohol in her bloodstream. She felt uneasy. She felt regret.

Hugo Boss rubbed the curves of her body, felt up her ass, was massaging her. She was going to move his hand away, but didn't. It felt good. Having a man touch her felt wonderful. She didn't like that it felt that damn good. That should have been someone else's hand on her flesh.

Attorney Marcus Brixton should have called by now.

No matter what had happened, she would've taken him back for one night.

A thirsty woman would always return to a familiar well.

But she was here, a stranger in a strange place with a unique man, his strange hands on her as if he were trying to learn the topography of her flesh and curves. He stopped massaging her. She sighed. She was glad she was at his place. It would be easier to leave abruptly, much easier than using him like that, then being rude, and telling a guy he couldn't stay the night at her crib, telling him he had to wash his dick in some other bathroom, making sure he left before the Mexican neighbors' roosters crowed or the first morning flights landed at LAX.

They lay there, not talking, but breathing, recovering, and absorbing the moment. She wanted to ask him to turn the ceiling fan on, or to open a window and let in some desert chill, but she didn't. She was in the middle of the unsure feeling a woman had when she'd been with somebody new, but someone old was still percolating in her system.

Eyes closed, a stranger's hand caressing her breasts, her nipples erect, Kwanzaa felt like she was resting in the middle of nowhere. She thought about her ex. Wondered where he was, wondered if they were both having meaningless sex at the same moment, wondered if the bitch he was with was the one who had given him the STD, wondered if the bitch wore Peruvian hair or wore it natural, wondered if she was as attractive as the stranger whose come drained from inside her to red sheets.

Her phone rang, Destiny's text tone, but Kwanzaa didn't pick up the phone. She couldn't tell if she was awake or dreaming. She felt like she had entered another world, one where dreams and fantasies came true. Where she was, everything felt intense: sight, touch, taste, smell, all she heard.

She throbbed in the spaces he had filled.

She was awake.

The inside of her mouth tasted sweeter than the icing on chocolate cake.

The diphallic man eased from the bed and went to the bathroom.

Kwanzaa positioned herself so she could have a clear view of his genitalia when he returned. She had been with twins, fraternal twins. She wondered if this travesty could be considered a ménage à trois between two people. He came back and gave her a towel. She went to the bathroom, a stark white bathroom that had no signs of a woman's hair on the floor. She ran hot water on the towel, used Dial soap. She could see the bed from the bathroom, could see the stranger resting on his back, stared a moment, still astonished. But soon she closed the door, still intrigued, still in awe, but not comfortable cleaning herself in front of him.

She was ready to put on her LBD and FMPs and go and find her trio of Blackbirds. No one would believe what she had experienced. She didn't believe it. Eight women had been waiting on him to come home. Now she understood why. This uniqueness could become an addiction for women who had a weaker resolve. Kwanzaa joined him once more, sat on the edge of the bed. She hand-combed her tousled mane, ready to execute a wordless exit. He put his hand on her shoulder. She gazed back at him. He pulled her back toward the bed and she lay on her back, let him kiss her and crawl between her thighs. Seconds later, with no discussion, Hugo Boss was inside her once more, deep in her pussy, being the boss of her, stroking, working part of his equipment toward firmness, turning her this way and that way, making her growl and grab sheets. He had her so damn wet. Again she was taken from behind. Her entire body trembled and shook with acute orgasm.

Chapter 44

Not long before midnight, nervous, Ericka Stockwell whipped her car from Stocker to Don Lorenzo. She whizzed past Terra Nova Town-homes where she had lived when she was a preacher's wife. She remembered her husband, the days when she was a first lady, her era of being regretfully married. Talking to Debra about her life over the last two decades had resonated, had caused her to hold up the metaphorical mirror and reevaluate her life all day long. She was over thirty and divorced. Hadn't seen that coming. It was still a shock to her system. She never imaged that would be the top line of her relationship résumé. But then again she hadn't seen cancer coming either. Still, the divorce and being childless were on her mind. She'd always thought that she and her ex would have a baby there, eventually lease out their townhome, then find a property on the other side of Stocker in View Park. What a fool believes.

On the half-mile-long, two-lane avenue, she curved to the left and arrived at the next set of properties in Baldwin Hills Estates, where Destiny's father had his townhome.

Each time she came this way she experienced déjà vu, felt nostalgic and foolish.

The memories of living in Baldwin Hills made her twist her lips and sigh. Hers had been a three-bedroom, three-bath in the 4600-something section of Don Lorenzo that had cost over $350,000. It was the newest development in Baldwin Hills. Mr. Jones was in the neighboring community in the 4650-something block of Don Lorenzo, the tan-colored townhomes built in the 1980s. He had scored a townhome—that now went for at least $445,000—at a fire sale price. The value of her property was upside-down when she divorced, so there had been nothing to argue over, not financially. She let the ex have the mortgage, removed her name from the debt, and focused on getting her credit score back to a respectable number and her health back on track. The downturn in the economy had destroyed some families, but others had taken advantage of the miserable moment in time and found unbelievable deals. At least she got to keep the cherry-red SLK, the two-door roadster. It was a depreciating asset, but at least she didn't leave the marriage childless *and* empty-handed. And maybe having no kids was all for the best. If she had requested child support, the man of God she had married would have snapped and the next thing you know there would be a choir singing "Ave Maria" at a funeral.

That from a man who was a minister of a congregation that saw him as God.

Ericka pulled over and slowed to a stop in front of Parkview Estates.

She turned Beyoncé off, put the top up, turned the heater off, made sure her windows were all the way up, and turned her wheels facing the curb. She checked her face in the mirror. She chewed spearmint gum for one minute, long enough for the flavor to sweeten her breath and saturate her tongue. Chewing gum also improved a person's mood, while decreasing anxiety and stress. Going to see Destiny Jones's dad this late at night had left Ericka anxious and stressed.

She put on lip gloss before she opened another button on her purple blouse.

Ericka nodded at her cleavage, then looked at her gray skirt, fretted about panty lines, then remembered she didn't have any on, but she had a thong inside her purse.

She tried to decide if she should put on high heels. Too obvious. She put on a pair of flats. Changed her mind. It was a Friday night. Friday night was made for heels. She put the five-inchers on, new shoes from ShoeDazzle. Sexy. Colorful. Mr. Jones probably wouldn't notice. And if he did, she would say it was Kwanzaa's birthday and they were going to hang out.

She looked in her rearview, checked Don Lorenzo for people and traffic, looked for the coyotes that came out at night, then with the Kaiser bag in one hand and a plastic bag with food sealed in Tupperware in the other, she hurried through broken light into shadows toward the gate. She walked with her wedding-ring finger stuck through her sorority key chain that held her house key, car keys, and two vials of pepper spray. Seconds later she headed up the concrete stairs and rang Mr. Jones's unit. Anxiety swelled. The buzzer sounded to open the gate.

She went up a dozen more concrete stairs, so nervous she almost stumbled.

The units faced each other, so anyone who was awake would see her. Cute little dogs barked. She walked by three units on her left, same number on her right.

Mr. Jones was there. She wasn't ready to see him yet, wanted a few more seconds. Destiny's father waited with the door open, the light from inside his home illuminating the back of his head. Mr. Jones was smoking, the tip of his rolled-up cigarette lighting up as he inhaled.

He blew smoke. "Miss Stockwell, is that you?"

"Good evening to you too, Mr. Jones. Nice to see you again."

Mr. Jones put out his smoke, its scent medicinal, and that triggered sensual recollections.

Explicit memories flashed before her eyes and she felt desire come alive as tingles.

She said, "You don't have to stop on my account."

"I was about done for now."

"You okay?"

"Skin was feeling a little irritated. That would give me trouble sleeping."

"Mr. Jones, you know if you eat a mango before smoking weed, it heightens the effect."

"Really? Will grab a few mangoes from Superior supermarket tomorrow."

"Just an FYI from an expert."

"You've learned a few tricks along the way."

"I swore by mangoes and several brands of Kush when I was going through chemo."

"Where is Destiny?"

"I guess she's at work. She sent a text for one of us to drop the medicine by ASAP."

"You look nice."

"Thank you. You look handsome as usual."

"Kwanzaa's official birthday moment is in a few hours. After two in the morning."

"You remembered?"

"Destiny programmed my phone with the alerts, and an automatic text."

"Of course."

"You came by yourself?"

"Coming by yourself is called masturbation, Mr. Jones."

"When the other Blackbirds aren't around, you're full of surprises, Miss Stockwell."

"So are you, when it's just me and you."

"You caught me red-handed."

"You're smoking like you just don't care."

"I just lit this about a minute ago. Only took six or seven puffs. I felt pretty good today, then was a little irritated."

"You're up late."

"Just made it back home."

"Hot date?"

"I go to the Nuart in Santa Monica for late showings."

"Really?"

"They showed *Raiders of the Lost Ark* tonight. I go almost every Friday night. Keeps me from sitting in the house with nothing on my mind but cancer. I saw *Dracula*, the one by Coppola, last week. I think I saw *Showgirls* the week before that, or might've been *Clue*."

"You like movies?"

"Movies and television. I watch everything. I've become a movie and television buff."

"You always impressed me as being so serious."

"A documentary about the Black Panther Party is coming to the Nuart, too."

"Really? We never really hear anything about them."

"The government was terrified of the Black Panther Party, ran a smear campaign. They sent in Uncle Toms and set them up to be assassinated. Get the public to hate them, so when you murder them the public will cheer. They applaud white militant groups with guns, but when the Black Panthers had guns, and were law-abiding with those guns, they were ready to change the laws. Anytime we get close to having a black messiah, anytime we've had anyone about to get us to the next level, they have been either discredited or assassinated. They did it to Marcus Garvey, Malcolm X, and to the civil rights movement. Keep the minorities from organizing and having true power. It's important because now we're seeing history repeat. The government and media are spreading propaganda and trying to use the same tactics to discredit the Black Lives Matter movement, only they can't control Black Twitter."

"I should go see the documentary so I can see the connection on that level."

"You should. I'm going to go with Vince."

"Kwanzaa's dad? You're going with Mr. Browne?"

"Yeah, we're going to check it out. It's going to play for three or four days."

She paused. For a moment she had thought he was asking her out on a date.

For a moment she had felt like a girl being asked to the prom by her secret crush.

Now she realized he wasn't asking her out, that he was only making conversation.

Mr. Jones said, "I wonder what it would be like if for every crime committed in the United States, if for every arrest, if for every shooting, if for every bombing, I wonder what it would be like if they never stated race, but only stated the religion of the so-called offender."

"That would be interesting. 'Christian shoots Christian at nine on CBS. Christian mom drowns Christian children. Another Christian enters schools and kills more Christians.'"

"Nah, they will never do that."

"It would tell a lot more than the hue of the epidermis."

"It would be different."

"Would love to hear those news reports on Fox News."

"Where red Christians tell lies about blue Christians."

They laughed. She loved his laugh. It was the sweetest sound she knew. Laughter dwindled as awkwardness rose.

He took the heaviest bag, reached for the other, but she said she could carry it. He nodded, then stepped aside and invited her in. Ericka moved by him, her body touching his, and she moved on, let him follow her quick sashay toward the living room. She realized that he had waited at the door to get the package. He hadn't meant to invite her inside, but she hadn't walked away. She didn't come this far to hand him the bags, then return home. Her thoughts raced as her heart palpitated. Her palms were damp.

Mr. Jones turned on the lights in the living room, made the space unromantic. In the living area there were two dozen framed photos of Destiny, prints of her when she was in diapers and reaching up toward the camera, of Mr. Jones holding her on his hip when she was about two. There were pictures of Destiny on her first bicycle, of her swimming in a pool, of her in school uniforms, of her over the years sitting in different Santa Clauses' laps at Fox Hills Mall. All were pictures of Destiny before the *incident*. It was as if Mr. Jones was trying to control time.

There were no pictures of Destiny's mother. That made Ericka feel easier, but not totally comfortable. She knew that Destiny had wanted her mother and father back together.

Sometimes she sensed that Destiny still hoped that would happen.

Her parents' breakup had scarred her. It had damaged her ideal view of the world. It had been a watershed moment.

Ericka looked at Mr. Jones. He wore slim Levi's jeans, a Dan L. Steel Engineering tee, no shoes. Even as he battled cancer, he looked better than most men half his age. He looked fit. He caught her staring. Ericka smiled at him, a smile that held a memory, and then she looked away.

He led the way and she followed him into denial.

She said, "Look at how much you love your daughter."

"My pride and joy. Best mistake I ever made."

They laughed.

Ericka walked back and forth, smiled as they started a conversation about nothing important, only otiose questions about traffic, the drive over, nothing serious. Her hands were twisting, folding and unfolding the top of the Kaiser bag in her hands. Last time she had dropped off something on Destiny's behalf, Mr. Jones had given Ericka a quick tour. It was a trilevel townhome, a home that had been all but destroyed by the previous owners who were enraged due to foreclosure and had stolen every appliance and fixture, then left profanity spray-painted on every wall. With the work Mr. Jones had done with his own hands, patiently, over the last five years, it looked sparkling and new. He was a true handyman, a degreed blue-collar man, and while Destiny was away at Hoosegow, to maintain his sanity, this was how he had stayed busy.

This was much nicer than the townhome Ericka had lived in when she was married.

Watching a man keep a spotless home and clean up after himself, that was sexy.

"How's Mrs. Stockwell?"

"She's fine, Mr. Jones."

He nodded. "Tell Mrs. Stockwell I said hi when you see her again."

She almost said that would be on the twelfth of never, but sighed and replied, "Sure."

Ericka took out her phone, did that to see where Kwanzaa had checked in on Yelp. The first check-in had been on Sunset, then the second had been near downtown. She wasn't home.

Ericka said, "I think the birthday girl is club hopping."

"Going to meet her?"

"Was thinking about it, but I walk in those house music spots, and everybody is barely twenty, so I look like I'm the older loser chick trying to get her cougar on. You ever club hopped?"

"We used to hit four clubs a night back in the day."

"You partied like that on a Friday night?"

"Friday and Saturday, from Orange County to Hollywood, then hung out at Venice Beach all day on Sunday with the chain saw jugglers.

Michael Colyar would be there telling jokes on the boardwalk. Used to take my gear and roller-skate almost all day on Sundays. I met Destiny's mom on Venice Beach. Saw her in the crowd. Thought she was the prettiest woman ever made."

"Who is Michael Colyar?"

"Shit. I am officially old."

"You met Destiny's mother on the beach?"

"Carmen was wearing a pink-and-blue bikini, had her skates on, and was spinning and dancing to 'Atomic Dog' with the crowd. Had to be a hundred people in that crew. I skated my way over next to her, and we got our bounce on. That used to be the thing to do every weekend."

"Love at first sight?"

"More or less."

"What does that mean? More or less?"

"Whenever a man looks at a beautiful woman, it feels like love at first sight."

"But is it? Was it?"

"Sometimes it is."

"Was it with Destiny's mother?"

"I married her."

"So I guess it was."

"I guess so."

Ericka smiled to hide her envy. She felt foolish.

He asked, "Would you like something to drink, Miss Stockwell?"

She presumed that was his way of measuring how long she was staying. She fixed her mouth to say that wouldn't be necessary, her body in the position of a runner, prepared to leave now, to take her anxiety and go, but then she looked at the sofa. When she gazed at the sofa a fiery tingle raced up her spine, and instead she exhaled slowly and answered, "Water will be fine."

Chapter 45

Ericka made herself comfortable on the sofa. To ease her nerves, she browsed fliers on the coffee table. All were for films at the Nuart. There was a card showing all the acts coming to the LA County Fair. Patti LaBelle. Chaka Khan. Ericka nodded. These were Mr. Jones's interests. She felt like she was intruding, learning more about him by being invasive, so she stopped browsing, then put the stack of fliers back the way she had found them.

There was also an obituary on the table.

Ericka asked, "Who passed?"

"Guy I grew up with. Prostate cancer. He wasn't even fifty."

"Sorry to hear. How long was he sick?"

"Ten years of suffering. He went from being able to lift a house to barely being able to lift himself out of bed. Changed his quality of life. Could barely recognize him at the end."

"Bet that was hard on his family."

"It is. Everything is redirected and you take them on that journey with you."

"Those who are willing to travel with you. A lot of people have to do it alone."

"No one should go that journey alone."

Ericka shifted, felt her own fear rise and subside. "I'm sorry for your loss."

"At least he got to see his grandchild be born. He saw his daughter graduate from Princeton, walked her down the aisle, and saw his first grandchild. He had a strong mind and made himself last that long. And three days after his grandson arrived, he let go and went home."

Mr. Jones opened two bottles of Aquafina. Room temperature.

He sat down a person's space away from her, placed bottled water in front of her.

She held the Kaiser bag in her lap, nervously bending the edges of the white-and-blue bag.

She yielded a nervous smile.

Mr. Jones asked, "What was in the other care package?"

"Food to make sure you stay healthy."

"Destiny cooked?"

"I cooked earlier. They've been gone most of the day. Indigo was supposed to come back home after she worked out, but she texted that she was getting chicken soup down in Venice."

"Then I will eat it when the munchies kick in. What did you make?"

Ericka laughed. "Salmon, mixed vegetables, and wild rice."

"My favorite meal."

"If you heat it in the microwave, sit a cup of water in there too so it won't dry out."

"Thanks, Miss Stockwell."

"Being bald works for you. Bald is sexy on a black man."

He rubbed his head, grinned, kept his thoughts to himself.

She motioned at the ashtray and the roaches. "What are you smoking this time?"

"Pineapple Express."

"Never tried that one. I prefer White Berry, Tsunami Crush, or Maui Wowie."

"I have more. Want to partake and see if this pleases your palate?"

"If I smoked, then I would have to stay the night."

"I have a guest room."

"Mr. Jones, you don't want me getting high, not around you."

"Because?"

"I lose control."

"We both do."

"Indeed we do."

"We smoke and lose control."

"I start to tell all of my secrets. I think I talked your head off when we did."

He said, "On this sofa."

"Right here. On this sofa. I guess you could say I showed you my secrets."

"Yeah. I showed you mine as well."

"Things got out of hand, Mr. Jones."

"Should we talk about that?"

"Should we?"

He said, "Or just keep pretending it never happened?"

"I don't know. You tell me, should we act like we didn't do anything?"

"I've been scared to be alone with you. Didn't know what to say."

"Same here. I had no idea how you felt about what had happened."

"But we are alone again."

"Yes, we are."

"On the same sofa."

"Yes. Back at the scene of the crime."

Chapter 46

Mr. Jones paused. "Sorry about that. All I remember is that we were partaking of the medicinal, talking politics, laughing, being serious. Puffing, passing. Puffing, passing."

"Puffing and passing became puffing and kissing."

"Yeah. Kissing. Not sure how we arrived at kissing."

"We were talking about the state of the black man and woman in America. Talked about how we lost our African richness and became second-class. We watched part of a video on YouTube. *Truth of How Slavery Started the Black Slave Trade and Racism.*"

"We do get deep when we smoke and talk."

"You get deep when you get deep, and I'm not talking about words."

"How did we get from point A to point B? How did we start kissing?"

"I started it. You said you had strained a muscle. I rubbed your shoulders, gave you a massage, and started it."

"I had the medicinal in my blood and when you massaged me, I made a bad choice."

"It was my choice. Never should have gotten high with somebody I had a crush on."

He grinned. "I couldn't believe it when you told me that."

"I was buzzed. Couldn't keep it in anymore. I've always had strong feelings for you, Mr. Jones. I had them as a girl, but they are more mature now, and I have expressed them to you as a woman."

He said, "Never saw you that way."

"What way?"

"In that way."

"What, like a woman?"

"Miss Stockwell, I remember when you were learning how to drive."

"You watched me grow up."

"You didn't feel weird about that?"

She chuckled. "First thing that weirded me out was you smoking with me."

"Was surprised you smoked. It weirded me out too."

"Cancer made us do it."

"Was still surprised. That wasn't the image I had of you."

"You saw me as being innocent."

"Still do see you as a church girl. In my mind you're still . . . still . . ."

"A virgin?"

"I know. Still are a few things I can't imagine you doing."

"Even after you've done those things with me."

"Seems surreal. And illegal."

"I was smoking at fifteen. When I was sent to Oklahoma, cousins back there introduced me to weed. That's all they do back there. I never did much. School. Church. Weed. Was trying to fit in and be grown."

"Trying to be grown before she was grown was Destiny's issue."

"It's every girl's issue, Mr. Jones. We're made that way, to seek out our independence, to seek acceptance. We want a place we can be ourselves and be loved for being who we are."

He said, "And you had a thing for me when you used to babysit Destiny."

"You weren't supposed to know."

"You were so quiet and studious. You were a younger version of your mother."

"Used to wish you'd kiss me when you dropped me off at home afterward."

"Your telling me that you had feelings for me threw me for a loop."

"Why?"

"You were so proper. Thought you saw me as an adult, maybe an older guy, if not an old guy, or even worse, with your religious upbringing, as some sort of heretic."

"I was so scared to tell you that I had so many intense dreams about you."

"Then straddling me the way you did so you could blow smoke up my nose."

"I straddled you to blow you a shotgun. Made you feel this heat on you."

"And after you did, you inhaled, then put your tongue in my mouth while you exhaled."

"You weren't ready for that. Weed made me bold. Never would have done that sober."

"The way you kissed me changed everything. You kissed me like you were full woman. It wasn't clumsy. It surprised me. You wouldn't let me pull away from you. You made me give in."

She said, "I guess I did. Once I got started, it was hard to turn it off."

"You're not a little girl anymore."

"I'm a grown woman now, Mr. Jones. We're two consenting adults."

"This old man got caught up in the moment and got carried away."

"You're not an old man, so please, if you're trying to turn me off, it's not working."

"Kicking fifty in the ass with steel-toe boots."

"You're in better shape than my husband was, and he was thirty-six."

"I was the older person. I really should apologize for allowing that to happen."

"Only if you didn't enjoy it."

"I did."

"I did too."

"That's the problem."

"Sure is."

The conversation paused, but the eye contact continued.

Mr. Jones asked, "You good? How's your health, Ericka?"

She made herself smile. "Last scan came back looking clean. Blood work looks good. Liver good."

"The process, the pain, it was too much for your husband."

"Ex-husband."

"He should've stuck by you."

"He should've. But his toy was broken, so he went and found a new toy."

"I heard he remarried."

"There is a new first lady in his life. May God bless both of them."

"That sounded petty."

"I need to work on my delivery. Still hard to sound sincere when I'm not."

Mr. Jones shook his head. "You married when you were twenty-four."

"Met him on a flight back from Argentina. We were on the same flight. Sat next to each other. He had been there doing missionary work. Wish you had stopped me from dating him."

He said, "Wish you had stopped me from marrying Carmen."

"Then Destiny wouldn't be born *and* you would've been locked up as a pedophile."

He laughed. "If only I had been a vampire that sparkles in the sun."

She laughed. "No vampires. But I would have waited for you to be released."

She was glad he found her to be humorous, glad he didn't say what she was thinking, that if Destiny hadn't been born, it would have saved her from all she had gone through.

She would rather a child not be born than to have to suffer some heinous things.

He said, "Timing is everything."

"You had to wait for this flower to grow before you considered plucking it."

"I think you did the plucking."

"I did the choosing, but when you had the space and opportunity, you did the plucking."

"That's your story?"

"And I'm sticking to it. It's a woman's right to blame a man for her bad choices."

He smiled. "You're a beautiful woman, Ericka Stockwell. A beautiful young woman."

"Got a few gray hairs now. Somewhere in this short fuzz is a lot of gray hair."

"At least you have hair."

"Gray hairs, fighting cancer, and divorced."

"We have the same résumé."

"I don't know about you, but I never saw this tsunami of bad times coming."

"No one does. When we're kids on swings, or boys chasing girls, no one predicts this."

Ericka squeezed the tingle in her thighs, felt her nipples rise, her breasts swell.

Mr. Jones sighed, squirmed where he sat, seemed to swallow his thoughts.

Ericka took a deep breath, twisting the bag in her lap, making it rustle, remembering how Mr. Jones had been a storm on this sofa.

Ericka sat on the spot where it had happened, on the memory.

The evidence of their transgression had been cleaned; not a spot remained.

As if Mr. Jones was feeling what she was feeling, remembering, he said, "This sofa."

"Like you said, since that evening, we've acted like it never happened."

"But it did happen."

"No one knows."

"The sofa knows."

"Yeah, it does. We almost broke the damn thing."

"I have stared at this sofa every day."

"Each time I look at Destiny, I feel a little strange now."

"Our secret burns in my chest at times, but I keep the words from escaping."

"Destiny is my friend."

Mr. Jones said, "You were there for her when shit was real bad."

"Because I love her. When I heard about that, I ran to find where she was."

He asked, "Should we tell Destiny at some point? Should I ask her forgiveness?"

"I'm not sure about that. It would change her image of her dad."

"And of you. It would change your friendship, or end your friendship."

She toyed with the bag. "Yeah. Could end our friendship. I wouldn't
like it if one of the Blackbirds slept with my father. That is gross in my
mind, so I know this will be gross in her mind. She's seen me naked and
she came from you. Indigo and Kwanzaa would be furious too."

"She's seen you naked?"

"Girls, we undress and get dressed in front of each other, walk around
topless, no biggie."

"I didn't see you naked."

"We didn't quite get to the part where clothes come all the way off."

"Too bad."

"Why did you say that? You want to see me naked?"

"That wasn't a request."

"I know."

"Was trying to be funny."

"I know. We sort of unzipped zippers and moved the panties to the
side and did it."

He paused. "I feel like I am taking advantage of you and deceiving
my daughter."

Ericka asked, "Do you tell Destiny everyone you sleep with?"

"Of course not."

"Then you're not doing anything out of the ordinary."

"Do you tell her your love life?"

"We're besties. We talk about men."

He said, "Our relationship is different. She's my daughter, not my
homie."

"She knew about the girl on the motorcycle. Billie."

He paused. "I can't tell Destiny about us, about this thing we did on
the sofa."

"We had sex on the sofa. You put your penis inside me. No need to
sugarcoat."

"I can't tell her. I wouldn't be able to let those words come out of my
mouth."

"It was just that one night."

"Just one night, but several times that same night."

"It was unexpected and intense."

"Very memorable."

"At least you were able to get the milky stains out of the sofa."

"We marked our territory very well. Used a lot of Febreze too."

"I don't want to pretend it didn't happen, Mr. Jones."

"I get it, Ericka. You had cancer. Cancer has a way of making the most arrogant become humble. You fought it and you won. A lot of people give up, but you fought it and won."

"I'm in remission. I've won the battle, but the war might not be over."

Mr. Jones said, "I have cancer now. You understand how it is. It's physical, but it's also mental. Does something to your mind just knowing your body is turning against you."

"You feel an invisible clock over your head."

"And you're doing your best to find a way to stop the countdown."

Ericka said, "People find out you're sick and some come closer, but many run away."

"Some people aren't built to handle being around sick people."

"Some are just self-centered."

"Some don't know what to say to a person whom they see as death personified."

"They look at the sick and don't want to see themselves, so they turn away as if to avoid some curse, as if staring at us too long will assure they will suffer the same fate we suffer."

"You know what that's like. You feel empathy. You went through it before I did. I think it would have been different if you hadn't already been tested. Your sex was an act of compassion."

"Is that what it felt like? Sympathy?"

"I assumed that you just got caught up in your emotions, and maybe you were giving a man who could end up dying from this shit, if it gets out of control, a dying wish."

"Mr. Jones, this pussy is not part of the Make-a-Wish Foundation."

He laughed.

She said, "I understand the journey, and how even though people support you, you're still doing this on your own, how no one can understand your misery, but it was not empathy. I would have slept with you if I never had been sick. There. Now you know. It was not an empathy fuck."

"What was it?"

"This was here before I was sick, before I knew you were ill. It was there when I was getting married, and if you had asked me to not get married, I would have listened. I have fantasized about you half of my life, and you never knew I was so hooked on you. And now I've become friends with your daughter. It's scary, but my feelings for you have always been strong."

She fell silent. She had said too much, and this time there had been no weed to blame.

There was silence. Silence was rejection.

He asked, "You okay?"

"Feeling foolish for being here. Thinking about cancer. My life had been a series of unfortunate events. Seems like God has punished me for being a foolish teenager."

"It wasn't God."

"What was it?"

"Not God."

"The other guy?"

"Wasn't my God. I'm divorced and my daughter . . . to have the child I was supposed to protect . . . be raped . . . videotaped . . . taken away from us . . . be imprisoned because she did to the rapists half of what I would've done to them if I had known . . . and now cancer for me . . . and I still worry about her fitting in the world . . . meeting the right boy . . . knowing people hate her . . . this isn't the work of my God."

Again silence.

He said, "You're one of her best friends, Miss Stockwell."

"I am, Mr. Jones."

"Is she doing okay?"

"She's overdoing it, if you ask me. Between school and working here, there, and everywhere, it's like she wants to keep busy so she doesn't have to think. She's avoiding life not by hiding in a room in the dark, but by keeping her brain occupied every moment."

"Any boys?"

"Boys? You know your baby is an adult, right?"

"I know."

"I'm teasing you, Mr. Jones."

He nodded. "She never mentions any boys, or men. Funny, when she was young I wanted to keep her away from men. Now I'm concerned because she doesn't have anyone in her life. She never talks about dating. Girls her age, that's all they talk about. Boys, boys, boys."

"She's dated a couple of guys."

"Good."

"It didn't last."

"At least she's trying. That's good."

"She's tried to be Destiny Jones with them, and they can't handle her strength."

"I want her to be okay, but I have no idea what to do. She didn't make it to Yale or Harvard like we had hoped, but she's at a great university. As long as she's at USC, she can do good in life, no matter what has happened to her. Shit like that happens and some women never recover. I didn't want my daughter to end up becoming a stripper and doing that to get by. That's not what she's doing at night, is it?"

"Of course not, Mr. Jones. Why would you even think that?"

"The hair. The way she dyed it. She always has money in cash."

Ericka laughed. "She's not a stripper."

"Well, nowadays it seems to be an honorable occupation."

"Based on music, one would think. But why would that even cross your mind?"

"I went to a strip club with some friends not long ago. Saw another one of my friend's daughters was working there. She made men create thunderstorms by throwing up wrinkled dollar bills and watching gravity pull them all back to a nasty floor. No matter how high a woman was from her performance, from the adulation, she still had to be on the ground, on the level of the lowest of the low, to collect her offering, as if she were a homeless or discarded veteran picking up money thrown on the ground. No dignity lives on the ground. When the dance was done, strippers bent over or got down on their haunches and picked up fallen dollars the way slaves picked cotton. The same way a slave smiled at a master, the stripper gave a bogus and insincere grin to her customers, her masters of the moment."

"Were you at a strip club or a spoken-word event? You're spitting poetry."

"It was a strip club. I was trying to not sound so damn ghetto about it."

"No need to try and impress me with your intellect."

"I know. But I do. I do try and impress you."

"Do you? You have two degrees and want to impress me?"

"You make me nervous. You make me aware of myself. So, now you know."

"Destiny would never do that, Mr. Jones. She'd never swing from a pole."

"No man thinks his daughter would do that, but the club is filled with daughters."

"Destiny is too cerebral to be a stripper. I know that there are strippers who have degrees, but your child is a rare breed. She'd be a Mensa stripper and if you wanted her to get naked, you'd have to answer Mensa-level questions. She would make them take a twenty-minute IQ test, and they would have to not miss a question for her to take off a sock."

Mr. Jones laughed. "Thanks. That will make me sleep a little better."

"You saw a friend's daughter, someone you knew as a little girl?"

"And there she was. She moved her moneymaker and men slapped it with worn and dingy dollar bills. Just made me wonder what my daughter was doing, that's all. A lot of those girls come from bad homes, or have had bad things happen to them in life. A lot of men see those girls as low-hanging fruit."

"It left you feeling something."

"A man sees the world differently when he has a daughter."

"When he loves his daughter. Only when he loves his daughter."

"Every man should love his daughter."

"You see the world the way it's always been, Mr. Jones. I'm a teacher. I see the scientists, and poets, and writers in the making, but I also see the next con, the molester, the next thief, the next stripper, and the girl who behaves as if she will grow up to be the next prostitute."

"Not my daughter. I just sat there wondering how I would've felt if I had walked in and found her working there to get enough money to pay her way through USC."

Silence returned and brought her friend, awkwardness.

Again crumpling the edges of the bag, the noise again causing Mr. Jones to look at her hands, Ericka said, "Well, here's the medicine Destiny asked me to bring you."

"It's prednisone."

"Be careful with the stuff you buy across the border. It's not regulated."

"Only take it when I have to, when it's impossible to be comfortable or to sleep."

"The side effects. The least being that I broke out and had skin infections, so I lived on antibiotics, which my stomach didn't like, so then I had to take something for that. I was taking layers of medication. Taking medicines to fight off the side effects of medicines. And my mood was never even. One day I would be sweet, the next I was calling people and cursing them out."

"We have to poison ourselves with chemicals and radiation to get cured of the poisoned food, the food with steroids and additives and preservatives that have already poisoned us all."

"The crap we take to cure cancer can cause cancer, just like the food they sell us."

"Vicious cycle. My feet and hands might swell in a few weeks. Skin will darken."

Ericka said, "Well, if you need me to drive you to your appointments, or if you're not comfortable with me taking you, let me or one of the other Blackbirds know."

"Thanks, Ericka. I will ask you."

"You can ask Indigo or Kwanzaa. Both have cars."

"I prefer your company. You would understand if my mood went crazy. Prednisone, too much of that shit and I might curse people out too."

"Anytime, day or night, if you need me, I'll come right over and let you curse me out. Where I grew up, I'm used to being cursed out."

He chuckled. "Thanks."

"And if you want, I can take some of your Kush and ask Indigo to make you some brownies so your house won't smell like you're living with Snoop Dogg and Willie Nelson."

"That would be nice. I could cure the munchies as I ate the medicine."

"Don't eat that much. You'll end up in the emergency room and they'll trace it back to me. *Sixth-grade teacher makes weed brownies on weekends, details at eleven.*"

Again they laughed.

She said, "I guess I should get back home and not overstay my welcome. I cooked Kwanzaa's dinner for the crew."

She stood to leave, trying to shake off the memory of a nirvana gone by, trying to ignore the euphoria a person feels when falling in love. It was time to let go and move on with the rest of her life. She extended the white Kaiser Permanente bag out to him. He reached and took part of the bag, gripped the edges. She didn't let her end of the bag go, hadn't intended to hold on, but couldn't free herself. She stared at Mr. Jones, the bag suspended between both of them.

"I miss you, Mr. Jones. Did you miss me at all?"

"I've been thinking about you, too."

He tugged the bag like he was trying to pull her to him.

He felt something. Now that scared her.

She resisted. "Jesus, we can't do that again."

"You're right."

"No more sofa."

"No more sofa."

"I think I just wanted to know that it meant something to you."

"It did."

"Did it?"

"It meant a lot."

"It meant a lot to me."

"You mean a lot to me."

"You mean a lot to me too."

Ericka exhaled, jittery. Being sexually aroused fired up the brain and caused the body to stay awake longer during the night. It was a good thing. She needed to stay awake.

She stepped away, began undressing.

He asked, "What are you doing, Ericka?"

She stood before him, her clothing pooled at her feet.

"You sure you want to pass this up? This is me naked, Mr. Jones. This is what you're afraid of. I'm a grown woman. This is not the body of a *child*. I am tall, slim where it matters, and thick where it counts most. You sure you want to let me walk out of that door right now? Do you?"

"Why are you doing this to me?"

"Because you do this to me."

Chapter 47

Hakeem knew I was Destiny Jones.

He knew.

Doing twenty over the posted limit, I sped past Indian Wood and came up to Raintree Condominium-Apartments. The walled, gated, guarded community where the mechanical engineer I had fallen for lived was built on the land where they had filmed *Gone with the Wind*.

I hesitated, checked my anxiety level before I made a left onto the property.

After I downshifted and cruised my motorcycle over the speed bump, I nervously jammed my key card into the slot and the gate eased up. It felt strange using the passkey.

I didn't want to come here.

Didn't want to be here.

Wanted to be able to hide from this and keep moving.

But lust was physiological, and I was beyond that, and into the philosophical aspects of being in love. This was not about sex. My soul ached like I'd never sleep again.

I was angry with myself for not telling him before he found out on his own. I was angry with myself because I had ended up in this horrible position.

I cruised over the speed bumps, picked up speed, felt my anger surging in waves.

His Ram 3500 was pulled up to the wall.

His sixty-thousand-dollar Big Wheel was here, so he was here.

Nancy's car was in a visitor's space.

That meant Eddie and Nancy were over getting Nancied and Eddied.

Eddie didn't have a car. Nancy had become his Kato and walking ATM.

They were here, together, and I knew Hakeem had told them, so they were talking about me. I would have to face them all. I would have to explain to them all. I felt so damn defensive.

I parked, turned off my CBR, took off my helmet, but kept my motorcycle gloves on. I spied something useful, picked up a piece of steel rebar that was on the ground, left over from construction. It was about fourteen inches of unforgiving metal. I swung it, made it go *whoosh*.

Nerves made me bat rocks. My mind told me to be Kismet. Let Kismet handle this.

I dropped the rebar, let it clank onto the asphalt.

I stopped where I was. I called Ericka to tell her what had happened, where I was. She didn't answer. I called Indigo. Her calls went straight to voicemail. I called Kwanzaa. She didn't answer. I called my dad. He didn't answer his cellular or his house phone.

I called my mother in NYC. She didn't answer.

I asked God what to do. There was no answer from above.

I asked every version of me ever created what I should do.

They did not respond.

The universes had abandoned me.

I was alone.

I called Hakeem again. He sent my call straight to voicemail.

His voicemail was still full from me leaving messages all evening.

I just wanted him to hear me out. He was denying me the chance to explain.

I wanted him to hear what was in my heart in my words.

The image of that billboard on La Brea flashed in my mind, only instead of the image of a brown-skinned boy I saw my face over the price of incarceration versus the cost of education.

There was also a cost of relationship for all those incarcerated, a cost of love.

I saw my face with a line down the center, one side with me as I am now, the other side with me as I was at fifteen, when I was young, naïve, and nice to so many undeserving people.

If I could only go back and talk to her, if I could tell her that it wasn't worth it.

I wanted to tell her that one day she would meet a man named Hakeem. I wanted to tell her to be calm, unflappable, and one day love would find her. I wanted to tell her to be honest and she would fall in love one day. I would tell her that here is where she would end up if she wasn't patient. I would tell her that she would end up heartbroken, afraid, angry, and unable to find anyone she loved to tell her what to do, to talk her down from her angst. I would make that hardheaded child listen.

I walked toward the building at an unsure pace. With each step my fear and anxiety swelled in my throat. I took deep breaths, tried to knock away bad thoughts, tried to mentally bat away my fear. But I could bat away demons all night. The fear wasn't going to leave. It had taken root, and it was deeper than the deepest root of a wild fig tree at Echo Caves in South Africa.

I felt different. I felt a change and I knew why.

Tonight I wasn't here as Kismet Kellogg.

Tonight I was Destiny Jones.

And being here as my true self, being here with the shame my name carried, terrified me.

Chapter 48

After the second session, after the panting that made her throat dry, after the echo of skin smacking skin like fierce soul-clap after soul-clap, after the vaginal contractions and guttural moans, after so many stages of arousal that had her writhing beneath him, when it no longer felt like she was suffocating, Kwanzaa had freed herself from the heat and rolled her sweaty body to the far side of the bed, needing to get away from that last wave of orgasms in order to survive.

She listened to the man who wore Hugo Boss, a man who was now wearing only his own skin, pant and struggle to breathe, his throat also too dry, exhausted.

No words were spoken as she wheezed, prayed for her spent body to cool down.

She gave into alcohol and exhaustion, and slept for ten minutes, maybe fifteen, until she was jarred awake by another round of sirens heading toward the homeless. It was hard to get comfortable in a foreign bed, in a stranger's apartment, downtown where the sounds of sirens rode on every breeze, where helicopters flew in the distance, where cars were broken into all night long, or even worse, where she felt like another woman might come in at any moment. Drunken sex. It had been drunken sex. She felt the lack of judgment, yielded a sigh, but the intact passion of lovemaking resonated. It still felt surreal.

She put her hand between his legs, amazed, not turned off, actually turned on. Still mesmerized. Still craving.

They didn't kiss. She thought about it. Hoped for it. Didn't happen. It wasn't necessary.

They were strangers who had met and fallen into a strange bed without a second thought. When this ended, they'd still be strangers. Strangers with carnal knowledge, but still ignorant of each other. The shallowness of sex was but a momentary salve.

She took a few breaths, felt clearheaded enough to leave, would be down Fourth Street to the 110 South, then off at Florence in a jiffy, and from there it was a short drive through a land with a mixture of signs in Spanish and in English, where her black world was turning more Latin every day. She was one of the few who both embraced and loved the change. There had never really been a Southern California, only a Baja Norte, and the people were reclaiming their land.

It scared white people because they would lose voting power. Indigo said that it scared black Americans because they had no land to claim as their own. The black man had always been a wanderer on this continent, displaced from his own culture, ignorant of his own true languages, running from the south to flee Black Codes and Jim Crow, running to the north to work in the automobile industry, running west to work in aerospace, only to find Black Codes and Jim Crow lived from coast to coast. Kwanzaa told Indigo the African fled Africa for the same reasons.

Kwanzaa yawned.

It was time to go.

She could be pulling up at her apartment building in twenty minutes, maybe thirty, unless there was an accident or construction. Outside of those factors, there shouldn't be any bumper-to-bumper traffic at that time of the night.

She stared at Hugo Boss for a moment.

This was done.

It was going to be awkward seeing him at Starbucks. She decided she would ask to get transferred immediately.

She kissed Hugo Boss, kissed Mr. Iced Coffee good night, kissed him and knew she would never kiss him again. She walked away as if she didn't need to be escorted to her car, and along the way took out her pepper spray. Kwanzaa did her brazen sashay out into the darkness of downtown L.A., heels *clip-clopp*ing hours before the arrival of the official hours of the Walk of Shame, the hours of a restless woman's walk of atonement.

The stink of gentrification and the putridness of the homeless were strong, but otherwise the street was empty. She had expected to see many women outside, waiting for Hugo Boss to open the door, waiting to be chosen to be next to experience his blessing. His *blessings*.

When Kwanzaa made it to her car, a dark blue Kia Optima, she made sure no one was following her, then sat in her car a moment, saw her dad had sent her a happy birthday text message, saw her stepdad had sent a message, saw her stepmom had sent a message, saw her mom had sent a video of her singing "Happy Birthday," and Kwanzaa smiled, felt special.

Then she stopped smiling, started thinking about her ex and an STD that sounded like it should be the name of a Greek goddess, remembered the breakup, the tears, acknowledging the worst feeling in the world was to feel used, but that she still would have met with him tonight if he had called. Good-bye sex could have been her closure.

She would have been with Marcus Brixton at two fifteen, at her birth moment. She had wanted to feel his lips on her neck, on her ears, on her inner thighs, wanted to taste him for the last time. She was hanging in there, trying to reconcile her emotions. If she had seen Marcus, it would have led to talking, to kissing, to being naked. To fondling, to him being inside her, to her coming, and she would have been beyond heaven, and then the sex would have ended, and she would be in bed with him, cooling off, remembering the pain, feeling confused, loving him, and hating herself, crying, arguing, fighting, then going back to her apartment, back to being alone, back to feeling lonely for him.

But instead she had had a one-night stand to protect herself from him.

She double-checked her phone; no messages from Marcus.

For years their thing had been to be in bed on their birthdays; their tradition had been to make love at that middle-of-the-night minute, his voice in her ear telling her happy birthday.

She wiped away a tear and whispered, "Happy birthday to me. Happy birthday to me."

She could go home, put on a smile, put on her outfit, kick it with Indigo and Ericka, let them see her glow, wait for Destiny to get in. Then they could all chit-chat for a moment as her girls handed her gifts, more than likely shoes and a vibrator, or gift cards and a vibrator, or a vibrator and a vibrator.

Then sleep alone.

Kwanzaa started the car, but then police sirens jarred her, made her realize how lightheaded she was. She looked back toward the loft, toward a fading memory. Kwanzaa stared at the renovated warehouse, gazed at the graffiti-covered building.

Her phone rang. The caller ID said it was Señora Brixton, Marcus's mother. Señora Brixton had been like Kwanzaa's third mother for the last six years.

Kwanzaa put a smile on her face and answered, "*Buenas noches*, Mama Brixton."

"*Feliz cumpleaños, mija.*"

"*Gracias. Muchas gracias. Cómo ha estado usted?*"

In Spanish Señora Brixton said, "I have been well, thank you. Tonight I tried to stay awake until your birth moment, but I am too old to be awake until that late hour."

"That's fine, Mama Brixton. It's so nice to hear your voice."

"I wanted to be the first to call my daughter. You will always be my daughter."

"You will always be my mother, Señora Brixton."

"You are a special woman to me. You learned to speak Spanish, and I respect you for that. Mexicans come here hungry for opportunity and the young ones learn English in a year. People here in California are surrounded by Spanish and can barely speak two sentences."

"Well, many people pick up the xenophobic ways of their oppressors and their nation."

"This is why you are so different than the others. There is no hate in your heart."

She told Kwanzaa she had missed her sorely over the last few months, and she would always love her, no matter what had happened to cause her son to break up with her.

Kwanzaa asked, "What do you mean? He told you he broke up with me?"

"I asked Marcus to forgive you, *mija*. I told him you are young and at times young women do foolish things. I do not hate you because of what you did. I was a young woman once upon a time in Mexico. I was young and foolish. I told him to not be so heartbroken and try to forgive."

"I'm sorry. What did I do to cause Marcus to break up with me?"

"My son told me and his father what you did, how you were with another man."

"Is that what attorney Marcus Jesús Delgado Muñoz Brixton said to his parents?"

"He said he found you in bed with another man, and for that, he broke the engagement. My son told me you had been seeing a student at UCLA for a very long time behind his back."

"That's not true, Mama Brixton. I am not that kind of woman. You know that."

"My son went to Harvard. He is a Christian. He is a man of character."

Silence fell between them. That silence told her whose side his mother was on.

When she was a teenager, Marcus's mother had paid a coyote to bring her across three deserts so she could work hard in sweat factories and clean filthy toilets in large homes to earn herself the American dream. She had knocked on Marcus's father's door, a funeral home director who would first become her client, then her boyfriend, and eventually her husband.

Wide-eyed, Kwanzaa said, "I love you, Señora Brixton, but your son cannot slander my name. *He* was with another woman. *He* was the one who cheated on me and gave me a disease."

"He has not said much about what happened at all, *mija*. You gave him a disease?"

"*He gave me a disease*. Your son didn't tell you about the Chilean client, the whore he had sex with on his birthday during lunch, then was with me the same evening? His cheating left me bleeding, having a discharge, and in pain each time I urinated. *He did that to me*. Your son slept with an unclean woman and poisoned my body with the disease the Chilean whore gave to him; did he not tell you? Did he fail to tell you that he risked my health and maybe my damn life and could have given me a million diseases? I kept thinking of all the diseases he could have had after cheating on me. Your son from Harvard, your precious son, he could have given me AIDS or herpes. And he didn't have the nerve to tell me he was nasty. My doctor told me, and *then* your son confessed. He confessed because he had to confess. Now that I think about it, he confessed because he probably didn't know from whom he got it and to whom he had given it. He was walking around with a nasty dick doing only God knows what to whom. I guess your precious son left that part out of the lies he told. I was *never* in bed with any other man, not for the six years I was with him. I never cheated on your son, and the lying bastard knows that."

"My God. *Mija*, there is no reason for a woman to talk that way."

"I'm sorry, Mama Brixton, Señora Brixton, but right now my tongue is on fire. Your son was the one who ruined what we had built between our families, not me. If what you are telling me is true, your son is spreading vicious lies about me, the same way he spread a damn disease. He is attacking my character. If I were at fault, I would be at your door begging for forgiveness. Your precious son is a liar and I swear on my dead ancestors' graves I am telling you the truth."

"My son has no reason to lie to his mother, Kwanzaa."

"He's an attorney. He is in the business of lying. He is a professional liar."

"I did not want to upset you like this, *mija*. This was not my intent."

"Let's be honest. His father was not faithful. You turned your head to all he did. You let him get away with it. Your son will pay for what he has done. He will pay for telling lies on me."

"Men will be men, *mija*."

"And a woman will do what a woman has to do, Señora Brixton."

"I only know what my son has said to me. My son has always been caught between two worlds, has always struggled to figure out where he should be in this world. Do not fault him for being a man and do not fault him for needing to know where he belongs in this world."

"I'm glad you called me. I am so glad you called me on my birthday."

"Let's not be angry. *Mija*, I can make you a beautiful pineapple upside-down cake this year too, if you like."

"No, that will not be necessary. You have already chosen your side in this matter."

"I did not mean to upset you on your special day."

Shaking her head, jaw tight, eyes burning, Kwanzaa held the phone as sirens blared down Fourth Street toward downtown, as sirens blared in the opposite direction as well.

"I just wanted to be kind and tell you happy birthday and talk to you in Spanish."

"Thanks for the call. It was nice to hear your voice, Señora Brixton."

"*Feliz cumpleaños.*"

"*Gracias*. Have a nice life, Señora Brixton."

"I hope to hear from you again, my daughter."

"May you live well and live long, Mama Brixton."

Kwanzaa ended the call, disillusioned once again, wounded once more, her mind going over six years spent with Marcus, over a time that was only the blink of an eye, tragically brief.

She sat there a moment, infuriated, sober, yanked down from her high.

She shook her head and cried, but she did not cry torrentially.

She had nothing to feel guilty about.

Abso-fucking-lutely nothing.

Then she laughed. It was so ridiculous, she laughed.

She wished she were still with Marcus just so she could cheat on him.

She wished she could cheat on him and let him find out about the betrayal. She wanted him to feel all she had felt.

They were to marry two years after she finished grad school, have their first child within four years, and depending on how much they liked the first child, maybe their second within six, and if they all got along, they would adopt an Iraqi war orphan to help them understand young people better. The second child based on how much they liked the first rugrat, and the Franzen-ish line about the Iraqi orphan had been their little joke, as Marcus was a huge fan of Jonathan Franzen, maybe of all successful white men now that Kwanzaa thought about it.

She was going to speed to Marina del Rey, race to Marcus Jesús Delgado Muñoz Brixton's condominium off Lincoln, the place she used to spend weekends waking up with a view of the world from thirty stories high, with windows open to the distant sound of the ocean, to a sweet salty breeze, and let the Destiny Jones in her incensed soul come to life.

She started her car and took to the streets, sped toward the freeways.

She was going to go after Marcus. She was going to take this to his front door.

She would go Straight Outta Compton on his ass, show him what she was really made of, stop being nice, and be the next one on the Gray Goose to Hoosegow.

She would lose all she had struggled to gain over what Marcus had done to her.

She trembled, recalling every soul-crushing word Mama Brixton had said.

A thousand curses left her mouth.

She had to pull over near Los Angeles Street.

She was too upset to drive.

Again, Kwanzaa cried, this time torrentially, her hands gripping the steering wheel.

She cried her eyes crimson. She cursed as she wiped away her tears.

If she did what she was thinking, she would end up in jail.

Marcus would be free.

There was no victory for her to have.

He had betrayed her, lied, fucked her over, and he would get away with it.

The storm ended. She was hot. Sweating. And then she made two right turns, drove east until she was back in the Arts District. She eased out of her car, took deep breaths, did her best to fix her hair, straighten her clothes, put on more lipstick and headed back toward the converted warehouse. She went back to the man she called Hugo Boss.

She returned to the door of a stranger.

She rang the doorbell, wondering if another woman had already been invited inside.

She knew he knew it was she. Kwanzaa saw the security camera above the door.

She knew he had seen her on a monitor before he undid his locks.

She turned to walk away.

Hugo Boss opened the door.

She stopped walking, turned around, went back to the door.

He smiled. His beautiful eyes made her eyes do the same.

He disarmed her external fury, but the storm raged inside her.

In a calm, soft voice she said, "My name is Kwanzaa Browne."

"I'm Cristiano Gonçalo Bernardo."

"Pleased to meet you."

"Likewise."

The smells of downtown enveloped them. They stood in silence for a moment.

He asked, "Are you okay?"

"Allergies. Just my allergies acting up."

"Are you sure you're okay?"

Kwanzaa wiped her eyes and asked, "Are you expecting someone else tonight?"

"No, no one is coming."

"Did I disturb you? What were you doing?"

"Was wondering why you left so soon."

"Oh."

"Did I turn you off?"

"Not at all."

"You sure?"

"I'm back at your door. So I would say it's the opposite at this point."

Again they stood in silence, the cool breeze and sirens blanketing the night.

Still strangers, only familiar with the anatomy and orgasm of the person they faced.

He asked, "Would you like to come back inside?"

"Would I be breaking protocol?"

"There is no protocol."

"Yes, I would like to come back inside, if that is convenient for you."

"Are you okay?"

"I want to sit down a moment, but I don't want to be on the streets in my car."

"Okay."

"I can't drive right now."

"Your allergies."

"Yeah. They're acting up."

"Tipsy?"

"Not tipsy. Just a little upset and can't drive at the moment."

"What's wrong?"

"Nothing to do with you."

"You don't look very happy right now."

"Don't want to sit in my car in the dark out here."

"Understood."

"I'll try to not cry in front of you."

"Allergies don't scare me."

"We don't have to talk."

"I will leave that up to you."

"I just want to sit down a moment and think."

"Would you like something to drink?"

"I need something strong and stiff."

"Really?"

"And make it a double."

Chapter 49

I was here as Destiny Jones, not as Kismet Kellogg.

I dreaded the moment I was about to face.

I walked nervously down the hallway, asked myself what I was doing.

I could admit I was in the wrong. I could vanish.

But he had photographed me naked.

I stood in front of Hakeem's condo for what felt like forever wrapped in eternity and stretched across infinity. Soon I heard Nancy on the other side of the door. Same as she had been doing many of the nights I had come by after work, she was making love as rap music played. Nancy was loud. Eddie was probably Eddying Nancy all across the living room floor.

I took the key out, then put it back in my pocket.

Kismet had been given an open invitation.

Destiny had not.

I rang the doorbell, interrupted love in progress. Waited. Heard angry, impatient footsteps. The door opened a few inches, wide enough for me to smell the scent of grilled salmon and maybe veggies and baked potatoes. I expected to see Eddie's sweaty face, maybe Nancy. It was Hakeem. When he heard the doorbell ring, he knew it was going to be me. I'd never seen such a disgusted, harsh look on his face before. I needed him to see my face, see my sincerity, see my fear, my pain, see my love, and hear the same in my voice.

Terrified, heart aching, I whispered, "Can we please go somewhere and talk?"

"You're Destiny Jones."

In a distraught tone I asked, "Who told you?"

"You didn't."

"I was going to tell you. I swear. Every day I wanted to tell you."

"Why didn't you?"

"*This.* I was afraid of this. I hadn't planned on loving you and didn't think I'd let you inside my heart. But I did and after I had, I was afraid of your reaction. I was going to tell you, eventually."

"I asked you to move in with me. No wonder you kept me from your family."

"Lying is shameful, yes, but everything else I told you was true. I go to USC. I work three jobs. I am *not* seeing anyone, and my mother *is* an attorney, my father *is* an engineer. Only the *name* was misleading, but that's the name I use with everyone I don't know. I was already using that name when I sell Fire Sticks. I use that name at my jobs. I didn't make up that name just for you. I'm still the *same* person, the same Kismet you've been kicking it with. I'm the same person."

"Look, Destiny Jones, I need you to get away from my door."

"Can we get past the lie I told? There is no chance we can work this out?"

"We're done."

He closed the door.

I knocked until Hakeem opened the door again.

Hakeem snapped, "What?"

Heart throbbing, barely able to speak, I said, "If we're done, give me my money."

"I don't have it."

"*Then find a way to get it.*"

"I know you don't want to have the police come arrest you, Destiny Jones."

He slammed the door in my face like that was our denouement, our epilogue.

Hands dank, fingers trembling, I used the key in my pocket to open the door.

The door caught at three inches. The silver security chain had been put on.

I didn't care if Eddie was Eddying Nancy into seventh heaven, or Eddying her into the floor, or if he was in that crazy position where Nancy milked him like he was a freaking cow—something I wish I had never seen. The disgusting way Hakeem said my name, that hurt, and the way he dissed me at the door like I was a solicitor for Jesus verified that he'd already told them all about my past. I didn't care what they thought. I didn't allow people to treat me that way.

My world became the hue of fresh blood. I was the sun.

None of the Blackbirds were here to talk me down.

I took a step back, grunted, and flat-kicked the wooden door.

The chain snapped.

So had I.

Chapter 50

Indigo coughed once, sat up and sipped more delicious chicken soup, then stared at the six-foot-tall Channel Islands surfboard in the corner, at the colorful bikinis hanging over almost every door, at perfume on the worn dresser, at classical European art on the dull walls, at candles, at two dozen pairs of dirty shoes scattered across the wooden floor, at piles of clean and wrinkled clothes thrown across chairs, at a closed laptop whose case needed cleaning, at a twin bed with four pillows and a gigantic teddy bear, then stopped evaluating Rickie Sue's life and evaluated herself. She gazed in a circular, unframed mirror on the wall as music played on Rickie Sue's phone, the sound piped through a wireless Fugoo speaker. Nina Simone sang "Do I Move You."

She picked up the phone, the one that was a clone of her father's.

He had many texts and emails, but nothing incriminating. He had messages coming to him from Japan, from China, from Nigeria, from New York, from Amsterdam, but all were on a business level. She scrolled back over weeks of boring correspondences. There was no evidence of any immoral behavior. Her mother had been wrong. She was happy her mother had been mistaken this time. Indigo put the phone back down, grinning, glad to know she had good news.

Soon she would need to see Olamilekan so she could clone his phone.

She wanted the specifics. She wanted truth beyond his lies.

She, like her mother, wanted to be able to sleep at night without worrying.

Indigo looked at her braids, the funky style that made her look like a fashion model, looked at what Rickie Sue had done with ease and minimal pain, then lay back on the portable massage table. Worn socks were on her feet. Vicks was on her feet underneath those huge, comfortable, man-size socks. She stared at the ceiling, hummed with Nina Simone, waited for Rickie Sue to come back from the kitchen and start rubbing her naked body again.

Indigo was sure the things Rickie Sue had done had ensured her a place in Nigerian hell.

Indigo's cellular rang, Olamilekan calling for the fifth time.

She didn't answer.

The diatribe her mother had given had put her in a mood.

One that was not positive so far as Olamilekan was concerned.

Rickie Sue came back into the small bedroom, nude, but she had on socks, the same sort of white, man-size socks that had been put on Indigo's feet. A man's shirt hung in the doorway between the living room and bedroom. It was obvious Rickie Sue really had a boyfriend.

Indigo's phone buzzed. Now there were twelve texts from Olamilekan.

She hadn't answered any of his messages. She hadn't read any of his words.

Indigo sighed.

She liked a challenge, and Olamilekan was the ultimate challenge.

Every woman wanted to tame the wild one. The wild ones were exciting, and always seemed worthy. But a subjugated scorpion would still sting you one day. It was in their nature. Maybe she needed to start over, find a man who would see her as she saw herself, not wait for him to change, not try to prove to him repeatedly she was worthy of love and monogamy.

She was tired of chasing a man who wasn't chasing her in return.

She was loving and supportive. She loved to cook and loved to cuddle. She didn't like to argue, but would if given a reason. Still she preferred peace to foolishness. She had her own everything and wasn't needy, had never been a clingy woman, was ambitious and had many goals, but would do what she had to do to spend time with her man. She longed to spend as much time with her man as she could, to be generous with all she had to offer, to give slow kisses and have amorous nights in every season. She didn't have to go out all the time, was just as content cooking her man dinner, making love, then cuddling naked and watching Netflix. She was a Netflix-and-chill kinda girl. She went out because she was restless, because her man was never available, went out to keep herself occupied, but never to look for trouble guised as a new lover.

She was honest. She was loyal.

In a soft voice Rickie Sue asked, "How are you feeling?"

"My coughing is easing up."

"You've sweated it out."

"Yeah. My fever is down."

"Am I the best nurse ever or what?"

"You're incredible, that I will admit."

"You've been under my care for three hours."

"Feels like I just arrived here."

"Someone is looking for you. They are ready for you to leave Wonderland."

"It's my bae. I'm ignoring him today and it's driving him crazy. He probably thinks I am out somewhere cheating on him. He probably thinks I have hooked up with my ex-bae as revenge."

"Wouldn't he be surprised?"

"Very. He would be very surprised. As surprised as I am that this has transpired."

"You're cheating on him."

"A woman can't cheat on a man with another woman."

Rickie Sue laughed at Indigo's silliness. "You really have a boyfriend?"

"Told you, I'm not a lesbian. I was with a woman once, out of curiosity, but I am not a lesbian."

"You were with a woman. Was she this attentive?"

"No, you're very attentive. I'm comfortable. Too comfortable."

"I make it do what it do. Did the woman you were with make it do what it do?"

Indigo paused. "I'm joking about being with a woman. This is my first and last time. I came for the chicken soup and you wanted to see if I tasted like chicken."

Rickie Sue laughed. "I don't think you're joking."

"You massage your bae a lot?"

"All the time."

"Bet he's madly in love with you."

"And your bae thinks you're creeping with your ex."

"He's jealous. I used to date a basketball player before I met him."

"Pro or college?"

"Pro. He plays for the Lakers."

"You're joking. You used to date a Laker?"

"We dated. Broke up. Dated. Broke up. Now I am dating another athlete. And we date and break up and date and break up and date and break up and date. Might have to trade him too. He's developed a thing for a model, some South African woman who recently came to America, and now needs a nose job and a new weave before she can seek gainful employment."

"I would think you'd be with a white boy."

"Why?"

"You're smart. You're sexy. Smart black women usually leave the black man's foolishness behind, especially when they realize a white boy will do anything for a black woman."

"Men will be men, no matter what race. All women, all races, all ethnicities have the same problems. If I dated a non-Nigerian, I would never hear the end of it from my family."

"A Nigerian Laker . . . hold on. Wait a minute. No way. *Yaba* is your ex-bae?"

"We dated. So much drama."

"Are you famous or something?"

"I'm just a girl going to university so that she can one day end up on the Supreme Court."

"Why did you and Yaba break up?"

"You know how ballers are."

"Too many options."

"Way too many."

"White girl?"

"Ethiopian."

"At least he stuck with a black woman. Most of the brothers start off broke with a loyal black chick, start off like Michael Jordan, then when all is said and done, the sister and his starter kids are in the rearview mirror and a white girl is at his side reaping the benefits."

"Magic Johnson didn't change up."

"Magic Johnson didn't have a choice."

"You have an interesting perspective. I don't agree, but it's interesting."

"Which baller are you seeing now? Another Laker?"

"I changed sports. Have you heard of a football player named Olamilekan?"

"Get the fuck out. You dated Yaba, and now Olamilekan is your *current* man?"

Indigo set free a mild cough. "You can pronounce Olamilekan's name with no problem?"

"I'm a *big* sports fan. He's fine as hell. I have his jersey in my closet, or in the dirty clothes, if I didn't leave it at my bae's apartment. Olamilekan? And he's your billion-dollar bae?"

"He's not a billionaire. Never will be. His debt-income ratio is out of control. I am more sensible. I would have him live modestly, invest wisely, and save tremendously, if I were his wife."

"You're getting ten-year, one-hundred-and-thirty-million-dollar-contract dick?"

"Never thought about it like that."

"That's at least twelve million an inch."

"You've turned his penis and income into a word problem."

"And I bet Yaba had more inches."

"One could assume, but one could be wrong."

"Does he?"

"When a man with a big penis is having sex with one, we only groan and do not complain."

"Girl, forget going to school and managing an apartment building in Inglewood, you better get pregnant by one of them and get out of the hood. Hey, get pregnant by both at the same time. Have twins by different daddies and get two checks. That could be your retirement plan."

Indigo laughed, then coughed more, still ill, but now not as congested.

"You like the soup?"

"Best soup ever."

"Like the way I braided your hair with the sides going back and the top like a Mohawk?"

"My hair looks awesome. You braid better than my Dominican beautician on La Brea."

"Like the way I make it do what it do when I did what I did when you were on your back?"

"I didn't like it. I did my best to resist your powers, but I failed. It won't happen again."

"You were tense."

"I've been stressed."

"You came so many times. You came so hard you almost fell off the massage table."

"No, I didn't. I am an epileptic with Tourette's and both were acting up simultaneously as I did the Holy Ghost dance and spoke in tongues. Sorry you mistook those incidences for orgasms."

"That stress came right out of you."

"Most of it. I feel lighter."

Rickie Sue laughed. "Now be honest. Am I your first?"

"I am not a lesbian. I have not been influenced by Western culture."

"I read in this magazine that one out of—"

"*One* woman. A college professor. She taught literature. I saw her twice. *Twice.* She was ten years older. She was well traveled, mature, beautiful, very ambitious, and experienced."

"Which one of us did you enjoy the most, her or me making it do what it do?"

"This was the bomb, but I don't want to become accustomed to being treated this way."

"And I don't want to get used to treating a woman like this."

"We're on the same page. I'm glad to hear that."

"You're very attractive, Indigo. Men and women find you very tempting."

"Of course they do, but I only notice men in a sexual way. I'm not a lesbian."

"You ride a motorcycle and you can change a flat faster than a mechanic on speed."

"I can bake a cake, clean a home, and sew a new dress too. What's your point?"

"But what about the fling with the college professor? Were you curious?"

"It was something *she* wanted. I think I was flattered that she was so enamored by me and she wanted to do *that* to me, so I let her have her way. Long time ago. Hated myself after. It's not my forte."

"Could've fooled me."

"You're a lesbian pretending to be straight, Rickie Sue. I know you are."

"No, I'm not. There is nothing lesbian about me, Indigo."

"You have a lesbian's tongue. You made me walk through heaven."

"I imitated my boyfriend. And I'm better at that with a man than I am with a woman."

Rickie Sue ran her vibrator across Indigo's breasts, then sucked Indigo's right nipple, sucked as she moved the vibrator south, suckled as she moved the hum inside Indigo bit by bit.

Indigo's back arched and her left hand raised, pulled at her braids while she bit her lips and tried not to roll her hips. The vibrator entered her, its song muffled. Tingles moved throughout her body. With each gentle movement, with each ingress and egress, with every measured stroke, the brightest hues flashed behind Indigo's eyes, sparkles that rivaled Venezuela's Catatumbo lightning, the everlasting storm with two hundred flashes an hour. Soon Indigo felt explosions so bright she imagined they could be seen for over two hundred miles.

She imagined she could be heard all the way back to Lagos.

Rickie Sue suckled Indigo's breasts, sucked her nipples, did that while multitasking with the toy, then with her free hand, pulled the towels away from Indigo, pushed Indigo's legs wider. Rickie Sue eased the vibrator in and out over and over until once again Indigo was an epileptic with Tourette's doing the Holy Ghost dance.

"Gbe fun mi gbe fumi gbe funmi."

Indigo's cellular started blowing up. Alessia Cara sang the ringtone for Destiny Jones.

"Fi si nu mi. Yes, yes, yes. *Fun mi fun mi fun mi fun mi."*

Indigo was in another place, too far away, was being tongue-kissed by Rickie Sue.

She gave smooth and even strokes with her vibrating toy.

"To ba je okunrin ma fe e."

A girl was kissing Indigo the way a man kissed a woman, and with her eyes closed, with full lips against her full lips, with a small tongue chasing her small tongue. Indigo gave in, enjoyed the tenderness. It had not been like this when she had tried this two times before. Just like men, women could be bad lovers, could be clueless, or were unable to adapt when they changed partners. Rickie Sue had adjusted, had adapted to Indigo's needs, to the way her body responded. Indigo hadn't had to tell her anything, hadn't felt uncomfortable all evening.

"Fun mi fun mi fun mi fun mi."

Indigo's orgasm was full-body, so intense she didn't hear the sounds of the cold ocean waves crashing into dirty brown sand, didn't hear inebriated people on Ocean Front Walk.

"Oluwa oooo. Oto oto oto oto. Monbo monbo monbo."

She didn't hear someone knock at the front door.

She didn't hear Rickie Sue's lover trying to enter the apartment.

He called out, "Rickie? Rickie? Rickie? Rickie? *Bent u in het huis? Wat ga jij doen? Bent u met een man? Open deze deur onmiddellijk.* Rickie, I know you are in there. Open the door."

Chapter 51

Indigo sat up, pushed Rickie away, eyes wide, fear and panic in her every breath.

Rickie motioned for Indigo to calm down, whispered, "Relax, Indigo."

"Who is that?"

"My bae. Jesus, Jesus, Jesus. Let me think. Wait. Yeah. Just stay where you are."

"Are you mad?"

"I have this under control."

"He heard us in here."

"Just don't move."

Indigo did what Rickie said, lay on her belly, the sheets over her, still nude.

Rickie Sue put three peppermints in her mouth and pulled on black and gray joggers and a worn *Fear the Walking Dead* T-shirt. There was only one door. There was only one way out.

Rickie Sue went to the door. Indigo heard the locks come undone. Rickie Sue kissed whoever was there, said a couple of things, could tell he was concerned with why she took so long to open the door, and she said she didn't hear him knocking. Rickie Sue brought him toward the bedroom. Indigo looked up and saw an athletic build, six foot three or four, blue eyes, blonde hair, a beach tan on a stunning man who looked like Brad Pitt when he was in *Thelma and Louise*.

He was in his early twenties, maybe a few years older than Rickie Sue.

He saw Indigo on the massage table, nude under a sheet, exhaled, and looked relieved.

Rickie Sue said, "Yorick Xander, I want you to meet my cousin from Africa. My cousin's name is Indigo. Indigo, I want you to meet the boyfriend I told you about, Yorick Xander."

Holding a skateboard, dressed in skinny jeans, a hoodie, and white tee with Luke Cage on the front, Yorick Xander waved, looked a little embarrassed, lost the anxiety that had been in his body language, and in a thankful, accented voice said, "Hello, Indigo. Nice to meet you."

Indigo coughed twice. "Hello, Yorick Xander. Nice to meet you. Rickie Sue has been talking about you nonstop and I am so glad I have a chance to meet you in person."

Yorick Xander looked astonished. "You and Rickie Sue could pass for twins."

Indigo said, "We have strong genes in our family. Tall women with beautiful skin."

Yorick Xander said, "Women with dark skin are underappreciated and amazing."

Rickie Sue said, "My cousin is sick and I was putting Vicks all over her to help her feel better. Anyway. Cousin Indigo has to fly out tomorrow and she needs to get better."

Yorick asked Indigo, "Where are you going?"

"First to Florida to see other cousins, and from there a twelve-hour flight home to Lagos."

"Your home is in Las Gidi?"

"You know Lagos's nickname?"

"The city of hustlers. That's what some say the nickname means."

"Yes, but I am considering moving here to the States. More opportunities here."

Yorick Xander said, "I've been to Lagos many times. The women are *beautiful*. The African women are so fashionable, so well dressed, so cultured. They are amazing."

Indigo coughed. "Your voice is beautiful. Were you speaking a different language?"

"I am from the Netherlands. Amsterdam. I love your accent too."

"Are you living here in the United States now?"

"I am living in the country of extremists. I have never seen so much hate."

Rickie Sue asked, "What was that you told me the other day, Yorick?"

"American extremism has created extremists around the world. America has invaded every country in the world, has created global poverty, and now does not want the immigrants to come here. If you burn down a man's home, destroy a man's country, you owe him refuge."

Rickie Sue said, "Well, they never fixed up Detroit so I know they're not fixing up Iran. They're not finding homes for the homeless vets here, so they're not going to do that for others. So far as helping those other countries, no one throws a parade for a losing team."

"Rickie Sue, my beautiful girlfriend, let's not argue in front of your cousin."

"You're right, Yorick. It would not be a good first impression, and she would think we were as different as chalk and cheese, but I will just say charity begins at home and leave it alone."

Indigo said, "You are a very interesting couple. I see the attraction between you two."

"He's atheist, but I'm not going to hold that against him. Right, Yorick?"

He said, "And I will not hold it against you for having a temperamental Sky Daddy."

"See what I mean, cousin? We agree to disagree. Plus when you date an atheist in California, you have a lot more fun on Sundays at the beach learning to surf."

Yorick Xander put his arms around Rickie Sue. "Do I smell something cooking?"

"I made some of my world-famous chicken soup for my cousin."

He asked Rickie Sue, "How much soup did you make?"

"A gigantic pot. I knew you'd come by and want some too. Hungry?"

"I'm always hungry for your chicken soup."

He followed Rickie Sue to the kitchen, talking and kissing, the sounds of wet lips resounding. Rickie Sue made him a ham sandwich, gave him that and a bowl of soup, then came back to Indigo, winked, pulled the socks from Indigo's feet and rubbed more Vicks on her soles.

Indigo whispered, "Rickie Sue, your vibrator is right there on the table."

"It's always there on the table. He probably didn't even notice it."

"You left it turned on. It was humming while your bae was standing in the door."

Rickie Sue laughed out loud, then nervously danced over to the toy, turned it off.

She said, "If he asks, I will say I was using it to massage your lower back."

"Our clothes are all over the floor. My motorcycle helmet and my jacket are right there by the door with my jeans and thong. Either he is naïve as hell, or you are a good liar."

"Lying is a survival skill. So is denial. Works best when they meet in the middle."

"Should I leave?"

"Stay right there."

Yorick Xander returned to the bedroom door, exchanged words with Rickie Sue. Indigo kept her face down, on the massage table, staring at the floor, wondering if Yorick was looking at her ass. Rickie Sue was massaging Indigo's back, the sheets exposing the curve of her butt. Rickie Sue stopped the massage, and Indigo rose up so she could see the Dutchman in the room. Yorick told Indigo that it was a pleasure to meet his girlfriend's beautiful cousin, said he hoped she felt better. Indigo thanked him, then faux-coughed twice. Rickie Sue went to the second-hand dresser, opened her purse, took out her car keys and some money.

Yorick Xander said, "If I didn't see you in front of me, Rickie, I would swear that was you on the table getting a massage. If your cousin had been here alone, I would have walked in and kissed her before I realized my error. There is a remarkable resemblance in all aspects."

Rickie Sue said, "My hoopty has a flat tire and I need a new one. See if you can find a used one. Maybe try that tire place on Lincoln by Alka Logic, the place we buy water. Buy some more water, too."

Rickie handed the keys and cash to Yorick before taking his hand and leading him back to the front door. Indigo heard them talking, laughing, kissing. Then they were in the kitchen, trying to be quiet. Indigo exhaled. Almost ten minutes passed before Rickie Sue came back.

Indigo whispered, "Where is Yorick?"

"He's gone."

Indigo looked up at her and said, "*Cousin?* We don't look anything alike. You don't look Nigerian. You look Ghanaian, maybe from the Ivory Coast or Liberia, if anything."

"To Willy Wonka we look like we came from the same chocolate factory."

"Your hair is a mess, you were sweaty, out of breath, have your T-shirt on inside out, and you put your joggers on inside out too, and here I am naked under a sheet in your bedroom."

"And he didn't have a clue I was making it do what it do while he knocked on the door."

"When will Yorick be back with your car?"

"Not for about five or six hours. He will spend the night when he comes back."

"I need to leave and get to Inglewood. I have a birthday dinner to help cook. I need to get a phone back to my mother. I need to call my boyfriend. I need to check on my ex-boyfriend too."

"Don't leave. I know I will never see you again. So don't hurry to go."

"I never should have come. What I am doing here, allowing you to do this, isn't right."

"You are still coughing. There is more soup. Rest a little longer."

"You are trying to become the devil again. I don't want to be in jail for fourteen years."

"More Vicks. More vibrator. More me. All you need to do is relax. Let me pay it forward."

"Your man from Amsterdam could've walked in on us. It could've become very ugly."

"You don't have to worry. If Yorick Xander comes back, he still has to knock to get in."

"He heard me through the window before he banged on the door."

"I told him you had cramps too, said you had them real bad."

"That was brilliant."

"Telling a man a woman has the cramps scares him shitless."

"Yes, it does."

"We're good. Plus, he knows my sick *cousin* is here. He will call first."

"Where does he live?"

"Santa Monica. He rode his skateboard down to borrow my car."

"When you were in the kitchen a minute ago, did you give him a hand job?"

Rickie Sue laughed. "Did it sound like I was slapping a wet steak in there?"

Indigo said, "You are the devil."

"So you're gonna kick it with your favorite cousin a little longer?"

"This will be my last time. This will not happen again."

Rickie Sue laughed at Indigo, undressed herself, and was once again naked.

Rickie Sue said, "Get off the massage table. Let's get comfy on the bed for a while."

Indigo got up, eased off the table, let the sheets fall away, and crawled onto the mattress.

Fresh sheets. Lavender scent. Twin bed. Indigo moaned when Rickie Sue eased onto the bed and put her skin next to hers. She craned her neck, looked back at Rickie Sue.

Indigo asked, "I am not trying to be in a relationship with a woman."

"Indigo, don't get me wrong. You just saw my man. I have a sexy man from Amsterdam who loves to surf and take me to Burning Man. This isn't nothing I do often, but you are so fine."

"Whatever you say, my black American cousin."

Indigo rested on her belly. Rickie Sue put more Vicks on her hands, rubbed them together, straddled Indigo, and then massaged Indigo's back again. Rickie Sue did a slow grind at the same time. Rickie Sue moaned as Indigo's cellular rang. It was Olamilekan's ringtone.

Rickie Sue didn't stop. She kept massaging, kept riding. Indigo felt her come, felt her tremble. Rickie Sue slowed, took breaths, then went to the bathroom, washed her hands.

Indigo stared at Rickie Sue. Rickie Sue blushed.

Indigo quivered. "That was sexy. I felt you on my back. Your energy went inside me."

Rickie Sue eased back into the bed, up close to Indigo, then masturbated Indigo by simultaneously rubbing her clitoris with the thumb and her anus with the forefinger.

"Indigo, when we first got here, did you like my head game?"

Indigo moaned. "Bet your boyfriend wanted to do that to you a moment ago."

"He wanted to do that and more."

"Too bad your sick African cousin was here cock-blocking."

"Well, my momma always said to take care of family first."

"Your skin is so soft."

"So is yours."

"You're coming."

"Yeah, yeah. I'm coming."

When the orgasm was over, Rickie Sue touched Indigo's face, stroked her dark cheeks, and touched her full lips. Indigo touched Rickie Sue's face, stroked her dark cheeks, and touched her full lips. Rickie Sue took Indigo's fingers in her mouth, fellated each digit. Indigo moaned and closed her eyes. Rickie Sue rubbed Indigo's clitoris and anus again, with thumb and forefinger. Indigo made her stop, then did to Rickie Sue what Rickie Sue had been doing to her.

Indigo sucked Rickie Sue's nipple as Rickie Sue came, writhing, holding her hand. Indigo held Rickie Sue like a bowling ball, stimulated by rubbing the thumb and forefinger on her clitoris and anus at the same time. Rickie Sue made faces like she wanted to cry. Her legs began shaking. Her back arched and she reached for Indigo's hand. Indigo didn't back away. Rickie Sue stopped panting, released her hold on Indigo's hand.

"Jesus, Indigo. Jesus. My God. You made me see dead people."

Indigo rolled away, heard her phone ring, Ericka's ringtone, followed by Destiny's ringtone, followed by Kwanzaa's ringtone, followed by her mother's ringtone, followed by Olamilekan's ringtone, followed by Yaba's ringtone, followed by her father's ringtone.

She wasn't in that world right now. She had escaped them all.

Rickie Sue's chest rose and fell for a while. She dragged herself to the bathroom and turned on the shower. She came back to the door. Indigo saw the serious look on Rickie Sue's face. Saw her aroused nipples. Rickie Sue motioned for Indigo to come to her. Seconds later, Indigo stood under warm water as Rickie Sue soaped their bodies. Indigo was washed from her neck to the bottoms of her feet. They rubbed their breasts together, nipples across nipples, and Rickie Sue kissed Indigo. Indigo panted as Rickie Sue's hand went lower. Rickie Sue put her hand between Indigo's legs, fingered her for while, then took Indigo's hand, placed Nigerian fingers where she ached. Indigo slid her fingers inside Rickie Sue while the same was being done to her. Indigo felt incandescent. Ethereal. As if she had floated up, up, and away.

Soon they were back on the bed, on fresh sheets, soft music playing.

Indigo asked, "How do you do this? How do you get me to do this sort of thing?"

"Well, this wasn't exactly the missionary work I thought it was going to be."

"How did you think it would be?"

"Not like this. You're good at this. So good, you've taken the lead."

"I'm not good at all. Feel free to take the lead back. Or kick me out of your place."

"I'm not kicking you out yet."

Rickie Sue kissed Indigo. Full lips pressed against full lips, soft like pillows. Indigo squirmed. Then she sucked Rickie Sue's breasts, made Rickie Sue squirm. Indigo pulled her between her legs, positioned Rickie Sue like she was a man, like she was Olamilekan.

Soon their heads were at opposite ends of the bed, legs crisscrossed as they made scissors, as vaginas touched.

Indigo stared at Rickie Sue, her hips rolling while her hands pulled Rickie closer to her as Rickie Sue did the same. Rickie Sue grinned, pulled Indigo closer, vagina to vagina. Lips kissed. On fire, Rickie Sue crawled to Indigo, climbed on her thigh, positioned herself on the muscle, on the bone, and did a slow grind, her breathing heavy. Rickie Sue leaned in, nibbled on Indigo's lips. Indigo pushed up on her elbows, positioned herself, and rode Rickie Sue's thigh at the same time, had situated her clit on the hardness of Rickie's leg, on her bone.

Soon Rickie Sue had Indigo on her back, was on top, had Indigo's long legs open wide, made scissors from a new angle, dominated, grinding, enraptured. Swimming in a good feeling, Indigo closed her eyes, her breathing heavy too, felt a woman's passion for her.

Indigo wished Olamilekan were this attentive.

She wished Yaba hadn't been so disappointing.

Rickie Sue licked Indigo's nipples, then went down on Indigo, put French kisses between her legs, massaged her with fingers, and massaged her with tongue. Indigo held Rickie Sue's head, and a thousand thoughts went through her mind.

The things her mother had said went through her mind. Ten years in jail in her homeland for breaking this law. But she felt so good, too good to think about laws or superstitions.

If only women could have babies with women, babies that shared the same DNA, her world would be perfect. Maybe in one of those far-away universes Destiny always talked about, that was a possibility. Rickie Sue stopped, sat back, her mouth moist, and little by little she grinned.

Indigo said, "I am glad you are not African. I am glad you are not Nigerian."

"If I were?"

"This would become addictive. This would become a problem."

Indigo crawled to Rickie Sue, then licked her lips, brushed her full lips over Rickie Sue's vagina, barely grazed Rickie Sue's lips over and over, drove Rickie Sue mad with anticipation. Indigo gave Rickie Sue's vagina soft kisses, slow kisses, kissed her there like she had all the time in the world, tested her, teased her, made her pull at sheets and sing each time she exhaled. Rickie Sue moaned, trembled, jerked, told Indigo how beautiful she was, told her how good she was making her feel. Indigo gave her intense kisses, then gave her fingers, and massaged her with her tongue, then played games with her using her tongue.

Indigo asked, "Am I doing this right?"

"Fuck yeah."

Indigo took a breath, then grazed Rickie Sue's sex with her tongue.

She moved her tongue back and forth over and over, still in slow motion. Soon she moved her tongue vertically, up and down, up and down. Then she opened Rickie Sue, explored her with the tip of her tongue. Indigo slid her tongue inside Rickie Sue as if it were her lover's sweet mouth. She went deep without going too deep, did the same thing she did when she kissed a man, when she sucked on his tongue. Indigo hummed and sucked on Rickie Sue. She sucked Rickie Sue the way she loved to be sucked by a man, and loved the way her tongue felt. Rickie Sue called out to her savior. Indigo took small breaths through her nose, same as she did when she kissed for a long time, when she had kissed and fallen into a trance, and gave Rickie Sue more of her tongue, gave her more soft kisses, then sucked gently. Gently kissing. Gently sucking. Gently licking. She took a break, paused for a few seconds, watched Rickie Sue squirm, heard her whimpers beg her to continue, then Indigo adjusted herself, put her hands under Rickie Sue's ass, leaned in and started again with the soft kisses before she reentered her with her tongue. As Indigo gave her perfect kisses and tongue, she used her hands, touched Rickie Sue's quivering body, massaged her legs, rubbed her belly, squeezed her breasts, pinched her nipples as she tongued her.

"Rickie Sue, should I stop?"

"What are you trying to do to me?"

"You like this?"

Rickie Sue held Indigo's braids as her answer.

Indigo closed her eyes, held Rickie Sue gently, slipped her tongue inside, pretended she was kissing Olamilekan for a while, then pretended she was kissing Yaba, sucking his lips. Rickie Sue was so sensitive, so excitable. Her thighs tensed and her back arched as she held Indigo's braids and sang her orgasmic song. Indigo made Rickie Sue come so hard her legs refused to stop shaking. Indigo made a woman come with her mouth. That was a first. She grinned. A moment later, Indigo stopped, backed away, looked at the ethereal glow on Rickie Sue's face. Seconds later, Rickie Sue followed Indigo's retreat.

Indigo said, "No more."

Rickie Sue whispered, "Yes, more."

Again Rickie Sue was between Indigo's legs as Indigo held Rickie

Sue's head. Right away, Indigo's song began and her legs shook. Rickie Sue was so much better. So much better. Better than Yaba. Better than Olamilekan. Rickie Sue made Indigo jerk and come. Shake and come. Moan and come. Talk to God and come. Rickie Sue moved her damp mouth to Indigo's breasts, then kissed her, gave Indigo African honey.

Indigo said, "If only you had a dick. You would be perfect for me."

"Girl, swear to God, I was just thinking the same damn thing."

Then they laughed. Laughs became tender kisses and rising moans as they fingered each other. Indigo held the sheets and orgasmed again, a small one, was feeling too good, then rolled away from Rickie Sue.

Indigo stared at Rickie Sue, stared, shook her head, bit her lip, then whispered, "You are the devil. You lie like the devil. You have a body like the devil. Your soup is the devil's soup. Your hands are the devil's hands. You tongue my no-no like the devil. You taste like the devil."

"Girl, please. You eat pussy like the devil."

Indigo laughed again.

Rickie Sue got up, danced, turned on jazz, picked up the vibrator, turned it back on, and smiled. She opened her drawer, took out as second vibrator, turned it on as well.

She tossed both of her humming toys on the bed next to Indigo.

Rickie Sue winked. "In case you want to reciprocate."

"I don't believe I'm going to ask you this. I really don't."

"Whassup?"

"Do you have a strap-on?"

"Wish I did."

"If you had one, this could get pretty interesting."

"Might have to get online and see if Amazon Prime makes one-hour deliveries."

"Have you not had enough of me for one day? Am I overstaying my welcome?"

"I'm a groupie. You're famous."

"How am I famous?"

"Are you serious?"

"No one knows who I am. No one knows my face or my name."

"Olamilekan is your bae. I do love to watch Olamilekan."

"Oh. That fame by osmosis thing. Famous for doing nothing."

"And I'm a Yaba fan too."

"So now you see me as another Amber Rose, a woman celebrated due to a man."

"I'm that close to being with two superstars. I'm touching the woman they have touched. This is exciting for me. They don't know you get down like this, so I know you in a way they don't know you."

"I'm only seeing Olamilekan, not both of them. I'm not like that."

"Still, I'm one up on them. I know that's strange, but it really has me aroused. You aroused me when I met you. I have no idea who you are, but I can tell you're someone special. The way you carry yourself, everything about you is different. You're smart too. Very smart. You're not ordinary. So, if I only get to do this once with you, I want all I can get before you go."

Again, as Nina Simone sang, the music down low, as vibrators hummed, called out to them, asked what did they want to do, Indigo licked her lips, stared at Rickie Sue.

Indigo whispered, "This goes against my heterosexual, Nigerian sensibilities."

"The offer for chicken soup was honest. I owed you. Hey, we can stop doing what we're doing, and I can rub you some more, feed you some more, get you comfy again, then we can chill out and watch *Survivor's Remorse*, or we can take a nap. I know you're weak."

"Me and you together is like mixing Nigerian coffee and dark chocolate. It's addictive."

"That combination could keep us up all night."

"I have somewhere to be, have a birthday to celebrate, and Yorick is coming back."

"Sweet, sweet chocolate. And good, good coffee."

"You did make it do what it do when you did what you did."

Rickie Sue said, "See? You didn't need to try to walk up all those stairs to work out."

"Soup. Massage. Vicks. You've been pretty damn awesome. Wish you were a guy."

"And I rebraided your hair and gave you a good scalp massage too."

"You are really the devil, you know that?"

"I can make it do what it do, and you're damn good at making it do what it do too."

"At the risk of being redundant, I'm not a lesbian. This is a layover, not my destination."

"Neither am I. We're just, as they say, two ships passing in the night."

Rickie Sue went to Indigo, pulled her to her, and began kissing her neck, her ears.

Rickie Sue whispered, "All this chocolate. And your fine ass is just as sexy as I am."

Indigo moaned. "So much sweetness between you and me that it's ridiculous."

"Now it's like I know what it's like when someone is with me, can see it, feel it, taste it, hear it from their point of view. It has to be amazing for a man to be with one of us."

"We are awesome, American cousin."

"So damn awesome, African cousin."

Chapter 52

Cristiano Gonçalo Bernardo asked Kwanzaa Browne, "Sleeping?"

"Smiling with my eyes closed and hoping this part of the night isn't a dream."

"Really?"

"You've made the worst birthday ever become the best birthday ever."

"Today's your birthday?"

"Today marks an anniversary of the moment I made my first appearance in the world."

"Happy birthday. I'm glad I had the opportunity to be a part of your special day."

A moment passed, before Kwanzaa asked, "Question, Cristiano?"

"What, Kwanzaa?"

"The guitars, the instruments, do you play, or are those just decoration?"

"I play."

"I play the guitar too. My stepdad taught me."

"We should have a jam session."

Kwanzaa chuckled. "We just did."

He laughed.

She said, "You must work in Inglewood."

"My job is not far from your job."

She didn't ask him to be more specific about where he worked, just let it go.

He said, "I was surprised to see you in Hollywood."

"I was just as surprised to see you outside of Starbucks."

"It's your birthday."

"Yup."

"You were clubbing alone."

"Yup."

"Where are your other friends tonight?"

"They're waiting on me to get back home so we can start the weekend of celebration."

"Boyfriend?"

"I'm single. My friends are all female. Three girls trying to live out loud, just like me."

"Are they single like you?"

"One is divorced. One is in limbo. One has a bae."

"For the ones who are single or in limbo, I have friends and could arrange a party."

"Are your friends built like you?"

"Does it bother you?"

"For a moment, I thought I was being Punk'd."

"It's real. It doesn't scare you or turn you off?"

"Not at all. I'm amazed. Are there many men like you?"

"About one in every six million men in the world."

"How many men are there in the world?"

"About three and a half billion."

"So there are a few more of you out there."

"One would assume."

"You're a double-barreled lover."

"I'd never thought of it that way."

"And both barrels are fully loaded."

"Yeah, they are. Others are like me, but not all are functional on both appendages. I'm a rare case amongst rare cases."

"Your friends know about your blessings?"

"Not everybody. It's not something I talk about."

"The women who were waiting?"

"You noticed. They know. Or they have heard."

"You've slept with some of them?"

"Most of them."

"Most."

"Sometimes they bring a friend."

"To watch or participate?"

"To watch, then participate."

"At least you're honest about it."

"It's not my thing. I don't want to become anyone's sideshow."

She said, "Thanks for this wonderful experience on my birthday."

"You're a great dancer."

"So are you. I had so much fun with you at the Club. Dancing with you like that, that made my night. Everything after was a bonus."

"I see you like dancing."

"Love dancing. I could dance until the club closed down and be the last one to leave."

"Can I get your number?"

"You don't have to ask for my number."

"What do you mean?"

"I saw the queue out front. It's Friday night and that's what Friday night is all about. Trying to live out loud for a little while. I wanted something. You wanted something. You got what you wanted. I got what I needed to get through the night. It was liquor and sex. I know how this goes."

"No, I really want your number."

"If I see you again, ask again, and maybe I'll give it to you. Not tonight."

"What do you do when you're not at Starbucks?"

"You're asking me about me?"

"I'm asking you about you."

"UCLA has most of my time."

"What's your major?"

"Pharmacy. Pharmaceutical sciences and administration."

"Smart girl."

"Needed to have a major that could get me where I want to be in life."

"You're getting dressed again."

"I should leave before my car turns back into a pumpkin."

"I'm enjoying your company."

"Same here, but I have to go meet my friends. The three girls."

"You're going to see them this late?"

"My friends do this celebratory thing on our birthdays, so I need to get back and change."

"Can I give you my number?"

"That's not necessary."

"May I have a few more minutes with you, Kwanzaa?"

"Want me to be your koala bear again?"

"Yeah. It was awesome."

"I really enjoyed that. Never had it like that before. Never imagined that was possible."

"I have a confession. I've always thought you were so beautiful."

"You never said anything to me."

"You always wore a ring. Tonight I saw you weren't wearing one. So I didn't know if that was something you did when you went out, when you were in a particular mood, or mode."

"Yeah. Well, my status has changed, so that altered both my mood and mode."

"Until when?"

"Until I meet someone new."

"It's not a temporary breakup?"

"It's the real deal. I'm free to do what I want and with whomever I choose."

"Sorry about the breakup."

"I'm not."

"Based on that bitter tone, sounds like a bad ending."

"I got to sleep with you, so it's not so bad. This is what I call a happy ending."

He paused. "You're the serious one at work."

"I have fun and dance with everyone else and act silly at times. Some customers hate it. We'd go crazy if we didn't have fun."

He said, "I've never seen that side of you."

"Well, when you show up, the climate changes. Every girl gets quiet and stares at you."

He said, "You always look so stush in the land of chavs."

"Really?"

"You never seemed approachable. Thought you were stuck-up."

Kwanzaa shrugged. "You didn't seem friendly. Was really surprised to see you in a club."

"I guess we read each other wrong."

"And I slept with you, of all people. I never expected this would happen."

"Do you want it to happen again before you leave?"

"Only if you want it to happen again."

"I want it to happen again."

"I was hoping you would."

They kissed. And kissed. Intense, ravenous kisses that left her breathless.

With two fingers he massaged between her legs, eased inside her. With both hands, she massaged his equipment. She thought of it as equipment, because he was well equipped.

She felt like a virgin, trying something new, unsure of what to do, how to please.

Kwanzaa's LBD from Forever 21 fell to the wooden floor, but her FMPs from DSW stayed on her feet. Feeling sexy, seductive, confident, Kwanzaa slowly took to her knees. As she held him in each hand, her phone rang. It was Marcus Brixton's ringtone.

"You need to get that?"

"It's nobody."

Licking her lips, she lowered her head and moved on with life, forgetting Marcus Brixton.

Chapter 53

With an explosion, splinters of wood took flight and the door flew open.

Hakeem bolted back into the living room in total shock.

Eddie and Nancy weren't in the living room getting Nancied and Eddied.

They were always in the front room. This was their unofficial Motel 6, where Hakeem always kept the light on for his homie. I stepped inside. I eased the door closed. Eddie wasn't in the living room. He wasn't in the kitchen. Then I heard Nancy freaking out in the bedroom.

I asked, "What's going on, Hakeem?"

We stood and looked at each other, both of us short of breath.

I said, "All of you are in the bedroom? You, Eddie, and Nancy are in the same bed? All of you are on the mattress I paid for?"

I pushed by Hakeem and went to see what the hell was going on, if he and Eddie were tag-teaming Nancy. Nancy made a sound of terror and her shadow hurried into the bathroom.

She was naked, panties and bra in her hand.

She dropped her sweatpants and hoodie along the way. The lock on the bedroom door didn't work, so she had fled to hide behind a door that she thought couldn't be opened.

Eddie wasn't there.

Food had been cooked, a meal for a king. Nancy was naked.

And Eddie wasn't here.

Tears in my eyes, jaw tight, breathing fire, I turned, scowled at Hakeem and snapped, "Wha de blood claat ah go on here?"

He barked, "I need you to leave, Destiny Jones."

I hurried toward the bathroom and beat on the door.

"I saw you, Nancy. Okay, we can do it this way or that way, but it's going to be done. You can come out of the bathroom and I'll be cool. I will be cool. I won't trip. Or I can kick the bathroom door down and make this get real, real ugly real, real fast."

The door opened one inch at a time on the face of the terrified nineteen-year-old.

She looked up and saw I had my phone in my hand, was recording this moment.

I announced, "I just walked in on Nancy having sex with Hakeem Mitchell."

"Put the camera down. Stop saying my name. Please, don't say my name."

"I walked in on Nancy having sex with Hakeem Mitchell. Nancy is Hakeem's best friend's bae. This *thot* is over here sleeping with her bae's boy. Look at this pathetic *thot*."

Behind me Hakeem shouted, "Please, please, don't do this. Not like this. Not like this."

I aimed my phone at him. "This is Eddie's best friend. He's screwing his homie's bae."

"Stop recording me."

"This is for my own protection."

"You, of all people, shouldn't want to record anyone."

"I'm only recording as a safeguard."

"Please, stop recording me."

I turned back to Nancy and called her every disgusting name I could think of.

She yelled, *"Protect me, Hakeem. Protect me. Please protect me."*

Hakeem yanked on a hoodie, grabbed his keys, and marched out the front door.

He left and didn't say a word. He just walked the hell out on both of us.

It was just Nancy, alone, facing me, shocked that he had abandoned her.

She pulled on her pink sweats and hoodie, then tried to sprint toward the door.

I stepped in front of her, asked, "Where do you think you're going?"

She cowered. "Don't hurt me."

"No one is hurting you. I have not *touched* you."

"You're Destiny Jones."

"I know who I am."

"Please, stop recording me."

"Eddie will love seeing this recording."

"Please, don't tell Eddie I slept with Hakeem. Eddie would kill Hakeem if he found out."

"I walked in on you sleeping with Hakeem."

"You weren't supposed to come over tonight. Hakeem said you weren't coming over."

"Thanks for the clear confession."

"Hakeem is just a friend. I love Eddie. I love Eddie more than you will ever know."

"But you had to have some Hakeem."

"Hakeem has a job. *I can't afford Eddie.* I've maxed out all of my charge cards and I needed to talk to Hakeem and ask him what I should do. We talked about Eddie not having money, and about you being who you are, and Hakeem told me about all the other girls Eddie is sleeping with, and I cried, and we cooked and had dinner, and then we ended up having sex."

I stopped recording the nineteen-year-old thot, then stormed to the kitchen and grabbed a butcher knife. She cowered again, set free a shriek of horror, like Jason and Freddy were after her.

I said, "Help me."

"Help you?"

"Help me."

We tussled and wrestled the mattress down the stairs. We got it to the ground floor and leaned it against the building. Then we went back for the box spring, which was easier to move because it was lighter. Nancy kept her distance. Brain on fire, anger unleashed, I used the knife and cut the mattress, I stabbed it over and over, killed it many times over, then cut it open from top to bottom, sliced it until it was unusable, then did the same with the box spring.

I wiped sweat from my face. Then I realized that it would have been much easier if I had cut them up inside the apartment.

I faced Nancy. I glowered at Eddie's girl. She shivered like she wanted to know if I was going to do the same to her.

I gave her the butcher knife handle first.

Her voice trembled. "I'm sorry about what happened to you."

I snapped, "How could you smile in my face, then be with Hakeem behind my back?"

"I didn't mean to sleep with him. I made him dinner and it just sort of happened."

"You're communal pussy, Nancy."

"That's a horrible thing to say."

"*Go, just go.*"

"Are you going to tell Eddie? I promise, I will never do this again. It was a mistake."

"*Get out of my face.* Get away from me."

Nancy ran to her car, but I think she realized she had left her keys in Hakeem's crib. She looked confused, then bolted toward the condo, ran crying, like she was trying to race back in time.

I headed toward my CBR. Saw my reflection in the window of a car.

Cotton was all over me. It was in my hair, stuck to my face, all over my clothes.

I was about to get on my motorcycle, but I saw Hakeem's Ram 3500 was still there. Wherever he went, he went on foot. The rebar I had dropped before was on the ground, feet away from me. I picked it up and hopped in the back of his ride, and then climbed on top of the cab. I raised the rebar up high, screamed out my frustration, stomped on the top of the ride like Michael Jackson did in that banned portion of his old-school "Black or White" video, beat the Ram 3500 like it had insulted my dignity. I beat the *F* out of his truck until I lost my footing and fell from the roof of the truck to the concrete. I fell fast and hard. I sat there a moment, shoulder aching. I waited for the pain to die down, breathing cold air through my mouth. I groaned and pulled myself back to my feet. When I dusted myself off, I saw Hakeem racing toward me.

"*Not my Big Wheel. I know you didn't touch my Big Wheel.*"

He was back. With money in his hand. Wherever he had gone, he'd bolted there and collected the cash to pay his debt. He sprinted to where I was, saw the slaughtered mattress, cursed, ran toward his truck, damned that damage, pulled at his hair and cussed a hundred times. I faced him, expected him to be on his phone calling the police.

Seething, he said, "You messed up my Big Wheel? *Why would you go and do that?*"

"You're a whore who has no compassion, and you're a pathetic user."

He barked, "I pay my bills. I am not a pathetic loser."

He extended his trembling hand, extended the fistful of money toward me. I didn't accept it. This was beyond financial reparations. I needed emotional reparations.

I said, "Sorry for giving you my pseudonym. Over the years people have said so many horrible things about me that I don't do social media. I don't read many posts. I keep it moving forward. You can drown trying to tread in a sea of negative opinions. I gave you the same name I give everyone when I am not with people who already know me. Even the people at my jobs call me Kismet. Don't flatter yourself. It wasn't a lie tailored for you. It was a name I used so I could fit in with the rest of the world. It's what I do . . . what I do to protect myself from any more pain."

"What else did you lie about? Does your dad really have cancer, or was that for sympathy?"

"What did *you* tell lies about, Hakeem? Why don't you be open and honest with me? You seemed like a decent guy. You were such a geek and a gentleman. You became an instant asshole."

My eyes watered, throat tightened, but I strengthened myself.

Hakeem took a deep breath. "Are you going to tell Eddie?"

"Nancy and you."

"I need you to not contact Eddie."

"Wow. I bet this has been going on a long time, if not the entire time.

You have the degree, the condo, so I bet you're more attractive to her in fiscal ways than Eddie."

"It hasn't. Just tonight. This wasn't planned. She called me and told me she had figured out who you really were, thought you were Destiny Jones, but wasn't sure. Funny thing is, I called your phone one Friday and an older woman answered it. I asked to speak to you and she said there was no one named Kismet Kellogg at the pool party, said she knew all of her daughter's friends at the party. She told me I had dialed Destiny's phone number, and then she hung up on me. I was confused, but didn't think much about it, assumed that somehow I had been connected to the wrong number. When Nancy told me, it all came together. You're a liar."

"You're trifling."

"Are you going to tell Eddie that—"

"*Hell yeah.*"

"Then I'll call One Time."

"No crime has been committed here, not by me."

"Really? I'll show them what you did to my door. That's breaking and entering. Look at this mattress and my damn Big Wheel. Destruction of property."

"The mattress belongs to me, just like your condo still belongs to the bank until you make the last payment. Just like your Big Wheel still belongs to the bank until you hand over the last payment. The mattress is *mine*. I destroyed what belongs to *me*, and that's the way it is."

"You kicked open my door."

"You think you have me in check?"

"I have you in checkmate."

"Really? You gave me a key. You gave me permission to enter. As far as they know, the chain was on, you didn't answer, and when I heard that moaning and calling out for Jesus, I assumed you had fallen and couldn't get up and in my mind there was a medical emergency and I broke the door open to save your life, only to find you in communal pussy. Checkmate, bitch."

"My Big Wheel?"

"You *Eddied* Nancy. That was for Eddying Nancy. I'm sure Eddie will do worse. He's gonna Eddie you up real good."

"Are you going to snitch? I don't want to have to call the police and bring up who you are, then see it posted on social media. Didn't have social media back then, not like now. You might trend on Twitter. Everyone will start looking online for that old video of Destiny Jones."

"Well, that was lacking in subtlety."

"I'm being straight up. I'm sure people still have that DVD in their collection."

"One night we're on the new mattress and you're telling me I'm the woman of your dreams, you're asking me to move in, saying you want to be married, not to mention you're asking to fuck my ass and come down my throat, and the next, this is where we are. You say you have no idea who I am. Well, obviously that goes both ways. No, I don't claim to be a damn saint, not tonight, but you want the world to once again laugh and share a video of an underage girl being molested to save your own ass, when you know you're the one the deepest in the wrong on this night. No matter how cool, no matter what kind of condo you have in whatever zip code, no matter how educated you are, how you treat people tells who you are in your heart. You have no integrity, no dignity, no self-esteem. You treat me like this, and you betray Eddie by getting with his girl. You're despicable. What kind of monster are you?"

"I call the cops and the *LA Times*, and when they come and make you Miss Rodney King before they drag you away to Bauchet Street and throw you in the Twin Towers Correctional Facility, this will be the talk of the town, Destiny Jones."

"This sure has changed. I thought that if I showed up, pled my case, was honest, you would see the good inside of me. I've been good to you since I met you the night Badu was on wax. I've been loyal to you. Take away what happened to me, take away what you saw on that damn DVD, and I am Kismet. The good parts of me, Kismet Kellogg, she still wanted to work this out. I will take the blame for this one, for being too afraid to be honest about all of my past."

"Are you a snitch? Should I make a call so you can end up at the world's largest jail?"

"Eddie terrifies you. He could rip your head from your neck. You Eddied Eddie's girl."

"We've been boys since we were children. He's my brother by another mother. Eddie loves Nancy, Kismet Kellogg . . . Destiny Jones . . . whoever you are. He loves her to death."

"No. I'm not a tattletale. Where I was incarcerated, it wasn't cool to be a snitch."

"Where does that leave us?"

Nancy hurried back out of the building, her pink overnight bag in her hands.

She had her pink overnight bag. This night wasn't random. This night with Nancy was planned. No matter what he said, I doubted that this was their first time. She was surprised to see I was still there. She was shocked to see Hakeem was standing near me and not freaking out.

She looked down at her overnight bag, then back at me, and she cursed out loud.

Women knew women. The biggest sluts had Disneyland looks and a princess smile to boot. Nancy hurried by us without a word. She paused when she saw the destruction to Hakeem's Big Wheel. She made a larger-than-life sound of terror, and then she sprinted to her car, saw that it was undamaged, and breathed a sigh of relief. She hopped in her car and sped away, a bandit never slowing at the speed bumps.

Tears in her eyes, the bitch left like she was making a prison break.

Nineteen years old, educated and foolish. I'll bet she was running to Eddie. She would need to damage my name, tell him her version of this night, do her best to discredit me, say anything I said would be a lie, do her best to shame me from a new angle.

I turned to Hakeem, my eyes telling him I wasn't stupid, asking why he screwed her, of all women, knowing it was stupid of me to ask why a man ever screwed another woman, or why a woman screwed another man. Hakeem was a man and Nancy was a woman. No, Hakeem wasn't a man and that bitch wasn't a woman. He was a dick and she was a cunt. So it goes. Some folks were built for infidelity. In a world where some of us wanted a friend to become our faithful lover, too many were naturally cheaters, accustomed to lying, enjoying the game.

Hakeem said, "Nancy knows how to take care of a man. She cooks. Whenever she was over here with Eddie, before she left, she cleaned up the entire condo. You never made up the bed once before you left. I took you out to eat many times; you've never cooked once."

"I work three jobs. I go to USC. I start my goddamn day before seven in the morning and leave FedEx at midnight. I don't have time to keep my apartment spotless, let alone be a man's personal chef or Molly Maid service. I'm trying to ensure my own success, not live off yours."

"Eddie tells Nancy he's hungry for a sandwich, and she gets up and makes him a meal. A woman who cooks for her man, that's attractive. A man has to eat three to five times a day. He can look at a woman who takes care of him like that and imagine her taking care of the family while he makes the money. My mom takes care of my dad in that way. Besides that, it was different with Nancy. You're all attitude. You're demanding. Yeah, I liked the challenge. When we met it was cute. You would be soft, sweet. Then you would get frustrated and change up on a bro. The first time we were in bed, you demanded I go down on you."

"If you can't get it up, you need to go down."

"The way you said it, it shocked me, and it was like I didn't have a choice. And then you asked me why I couldn't get it up. *I was nervous.* Women don't ask men those kinds of things."

"I intimidated you. I questioned your virility, your manhood, and frightened you."

"That is not the issue. I'm just saying Nancy lets Eddie be a man."

"You can't handle me."

"That's not it."

"And finding out I'm the infamous Destiny Jones, this is your way out. I applaud you, Hakeem. Kudos. You have found a convenient way of blaming the victim. This is my fault."

"I was in high school when you were on the news. My senior year. That was what the guys talked about, Destiny Jones, her night of terror, and that DVD everyone wanted to see. After you were arrested, you were the talk on the Shaw. Seems like yesterday they were slangin' that DVD from Inglewood to Palm Springs to Tucson. They were selling them right outside of my granddad's barbershop on Crenshaw, curbside, right across the street from McDonald's."

"Nice to know they were selling Happy Meals and porn for pedophiles on the same block. I get it. Be honest. All of that bull about cooking and me being better in bed than you are didn't matter a few days ago. Keep this shit real. You know who I am. You saw the DVD. You saw the things that people did to me. You know I've been assaulted and you know other people know. You don't want to be with that girl. It's hard to unsee what you've seen."

"I can't take you home to my mom . . . and she finds out . . . you made a DVD like that."

"You make it sound like I chose to be humiliated and recorded while I was unconscious."

"Why go to a motel room with that crew if you didn't go there to get fucked?"

"I went to have fun, to make friends, to dance, not to be drugged, robbed, raped, and recorded."

"You went to have sex. No one went to a motel with those cats unless they were going to have sex. Don't act like you didn't go to have sex."

"Wow. I was fifteen. I was naïve. You think I went to have sex with those creeps?"

"I'm just saying, that's the way it is. You had sex, didn't like it, and got mad afterwards."

"You saw the video. Did it look like I was into what was being done to me?"

"I saw the gang bang. I saw you doing shit you wouldn't do with me."

"Wow. Jesus. You said that like I gave out invitations to come assault me."

"Some people said you did all you did just to get attention from the media. I can't . . . I can't take a girl like you home to my parents."

"A girl like me. Nobody wants *that* girl. I get it. I don't want to *be* that girl. But hey, I sure as hell don't want to take a motherfucker who will Eddie his best friend's girlfriend around my friends either. I would never contaminate them with your presence. You have *no* character."

"And you do, *Kismet Kellogg*?"

"I never messed around on you. I never cheated. I don't just get in bed with any man."

"How would I know? You would swing by, have sex, and go. How would I know?"

"You're redoing our history. Wow. You're trying hard to justify being caught with Nancy."

"You were the one playing the game."

"When I told you I loved you, I meant it. I meant it, dammit. I fucking meant it. I am the same person. So which one of us do you think is really the backstabbing monster here?"

"You are. I read the blogs. I read what you did online. They called you a monster."

"Remember that story I told you about breaking up with hip-hop? The way my heart had beat for my culture, for the music that was protest music? Up until today, it beat for you the same way. You had me, Hakeem. Once again I have ended up feeling betrayed and with a bitter taste in my mouth. Once again, I was a fool, nothing but another starry-eyed fool needing someone to love me."

My expression was cold, as hard as the rebar I had held in my hands.

Voice shaky, he asked, "Think I can get the card for the gate back?"

I threw it on the ground near his feet.

He swallowed before he asked, "Key to my apartment?"

I threw that on the ground too.

He picked both of them up. "Your name isn't on the list at the gate anymore. Actually, now that I think about it, it never was."

"After this, I guess you and Eddie will draw straws to see who's on first with Nancy."

"Can I get you to erase what you recorded? I'm not comfortable with you having that."

"Right, Eddie doesn't approve of you Eddying Nancy and having Nancy Nancy you."

"Leave this between us. I want to protect Nancy. She's innocent in all of this."

"Wow. So you want to protect the one with questionable morals?"

"She's nineteen. I'll take the blame."

"Wow. Was the sneaky little bitch's pussy that good?"

"She made a mistake. Let's not do this to her."

"I need that inappropriate picture of me erased from your phone."

"I need that video you took of Nancy and me deleted from your phone first."

I shook my head. "You took a picture of me naked, my breasts exposed. You're disgusting. I need that and any other photo you took of me. I was *naked*. I know you took more than one. I know you did."

He said, "Don't you find this ironic? You hate to be photographed, but you just recorded Nancy."

"From the man who was caught having sex with his best friend's jump-off, being called a hypocrite has no fucking impact. And that is not the definition of irony. Read a book."

"Regardless, you know what I mean. Don't do this to Nancy. She's young. Come on. You of all people should know the power of one video, how it can destroy a person's life."

"I was violated. My spirit was violated. My soul was violated. She was being a whore."

"On the video you were being a whore too."

"I don't remember anything that happened. I was drugged."

"Look at the DVD, bitch. You got ass fucked. You swallowed nuts like a damn squirrel. Before you call Nancy a whore, review your own fucking DVD, Destiny Jones."

Life drained from my face. I had been drugged, but I had seen the video, had seen what was done to me while I was drugged, when I was not conscious. I went numb, my expression hard as the rebar. Hakeem stood like he was trying to think of what to say next, of his next insult.

He said, "Don't just look at me like that. Say something."

My inability to blink and my thick breathing told him that his words had cut deep.

He had cut away my tongue.

He looked at me and chanted, " Do the Moe. Do the Moe. Do the Moe."

My soul had convulsions. Fissures in my heart widened. He chanted the song my rapist had chanted that night.

Hakeem Mitchell said, "You did the Moe, and you did the Moe real good, Destiny Jones."

I had nothing to say. I felt as defeated now as I had felt in court. Again I had been abused.

He growled. "Crazy bitch."

He jogged back toward his mattress-less apartment.

I took hard breaths, made the wall between me and the rest of the world touch the sky, fortified my emotions and made myself colder and thicker than two miles of ice. I became harsh land, my vulgar mumbles crueler than winter in Verkhoyansk, Russia. Hakeem was the third guy I had dated since Hoosegow. Loneliness, the need to be touched made us all susceptible, made us all let the walls down. It was inevitable. This was just another failed attempt at fitting into the world. Hakeem was nothing new, but that didn't stop it from hurting.

My throat tightened, face became red-hot, and again it was hard to breathe.

My phone buzzed. Ericka. She'd taken the medicine to my dad. Indigo had texted me wanting to know where in the world was Carmen Sandiego. I didn't reply. Right after that, my phone kept buzzing. Kwanzaa called me back. I didn't answer. My dad called. I didn't answer. My mom called. I didn't answer. Indigo sent another text message. I didn't bother looking at it.

I scowled at the damage I had done in a matter of moments. Hakeem should've apologized for the way he had reacted to my shame. He never should've slammed the door in my face like a master dismissing a slave. You don't have sex with a woman, tell her you love her, get her to love you, wine her, dine her, give her a key, ask her to move in, talk marriage, get busted in bed with another woman before the dust had settled, and then treat her that way. I'm not a dog. That bitch with balls should've manned-up, paid me what he owed, deleted the picture, and I would have left him alone. I never should have said I was Kismet, but then again, I shouldn't have to live in the past. But my past was tethered to me. Tonight it had its fangs deep in my flesh. Each drop of sweat that fell from my forehead and neck felt like blood coming out of my pores.

Once some bridges were crossed, this fucked-up world never allowed you to come back. For some people, the world was their Hoosegow.

I didn't have to be Kismet anymore. Not here. Not with Hakeem Mitchell.

I could kill him for that photo he'd taken of me when I was in his bed, unconscious, sleeping. I could kill him dead.

Rebar in hand I dashed back toward his condo, up the stairs.

He was unable to lock his door so I pushed my way inside.

He saw me the way the others had seen me when I went to get my revenge. He saw the anger in my face. He saw the rebar in my hand.

I said, "Too bad you didn't delete that photo. That was all you had to do. Blood claat, that was all you had to do."

With the heel of my boot, I pushed his damaged door, kicked it and closed it the best I could, smiled a nasty smile, then sprinted toward Hakeem Mitchell, swung the rebar and showed him Destiny Jones.

I showed him the crazy bitch.

Chapter 54

Mr. Jones pulled Ericka closer to him, held her awhile, exhaled, studied her face, gazed into her eyes. She felt him shake, felt his nervousness now, felt his guilt, yet felt his desire, felt that chained desire, same as she had the first time. She felt him about to back off, pull away.

She took his hands, placed them on her butt. He sighed like an angel losing his power to an imp. She touched his face, the face of her friend's father, a nervous man who looked at her like she was Lolita. There was no manipulation, only love. This was her heart talking, not her loins. He was the man who made her laugh, the man who made her smile. She took one of his hands, placed it on her breast, on her heart. She moved the other hand from her butt, put his fingers between her legs.

He kissed her neck, massaged her breast, and hummed an old-school tune. Ericka tingled, lost her breath when Mr. Jones pulled her closer. They kissed. They kissed again.

Just like that she became a star collapsing under gravity, ready to burst into a gigantic super nova. His kisses made her want to explode. So wet.

She was hotter than the surface of the sun and soon she would become a waterfall.

She held his hand as he went to turn off most of the lights, her eyes on his strong arms, on the sexy tribal band on his right arm, and she followed him back to the sofa, to that magical sofa. Things quickly moved from her breasts being nurtured, to her nipples being suckled while she measured him with two hands. She masturbated him with both hands. She sucked him, sucked and his precome was sweet, nutty, like raw hemp seeds. As they sat on the sofa, it evolved from him pulling away his clothing, to one finger being inside her, to two thick fingers being inside her, to feeling a blinding light, to feeling his weight on hers, to being penetrated, to having sex, having sex on the living room sofa, to sliding from the sofa to the cool living room floor, to neck grabbing, hair pulling, tongue sucking, back scratching, neck biting, to Mr. Jones savoring her pinkness, to Ericka feeling him at the back of her throat, to having her legs around his waist while he stood, his big cock deep inside her as he carried her. She held on to his arms. He was still strong. If he was this strong now, twenty years ago he had to have been hell in the bedroom. They had sex in the hallway that led to the stairs that led to the bedroom, and that shifted to them having sex against the wall, morphed to them having doggie sex on the carpeted stairs on the way down to the master bedroom, then to having sex in the bedroom's door-frame, to having sex at the edge of the bed, to having sex in the middle of the bed, to him pinning her down and making the bed squeak and squeak and squeak, to her riding him, riding and moaning. He took control, took her through five different doggie-style positions. They moved, initiated having sex in a chair. Her phone vibrated as expected, probably Indigo. Or it was Destiny calling to make sure the meds had been delivered to her dad. They all had the same ringtone, the song "Blackbirds," the version from the movie about a suicidal pop star. Her fear was Destiny walking in her dad's front door unannounced. She would have seen her red SLK parked out front, a car that would be hard not to notice, and thought nothing about it. There was no reason to think anything about it. Destiny would come into the townhome and hear Ericka knocking boots with Mr. Jones.

She didn't want Destiny to see one of her Blackbirds and her dad in the middle of doing the *bow chica wow wow* all over the place. But it was in motion; the passion didn't slow down.

Some fires could be extinguished. Some had too much power. The fire she felt had grown hotter and more dangerous. Pent-up emotions were the fuel. To her, it was as inevitable as it was unavoidable. And even after the flames had died, it could still smolder for years.

The fire burned and the updrafts were powerful.

There should have been clouds in the bedroom.

The fire owned her.

When she was with him, she could feel her heart beat in her chest.

She didn't want to die.

She wanted to fight and live.

She wanted to get to the other side of cancer and fall into the fantasy in her head. While eating oatmeal and turkey sausage at CJ's Café on La Brea with Mr. Jones after he took her to chemo, her crush evolved into the deepest love. When Mr. Jones was diagnosed with cancer, Destiny had cried, Indigo had cried, and Kwanzaa had cried. But Ericka had broken down. She had cried the hardest. She had thought about Mr. Jones dying and not knowing how she felt. She had opened herself up, she had taken a chance, and she had made her feelings known, hoping he had felt half as much for her as she did for him. The sex evolved to her being on her knees on the same chair, and moved from there to the thick Oriental carpet. She only saw it as making love to a kind man. She saw it as finally reconnecting with a man who, despite any perceived fault or disease, in her eyes, was perfect.

This felt like a one-of-a-kind love.

This was part of her bucket list.

She wanted Mr. Jones to hold on to her. She wanted to hold on to Destiny's hardworking, super, totally cool, hot dad. She wanted to hold on to the man she saw as a gift from God.

What she felt for Mr. Jones she had never felt for her ex-husband.

She loved Mr. Jones, and the love she had for him was as poignant as it was full.

She finally knew what being happy felt like.

Chapter 55

Leather belt around Hakeem's neck like it was a noose, my heeled motorcycle boot against the back of his head, pushing, strangling him, Hakeem beat the floor in submission, begged me to stop. It had taken a minute, maybe two, but we finally had an understanding.

Do unto others. Make them remember. I had learned that in Hoosegow. That was how a naïve fifteen-year-old had learned to survive in Hoosegow. Be an angel to those who respected you. Those who dissed you, make them wish they'd met the devil instead.

I let him go, left him gasping for air. I stepped over overturned furniture, over a broken coffee table, over fallen family pictures, and went to the kitchen, took another sharp knife, and while he scooted back, tried to crawl away from me, I carved a profound message in his front door, left a warning letting all others know what kind of philandering man he was. It was the kind of message no man wanted the police to see, the type of message no man wanted in a police report. They would see the artwork and know he'd treated a woman wrong, and no matter how severe the damage, they would fault him, they would blame the victim who reported the crime.

I dropped the knife, was about to leave, but remembered I wasn't done here. I went to the bathroom, retrieved my toothbrush and tongue brush, then went to the pantry for my box of Honey Nut Cheerios. I glowered at the condo I'd never visit again, at the man Kismet's heart still loved. I snapped a photo of Hakeem, on the floor, beaten like he'd never been beaten before, bested by Destiny Jones. Then I snapped a photo of the message engraved in his door.

I made the Vulcan salute, and said, "Live long and prosper, bitch."

We held eye contact. He was too terrified to utter a word.

Whatever we'd had was upside-down and inside-out now.

I walked out the ruined door, eased it closed behind this broken affair.

Hakeem's phone in my hand, I headed back downstairs, deleting all photos. He had taken over thirty shots of me sleeping in the nude, from every angle possible. When I was near his damaged Big Wheel, I dropped his phone on the pavement. I expected to hear sirens, to see police, same as it had been on that night a long time ago. Scared because of what I had done, and at the same time trying not to be girly and break down, I threw my Honey Nut Cheerios, toothbrush, and tongue brush into the garbage bin. With my phone, as tears rolled from my eyes over my cheeks, to my chin, I sent the video I had taken of Nancy and Hakeem to Eddie. I hoped Eddie came over and kicked Hakeem's ass too.

Chapter 56

The Kismet Kellogg inside me ached. I had broken up with Hakeem.

The Destiny Jones part of me was afraid. I had committed a crime. I rode not knowing if Hoosegow was once again in my future.

This could be the road where my freedom ended.

I zigzagged streets doing the speed limit, heard sirens yelling from all directions, heard the wails of those who were sworn to protect and serve as I white-lined traffic and fled east. When I was caught at a light, I was startled when another biker pulled up next to me, rolling in neutral, the engine revving to get my attention. Pink CBR. Pink Shark helmet. It was Indigo. She gave me the thumbs-up, then pulled her helmet up on top of her head for a second, took out tissues, and blew her nose.

I flipped up my face mask and asked, "You still feel bad?"

"I feel pretty good now. Just the end of the congestion, I think."

"You shouldn't be riding in the night air. You should be either in your Rubicon or rocking the BMW with the heater on."

"I'm happy to see you too."

It was dark so she couldn't see my red eyes.

I didn't ask her where she was coming from, or why she was riding in the chill of the night when she knew she wasn't feeling well. I guessed she had been to Bel Air to spend time with Olamilekan. Or had crept to the Palisades to be with Yaba. Life was that way for the unsettled.

Police cars whizzed by, lights flashing.

My heart raced. I thought about Hoosegow, the one for adults.

Indigo and I headed south, sped against the crisp night air, rode against the wind, and I drove with a few tears falling, still trying to out-run Kismet's unwanted emotions, her undeserved heartbreak, trying to speed away from the pangs of my past, trying to get away from a false love. Indigo kept up. When we hit Crenshaw, we caught up with Ericka. She was heading home too. As we all turned left into our four-unit apartment complex, Kwanzaa's car came from the opposite way, had come up West Century and turned north on Crenshaw. She flashed her lights and blew her horn at us and let us all go before her, then turned right inside the gate behind us, the last to enter Little Lagos.

Colorful balloons were all over the rails, more than I had left out this morning. Ericka had hooked it up real nice.

Thirty seconds later, we were all smiles, checking whatever issues we had at the gate, singing "Happy Birthday" to Kwanzaa Browne, first the traditional version, then the Stevie Wonder version. We all went to our individual nests, and took quick showers. I did the last of my crying in the bathroom, cried and gave those tears to the ocean. We all dressed in inexpensive costumes we had bought in Santa Monica. This was what Kwanzaa wanted us to do. It was silly, but it was her birthday and she wanted us to dress up like characters from *Ever After High*.

Kwanzaa wore a Cerise Hood costume. Cerise Hood was the daughter of Red Riding Hood and the Big Bad Wolf. Indigo was Raven Queen, the daughter of the Evil Queen and the Good King. I was blessed with the attire of Apple White, the daughter of Snow White and her king. Two days ago, I would have seen my costume as the perfect costume, but I thought I had found my *muh-fukin'* king. Hakeem had turned out to be just another court jester. Ericka became Briar Beauty, daughter of Sleeping Beauty and the prince.

All the characters from *Ever After High* were rebels and friends.

We reconvened in Kwanzaa's apartment to open wine and share a bottle in celebration.

As always, I became James Van Der Zee. They gave me their phones and I took what seemed like a hundred photos of my Blackbirds. They posted their photos to social media right away. I shot a video for Snap-chat. Kwanzaa used a feature to make them all look like raging demons that needed an exorcism. It became laughs, hilarity, and silliness real quick.

The food Ericka had cooked earlier was put in the microwave and a small birthday cake from Hansen's was on the table. We sang to her again, this time with me recording the moment. It felt like I needed two bottles of wine for myself. Indigo had carried homemade chicken soup in her backpack, the soup in a Tupperware bowl, the sealed Tupperware wrapped in Saran wrap.

Her hair had been rebraided and it looked awesome.

Kwanzaa asked, "Did you go see the Dominicans?"

"I got it braided on Venice Beach."

Indigo was in a good mood and had a fresh bruise on her neck. As melanin-blessed as she was, Olamilekan or Yaba or some new dude had to suck hard for that to become visible. My guess was the American footballer had scored a few touchdowns tonight.

Kwanzaa had a hickey on her neck as well. No one else noticed. I refused to ask her if she had seen Marcus Brixton. Most surprising of all, Ericka Stockwell's neck looked discolored too. Her hair was too short to hide the mark. That was twice in a few weeks I had noticed that sudden rash. A woman with her complexion, her skin told stories.

Indigo asked, "Destiny, are you okay?"

"I'm great."

"You look intense."

"Why do you look like you've been shaken up and stirred?"

Indigo shrugged. "Did you stop by Hakeem's? You look shaken and stirred too."

"Yeah. I went to see him."

"Your eyes are bloodshot."

"Might be catching what you've got."

"I hope not. We don't need two of us with this issue."

Kwanzaa said, "Destiny, is Momma Jones back in the country?"

"My mom should be here in a few days. Whassup?"

"Marcus lied about me. But I don't want to get into it right now. Your mom knows how to handle things. Your mom knows people. I need to get in contact with Momma Jones."

"I won't be angry, but are you sleeping with that scum Marcus Brixton again?"

"Hell no. He won't ever see, touch, taste, smell, or hear this again."

"He can hear it? Does he put your conch up to his ear and hear the roar of the ocean?"

"Marcus has messed with the wrong one. Just get me in touch with your mother."

"How bad?"

"This is worse than Hurricane Katrina and the crash of the *Exxon Valdez*."

"Damn."

"He has messed with the wrong one. And on my mammy-sucking birthday."

I nodded, felt her anger, left that issue at that, said, "Ericka?"

"Hey, Destiny."

"You okay?"

"I'm trying not to laugh. Marcus will never hear the roar of the ocean again."

I hand-combed my locks, then asked, "Who dropped the package off at my dad's?"

Ericka raised her hand, like in a classroom. "Oh, yeah. I was your drug runner tonight."

Ericka ate a bag of potato chips at record pace, then jumped up, danced while she sipped wine. Her skin was flushed, her hair smelled like weed, and she had the munchies.

Kwanzaa got up, started dancing to "Uptown Funk" with Ericka.

Suddenly Kwanzaa had a broad smile, and as deep brown as her skin was, a sweet glow. Cerise Hood and Briar Beauty were getting down like they were Bruno Mars. Indigo joined in, and the Raven Queen danced like she was the happiest of the lot.

She asked, "What's the plan, birthday girl?"

Kwanzaa said, "Okay, tomorrow we're taking the tops and doors off your Rubicon and going to Belmont Shore. We're having breakfast at a bistro on Second Street with my dad and my stepmother. I want to go to La Creperie Café. Then we're going to say good-bye to them to kick it at one of the beaches between there and Huntington Beach with my mom and my stepdad. We'll be low-key, so bring your suntan lotion and reading material, and after I kick my mom and bonus dad to the curb, on the way back we're stopping in Long Beach and we're going to For-ever 21 at the Pike to see what's on sale, maybe go by H&M and see what's on sale too, and we're riding the Ferris wheel. Then we're bowl-ing at El Dorado Lanes on Lincoln in Westchester."

Kwanzaa stopped dancing and sat back down. Indigo sat back down too.

Ericka danced around the living room and said, "Get up and dance, y'all. Destiny, grab a phone and take some more photos. *Hot damn.* We should have gone out dressed like this."

Kwanzaa laughed. "What did you do today that has you bouncing off the walls?"

Ericka laughed. "Went to see Dr. Dubois. Got that out of the way. I still can't believe she remembered me and Mrs. Stockwell."

Kwanzaa asked, "Do you ever call the woman who gave you life your mother or your momma?"

"The only place it will say she is my mother is in her obituary, and on my copy it will be scratched over or blacked out or I'll use Wite-Out or chew her name out of the program."

I asked, "Did you see the doctor after you dropped the meds off at my dad's crib?"

"Before. Indigo pulled a disappearing act on me and I was left hold-ing the bag, so after I spent some time at Debra's office, I had to come all the way back here to get the package. I made dinner, cleaned up my place, then I took it to your dad's crib. Feels like a ton of stress has been lifted today. I feel light. Now get up and dance, Apple White. Get up and dance. Stop acting like Hakeem wore your butt out."

"So how was the visit with Leonard's mom? What did she write about you and your mom?"

Ericka stopped dancing and smiling like it was the morning after a good night.

She said, "She was real cool, real nice to me, but I am still scared to read whatever she wrote about me and the wicked witch."

Ericka said that she had the pages that Debra Dubois had given her in her apartment. She wanted one of us to read them before she dared to revisit her past. Ericka handed me a card that had Leonard Dubois Jr.'s cell number on the back.

She said, "Your name came up. Your first love wants to get in contact with you."

"He wasn't my first love. He was my only one-off, and should have been a never-off."

"Your first lover is still crushing on you after all these years. That's so cute."

"The way he was carrying on, are you sure that number isn't for Indigo or Kwanzaa?"

Ericka laughed like she was buzzed beyond belief.

Indigo asked, "What kind of juice are you on, Ericka?"

Ericka kept on singing and dancing.

We sipped wine like queens without kings. We celebrated like we'd never had an issue in the world. We danced like heathens. We sat at Kwanzaa's kitchen table, ate more food, became the characters from *Ever After High*, played Scrabble and partied geek-and-nerd style. We cleaned up, grabbed pillows, and got comfortable on the sofa and floor.

Kwanzaa turned on the television, used the app I'd installed and streamed *Medicine for Melancholy*. Ericka fell asleep ten minutes into the movie. Then Indigo gave in and the Raven Queen was out like a light. About three-quarters through, Kwanzaa pulled her hood over her head, and soon feel asleep texting someone. Her phone dropped from her lap. When the movie ended, I peeped at her screen. She had thanked some guy named Cristiano for kicking it with her at the Club. She also had been online looking at photos of men who had been born with a condition known as diphallia, resulting in them being born with two penises.

I guess that was the type of porn she needed to play the fiddle and get through the night. I guess she craved a unicorn.

Made me wonder about Marcus. There was a message from him as well.

I was tempted to scroll up and read the exchanges between her and

Marcus, but I didn't give in. I respected her privacy. As a friend I supported all her decisions, good or bad.

I was a ride-or-die friend.

I turned the television off, collapsed on the sofa with Ericka, our heads at opposite ends. She had been so happy tonight. The same way I had felt when I had started with Hakeem.

I hadn't seen Ericka with that kind of glow but once since we'd all been living in the quads, and that was a few weeks ago. I bet she was seeing some guy at her job as a booty call.

I tried to sleep at Kwanzaa's place, but kept tossing and turning, kept sitting up, kept feeling the angst breathing in my chest, felt the downside of love burning in my bloodstream like a hot poison, so I stood outside awhile. Dressed like Apple White, probably looking either silly or like a hooker to anyone who looked up and saw me leaning against the railing, I took in the night air, listened to the noises of the restless city, to the cars, to the sirens, to the echoes of danger, to society gone bad, to culture gone wrong, to a gluten-free world abandoned by its savior. The din was overshadowed by the rudeness and loudness of music bumping as carloads of inconsiderate fools went by.

I'd get over Hakeem. I would get to the other side of this bad feeling, same as I have other things.

I sat on the stairs trying to freeze myself in the desert air, then finally yawned, gave up on punishing myself, and ended up walking back to my apartment, to my unmade bed.

I pulled myself into a fetal position.

I wanted to erase Hakeem from my mind, never mention him again, and move on.

I suffered the same intense feelings for Hakeem that Kwanzaa had had for Brixton.

We didn't make it to my birthday. I had wanted to tell him who I was before then, and had hoped he would have accepted me as Destiny, had hoped I could have paraded my happiness in front of my girls, in front of my dad, in front of my mom, in front of the world that had belittled me.

Beyond our walls, beyond our gates, the scream of sirens resounded.

Each cry reminded me of when they had come for me. It reminded me of when they had thrown a fifteen-year-old on the ground like she was a terrorist, handcuffed her in front of her mother, father, grandparents, perp-walked her in front of the entire community, and with local news recording every precious moment, they had dragged her away, her mother and father yelling, grandparents screaming and crying in the background. Her face had been blurred on the news, but the community knew which private school girl had taken a sudden fall from grace.

The rest was in court records, seventy-four pages of my life in black and white.

Being arrested was only the tip of the iceberg. That was the kindest thing that had happened during that twenty-four-hour period of my life. Hakeem had gotten off easy. This season, I had been nice, the Kismet that lived inside of me had ruled.

He wasn't a prize, but Kismet had loved him, and love was powerful.

Love made you give an unworthy fool an undeserved break.

I whispered, "Bye-bye, Kismet. Bye-bye."

Chapter 57

Three weeks later, Ericka Stockwell was back at Kaiser on Cadillac.

She was in the basement, in a chair, giving enough blood to fill twelve vials. Tests had to be run. The next day she was back, in the Alliance Imaging trailer that came twice a week, for a positron emission tomography scan. It wasn't her first time having her body injected with a radioactive substance so they could look for disease in her body. After the injection, she had to sit in a cold room alone, wait an hour, thinking, anxious, and then lie on a narrow table that slid into a tunnel-shaped scanner. Ericka closed her eyes, struggled with mild claustrophobia.

She thought about life. She thought about death. Hospitals made people think of both. The same places where babies were born and cried also had freezers in the basements, those rooms quiet. Everyone with the horrific disease was forced to think about the inevitable.

The doctor told her the PET scan would detect signals from the tracer in her blood stream, and a computer would convert the signals into 3-D pictures. The images would be displayed on a monitor for her oncologist to read. She had done this before so she already knew, but she listened anyway. She had to lie still during the test. Too much movement would blur images, cause errors. She wondered why this, of all journeys, was her designated journey.

Kwanzaa's grandparents had both died from cancer; her grandmother had had colon cancer and her grandfather had had throat cancer. Both died long before she was born.

It frightened Ericka. Knowing so many people whose bodies had all but eaten themselves alive, it terrified her like nothing else.

When Ericka left the trailer, she was surprised to see Mr. Jones seated on the patio between the main building on Cadillac and the building on Venice. She had told him she had an appointment, but hadn't expected him to be outside waiting for her. He looked handsome. Tan jeans. His 1000 Mile boots. He rocked a tee that read PUT DOWN THE GUNS AND PICK UP GLOVES. The image of a gun and boxing gloves in the ring was across his chest.

He gave her a hug.

He touched her and all her emotions rose to the surface.

She didn't want him to let her go. She wanted to cry, but didn't.

She asked, "What are you doing here?"

"I missed you."

"For real? You missed me?"

He said, "I know you had to fast before your PET scan. Thought you might want to go over on Pico for some chicken and waffles, or go around the corner and eat at Sabores de Oaxaca. If you have time, we could go to the Mad Carrot. Sweet spot I found right off the beach in Playa del Rey. We can walk around after."

"I would love to kick it with you and add fat to my butt and thighs, Mr. Jones."

"Scared?"

"Yeah. I don't want to go through this cancer shit again. I can't handle this again."

"I meant scared of being seen in public with me."

"Oh. I feel silly now."

"We're going to be okay, Ericka."

"I'm trying to not act like I'm concerned, but I am."

"We're going to be okay."

"And to answer your question, I'm not scared to be seen with you."

He said, "I don't want you to be uncomfortable."

"It's not like we're cheating on anyone."

"If we're going to kiss, we'd better kiss before we're in public."

Ericka grinned. "Oh, you want a kiss too?"

"I will at some point. If that's okay with you. Been thinking about kissing you all morning."

"Can we negotiate the terms?"

"Like it or not, I'm going to kiss you when we get in the garage."

"If you're going to get a kiss, you have to get a kiss right here."

"Right here?"

"Right here."

"You think I won't?"

"Right now."

"Are you daring me, Miss Stockwell?"

"I'm ordering you. I need you to kiss me. I'm scared."

Mr. Jones held Ericka Stockwell's face in his hands. As people passed, walking from building to building, as people were pushed in wheelchairs, as ambulances arrived, as people limped toward Urgent Care, as people exited the parking garage, on a clear day, he kissed her.

She asked him, "Do you think we ever get to a point in life where we are as healthy as we will ever be? Where we are as beautiful as we will ever be? When we are as strong as we will ever be? Where anything good that is going to happen to you has already come and gone?"

"You're kissing me. So that means good things are still coming my way."

Mr. Jones wiped away the tears raining from Ericka's eyes, then kissed her again.

DESTINY'S BIRTHDAY

Chapter 58

Ericka escaped her nest, was spending the day with Mr. Jones.

It was three weeks before Destiny Jones's birthday.

That Friday morning, as they rode I-15 through San Bernardino County toward the sunrise, when they were six miles southwest of Baker, California, and one hundred miles from Las Vegas, Nevada, Ericka stopped singing, peeped over her shades toward the Mojave, and saw an exit sign that led to an unincorporated community in the unofficial middle of nowhere.

Excited, she pointed at the sign and shouted, "Z for Zzyzzx. *Z for Zzyzzx. Boo-yow.*"

Dressed in jeans and an Iron Man T-shirt, Mr. Jones laughed, rubbed his shaven head, and said, "Damn. I was hoping you missed that *stupid* exit sign. Thought I was going to catch up."

"You know why the man who lived that way named his street Zzyzzx?"

"To make people spit when they asked for directions?"

"No, but that's probably a better reason than the truth."

"No idea why anyone would pick that unusual name for an exit to nowhere."

"So it could be the last word in the English language."

"The things we do for attention and to feel immortal and smart."

"I've beat you at the word game four times in a row. I'm bad; I'm bad; who bad? I'm bad."

"Remind me to bow at your feet."

"Suck my toes while you're down there."

"You know I will."

"That's why I got a pedicure. That foot fetish of yours."

"I'll stop sucking your toes."

"You better not. You stop sucking, I stop sucking."

They were in Ericka's roadster, riding I-15 north toward Sin City to add a little more sin to the city. As Ericka relaxed in the passenger seat, they listened to Babyface and Toni Braxton sing about marriage and divorce. Ericka sang off and on, and at the same time they had played the alphabet game, where they had to find the letters of the alphabet sequentially on objects, buses, cars, billboards, exit signs. *A* is for Arby's. *B* is for Burger King. *C* is for Cudahy.

It was silly, but it was simple and idiot-proof.

Ericka had taken a day off work, had planned the day off two weeks ago, but hadn't told the Blackbirds. She and Mr. Jones had left his condo for Las Vegas at five in the morning.

They had planned to spend the day, eat at the Bacchanal Buffet at Caesars Palace, play Blackjack, maybe take in a show, eat at the Bellagio, walk the Strip holding hands, and spend the night kissing, nude, in each other's arms. Ericka smiled. It was their first real date. They were taking a trip together. It would be their first time spending the day and the night together and not worrying about being seen.

They would shower together. They would share a bed.

She asked, "How is your energy?"

"It's not too bad."

"I can drive. I don't mind driving."

"I want you to relax, Ericka."

"I'm fine."

"How is your energy?"

"The Blackbirds keep me busy, in a good way. Last Saturday morning we did the stairs at Santa Monica, and after that we were on Venice Beach playing two-against-two volleyball in the sand for about an hour and a half, then we drove to Santa Barbara and ate at the Honor Bar. Sunday we went to Racer's Edge and rode the go-karts. The Blackbirds are so competitive."

"You overdid it."

"Maybe. I felt a bit exhausted."

"How's your sleeping?"

"My sleep has been off. Well, not off. Just been giving you all of my extra energy."

"Don't blame me."

"The Blackbirds had so much fun last weekend. Two weeks before that, Indigo, Kwanzaa, Destiny, and I were all part of the solidarity walkouts at the Southern California universities."

"West Coast is emulating the black student movement on the other side of the country."

"The Blackbirds are supporting positive change, protesting the system."

"Stand for something, or fall for anything. Many leaders have cried that out to the people."

"Next week we're going to Loyola Marymount University to listen to professors, lawyers, all types of scholars and activists talk on the caging of the black woman in America. Love my Blackbirds, and I want the world to change, but I need some private time with you. I need to get away from protesting, grading papers, lesson plans, and give you my full attention. Today, I just want to chill out and be a woman with a man doing things a woman does with a man."

Ericka had been sneaking away from the Blackbirds and spending time with Mr. Jones, as much time as she could. Midnight movies at the Nuart, eating popcorn, chicken empanadas, veggie dogs, and curly fries, while sipping red wine from Argentina and drinking West Coast IPA, then leaving the movie hand in hand. They had gone to a Sunday matinee to see *The Black Panthers: Vanguard of the Revolution*, then sat in Starbucks and critiqued the portrayal of Huey Newton as a borderline psychopath. They had gone to the Hollywood Horror Museum, to see Sonia Sanchez at the American Film Institute, to cafés along the beaches, and to concerts.

She had spent many evenings with Mr. Jones, and not always at his condo.

One evening they had met at Deano's Motel on Sepulveda off the

405 at Venice, where they had cable television and telephones, and the worn signs on the building looked like they had been up since the '70s. Having sexy time in a trashy motel had been on Ericka's bucket list. People at the motel probably thought Mr. Jones was a perverted client because she had dressed up like she was a student from Gryffindor. They had visited three other local motels. She was a hooker from Hufflepuff when they had gone to the Jet Inn on Slauson near Overhill. At the Sea Way Motel on Venice next to Kaiser, sixth-grade schoolteacher Ericka Stockwell was dressed in her provocative Ravenclaw attire. At another motel near LAX she was a sexy student from Slytherin. She was enjoying life. For once she was enjoying the sensual aspect of living.

Great loving and good laughs with a partner in crime who was capable of epic conversations, and gave her friendship, was more than she had ever expected from Mr. Jones.

It wasn't fair that it had arrived this late in her life. She hung on to her denial, refused to let her heart accept what her mind already knew. She would not ruin anyone's birthday. She would pretend until the end.

She looked at the sky, fell into nephelococcygia, the term that meant one looked for and saw shapes in the clouds. She saw hearts. She saw beautiful hearts.

Ericka wore jean shorts and double wifebeaters. She wanted to be sexy for Mr. Jones. Her tennis shoes were off and her right foot was on the dash, seat all the way back, as Mr. Jones drove her toward what felt like a honeymoon retreat. Her legs spread just enough to give her lover a glimpse of the makings of the Promised Land. Ericka had been smiling and laughing and flirting since she had arrived at Mr. Jones's home early in the morning. She had had sex with him to start the day, a nice ten-minute groove, showered, and headed to the car so they could beat as much traffic as possible. She used to be quiet around Mr. Jones, timid, but now she felt like she was full of words, had so many things to say to him, wanted him to know everything about her.

A little nervous, she asked, "Where did you tell Destiny you were going?"

"I told her I had to go out to Palm Springs for an engineering conference. You?"

"I haven't told the Blackbirds anything. I packed my bag three days ago and left it in my car, so when I left this morning, all they saw me carrying was the usual stuff I take to work."

"So, I guess you're being bad and metaphorically sneaking out of the window."

"I guess I am. I guess at some point everyone needs to get away from everyone."

"You need to tell them something."

"Jesus. We act like we're plotting against the government."

"Overthrowing the government might be easier."

"I'll group text and say I met a handsome man and I'm going to screw his brains out."

Mr. Jones laughed. "I think you did that a while ago, Miss Stockwell."

Ericka said, "They are so busy studying, they won't miss me."

They rode a few miles, music playing, and for a while Ericka talked about work, the inner-city children, the problem children with problem parents, the incompetent teachers, the stress management that received little to no accolades, explained to Mr. Jones how she was a counselor and a mother to not only her classroom, but also to almost every black child on the campus. She had become a mother to many. At times she felt she was the sage Blackbird.

They were on a tract of two-lane freeway where everyone was doing at least ninety miles per hour in the slow lane, a stretch where rest stops were at least fifty years apart, gas stations two galaxies apart, and signs said BEWARE because TRAFFIC was being MONITORED BY AIRCRAFT. It was so hot that Ericka bet the devil himself was inside a CVS drugstore, under an air conditioner, resting in a hammock, eating a double-dip praline pecan ice cream cone, and reading a book.

Being in a car, riding through the 110-degree heat with nothing to see but freeway, dirt, and mountains, nothing to look at but each other, no one to talk to except each other, for close to five hours, in a tight roadster, the world could become cramped, claustrophobic.

It definitely let a person know if they got along with whomever was riding in the car with them. Ericka and her ex-husband had made this trip once. It had been a five-hour drive from hell. They had argued the

whole way. They never had been able to get along when there was silence, when there was truth. Ericka and her ex-husband had gone crazy
and cursed each other out and ended up breaking up on the road, only
to get back together, only to end up getting married. But she wished she
had hit him in the head with a shovel and buried him in the middle of
the desert, in one of those dirt mounds on either side of the highway,
like they did in that Vegas movie Robert De Niro and Sharon Stone had
been in once upon a time.

With Mr. Jones, time was flying.

She wished her car were smaller so they could be closer.

Ericka said, "Mr. Jones?"

"Yeah?'

"Is it okay if I tell you something at the risk of offending you?"

"You can tell me anything."

"I love you, Mr. Jones. Don't say anything back. I wanted to say that I
love you. I want to put that in the air, let the universe absorb those words
as I say them out loud. I love you. I expect nothing. Nothing at all. Just
wanted to tell you how I feel about you at this moment. I love you."

Mr. Jones smiled. "May I say something?"

"Don't say what I said. You can't say what I said, not even using a
synonym."

"It's not the same thing."

"Okay. As long as it's not the opposite."

"I remember when I saw you at your wedding. I had known you
forever, but when I saw you at your wedding, I didn't see you as a child
anymore. That wedding dress, and your body, the way it fit and made
you look like a princess, I will never forget how it made me feel, how I
stared at you, and on your wedding day I wanted to be your prince.
You'd become a woman, and I had no idea when that had happened. You
were a woman under the rules of the law, no longer walking the rim of
adulthood. I saw you at your wedding and lust filled my heart. Maybe it
should have bothered me, and it did, but it never bothered me enough.
I looked at you at your wedding, when you were smiling, when you
looked happy, and you captured something in my heart, and in that
moment I felt powerless, because I wanted you to smile for me like that,

but I had felt that I was asking for the wrong kind of love. I had known you since you were a child living under your parents' roof, since I was a married man myself, and when I saw you at your wedding I did the math, the age difference. I was already having sex when you were born. When your mother screamed in pain as she gave birth to you, I was probably somewhere trying to make some girl scream with pleasure. But when I saw you at your wedding, all of that went away. I just saw a woman. That's what I see now, Ericka, and that's how I see you, as a woman. I talk a lot, imagine other worlds, and maybe in one we were born closer to the same age, and in that world we found each other too."

"You should've pushed my ex-husband aside and demanded I marry you instead."

"That would have gone smoothly."

"Maybe in one world I am Destiny's mother. Or at least her step-mother."

"I hope so. But I'm trying not to get too used to you being around in this world."

"Don't bury me yet."

"That's not what I am saying. Don't be morbid."

"What are you saying?"

"I'm saying that I'm glad you're in my world. I don't want to lose what we share. And at the same time, I am glad that you are my daughter's friend. I don't want her to lose you."

"I've found you, Mr. Jones. I've found love. I don't want to lose you."

He asked, "Does it scare you? This secret thing we have, does it scare you?"

"It does. It took me years to find friends, good friends, and now I'm the one not worthy."

"You're worthy. If there is anyone to blame, I take the blame."

"May I make a suggestion?"

"Sure."

"Let's enjoy our road trip, Mr. Jones."

"Seize the day, Miss Stockwell."

"YOLO."

"I have no idea what that means."

"It means carpe diem, only in a very irresponsible way."

"Be impulsive, thoughtless, reckless, and pray you don't live to regret it."

"Bingo."

"Are you ever going to call me Keith?"

"Never."

"Why not?"

"Calling you Mr. Jones makes me feel so damn naughty."

He laughed. "I understand, Miss Stockwell. I understand."

Fifty more miles of desert went by. Las Vegas was on the horizon, and the PET scan was on her mind. Her life was on her mind. She had always played life safe, never taken any risks, not until she'd met Indigo, not until she'd reconnected with Destiny, not until she became best friends with Kwanzaa. Ericka had always been so predictable. She had been tofu. Even with what had happened when she was thirteen, even with her forced stay in Oklahoma, her life had been tofu.

Ericka's cellular rang. She looked at the ID. It was Kaiser calling. They had called her a dozen times since she sat in the office and was given the bad news. She rejected the call. She rejected the truth.

She rejected them and looked at the clouds again, searched for hearts, for the images of love. Ericka reached for Mr. Jones's right hand, put his fingers between her open legs. As they rode along doing one hundred miles an hour, he rubbed her where there was heat.

Feet on the dashboard, Ericka adjusted herself the best she could. As they headed downhill, the Las Vegas Strip thirty minutes away, his finger rubbed her spot. He had learned how and where to touch her.

She whispered, "Faster, Mr. Jones. Faster."

Chapter 59

Two days later, Ericka met Mr. Jones at Angelus Funeral Home to say good-bye to one of the people she had befriended when she was going through chemotherapy at Kaiser. The thirty-year-old woman's cancer had returned, and it had been aggressive, and in a matter of days the body had started shutting down. She had been in hospice, the inevitable had occurred, and she had been called home. Ericka hadn't spoken to her since right before Indigo's last birthday.

Ericka had been notified of the loss when she was leaving Las Vegas with Mr. Jones.

He had comforted her. Once again he had been there for her.

After paying respects to a fallen soldier, Ericka dried her tears, suppressed her fears, and followed Mr. Jones to Venice. They parked their cars near Abbot's Habit, then walked through the eclectic neighborhood hand in hand, ended up on the promenade at Venice, first using their medical marijuana cards and visiting a dispensary who sold outstanding Kush, then stopping to look at artists in action, freak shows, T-shirts, the Pacific Ocean only a few hundred yards away.

Mr. Jones told her that when his parents were growing up, they had been part of the Great Migration, that time after World War II when blacks fleeing the mistreatment in the South came to California in search of unionized work and wages that were strong enough to support a family. Black L.A. was art and jazz back then, and Central Avenue was the place to be. Hattie McDaniel had to sue because it was against the law for blacks to own a home in the same areas that had become the epicenter of black culture.

Ericka said, "I wish I could have seen it back then."

"It was less integrated."

"Was that any better?"

"In some ways it was."

"We're so spread out now. In the Valley, in the Inland Empire, down to San Diego."

"I took a lot of black L.A. for granted when I was growing up."

"We're too busy living and trying to survive to have many of those reflective moments."

"See it now. It's changing. See what's left before it fades away."

"Every day I look at things I never want to forget."

"Laws changed and the white people ran away, but black folks haven't laid claim to the area. All the names they use are the developers' names. Leimert. Baldwin. Crenshaw. Blair. This is no-blacks-allowed-after-dark territory. Come sundown, you'd better be on the other side of Central Avenue, or you'll become some policeman's play toy. Black neighborhoods should have more than a street named after MLK. All we have around here that's official is Little Ethiopia."

"That's two blocks along Fairfax. Not even close to an official black area."

"I'd love to see a memorial as large as the tribute to the African Renaissance in Dakar. Something that makes a statement and was made by black hands. I would love something ethnic you could see as far away as the 10 freeway. It would be a black man, black woman, and their child, an unbroken family, and it would point toward Africa, back toward the Motherland, maybe toward Liberia, where some of the enslaved blacks went after they left here."

"They should have one just as prominent in Oklahoma, in Greenwood, where they held a terrorist attack on the Black Wall Street. They should have a brother or sister memorial there too."

"If no one else, they were owed reparations."

"I love talking to you. Love talking to you about race, ethnicity, demography, and family."

"Destiny says I talk too much about the same things. She thinks I'm angry. I'm not. I'm enlightened, and because of that, I'm passionate. She just says I talk too much."

"Destiny is wrong. But then again, she probably thinks I talk too much too."

Ericka and Mr. Jones moved on, but when they turned down a side street to make the long walk back to their vehicles, Ericka saw a familiar pink CBR parked in an alley.

It was Indigo's motorcycle.

It was one of a kind, easily identifiable.

Ericka panicked, looked back and forth, but didn't see Indigo anywhere in the crowd. She imagined Indigo seeing them, telling Destiny, then Destiny being infuriated. Ericka told Mr. Jones she thought it would be best if they walked separate streets, took different avenues to get back to their parked cars. Mr. Jones hesitated, but didn't argue.

They took separate routes to their vehicles.

She followed Mr. Jones back to Baldwin Hills.

Ericka hurried in through Mr. Jones's garage, undressed as she went up the stairs.

Mr. Jones asked, "What would Indigo be doing at Venice Beach on a weekday?"

"Maybe she's with Olamilekan."

"Didn't they break up?"

"They always break up. He dumps her if he thinks she's said two words to Yaba, and she dumps him if she thinks he's still seeing some South African girl recovering from a broken nose. They should call fake breakups *fake-ups*. They fake-up too much. I've stopped caring."

"So they got back together after their last fake-up."

"They're talking. He's sending flowers. He's sending gifts. I think they're cool again. He was over last week. Or maybe she's kicking with Yaba. He's been over to see her too."

"If she were with Yaba, as tall as he is, we would have seen him a mile away."

"Not if he was sitting down, maybe at the café by the bookstore, having lunch."

"Yaba lives this way?"

"Yaba's estate is in the Pacific Palisades."

"And Olamilekan?"

"Bel Air."

"Both live a long way from here."

"Both live near better beaches. The properties they have and their amenities make going to a public beach seem like slumming. And both would get mobbed by sports fans."

"Yeah, we'd see the crowds first, long before we saw one of them."

"So that means she's not with one of them."

"Is she with Destiny delivering Fire Sticks?"

"Only saw one CBR."

Ericka checked her phone. There were no messages from Indigo.

Ericka hoped that meant Indigo hadn't seen her being romantic with Mr. Jones.

Mr. Jones called Destiny, started a conversation, talked for two minutes about attending a cancer support group in Inglewood on the following Saturday morning, then ended the call.

He said, "She has no idea. She's busy delivering Fire Sticks around town."

"I haven't received any messages from the rest of the other Blackbirds either."

"What do you want to do?"

"I want to kiss and kiss and kiss. I want your lips on my lips."

"You want me to stop talking."

"I never want you to stop talking, but I need you to start kissing."

Soon they were nude, on the sofa, a cloud of Cataract Kush floating over their heads.

People around Ericka were dying. She wanted to live. She wanted to do the things she had always been too afraid to do. She didn't want to die regretting not doing things.

Sex with Mr. Jones was beyond being physical; it was an affirmation of being alive.

When Ericka woke up, showered, and dressed, she noticed her missing earring sitting in the middle of the sofa. She smiled, felt relieved, and put it in her bag, did it without asking Mr. Jones when and where it had been found.

Chapter 60

Kwanzaa was in Cristiano's bed, naked, cuddling, chatting, getting to know each other better. With him she had the desire to be naked in bed, to use him to gain relaxation and comfort, and it didn't matter if it was light or dark outside, because being with him gave her peace of mind.

He was always available for her. She couldn't say that about her ex.

Her cellular hummed. Marcus's ringtone. Kwanzaa put her phone on silent.

Kwanzaa crawled back to Cristiano, said, "As I was saying, I'm just trying to make sense of this anti-intellectual, anti–critical thinking society, and in the meantime I keep myself busy by studying chemiosmotic coupling, dehydrogenase, and the Henderson-Hasselbalch equation—which describes the derivation of pH as a measure of acidity—and at the same time mastering the theory of linear versus nonlinear differential equations."

"Okay, wordsmith, stop showing off. You're a bluestocking."

Kwanzaa laughed. "No one has ever called me that, but I guess I am a bluestocking."

She sat up, turned on her iPad, took out notes, studied for a couple of hours, then browsed the web. Cristiano was next to her, working on a business plan, at times texting.

He didn't talk much. The silence between them was comfortable.

It was so hard to not be distracted by a naked man in bed with her.

Her feet rubbed against his muscular leg.

He put his work down, took her breast in his mouth. A moment later it was too much to bear and they rolled on their sides, her feet at his head, mouth to each other's genitals. They were unhurried. He had her spread open, explored her. She used her mouth and hands, tried to drive him mad, went on until she couldn't take it anymore.

Soon she was in the position she loved the most.

She became his koala bear again.

After a nap, they bathed, washed each other's bodies, then talked as they put lotion on each other's skin. Nude, Cristiano took one guitar down from the wall, handed it to Kwanzaa.

He took down another. They played awhile, had a jam session.

Kwanzaa sang a number by ZZ Ward, then another by Nina Simone. Next she sang a Spanish song by Carla Morrison, "Tu Orgullo." Cristiano played and sang two numbers by Damien Rice, then two more by Ed Sheeran, the last being the one about Alzheimer's. Cristiano's father had died from Alzheimer's three years ago and that song struck a chord.

Kwanzaa said, "Those songs are amazing, heartwarming, heart-wrenching, inspiring, eye-opening, poignant, and tragic. If I could write songs, that's my style, the type I would write."

"That's the sum of what life is. Life is the ebb and flow of the good and the bad."

Kwanzaa asked, "How many other instruments have you mastered?"

"I have learned to play the piano like a second-rate Bach."

"Well, you play a vagina like Beethoven performing 'Ode to Joy.'"

"You're an excellent musician yourself."

"Yeah, I can fellate and make you sing David Sanborn's 'The Dream.'"

"Yes, you can."

"The sounds you make when you're in my mouth turn me on."

"I'm getting aroused."

"Me, too."

"We'd better get out of here."

"Yeah, or we'll end up back in bed."

"Or you'll be bent over the desk."

"We better get out of here fast."

They dressed in jeans and tees, his Hugo Boss and hers Forever 21, and left the loft, walked out into the sun, into the heart of urban gentrification. Holding hands, they chatted and strolled by the converted warehouses covered with roof-to-sidewalk murals to Traction Avenue, laughing about something irrelevant as they went inside the Pie Hole, a local spot where the menu always changed and was written on the rolls of brown paper. Yesterday afternoon, after they had ridden to San Pedro and back on Cristiano's Harley, Kwanzaa had had the apple crumble pie with black coffee. Here Cristiano didn't order iced coffee, but either had Earl Grey or Thai tea, and he loved the maple custard and blueberry crisp.

Kwanzaa glanced at her phone. Over a dozen missed calls from attorney Marcus Brixton. She knew what that meant. Her ex was desperate to see her.

The small eatery had a rustic charm, exposed bricks, a unique ambiance. Kwanzaa found a table in the seating area. She loved the cozy café feeling. Ten minutes there and she was pro-gentrification. She wished Crenshaw Boulevard could be renovated and have coffee shops and a variety of restaurants that offered healthy food choices. It would be nice to see the Shaw become a peaceful environment and a safe walking area from end to end. Paying six dollars for a slice of pie was a bit much, but it seemed worth the atmosphere.

Kwanzaa looked around. They sat in a room of hipsters, all wearing cuffed jeans or yoga pans, most of them using Macs. Some carried their cute little dogs like they were babies.

Cristiano leaned over to Kwanzaa and whispered in her ear, "I will tell you why I like the blueberry crisp so much. The blueberry crisp is like going down on you. It's nice and warm and juicy, flavorful, and not overly sweet, has a very nice balance. I could eat it, or taste you, all day."

"We better get this pie to go."

"Not yet. Let's sit here, enjoy the moment."

"I love this spot."

"Tell me which pies you like and why."

She smiled, loved his game.

She said, "The apple pie is rich, buttery, like cinnamon, sort of tart, sort of sweet. It tastes like you taste when you're in my mouth, when you're coming in my mouth, when I swallow. I love the aftertaste. It's intriguing with lemon and vanilla innuendos. The sweetness is perfection."

"The Earl Grey pie is topped with pistachios on a white fluffy layer of godliness. Took my first bite and I was sent to heaven. It was that way the first time I opened your legs and licked you. The moment your rich succulent pie touched my lips, it was like I had an orgasm while savoring. I loved the silkiness, the consistency, the taste, the sweetness level of you."

"Sometimes when you orgasm, it's rich, like whipped cream and cinnamon. It startled me, but it was a pleasant surprise. Another time it was airy, frothy with a slight tea taste."

"You taste like a peach, like peach cobbler with the right amount of butter. But I can taste hints of chocolate. If my tongue goes deep enough, there are sweet, bitter notes of the chocolate."

That went on for a while. It went on until Kwanzaa squirmed in her seat and craved another sixty-second orgasm.

She said, "Okay, you can't talk to me like that and expect me to sit here and focus. How can you do this to me with words about food?"

"We have to sit here and eat and have at least one cup of tea."

"You're trying to keep me in my clothes, when you know I want to be naked."

"As long as I can. You look nice in clothes. Let's mix with the world for a few."

"Of course. We must be civilized."

Kwanzaa glanced around the room.

People stared at her, at Cristiano.

They knew.

They had heard the rumor.

And now they had seen her with him every weekend.

She smiled.

Back at the loft, again nude, Kwanzaa used the maple custard to paint her lover's nipples, to smooth over his fraternal twins. She licked the pie away from one, then sucked pie away from one, added more pie, then sucked one as she stroked the other. He was a dessert so sweet.

He took Kwanzaa, made her his pie, and pampered her with his tongue. It was therapeutic, better than a steam, a facial, a shampoo and condition, and a deep-tissue massage. Then she pampered him, stroked and sucked until he gave her his orgasm, and it was like sweet red wine, a delicious cocktail, like eating sliced fruit and little mini bites of chocolate while listening to invigorating neo soul.

Chapter 61

Kwanzaa arrived at work at six in the morning to find Marcus Brixton already there, parked, waiting. As soon as she pulled into an empty space, Marcus jumped out of his Maserati and hurried toward her.

Kwanzaa was dressed in Starbucks black from head to toe, the weave removed, now in her natural hair phase.

Marcus wore a light gray suit, a conservative, colorful tie, and his eyeglasses.

He also held a dozen red roses. She had expected him to arrive with a loaded gun.

Opening and closing his free hand, in Spanish Marcus said, "Kwanzaa, we need to talk."

In Spanish she replied, "Did I know you were coming to my job? Did we schedule a meeting? Did your attorney call my attorney and pencil you in and you assumed you had been inked in for a conference?"

"You won't take my calls. You won't respond to my messages."

"Why would I? My attorney is very competent and articulate."

"Kwanzaa, just give me a couple of minutes. Let's sit down and talk."

Kwanzaa looked into Marcus's eyes, in his pretty brown, soul-stealing eyes. She gazed into a well that held six years of memories.

He said, "Oh. Yeah. The roses are for you."

Kwanzaa took the roses, and a small memory-based smile rose on her face.

Marcus smiled, his smile the anxious smile of hope.

He said, "I've missed you. I miss all we had. I miss all we were building."

"Give me a moment, Marcus. Morning is the busy time and you know people are always complaining about the service here, but let me see if I can start a few minutes later so you don't come here and make me lose my job."

He stood and waited. Kwanzaa was back in five minutes, her green Starbucks apron around her waist, her signal to him to make this quick because she had to get to work.

Marcus said, "Your hair looks nice."

"I really should not talk to you without my attorney present."

Marcus sang the same song he had now sung on countless messages. The Chilean had been a mistake. He missed Kwanzaa. They had had a solid six years, and he had made but one misstep. He told her that being a Christian was about forgiving. He had fallen short. He needed forgiveness and wanted to win her love back. He said that even Jesus had a period of his life that was not recorded, and he assumed that even the child of God had done things, human things, and made errors on his way to wisdom. Marcus said he had come into the era of his life where he made mistakes. And now he was on the other side of those foolish days. Marcus said that now he was a man. A real man. But a man was nothing without a woman. Marcus said he was the kind of man who needed a woman like Kwanzaa at his side.

He said she was brilliant. Sophisticated. Classy.

She was a woman who had, well, *Je ne sais quois*.

Marcus gave Kwanzaa never-ending praise, and said she was the best of the best of the best. He told her that he would do whatever it took to get her back. He wanted her to go away with him, for a weekend, to Napa Valley. Or finally take her to Paris, when she had a break. He would take her anywhere in the world.

He wanted to work things out. He wanted her to be engaged to him again.

She let him finish his flattering, wheedling talk; she let the cajolery die down.

She wondered if Marcus, if Olamilekan, if all men used the same Internet site to buy the Easter speeches they gave once they had fucked up a good thing and wanted to come back home.

She knew Marcus wanted this to end for him as it had between In-digo and Olamilekan.

But he would not be allowed to open any gate, be it metaphorical or real.

She knew why he had come to her running, and now on bended knee.

He wanted her to drop the lawsuit.

In response to all Marcus offered, Kwanzaa said, "Don't make me vomit in my mouth."

"I'm serious, Kwanzaa. I love you. I'm here begging you for another chance."

"I have to get to work. I don't make four hundred an hour, but it's honest work."

"You told me you loved me."

"Just because I used to love you, don't mean I always will. I'm not Whitney Houston."

She told him to tell his sweet mother she sent her blessings.

She said, "Don't come back to my job. Don't keep blowing up my phone. This is a legal matter. Therefore, you know better than to talk to me and not to my attorney through yours."

"We don't need attorneys between us."

"We needed a condom between us. That was my first mistake."

"We can come to an agreement without using an attorney."

"So what do we need, an arbitrator? Judge Judy? Jerry Springer?"

"We can come to an agreement without clogging the court system or using some other form of mediation."

"I had hoped the next time I saw you face-to-face, Marcus, we'd be in court. I've always wanted to be in front of a judge with you, but I had assumed it would be for marriage, not for what feels like a divorce. You know what you did to me. You know the lies you told and to whom."

He told her the lawsuit would never stick. She did not know the power she was up against. With a big smile, and in perfect Spanish, she told him to fuck off in Chlamydia-ville.

"Sure you want to take this route?"

"Oh yeah."

"You had me served at my job."

"Hope that didn't ruin your chance to ever become partner."

"A million dollars? For a curable infection? No permanent harm was done."

"I could cross that part out and write one billion. A woman's health is priceless."

"You'll never win."

"I don't have to win. You gave me an STD, then lied to your mother, and lied to everyone. A member of a prestigious law firm gave his fiancée an STD. I wasn't a side chick. I wasn't a girlfriend. Being engaged implied commitment. You fucked a client. You used your prestigious law office as a casting couch. You're educated and know about STDs, HIV, AIDS. You engaged in behavior that was potentially dangerous to your health, then knowingly engaged in sex with me without either informing me or using protection. I am a responsible woman, a former military brat, a woman who is in college, a woman who was with you for six years, and not until the second year we were together did we consummate the relationship. We did not have sex for a year. That speaks to my character. We didn't have sex for the first year, and not until the third year, after you put a ring on my finger, did we have unprotected sex. You were my future husband before I put my health on the line."

"You can't prove any of that."

"I can prove every word."

"How?"

"I will use your words to make my case."

"Is that right?"

"I will open my phone records and have yours subpoenaed."

He laughed a bluffer's laugh that had to have been learned at Harvard.

Kwanzaa smiled. "Enjoy that laugh. When we're in court and they are reading how you begged me to make love to you for a year, and how you told me you loved me, and how you had lied about cheating, then confessed about sleeping with your Chilean client, all done by texting because you didn't have the nerve to see me face-to-face. Bitch-ass coward. Six years of phone records will show I have done nothing inappropriate. Every woman I work with or have befriended can be called as a character witness. So, be ready to open up your life. Be ready to see your name and your law firm's name in legal documents, in the news, online, everywhere."

"A million dollars?"

"I should double that number."

"Do you really think you're in the catbird seat? You won't win."

"I don't have to win for you to lose, Marcus. We will call the Chilean to the stand and your business will be put on record. Did she think sleeping with you gave her a better chance at winning her case? Makes me wonder what you said in your position of authority to get her naked. We'll get to the truth. It will be real funny when it comes out that she had been lied to, that she was told I was the one cheating on you, that it was my fault she was given an STD."

He chuckled, shifted, paused before he asked, "What are you talking about?"

"I talked to her, Marcus. Well, my attorney has talked to her. That's why she's not returning your calls anymore. We have the same attorney. She is suing your ass too."

His nostrils flared. "Shit."

"Yeah, playboy. Shit. You lied to me and you lied to her, the same way you lied to your mother. How could you lie on me? How could you assassinate my character with your mother? You told your entire family a lie. How dare you put this bull on me? How dare you."

"Don't do this, Kwanzaa."

"Write a check and walk away, and no, we will not kiss and say goodbye."

"A million dollars?"

"Destiny Jones's mother is representing me. She's not a cheap date."

"You've pulled attorney Carmen Jones back into the game."

"Yeah, that ruthless bitch. Isn't that what you used to call her? You said she was a ruthless bitch, and her daughter was just like her. We all need ruthless bitches as our friends, Marcus."

He took a breath, said, "Ten thousand."

"That's not even a decent counter offer. Six years, Marcus. Three years engaged. One year shy of being common law. Two years shy of being at the altar. Four years shy of having our first child. Six years shy of having our second. You made promises and we made plans."

"Fifty thousand."

"Two hundred and fifty thousand."

"Sixty-five thousand."

"Three hundred thousand."

"That's not how you negotiate."

"Three hundred and twenty-five thousand."

"Okay, stop."

"Three hundred and seventy-five thousand."

Marcus paused. "Are you really going to do this to me?"

"Now you're the one wounded?"

"Are you?"

"*Hashtag*, I kept the text messages. *Hashtag* admissible in court. *Hashtag* your mother will be able to read the truth about her son. *Hashtag* the black chick wasn't the slut. *Hashtag* let social media be the judge. *Hashtag* will get very interesting at your law firm. *Hashtag* disbarred."

He nodded. "I will need a confidentiality agreement."

"Sure. You will be able to pay, rise in your career, keep your pretty face on billboards, be the bridge between two marginalized communities, work tirelessly on immigration and pointlessly for reparation, run for Congress, run for mayor, run for governor, run for Senate; you can do all the things you told me you wanted to do, and that confidentiality agreement will ensure that the contract runs in both directions. It will never be talked about again. Dollars make it vanish."

"Jesus. Three hundred and seventy-five thousand dollars."

"Plus legal fees."

"This is blackmail. You're extorting me."

"Well, let's just put the case on the dockets, then break out the medical records and messages, and see how a judge feels. Get ready to join the long list of nasty jocks and celebrities who have been sued for being trifling and disgusting, like you. Maybe they will give you a plaque."

"You've always been a smart woman."

"Smart where it matters most."

"I guess we should celebrate your victory."

"When the money is delivered, then we can find a bar and do penicillin shots together."

"That's a lot of money. I will have to pay it in installments."

"Missed payments will be subject to late fees, penalties, and interest, as you will be denying me the luxury of that which I am entitled. A missed payment will also end the confidentiality agreement on your end without terminating an agreement in the other direction."

Marcus paused. "Let's not do this. I still love you, Kwanzaa."

"I love you too, Marcus. I love the spirit of the promises we made to each other."

"If we love each other, then this is fixable. Couples have problems. Let's not do this."

"It's too late to not do this because this is being done."

He nodded. "Too bad this didn't work out."

"Yeah. Too bad you got busted. Too bad I was freed from a six-year lie."

"I'm not a bad guy. You know me better than anyone, Kwanzaa."

"I disagree."

"I made a mistake."

"Was the mistake the infidelity, or getting caught, or infecting me?"

"I was weak and had a lapse in judgment."

"You're an attorney, Marcus. You're going to have to become a better liar if you're going to swim with the sharks and become a politician. You can't even cheat effectively. You're weak. Barely got out of Harvard. Barely passed the bar. Get out of the lying business while you can."

"So what now?"

"Glad you asked."

Kwanzaa dialed a number and handed Marcus the phone.

He asked, "The Chilean?"

"Carmen Jones, esquire. Let's keep the legal ball rolling."

Marcus started a conversation with attorney Carmen Jones, with Destiny's mother.

As a homeless Rastafarian pushed a shopping cart overloaded with plastic bottles across the parking lot of the strip mall en route to the nearest recycling center, Marcus ended the call, head down, defeated, seething, upset.

He told Kwanzaa that he wanted the engagement ring returned. He said that if they had no chance of being together, he wanted the ring back.

She laughed harder. "Sue me for the ring and see how that works out."

"Be fair."

"You're going to ask for my ring back, so you can pawn it, then use the money to pay me part of what you have agreed to pay me? That's cold. It's not until you break up with someone that you get to really see what they are. Love puts on blinders. I cried over you so many nights."

"I guess it's my turn to cry. Is that what you want? To see me cry?"

"Oh, you will cry. The Chilean will want just as much money."

"This will ruin me financially."

"Be careful where you put your dick, Marcus. You should've learned that at Harvard. If you didn't, well, consider this part of your post-bar education."

"Are you serious? I mean, are you really serious about this?"

"Everything comes at a cost. I've paid emotionally, have paid with my health, have almost lost my mind over this, and now you're going to have to pay financially. There might not be reparation for many, but there will be restitution for one, as is the way of the USA."

They knew each other well. After six years they knew each other very well. Yet Kwanzaa felt like she didn't know him at all. The man you break up with, the man you slap with a lawsuit was not the man you had made love to for years, not the man you had planned to marry. And she was no longer that nice fiancée who had done her part and tried to amalgamate families and two cultures to make a real-life American-born fairy tale come true.

She asked, "Why, Marcus? What went wrong?"

"I guess, sometimes, you know, I feel like I'm caught between two worlds."

"There is only one world, but I get your point. The world has many compartments."

"I try to please so many people. Between Africa and Mexico, I get mixed up at times."

"You don't know if you want the black girl or the Latina to become your wife."

"I'm both. I am African. I am Mexican."

"You don't know if you want to be Marcus, or if you want to be Jesús."

"And at the same time, I am neither."

"My being black and knowing your primary culture, speaking Spanish, trying to make you comfortable in two worlds, that wasn't good enough for you, is that what you're saying?"

As blues played from the sound system in Starbucks, Marcus stood there, stunned, blood draining from his face. Kwanzaa looked inside Starbucks. The line wasn't too long, but it was steady. The Latinas inside knew she was having a quick meeting with Marcus. They were ready to dial 9-1-1 if the meeting turned ugly, a meeting that was being recorded by a coworker as she sat at a bistro table on the same side as the drive-thru. Kwanzaa sighed toward Marcus Brixton again, blew stale air at the man with whom she was once engaged.

Marcus adjusted his necktie, then walked away, across the lot, across the strip mall of pizza joints and doughnut shops to his sparkling Maserati. Kwanzaa wondered how much he could get for that car at CarMax. It wouldn't be enough. During the period that Marcus had been with her and the Chilean, he had been in bed with at least five other women. Marcus had no idea that attorney Carmen Jones had used her connections and contacted all of them.

Kwanzaa watched Marcus leave, that walk now with diminished swagger.

Actually, it was *swagger-less*.

She wondered what Marcus would tell his sweet mother now, wondered what the Harvard man would tell his proud father. Kwanzaa was sure a way would be found to blame her for what Marcus had done. That was always the way it went. Always blame the black chick.

A second barefoot Rasta man pushing a shopping cart holding at least a thousand plastic bottles moved across the uneven parking lot. As the homeless woke up at bus stops and in storefronts in the Southland, Yukons, Toyotas, Mustangs, Fiats, Mini-Coopers, and BMWs pulled into the long line for the always-congested drive-thru, some stuck in line as long as fifteen minutes, some as anxious as drug addicts, some like rabid pit bulls, many complaining on social media about the wait.

Unconcerned, a little emotional, Kwanzaa checked the time on her phone.

She had over three hundred thousand reasons to chill out for another moment. She waved at customers, smiled. One heavyset sister was always there when they opened and sat in a corner all day. She had to be homeless, her life in a pink backpack. This was part of Kwanzaa's world. As had been Marcus Brixton.

Seconds later, Cristiano pulled up in the strip mall's parking lot.

Kwanzaa smiled, waited on the patio next to the crowded drive-thru section. She felt odd being the Starbucks girl again. She looked across La Brea toward Centinelia, looked over at the billboard of Marcus Brixton and the other powerful attorneys in his law office.

She hoped they removed that billboard soon.

With a big grin on her face, Kwanzaa waited for the handsome and genial man who was blessed like one in five million. That blessing he had didn't matter.

Well, it mattered. It really mattered.

But Kwanzaa saw that extra part of him as a magnificent bonus.

He had turned out to be the type of man she wished Marcus could have been.

Cristiano carried a large Hugo Boss box with him. He greeted Kwanzaa, kissed her cheek, then sat the box on the wrought-iron table, and pulled her closer for a better kiss.

He kissed her right there, in front of Starbucks, with all the Latinas watching. He kissed her while customers complained about there not being enough employees working the counter.

Kwanzaa asked, "Have you gone shopping?"

"Surprise."

"This is for me?"

Cristiano said, "This is for you."

"What's this?"

"Happy belated birthday. More like super-belated."

"Are you kidding me?"

"I looked in your clothing, learned your sizes, and ordered you a few things."

She opened the box. There was Hugo Boss clothing top to bottom. Pants and jeans that cost three hundred dollars, two-hundred-dollar blouses, and dresses that cost a thousand.

She asked, "Are you serious?"

"Happy belated birthday."

"This is amazing."

"Anything you don't like, I'll take back and find something else."

"Are you mad? I'm keeping all of this. If something is too big, I will gain weight. If something is too small, I will lose weight. This swag is awesome. You have impeccable taste."

"You deserved more than drunken sex on your birthday."

"Don't make it sound like that's all we did. We danced before we had sex."

"Yeah, we danced. And then you were bent over my desk. You knocked everything off of my desk. You broke a few things that are irreplaceable. You destroyed my personal belongings."

Kwanzaa laughed. "You're never going to let me live that down, are you?"

"So, I hope this isn't too much."

"Nothing is too much, not with you."

"Is that right?"

"That's right and left, and you know that's right and left."

They kissed and kissed and laughed, then put the box in Kwanzaa's car.

She went inside Starbucks, made him an iced coffee, smiling, dancing, happier than Pharrell.

He asked, "Want to go out tonight?"

"It's Destiny's birthday weekend. Have to be a Blackbird until Sunday night."

"Which one is she?"

"She's the one who goes to USC. She rides a motorcycle."

"The African?"

"The other one. The one with white dreadlocks."

"Big plans?"

"Too many plans. They try to outdo each other on their birthdays. I keep mine simple."

"Girls gone wild."

"Blackbirds gone wild."

"You're going to be busy. I will have to be patient and wait to hear from you."

"You know I have to kick it with you at least one day on the weekends, if not both."

"I miss you already. I've gotten spoiled having your company."

"I'll see what I can do. I'll try to get away for a couple of hours. If I do, I'll have to come your way in an Uber. We're probably going to end up doing a few shots somewhere."

"Enjoy your friends. I'll be here for you. I'm not going anywhere."

"Really?"

"Really."

"I'd rather be with you. Being a koala bear."

He laughed. "Call you later."

"Okay. Have a good day, babe."

"You too, babe."

He blew her a kiss.

She blew him a kiss.

There was much noise on La Brea, but there was stunned silence in Starbucks.

Kwanzaa looked up and every woman was staring at her. Coworkers who usually gossiped like a van full of jaw-jacking cheerleaders after a Pop Warner football game were quiet, brown eyes turning green.

Their envy was as palpable as Kwanzaa's joy.

The girls at her job ignored the long line of customers, asked her question after question about Mr. Iced Coffee.

She told the girls to focus on the customers, to work faster and hope someone posted something nice about them on social media. But the girls persisted, wanted to know what was up.

Other than saying he managed two Hugo Boss stores, one in the South Bay and the other on Rodeo Drive, Kwanzaa didn't answer a question. She smiled, danced, sang, and made brewed coffees, vanilla lattes, and caramel macchiatos.

Chapter 62

That night the Blackbirds were in Hollywood at the Dragonfly Bar for *Stripperaoke*, where everyone performed karaoke while strippers danced. Shades on, locks hiding her face like Sia, Destiny sang her new mantra, "Here" by Alessia Cara, and with two cosmos in her blood, tried to blow the roof off the spot. Ericka killed Adele's "Hello." Kwanzaa slaughtered Alice Smith's version of that *rapey* self-professed pervert Cee Lo's "Fool for Love" and followed up with Adele's "Someone Like You." Indigo brought down the house with ZZ Ward's "365 Days." Later they took to the stage together, channeled Lauryn Hill, became four soul sister diva-fied fools, and earned a three-minute foot-stomping, hand-clapping, standing ovation belting out Nina Simone's "Feeling Good." The jovial multicultural strippers jiggled their breasts and twerked to the beat.

By midnight, they were all back in their individual nests.

Destiny, Indigo, Ericka, and Kwanzaa; everyone claimed to be over-exhausted.

Indigo Abdulrahaman eased on her pink CBR and left in the middle of the night, let the restless roar from her iron horse blend with the sirens and the beat of helicopters flying overhead.

Kwanzaa Browne left a few minutes after Indigo had disappeared.

Destiny Jones stood in her window, watching the gate open like anxious legs.

Not long after, Ericka Stockwell was in her convertible, top down, leaving the property.

Destiny showered, then tossed lube and two vibrators on her bed. She was a vibrator virgin. Tonight would be the first time.

Just to ease the stress, just until she was able to forget about Hakeem.

A man never had to be good to a woman for her to miss his touch in the midnight hour.

In the midst of her exploration, her cellular vibrated. She paused, trying to please herself, grumbled, cursed, and grabbed her phone. It was a text from Eddie. He had texted her every day.

She had ignored him every day.

There was a physical attraction. Only physical. There was no mental stimulation.

Too bad Eddie didn't have Hakeem's potential.

Or too bad Hakeem didn't have Eddie's pills and skills in the bedroom.

Too bad Hakeem wasn't a bedroom bully.

Then she would have something to miss.

The Kismet part of Destiny would have loved him and helped him out with that problem. She would have driven to Mexico and bought him crates of little blue pills if that's what he needed to up his game. She would have bought books on Kama Sutra.

They could have worked on his issue as a team.

Now removed from the wealth of emotions, but not trying to revise history, he had made her come, but she could give him only two out of five stars in bed.

She resumed trying to please herself. It wasn't planned, but she imagined she was with Eddie. She imagined Eddie came into her room, saw her doing what she was doing, and showed her something better than a toy.

She imagined well-built Eddie began Eddying her like she was Nancy. In her mind, she Nancied him like he'd never been Nancied before.

Writhing, moaning, creating a wealth of sensual scenarios, Destiny came.

Chapter 63

At sunrise, the Blackbirds left in the Rubicon on the way to San Pedro with Indigo at the wheel, Ericka her copilot, Destiny and Kwanzaa in the backseat sipping on their lattes.

Destiny asked Ericka, "You talked to Mrs. Stockwell regarding those chapters as of yet?"

"No, I have not talked to the lovely Mrs. Stockwell since she left Indigo's party."

"You should talk to Mrs. Stockwell, Ericka. That's my birthday present from you."

"Not gonna happen. Bring it up again and I will curse you like you stole something."

Kwanzaa said, "Mrs. Stockwell needs to read those poignant chapters."

Indigo said, "Had no idea what you had gone through, Ericka. Made me cry. I read those pages ten times. Each time I saw something new. That's why I came to your apartment and hugged you until you made me let you go. No one should have to go through that. No one."

Ericka rubbed her nose and whispered. "Made me cry too. Made me remember and cry."

As Destiny finger-combed her sisterlocks, she noticed another bruise on Ericka's neck.

She also noticed a couple of faint bruises on Indigo's neck as well.

Same for Kwanzaa. Last weekend, Kwanzaa left on Friday evening and didn't come home until Sunday night. She hadn't mentioned Brixton's name once in quite some time.

Destiny said, "Let's see some hands. Who was the last person in this ride to have sex?"

Indigo and Kwanzaa laughed. Ericka diverted her eyes, became uneasy.

Destiny said, "Why do I have the feeling I am the only celibate one in this Jeep?"

Ericka said, "Not long ago, you were the only one with her hand up high."

Destiny asked, "Kwanzaa, who are you sleeping with? Where have you been at night?"

Kwanzaa laughed and blushed. "I'm saving myself until I get married. You know that."

"You're a fucking liar."

Kwanzaa laughed harder.

Indigo asked Destiny, "Since you seem to be home nights after work, and you're frowning and cranky all the time, you ever going to tell us what happened between you and Hakeem?"

"It didn't work out. Someone else is riding his Big Wheel. Let's just leave it at that."

Kwanzaa said, "A man is like a shoe. You have to try him on before you buy him. I guess Destiny went over there and caught another woman wearing her shoes."

The Blackbirds laughed, all except Destiny Jones.

Raising her middle fingers, Destiny said, "Laugh at my pain; just cackle at my pain."

Indigo howled. "Hope you didn't get foot fungus like Kwanzaa did."

Kwanzaa cursed Indigo. Indigo cursed her back in Yorùbá.

Destiny said, "Yeah, and I bet Kwanzaa has been wearing some new shoes."

"I might have a new pair of shoes. A real nice pair."

Ericka said, "So you've been out breaking them in."

Kwanzaa giggled and blushed. "I don't know what you're talking about. All I do is work, study, and sleep."

Indigo said, "Forget about Kwanzaa's lying ass. Destiny Jones, I want to know what happened between you and Hakeem Mitchell. You went from being madly in love to nothing."

Destiny snapped, *"Let it go*. It's my birthday. So let it go, let it go."

On that note, Ericka, Indigo, and Kwanzaa sang that irritating "Let It Go" song at the top of their lungs. They were not going to let the issue go; they were not going to stop singing.

Destiny shouted, "Okay. Okay. Just stop singing that song. I *hate* that song."

Destiny took them down that stony road.

The Blackbirds were flabbergasted.

"The asshole was screwing his best friend's booty call and tried to slut-shame you?"

"You should've told us and we would've gotten our dads to kick his ass."

"I'm glad you beat the hell out of his Big Wheel. I guess that truck was his way of compensating for his shortcomings, or quick comings, not-making-you-comings, or whatever."

"You choked the engineer geek half to death with a leather belt?"

"That's some classic S&M shit. Bet that got his pecker hard."

"Did you really jack his front door up like that?"

"That was one foul message you engraved in the wood. Good Lord."

"And I'll bet she spelled every expletive correctly and had proper punctuation."

"Our girl has balls."

"She's so gangster that gangsters step off the curb when she walks down the street."

"Put a cape on her and let her fly around L.A. because she's my damn *shero*."

"Did you get your five hundred dollars back?"

"What five hundred dollars?"

"Please don't tell me Destiny loaned the player some money."

"She'd better take him to small claims court and get her ducats back."

Destiny shouted, "Calm down. It's handled. Shut up. Stop, stop, stop, just stop."

They started singing "Stop! In the Name of Love" at the top of their lungs.

Destiny screamed.

Chapter 64

In San Pedro the Blackbirds unloaded their gear and cameras, then took a helicopter ride. Soon they were twenty-six miles off the coast of Long Beach at Catalina Island. An hour later, Destiny and Kwanzaa were at least eighty feet under the ocean, scuba diving. They were careful, knew how to use the equipment so they didn't burst an eardrum, get the bends, or pop a lung. Ericka and Indigo dove deeper, went about one hundred and ten feet. Ericka had never gone that deep before.

Four black women, scuba diving, living outside preconceived notions, always garnered much attention. At 2:47 in the afternoon, they all sang the birthday songs to Destiny.

As they headed back to the helicopter, Destiny checked her messages.

There were three.

One was from her dad.

The second was from her mom, who was now in Paris. She had tried to make it back, but weather had caused all flights to be canceled. Still she had paid for Destiny's wonderful outing.

Hakeem's friend Eddie had sent her a birthday blessing as well. He said that he was no longer kicking it with Nancy. Again he thanked Destiny for letting him know what kind of friend Hakeem had been. He asked Destiny if they could meet for coffee. Eddie was looking for a new Nancy. Or wanted to crawl inside Destiny Jones so he could achieve a pyrrhic victory against Hakeem by bedding his betraying buddy's ex-lover.

Being with Eddie could be better than the night she had fantasized about him when she had used her toy, and if it was near as exciting as Nancy had made it sound when she was being Eddied, it could be the night of her life. She could let Eddie Eddie her, and Nancy Eddie in return, then rub that in Hakeem's face, let her ex know she'd experienced a man who could keep it up.

Shaking her head, not one to trick herself into thinking a woman could sleep with a man's friend and it never be seen as revenge, she deleted that message as well.

Hakeem and Eddie and Nancy could seek counsel under the covers with people like themselves. Destiny didn't have a high tolerance for drama, for fake people, for liars and cheaters. Besides, according to her Nike FuelBand, she'd masturbated for three miles last night.

Tonight she might try for a 10K.

Chapter 65

Ericka's cellular rang as they headed back for the helicopter. Kwanzaa and Indigo had gone to the bathroom. Ericka took the call, then called out, and waved for Destiny to slow down.

Ericka said, "It's for you."

"My dad is calling me on your phone?"

Surprised, Ericka said, "It's not your dad. Why would your dad call on my phone?"

Destiny took the phone and asked who was trying to reach her.

He said, "This is DJ, DJ."

"Dubois Junior, or some Dumb Jerk who is turning into a stalker?"

"This is Dubois Junior calling for Destiny Jones."

"How did you get my friend's number?"

"I sort of accidentally-on-purpose borrowed Ericka's number from my mom's phone."

"Why are you calling my friend asking for me?"

"I decided to take a chance and call to tell you happy birthday."

"Who told you it was my birthday?"

"You did. A long time ago."

"You remembered?"

"Yeah. I remembered. I've always remembered your birthday."

"Why?"

"Told you. I've always remembered you."

"You never called."

"I thought you hated me."

"You thought correctly. Ain't even gonna try and fake the funk."

"Well, I guess that means you don't want to come to the show."

"What show?"

"We're doing Red, Black, and Bruised again. Last weekend we were at the Laugh Factory in Long Beach, and this week we're taking it up on Sunset to the Comedy Emporium. I called to invite you to the show later on, if you're not too busy being rude to nice people."

"Can I do a plus-three?"

"You're bringing the Blackbirds?"

"You wanted me to come alone?"

"Yeah, that's the direction I had hoped this was going."

"That would be a date."

"I know what it would be."

"After what you did, you're calling a hundred years later to ask me on a date? I'm not dating you. I wouldn't date you if you were the last man on earth."

"Okay, no problem. You can buy your own ticket, if you decide to come."

"Wait. It's my birthday."

"So you want the ticket?"

"I will need four tickets."

"So you're coming?"

"If the Blackbirds can get in for free, we'll come by and check out the spot."

"Happy birthday, DJ."

"Thanks, DJ. Are we done? Can I hang up now?"

"And my mom told me to tell you the same."

"Tell Dr. Dubois I said thanks."

"She still wants to see you and talk with you."

"Maybe I'll stop by her office next time Ericka goes to visit her."

"I really hope I get a chance to see you later."

"DJ, dude. You really need to quit."

"What's the issue?"

"I don't need you stalking me."

"I'm not stalking you."

"Yes, you are. This is very stalkerish."

"I'm just calling to wish you happy birthday."

"And to try and get a date."

"That, too."

"Do you have a girlfriend?"

"Nope."

"Fuck buddy, suck buddy, masturbation partner, jump-off, or booty-call situation?"

"Nope."

"Bisexual?"

"Straight."

"Do you vote?"

"Sometimes."

"That's a turnoff."

"Really?"

"Strike one."

"Well, I refuse to go to the polls to choose the lesser of two evils for black people. When you have to choose between the lesser of two evils, you're still choosing evil."

"You still have to vote."

"Nothing has changed and that which has changed has changed too damn slowly."

"Okay. In that case, with that logic, I'll make not always voting half a strike then."

"Well, if you're voting for what the country is offering, I should give you two strikes. No matter who you vote for, they all have the same puppet master living at 740 Park Avenue."

"What happened to your last girlfriend, Mr.-Morehouse-going-to-Pepperdine?"

"She broke my heart. It's in the past. I'm over it."

"Two have broken my heart, the first one the most, but continue telling your story."

"Two broke your heart?"

"You were the first, if you must know."

"Me?"

"Pat yourself on the back."

"I had no idea. DJ, I'm really sorry if I hurt your heart."

"You hurt more than that."

"Sorry about that too."

"You piece of shit."

"Wow. Okay, I deserve that."

"I hated you for so long."

"Did you?"

"Hated you like I hate traffic on the 405 North."

"And now?"

"I hate you like traffic on the 405 South."

"Well, I've never hated you."

"I never gave you a reason to hate me."

"But now I understand the disdain. You don't have to come to the show."

"Four tickets. And you need to buy me and the Blackbirds a drink."

"You're coming to the show?"

"Maybe. But don't hold your breath. I'm still not crazy about the 405."

"I still would like to take you out for your birthday. We could do lunch."

"Why, Dubois? Why?"

"I want to go out with you."

"I just broke up with someone, so I'm not in that frame of mind at the moment."

"So did I. We're both free, so let's take advantage of this chance to be friends again."

"We were never friends."

"We were more than friends."

"For two minutes."

"You're killing me over here, Destiny."

"You had an objective, got want you wanted, then disappeared."

"We were friends, DJ."

"We were one-time lovers, never friends."

"I want to at least be able to be cordial with you, if nothing else."

"What's your objective? To get inside my head so you can get between my legs again?"

"I want to date you, but I see that's not possible. But I still want to go out with you."

"Dating is a job."

"And we're both unemployed."

"Before you date someone, they should show up with a résumé, fill out an application, and have references. I think I should be able to call up four women he's dated, ask questions, get some information, find out where the truth ends and the lies start. Men are so duplicitous when all they want to do is get laid. Why can't men just be up-front?"

"I didn't mean to hurt you back then. Am I allowed to take you out for your birthday so we can talk about it?"

"Knowing how I feel about you, is that what you really want to do?"

"I'm practically begging over here."

"You don't know me, DJ. I'm not the same Destiny you knew."

"I think you're the same."

"I'm not. I live in a different universe now."

"Then tell me who you are. Who is Destiny Jones now?"

"I'm not a child anymore. Sometimes I think about what happened too much and I battle melancholy. I'm trying to know what it's like not to be afraid. I've been my own worst enemy. I work hard to elevate my mind and find enough speed to escape my own gravity, to escape my own anger and rage, to get away from the fire and violence and pressures inside of me so I can fly so high that when I look down, I'll barely be able to see a small rock called Earth. I battle to arrive at a higher class and be respected as a black woman in a colonized world that praises a country that used to love to send postcards of strange fruit hanging from its Southern trees. I am a black woman, overworked, stressed, abused, and I have demons. Oppression, fear, being marginalized creates demons. Every black person in America should have demons, or they are spiritually dead. You'd have to be crazy to not have a breakdown. That's how I am doing today. I'm a descendant of Africa, grandchild of Jamaica, part of the lost race of stolen, young, and gifted blacks in a country that is finally starting to take down flags that never should have been raised. Does that answer your malicious Q to your satisfaction, or should I elaborate?"

"I think you did elaborate."

"This is where we say good-bye and go our separate ways."

"Well, as a birthday present I'll leave four tickets and see what happens."

Destiny paused, sucked her lips. "And you will buy four drinks?"

"If you show up, text me at this number, and I will handle it."

"So, now you're trying to be slick and give me your digits, and then if I text you, then you will have my digits, then you can blow up my phone all day and night and get cursed out."

"I'm being up-front about it. No shame in my game."

"I'm not the girl you once knew."

"And I hope that as a man, I am much better than I was when you knew me as a boy."

"You're still a boy. Women mature faster. You still a horny little boy."

"Whatever. You really need to ease up. Your Jamaican is showing."

"*Four* tickets. *Eight* drinks. And not at the table by the bathroom."

"Will see what I can do."

"Ericka will text you from this phone, so we don't have a misunderstanding."

"No problem."

When Destiny finished her call she handed the phone back to Ericka. Ericka put her arms around Destiny, held on to her. Ericka said, "He was your first."

"Well. Technically he was."

"What did you leave out?"

"Dubois Junior was the first who penetrated me. Well, I messed around with this other boy, a dude who was in high school, but he just gave me oral and I gave him oral and he fingered me and I gave him a hand job. I had never seen a boy come and I wanted to see what it was like, so I made him come. We never got to the part where he put it in. I think he was too scared to go all the way. We did that once, and he never tried to hook up with me again. Plus I was living with my parents, and they were going through a breakup, and I was being shuffled from house to house, was going to private school in Bel Air, had so much homework, no free time, and he went to school in a different area, so that dude and me just never really had the chance to be alone again. I guess high school girls were easier. He was cute, but I didn't like him. I mean, I liked him, but not like I liked Dubois Junior. My hair was long and straight back then. I was too cute. Dude loved my body and thought I was the prettiest girl on the planet. This body has always gotten me too much attention. Anyway. Can't really call that licking, sucking, fingering, and jerking a one-off, not by the Bill Clinton definition of sex. It was just a lot of heavy petting, I guess. He came all over himself. It was yucky. I felt good, but I didn't come. If I don't come, it doesn't count, right? And before you ask, and I know you will, I never talk about it because I never think about it. It was nothing."

"You're complex and seem to have selective memory."

"So, now when I think about it, it was intimacy, but it wasn't really sex. I used to think that dude was my first. That dude didn't get the cherry. Dubois Junior was the first to go balls deep. He was the one who earned the bloodied-sheets award. I was still a virgin until Dubois."

"You have so many layers."

"Well, I'm not as complex as you. You have more secrets."

"What does that mean?"

Destiny pulled away, said, "I see you found your missing earring."

"Yeah. I did. I found it in my apartment."

"You are a horrible liar. You found it where I left it."

"What do you mean?"

"I left it at my dad's condo."

Ericka paused. "When did you do that?"

Destiny took a breath and rocked. "You should start calling my dad by his first name."

Ericka paused again. "Why would I call Mr. Jones by his first name?"

"Are you really going to do this? I'm not stupid, you know."

"Destiny, tell me what you're talking about."

"I left the earring at my dad's. You were there."

"I was there?"

"Naked. In my dad's bed. With my dad. Should I fucking say any more?"

Chapter 66

Ericka's voice softened and trembled. "Oh, my God."

"You and my dad, Ericka Stockwell? You and my dad? You had sex with my dad?"

"No, no, no, no, no."

"Yes, yes, yes, yes, yes you did."

"You saw us?"

"High. Sleeping. Naked. Really? What kind of fuckery is that?"

"Are you mad? Are you angry?"

"Do you think this is my happy face?"

"Jesus, you're mad."

"Yeah. I am mad. I am disappointed. I feel betrayed. I am angry. I feel used and stupid."

"You hate me, don't you?"

Destiny wiped her eyes. Ericka wiped her own eyes.

"How long has this affair been going on, Ericka?"

"No one is married. It's not an affair."

"How long have you been screwing my dad?"

"We're having a relationship."

"How long has this *relationship* been going on behind everyone's back?"

"Not long."

"How long?"

"Before Indigo's birthday."

"How long before Indigo's birthday?"

"Started the night I took him the medicine, the first time I went there alone. It wasn't planned."

"This feels like an *Inception* moment. Like I'm in a dream in a dream in a dream."

"But, to be honest, I pushed the relationship, so I have to take responsibility."

"You're telling me that all of this happened not too long ago."

"Not too long ago."

"My dad came on to you?"

"He didn't. I just said he didn't. Are you so angry you can't hear?"

"You initiated it?"

"Yeah, I did."

"You're joking."

"I feel so bad about it now."

"It's not as bad as I thought."

"What did you think?"

"I was scared that this had been going on since I was a child, that it started out as some Humbert Humbert and Lolita shit. If my dad had been with you when you were my sitter . . ."

"What? You thought your dad was a pedophile?"

"I didn't know what the hell was going on, but I didn't like it. I was thinking you were with him while he was with my mom, and you were the reason he pulled away from my mother."

"Are you crazy?"

"What would you think?"

"Nothing like that ever happened. We did this as adults."

"I can only take your word as the truth."

"I'm not a home wrecker. It's not about sex, but it's become a sexual relationship."

"Gross."

"I'm just saying."

"No."

"I fell in love with Mr. Jones."

"You can't be in love with my dad."

"I fell in love with your dad."

"Well, I was thinking my dad had been the one who . . . you know . . . got you in trouble."

"Wait. You thought Mr. Jones was the one who . . . when I was thirteen?"

"When I saw you in dad's bed, that came into my mind."

"That's a horrible thing to think about me, Destiny."

"Plus you've never said who you were with, not that it's my business, so I assumed the worst and thought . . . Dad. Well, I'm friggin' glad that you weren't with my dad way back then."

"Gross. That would have been so wrong and gross."

"Yeah. Gross then. Still gross to me now."

Ericka laughed like it was the most ridiculous thing she ever heard.

Destiny laughed a little. "That would have been horrible. Yeah, I would hate you for that."

"I love your dad, Destiny. I loved him from afar. And . . . things have suddenly changed."

"I know. This is awkward. I wish I hadn't told you I know."

"I feel stupid right now."

Destiny whispered, "You were afraid of rejection."

"Yeah. I was. I was afraid of it most coming from you. I respect you more than anything. But nothing happened until recently. Your dad, not one touch, not one kiss, not one hug that was of the wrong kind, and not one inappropriate comment ever came from him."

"I don't get it. My dad saw you as his other daughter, at least that's what he told me."

"He did. But I was goo-goo-eyed, wearing braces, and never saw him as a dad. Even then I had a crush on him and looked at him the way little girls looked at the Jackson 5."

"There were five Jacksons?"

"Five Jacksons and five Osmonds."

"What's an Osmond?"

"Stop it."

"So this happened right under my nose. Who made the first move?"

"Serious, I did. I am the one to blame for this. Be angry at me, not at Mr. Jones."

"Unbelievable. You fucked my dad."

"I make love to him."

"My dad was in your no-no. No wonder you keep getting Brazilians."

Lips pulled in, again feeling thirteen, Ericka looked at Destiny. Ericka said, "I'll stop seeing Mr. Jones."

"It *never* should have started."

"I won't tell him you know."

"He'll know I know because he's my dad and knows me too well."

"He won't know if we don't tell him. I can tell him I don't want to see him anymore."

"We? So, now you've lied to me and you want me to fucking lie to my dad?"

"What do you want me to do? And lower your voice."

"You've lied, and now you want to hurt my dad?"

"Fine, then call him. FaceTime him and we will break the news together."

"I should have taken him that medicine my-damn-self."

"I'll break it off today."

"How could you be with my dad and think I'd never find out?"

"We can go back to being friends, me and Mr. Jones."

"It never goes back. It won't go back for me and Hakeem, it won't go back for me and Dubois, won't go back for Kwanzaa and Marcus, if Olamilekan and Indigo can't get it sorted, their shit won't go back to being friends, and, Ericka, it won't go back for you and my dad."

"You're cursing a lot."

"I'm fucking angry."

"Me and your dad, we understand how it goes. We've both had marriages and divorces. This isn't our first rodeo, albeit he's had more than I have had. We're realistic about this."

Silence wedged between them.

"You fucked my dad."

"That's been established."

"You fucking fucked my dad."

Ericka shook her head, rubbed her temples, chewed her bottom lip.

"Don't hate me, Destiny. If you hate me, that would kill me on the inside."

"Ericka, you are my friend, one of my sisters, and I don't want you to be alone."

"What does that mean?"

"Don't hurt my dad, Ericka. He's my best friend. I can't be there for him all the time, not the way I want to. If you're going to be there for him, be there for him. I know he's going to be okay, I know he is, but I don't want him to be alone. I want him to find himself a good love."

"And I repeat, what does that mean?"

"I don't want you to be alone. You should be with a good man for a change."

"So, you think you might be able to be cool with this?"

"Not all at once, not right away."

"This is another joke."

"This has to grow on me. This has been planted, so it takes time to take root."

"I see the light of the Lord in you."

"Don't push it."

"Understood."

"Why my dad?"

"He makes me feel beautiful."

"That's all you got?"

"Mr. Jones looks at me and sees what is beautiful. With him I don't feel lonely. I don't have to be with him all the time, and not in a sexual way, but just knowing he exists, that he's there for me, and I can be there for him in some way, on some level, because he's been there for me while I was sick, on this journey, well, I love him and I want to be part of his journey as well."

"He's older. The age difference, Ericka."

"We feel connected. You know women, Destiny. I'll be honest. I'm physically attracted to him too. Women want sex just as much as men want it, but we want love as well. We want to have sex with someone we can love."

"You can stop talking now. We're talking about my dad. That's TMI."

"So, what do we do now? Are we no longer friends?"

"You and my dad have been slick and sneaking out the window on me on this one."

"We're still sisters, Destiny."

"No, we're not."

"I don't want to lose that. That matters the most."

"You've messed that up."

"We are sisters."

"When you say that now, it sounds like incest." Destiny paused. "Do me a favor? Until I can handle this, can you do me a favor?"

"What do you need me to do?"

"Just let me know when you're with him, so me and you don't bump heads."

"Okay. Wow."

"And don't tell him we had this conversation."

"Wait."

"I don't need to be over there when you're with my dad."

"Did you just give me permission to keep seeing your dad?"

"I walked in on you naked with my dad and that scared the hell out of me. It looked like y'all had been robbed, stripped naked, and the bodies tossed on the bed every which-a-way."

"Sorry. We had had some top-shelf Kush."

"I'm just glad I didn't walk in any sooner."

"Yeah."

"If I had seen you and my dad . . ."

"That would have been traumatizing for all of us."

"You and my dad were cuddled up like fraternal Siamese twins in a red cocoon."

"I guess we were knocked out."

"Snoring. Drooling. Buck naked. I have to bleach my eyeballs now." Ericka took a breath. "Should we tell Kwanzaa and Indigo?"

"That's up to you."

"I will."

"Now that I think about it, nah, I wouldn't."

"So, don't tell them?"

"Nah. Let's see how long before they figure it out."

"Should I tell your dad that you know, that you walked in on us sleeping?"

"I just said don't tell him. I'm not ready for that conversation."

"Will you put him on punishment?"

"I might ground him for life. No television, no Internet, and no Malcolm X recordings."

Ericka paused. "I just want to be sure that you are sure that you are really sure."

"I sure in the hell ain't gonna tell *my dad* I saw him *naked* with your yellow ass."

"We had too much Kush. And my ass is red, not yellow."

Destiny hesitated. "You're amazing, Ericka."

"This is a joke, right?"

"You're pro-women. You stand up when it's time to stand up and let your voice be heard. You're an educator. You cultivate the life you enjoy. You make your money to get what you want. You have self-deprecating humor, but in reality you never put yourself down. You worry about what other people feel. You know when to walk away, even when you're sick and people think you're down for the count. You hang out with three amazing women and never try to compete. You're generous. You invest in yourself. You're beautiful and never act like a diva."

"Wow. Is that how you see me?"

"That's how I see you and the Blackbirds."

"You are that way too. You are the same way, Destiny."

"I'm the weak link. I'm afraid. I lie. I hide behind a helmet so no one can see my face. I was raped. I shot a man and blinded a woman. I had a relapse and damn near choked Hakeem to death. I'm out of control again. I doubt if I'm worthy of being in the group at times."

"I'm the weak one. You're the strongest link, and you don't even realize your strength. You don't take no shit. You wear a helmet not to hide, but to avoid conflict, and that's different. You wear a helmet to protect stupid people from winning a Darwin Award by messing with you."

"I need to get used to being alone."

"Don't say that. You will have success."

"I'll have to leave Los Angeles, maybe leave America and go somewhere where English isn't their primary language. The people here say they forgive you, then feed you to the lions. Even after you have done your time, you leave whatever form of institution and you are constantly treated like a criminal. These so-called Christians are Romans nailing folks to the cross every chance they get. I wish you could have heard the disgusting things Hakeem said that night."

"That bad?"

"If I had been able to carry a body and knew where to bury it . . . yeah. That bad."

"You're awesome and you want a partner. We all do. We can be as feminist as we want to be, we can march and protest, and sky-dive, and snorkel, and sing karaoke all night long, but at the end of the night, we all want a partner. Not a part-time lover, not a sometime lover."

"Not everyone will get that. You're better at dealing with relationships than I am."

Ericka said, "I've had wrong, I've married fake, and now I am experiencing something real. What I feel now, this was on my bucket list. I feel what I have never felt before."

"Maybe you and my dad can see how it works out, or just keep doing whatever you're doing. Maybe it's none of my business. Maybe I never should have said anything."

"Destiny."

"I'm here for you, and I am here for him, no matter how it turns out."

"Jesus."

"You're adults. What you're doing is as legal as the Kush you two smoke."

"So, we're still friends."

"No."

"Okay."

"You're still my sister."

"Did we just have a fight?"

"Sisters fight. Say their piece. Make up. Keep it moving."

"You're making me cry."

"As far as I am concerned, it will be two less people I have to worry about."

"Thanks, Destiny."

"I had to let you know I knew. I can't be phony. I can't be fake, not for long."

"I feel so much better knowing that you know."

"I don't."

"Sure you're not angry?"

"This cancer shit. Guess it tears some folks apart and pulls others closer."

Ericka paused. "Yeah. I guess feeling like life is short, seeing others die, the way I suffered and felt like the walking dead, it made me feel like I deserve to have at least one thing go right in my life, and that thing was your dad. It made me a lot bolder than I normally am. I guess he took care of me when I needed help the most."

"Dad told me his biopsy came back negative for prostate cancer."

"I know. I was so damn happy when he told me that. I was so stressed not knowing."

"He told you before he told me? Are you saying he notified you first?"

"Sorry about that. I think you walked in on our little celebration. We had a good time. He's better. He will be better. He'll be cured all the way. I wanted to celebrate that with him. I needed him to have that memory of us that day. I wanted to celebrate life and love and give him any sexual fantasy he wanted."

"Ericka Stockwell, no, no, no. Refrain from implying anything sexual about my dad."

"Sorry."

Destiny said, "And don't expect me to call you Mom. And please, no sex stories. And never ever bring him to your apartment to spend the night. That would be both gross and weird, especially if I have company. My company walking out of my apartment, and my dad walking out of your crib at the same time. That would be so damn creepy, the sun might explode."

"You're already seeing someone else, Destiny?"

"I'm done dating. I'm serious. Might have to have the occasional one-off. Or go back to being Kismet Kellogg, if it gets to the point that I just have to have some male company."

Ericka said, "Just don't give up. We will have trials and tribulations, we will be tested, and if we stay in the game, if we press on, if we believe in ourselves, we will win. Victory might not come as fast as you want it, or in the way you want it, but if you press on, you will win."

"And this is why I love you, Ericka. This is the part of you I wished was inside of me."

"Dubois tracked you down. That is kind of romantic."

"That should be illegal. We should turn his mother in for letting him steal your number."

"He remembered your birthday."

"Yeah, well, I remember his too, but have I ever called him? Not once in ten years."

"So, are we going see some comedy later?"

"Nah. I'll stand him up."

"You're going to stand up the stand-up while he's performing stand-up."

"Stop it."

"You're going to leave him hanging."

"That's basically what he did to me ten years ago."

"Now he sees the ugly duckling has become a beautiful swan."

"With the classic ass."

"You can't spell *classic* without having *ass* in the middle."

"I was never ugly, but I do look very hot now compared to the way I looked back then."

"Your life would have been different if he had never gone away."

"My life would have been different. One phone call from him back then, after I had given him my virginity, after I was scared and thought I was pregnant, but wasn't, and everything would have been different. In one of those universes, he called, he came back, and we dated. We might have broken up later, or married and had kids, then divorced, or still be happy, but we dated."

"The things we carry. The hopes, the fears, the memories, the night-mares."

"It's in my bags with the rest. Not the heaviest thing, but it's heavy and I would love to put it down, be done with it. Actually I had put it down. But it came back like a boomerang."

Chapter 67

Kwanzaa and Indigo came back over, laughing and pushing on each other.

Indigo said, "Kwanzaa is dating a customer at Starbucks, *dating* being a euphemism."

"You said you weren't going to tell until I said I wanted to tell."

"That's where she's been hiding when's she MIA. He's gentrifying her coochie."

Ericka asked Kwanzaa, "Well, who is this guy who has made you so damn secretive?"

"His name is Cristiano. We can talk about him later."

"You like him? You're over Brixton?"

"Cristiano is twice the man Brixton was. And he's kinder. And he's fun."

"Look at that smile. Do we need a wedding planner?"

"Shut your face. This is a month-by-month thing. Maybe week-by-week."

Kwanzaa took out her phone, put it in camera mode, and handed it to Destiny.

Kwanzaa said, "Since we're snitching like witches, Indigo got her passport stamped."

Indigo snapped, "Be quiet, Kwanzaa. I confided in you, and this is what you do?"

Ericka asked, "What does that mean?"

Kwanzaa said, "She went back to Britain. She's working on her dual citizenship."

"It was just a field trip. That's all it was. It was a much-needed vacation and I have gained perspective on life, warded off being burned-out, and my creativity has been enhanced. I needed some moments away from everyone, especially Olamilekan and Yaba. I needed to be away from my parents, away from Nigeria, and away from you three drama queens. I rested my body and expanded my mind and I appreciate all I have. I allowed a friend to appreciate me. I behaved like a criminal, but I'm back home now. Back home for good. I love men, but I can understand why women need a break from men."

Kwanzaa sang, "She licked a girl, and she liked it."

Indigo said, "I had a moment of reflection and lasting appreciation. If you say a word, if you make a joke, I will wave your panties in the air."

Ericka asked, "Same girl?"

"No. Someone else. An American girl who can't find Africa on a map, but she is sexy."

"Was this at Venice Beach?"

"You saw me?"

"I saw your motorcycle."

"What were you doing at the beach?"

"Buying Kush."

Indigo said, "I am not a lesbian. I think I was angry. And this girl made an offer."

"Are you still seeing Olamilekan?"

"Of course I am. I just had a diversion, as he has had many diversions."

Destiny said, "Let Indigo be Indigo and let it go."

Ericka handed Destiny her phone, then Indigo did the same.

Indigo said, "Destiny, take a lot of photos of us. Ericka, Kwanzaa, since we are half naked, and wet, let's get our *Charlie's Angels* pose with the ocean and the boats in the background."

Ericka said, "We have to take one posing in front of the helicopter too."

Destiny held the camera as the girls posed, but didn't take the shot. Instead she looked to the sky as if she could see all the galaxies, all the universes, and imagined that version of her she wanted to become, the one who was happy and didn't know she was happy.

She lowered the phone, looked at her confident girls.

Destiny shook her head. "No, I'm not taking the picture this time."

Indigo said, "And why not?"

"I don't want to be the group photographer anymore."

Ericka asked, "What's going on, Destiny?"

"I don't want to be an outsider taking your photos. I'm done with that."

Kwanzaa asked, "Are you offended because we always ask you to take the photos?"

Destiny said, "I don't want to be behind the camera. I want to be in the picture."

The other Blackbirds paused, stood where they were, three Nubian statues in the sun.

"Are you serious?"

"Destiny, you're joking right?"

"You don't take pictures. We respect that. You know we do."

Destiny snapped, "I want to be in the pictures."

Indigo asked, "Are you having a breakdown?"

Destiny kept her eyes to the sky as if she could see the version of Destiny who never left her grandparents' home that night; the girl who was never drugged, raped, recorded; the girl who never saw how ugly the world could become in an instant; a girl who never had to seek revenge.

She saw the version of herself who had never gone to Hoosegow.

She saw the version of herself that she would model herself after.

That version of herself was smart, enrolled at Harvard, took selfies, and never hid from the world.

Destiny looked across the universe, saw that version of Destiny, and she smiled.

Ericka went to Destiny. Indigo did the same, with Kwanzaa hurrying behind her.

They put their hands on Destiny Jones. The shared, they absorbed, they healed.

Destiny wiped her eyes. "I'm going to stop being afraid."

One by one they all started to cry. Soft tears. Tears of joy.

Destiny said, "I'm not going to keep being afraid. There. I said it. I claim it. I am longer afraid to take a photo."

Kwanzaa wiped her eyes and asked, "Are you sure?"

She said, "I'm sure. They don't like me, fuck 'em. Fuck Hakeem. Fuck the guy before him and the guy before that asshole. Fuck the people who did me wrong and fuck the people who cheered when I was sent to Hoosegow and fuck every bitch who booed me when I walked in Hoosegow and fuck every fucker who jeered when I was free again and fuck every fucking blogger and reporter that had shit to say and fuck every asshole who watched the video and fuck every fucker who made a joke about me being raped and fuck every fucker who fucking blamed the victim and fucking fuck 'em all."

Ericka said, "Destiny—it's just as powerful if you say *bless* instead of *fuck*."

"*Fuck* leaves no room for ambiguity. I would hate for them to get a *fucking* blessing because I was not clear in my use of the English language. Ice Cube didn't say *bless* all y'all, he said *fuck* all y'all, and then he went after them with "No Vaseline." I'm not using Vaseline."

"Point taken. But are you sure you're ready to take photos, or be on camera?"

Destiny pulled her bleached sisterlocks back from her youthful face, then wiped her eyes.

"I said I'm sure, dammit. That means I'm *blessing* sure. Now bless me with the camera."

Indigo took a breath and said, "Well, alrighty then. Destiny Jones has been mistreated like Miss Sofia in *The Color Purple*, kicked ass like Miss Sofia in *The Color Purple* wished she could have, has been locked up like Miss Sofia in *The Color Purple*, and now our girl has woken up like Miss Sofia in *The Color Purple*, and she has spoken. All her life she done had to fight."

"From now on, I want to be in *all* group photos. I'm not going to keep myself trapped underground like a Chilean miner. I am out of the cave. I exist. I exist. I fucking exist."

"We post them, Destiny."

"And?"

"We use Instagram. LinkedIn."

"And?"

"Snapchat. Pinterest."

"And?"

"Twitter. Tumblr."

"And?"

"We post them on all of our Facebook pages."

"I don't care. If you're not ashamed of me, then I'm not ashamed to be seen with y'all."

"We should make a Blackbirds page on Facebook."

Destiny said, "Make it happen. The world can see me. They can say what they want to say. They don't own my universe."

For the first time since Hoosegow, Destiny stepped up front and revealed herself to the camera. Then they were better than Charlie's Angels, they were Blackbirds, women who had lived through regrets and pain, smiling, laughing, being photographed over and over by a stranger.

Soon they were back in the helicopter, flying over the Pacific Ocean, still taking photos.

Only now they were all in the selfies.

Chapter 68

When they landed, they zoomed to I Love Lulu hair salon on La Brea, to visit the Dominicans and let them work their West Indian magic as no other beauticians could.

Ericka had her hair cut short like Amber Rose, short like the fuzz on a peach, and dyed blonde. No one asked her why she cut all her hair off. The Blackbirds were preoccupied, talking, on cell phones, sending text messages, web surfing, and no one made mention of when Ericka had endured chemo and was bald, just said she looked amazing, stunning, had the right-shaped head and face to make that almost-bald cut hot and feminine. Ericka made herself smile, the results from the PET scan on her mind, and she hung on to her denial, kept the day joyous, kept talking as if she would have many tomorrows, took selfies and sent them to Mr. Jones, thinking, wondering which photo of her would be her last, which smile her last smile before she danced with Hemingway.

Like her girls, she kept many secrets.

Indigo had her braids taken down, washed, and then had her mane pressed, something she hadn't done in a long time. She sent those transitional images to her mother and father. She also sent the first images of her freshness to Olamilekan, paused, then sent the same images of her transformation to her ex Yaba. Finally, to one other person, to Rickie, someone not a lesbian.

Not that she didn't always look girly, but Indigo wanted to look more feminine so other women didn't see her as temptation, so she would no longer be tempted, and since Olamilekan seemed to fancy women with long hair, maybe he would see her and have a stronger desire.

She thought about Olamilekan, but she was busy texting Yaba.

Rickie Sue sent her smiley faces and sexy photos. Indigo deleted them all, then blocked Rickie Sue's number. That had to be done. She had to be stronger than a wicked desire. She reminded herself she was a true Nigerian. She was a real Christian. No more trips to London. Her vacation was over. She didn't need to get her passport stamped again.

Kwanzaa wanted a brand-new look, something of which she knew Marcus Brixton would not approve, and as she chewed gum she found an edgy, curly style as unique and sexy and beautiful as the blessed and gifted man she was seeing. Kwanzaa decided to rock a teeny-weeny Afro with defined curls, one that made her look very much like Lupita Nyong'o. Compliment after compliment went her way, and she took selfies, sent them to her double-barreled lover, hoping what they had lasted for a long while, not forever, just for a long while, because like Indigo, their closet ailurophile who violated Nigerian law every now and again, for Kwanzaa, being with Cristiano was her vacation.

Destiny was no longer on the run. Her hair would no longer be used as her mask. She dyed her hair, was done with the white sisterlocks, and had her back-length mane taken back to its natural color. Once again her hair was dark brown, but she added golden highlights to the tips of her locks. She had it styled, back away from her face. Destiny Jones was no longer hiding. She used her phone and took selfies, sent them to her dad and to her mother. She sent one to Hakeem with a message. *Yeah, I'm Destiny Jones.*

Chapter 69

Hours later the Blackbirds were at the Comedy Emporium, a comedy club on the Sunset Strip near the House of Blues. It was the designated black folks night at the world-renowned club. Security was tripled. People were being searched before they could go inside. Purses were checked. Drink orders were aggressively taken before people could get comfortable, and the two-drink minimum meant you had to order both drinks right away or leave, no ticket refund given. Tips were automatically included in the price of the food and drinks, and you had to pay upon ordering, the same way Denny's treated black people in the '80s and early '90s.

All the tables had white tablecloths and candles, barely enough room left to fit a fly.

When the Blackbirds entered the overpacked club the bouncer inspected the four of them, studied their dresses, pants, and fitted skirts, took in their grown-woman cleavage and hair in four funky styles, smiled at their made-up faces, held his balls as if that was the ultimate sign of approval, adjusted his desire, then licked his lips LL Cool J–style.

They looked so good that as they passed tables, men were astounded, gazed at them, and made faces like they were one suck way from having an orgasm, swallowed their thoughts like they were testing their own gag reflexes. They watched the asses ticktock.

Indigo snapped, "I didn't want to sit up front. Why in the world did they put us up front?"

Destiny snapped back, "Did I complain *once* on your birthday, Indigo? Did I?"

Indigo was vexed. "Why did we get searched? I would receive better freakin' treatment if I went to the airport wearing a hijab. What are they expecting to jump off in a comedy club that we need to be searched like that? Bullets don't use GPS and don't have a name."

"Shut up."

"I don't want to wake up with four million Africans that died during the Middle Passage."

"*Indigo Abdulrahaman*, stop acting like the Queen of Sheba and *shut your mouth*."

"Destiny *Slave Name* Jones, for your information the *Queen of Sheba* was *Ethiopian*."

Ericka said, "We're getting the best seats in the house, Indigo."

Indigo sucked her teeth. "I don't want to be up front. I don't like being teased, and if a fight breaks out, like they always do in these places, I don't want to be trampled trying to escape. What if the place catches on fire? Can we at least get a table by an exit? And they are really charging thirty dollars to get in? And each drink costs at least ten dollars? Even water cost ten dollars? Plus twenty to park? This is why women date ugly men, to avoid paying for nonsense like this."

Ericka snapped, "You're always complaining about something, Indigo."

Indigo said, "Next time we go swimming, *Baldilocks*, you will accidently drown."

"I'm not afraid of death. Death can only get you one time. *I deal with you every day.*"

Irritated, Kwanzaa said, "*Children*, don't start fighting. You two are always fighting like it's some damn light-skin, dark-skin war, and Ericka you know light skin can't beat the melanin."

Ericka snapped, "That curling iron fried what was left of Indigo's brain."

Indigo retorted, "Don't make me smack your bald head."

Nostrils flared, Destiny growled, "Don't wreck my birthday. Understand, Boo Boo Kitty? Sit your African ass down and shut up."

Chapter 70

Wearing a black NO JUSTICE, NO HEALING tee with an image of an upside-down US flag across the chest as a form of protest and a signal of dire distress in instances of extreme danger to life or property, to the lives of America's second-class citizens at the hands of those sworn to protect and serve more than the interests of the Koch family, Dubois opened his act with a sidesplitting bit about the reality of police brutality.

When the laughter died down, Dubois said, "We are beyond Driving While Black. We are past DWB. They are on the next level. BWB. *Breathing While Black*."

People laughed, but most of the room applauded. A few shouted. They understood that Jim was still Crow-ing all over the United States. They knew that wasn't said on CNN or on Fox.

"DWB leads to being the other DWB—Dead While Black. As long as we breathing, they keep on beating. Mexicans don't beat piñatas as hard as the police beat black men."

Laughter arrived like the gentle storm that was the harbinger of a hurricane.

"Those motherfuckers must think we're filled with *galletas*, *dulces*, and *chiclets*."

Outrageous laughter erupted and the gentle storm suddenly became category 1.

"They are shooting brothers to death over child support. That's messed up, but you know the next day a lot of brothers were running to get caught up on their payments. Brothers were paying in advance. *Here, take the money for the next eighteen years.* Cops are putting the *dead* in deadbeat dads. Mommas had their kids calling up their daddies saying, *Cops find your ass, you will be dead on his beat, Dad. Pay me what you owe me. Don't make me call the cops.*"

On the last part, when he imitated Rihanna singing "Bitch Better Have My Money," the foot-stomping laughter in the earthquake-proof building made walls shake. Over three hundred people tried to catch their breaths. Kwanzaa had never laughed so hard. The bit had been so outrageous Ericka had snorted and had to pick up a tissue to wipe a gallon of tears from her eyes. Indigo's sides were aching and Destiny couldn't stop cackling long enough to make the pain go away. The Blackbirds guffawed like they had been fed the same laughing gas.

Laughter was an airborne virus.

Soon the level of enjoyment eased down and the room applauded Dubois like he was the next Dick Gregory/Paul Mooney/Robin Harris/Eddie Murphy/Richard Pryor/Leonard Dubois Sr.

The son of Leonard Dubois Sr. transitioned to his hilarious routine about Mars and Venus, about the tribulations of dating, then did witticisms about Atlanta, Confederate flags, Morehouse, black frat life, Bill Cosby, Donald Trump, Hillary Clinton, the television show *Empire*, and the movie *Straight Outta Compton*. He had damn near everyone in the room in stitches.

Dubois and Destiny made eye contact for a second. She felt him checking out her face, her makeup, and her sisterlocks. He recognized her, saw her new hair color, saw her not in sweats after a strenuous workout, but in full glam, dressed in the clothes of a chic woman, the accoutrements of a sensual woman, a woman who had jaw-dropping cleavage, the kind that made women cut their eyes at Destiny Jones. The boy she had known when she was barely a teenage girl, the boy who had become a man, he paused and smiled.

Destiny didn't smile. Her nostrils flared, but there was no smile.

Destiny shifted, adjusted her clothing, touched her hair. The sides of her sisterlocks were braided; the top left wild and free, Mohawk style, the way Indigo had worn her hair a while ago.

Destiny cringed when Dubois turned his attention toward the Blackbirds.

"Look at this table filled with fine sisters. Put the spotlight on this table. Look at those sisters. Fine like four Bond girls. Octopussy, Honey Rider, Pussy Galore, and Holly Goodhead."

Based on her complexion, he called Destiny *Honey Rider*. Named Ericka Stockwell *Octopussy*. *She walked in the club like what she has is better than eight coochies.*

When that wave of laughter subsided, he christened Kwanzaa Browne with the name *Pussy Galore*. He said he bet she knew how to make a brother feel *glorious*. Last but not least, because of her full lips and hot-pink lipstick, Indigo was given the nickname *Holly Goodhead*.

Indigo raised two thumbs when he said that and yelled, "Damn right. Now get Idris to play Bond and he can get some octopussy and a glorious good head from the honey rider."

The room laughed. Indigo's accent had made what she said just as hilarious.

Dubois did an Eddie Murphy as Axel Foley impersonation and shouted like he was outraged, "In Hollywood, if John Wayne can be Asian, Mickey Rooney can be Chinese, Charlton Heston can be Mexican, Angelina Jolie can be a black woman, Sir Anthony Hopkins can be a black man, and Laurence Olivier can do an Al Jolson and put on blackface to be Othello, then Idris Elba, a British man who happens to be black, can play James Bond. His name is *James*. *James* is a black man's name. James Evans, motherfucker. James Earl Jones, motherfucker. What kind of mind-fuckery is that bullllll-shit? We will trade you Zoe Saldana as Nina Simone for Idris as Bond. We will even throw in Tiger Woods, Bryant Gumbel, and a banana in the tail pipe."

Then he imitated Eddie Murphy's trademark laugh. "Eh, eh, eh, eh, eh, eh, eh."

A few women got up and hurried from their tables, laughing so hard they had to run to the bathroom and pee. Again Destiny's sides hurt from laughing.

All dimples and smiles, Dubois continued his foot-stomping, belly-aching act.

Destiny Jones, the woman who was hard to impress, was close to being impressed.

Dubois started to sing, made all the women swoon as he did a few song parodies. The women with wedding rings on their fingers smiled the hardest, their wishes and wants sent more than enough electricity to light up all of California. He was finishing his act, had done forty minutes of jokes and songs, had ranked on the world, had made people wonder what it would be like if the Native Americans had a GOP attitude and wanted to take their country back, had made people who knew nothing about politics laugh about Syria, about racism, and had cracked jokes about the Mexican people at the Chinese cleaner who didn't get his laundry to him on time.

Dubois made forty minutes feel like they had been on a roller coaster going through a fun house. It had been exciting and hilarious. It had been as orgasmic as jumping out of a plane.

They loved his talent and loved him.

Destiny remembered being in love with him too.

Dubois said, "Before I leave the stage, I'm going to need some help from the crowd. I'm gonna do the history of dance from the 1900s up until today with Jimmy Fallon on his show in a couple of weeks, and I need to work on a few steps. Hey, James Bond girls. Since you ladies are close to the front, any one at your table want to come up here and help me with this routine?"

Destiny froze. She knew he was about to call her to the stage, in front of the world.

He said, "Come on up here, Holly Goodhead. Get your freaky ass on up here."

Indigo cursed, didn't move at first, but smiled and gave in to the applause from the crowd. She was helped up the stairs to the stage and stood in the spotlight with Dubois.

The deejay played some beats and the tall Nigerian in five-inch heels loosened up and had fun. She did dances with Dubois, then the deejay kicked in a Nigerian number, Yemi Alade performing "Johnny," and Indigo shouted that was her favorite song. She took over, showed Dubois a few Nigerian moves, took him back to Africa. Indigo did tribal-meets-contemporary dance moves that made her dress hug her bubble and breasts, wicked moves that had men staring and calling out at Indigo like she was the hottest of the hot. As she moved her African waist and showed how Africa moves, one guy ran to the stage and threw all of the money in his wallet at her feet. He made it rain like it was a hurricane.

People laughed, some stood and clapped, then other men did the same, threw money and whistled.

Destiny saw Yaba the Laker first, said a bad word, then touched Ericka and Kwanzaa.

Yaba the Laker was here, in the club, backstage, watching Indigo act out.

Indigo was so preoccupied she didn't notice her ex-lover come on stage, didn't see her ex-boo ease on the stage from behind the curtain. Yaba the Laker appeared and the room was taken off guard. L.A. was a basketball town. L.A. had the Clippers, had had the Raiders and the Rams, had the Angels and the Dodgers and the Kings, but those sports were all the stepchildren, something to do when the big boys weren't playing, because it was *Lakerville*.

Everyone started applauding like it was an award show at the Kennedy Center.

Indigo thought they were hand-praising her wicked dance, but had a rude awakening when she turned around. She turned around as she did a sweet Nigerian hip-hop move, and Yaba was there, with a cordless microphone in hand. Indigo stopped moving, pulled the edges of her skirt back down. The music lowered to a whisper. Yaba frowned, then barked into the mic in a strong Nigerian accent, sounded angry. He said that he was pissed off that Leonard kept calling her Holly Goodhead.

Then he added, "You know you should be *Pussy Galore*."

People laughed.

Indigo look confused, embarrassed, but was not going to back down. She folded her arms across her breasts and was ready to bark back at Yaba for being rude and humiliating her in front of a room filled with black Americans. She was shocked to see him appear out of nowhere.

Yaba took her hand. Indigo thought he was about to pull her from the stage.

The music changed to a song by a Nigerian singer called Davido, a song called "Aye," a song that told a tale of love between different classes. Yaba sang along, sang as if they were the only two people on the planet, sang his love for Indigo to the room. He let her hand go, then the giant danced and took her hands and danced with her, and Indigo danced with him, her body already moving when the Nigerian song started, and she fell into the soft African-inspired beats, the mesmerizing music from back home, their dance cultural, powerful, sensual. People in the room did a soft clap along with the music.

Kwanzaa shook her head. "Had no idea. I guess she told him she was going to be here tonight, but I don't think he told her he would leave his castle and come down here for this."

Destiny said, "Look at her face. She didn't have a clue either."

Kwanzaa said, "I guess Dubois and Yaba have been friends since Indigo's party."

Ericka said, "I hope like hell Olamilekan isn't up in here too."

Yaba the Laker gave a short speech, the strong Nigerian accent now gone, his voice crisp, clear, articulate, Princeton, and he told how he had met Indigo at Starbucks when she had dropped her friend Kwanzaa off at work one day when she had car problems.

On that morning, Indigo was in her car, backing out of a space, and had surprised him when she cursed him out because in his rush to get a cup of green tea he had parked his Range Rover crooked across two parking spaces. He said Indigo snapped at him real good, asked him who the hell did he think he was that he could be so inconsiderate and park that way, was bold, was mean, and was arrogant. He said that he thought she was a crazy person.

People laughed.

He added that she was the most beautiful woman he had ever seen, and right away he knew she was a Nigerian woman. Yaba said that instead of returning the hostility, he saw the loveliness in her face, the frustration in her eyes, and asked what he could do to make her day better, and she had turned her frown upside down and said that he could tell her to have a nice day, then straighten his car out so other people could have room to park, and at that moment, when he saw her smile, he had asked her if he could give her a hug and a kiss on the cheek to help her start her day off right. She told him he could, told the room that Indigo had eased out of her car, and as they blocked traffic, she had let him hug her and kiss her cheek, and that hug and kiss changed into a real kiss, a passionate kiss between two people who didn't know one another's names. Well, she knew who he was, since everyone in the parking lot was yelling out his name, but Indigo was not impressed. To her he was just another guy, and he liked that. That was why he loved her right away. He asked for her number. They ended up texting all morning and into the night. He took her on a date, a restaurant in Silver Lake.

He told everyone that she didn't kiss him on the first date.

The room got the joke, and almost everyone laughed.

And now she was the love of his life.

He told the room she was his best friend.

He told the room she was the one he couldn't live without.

He said that he had changed his status online from "single" to "dating" when he kissed her, and now he wanted to upgrade his status again. Voice trembling, on the verge of crying, trying to man-up and be strong, he cleared his throat and told Indigo he wanted her to become his wife.

Yaba the Laker eased down on one knee and took a small box out of his pocket. A collective gasp filled the club and carried out onto Sunset Boulevard.

Over and over Destiny said, *"Holy Jesus."*

Ericka Stockwell's mouth dropped open.

As the crowd looked on, Yaba opened the beautiful golden box, and the obese diamond ring sparkled.

Yaba asked Indigo to marry him.

He asked her to be his for the rest of his life.

She said yes. Indigo said yes. She hesitated, and then kissed her fiancé. The room erupted in applause. No one had clapped that hard all night.

Waves of emotion and energy moved through everyone, like at a wedding. Women raised their glasses and cried as if they had seen a real-life Cinderella.

Nigerian music played and they danced, soft and easy.

Indigo raised her hand, so everyone in the room could see her ring.

The room became their paparazzi, cell phones flashing and recording.

Indigo and Yaba left the stage holding hands, went through the curtain to the back.

Kwanzaa looked around the room, read the faces of the people.

Tipsy women cried. A few women had sobered up and gave the guys they were with the side eye of unhappiness. It was going to be a good night for some, but a long night for more than a few brothers who had come up short. A public proposal made jump-offs want to upgrade.

Kwanzaa said, "Olamilekan is not going to like this mess; not at all, not at all, not at all."

Destiny said, "Oh, damn. This is not good."

Kwanzaa asked, "What?"

Ericka said, "You didn't notice what just happened, Kwanzaa?"

"Notice what? I was checking out the crowd. What did I miss? Did they get married?"

Destiny said, "Indigo wasn't crying. Every woman in the club cried, even the mean waitresses that have been acting like pit bulls. Every woman cried except the girl with the ring."

Ericka tilted her to the side and made a curious sound. "Not one tear in her brown eyes. Yaba cried. His lip trembled. His voice cracked. He was sincere. Indigo wasn't fazed. She was unemotional and composed the entire time."

Kwanzaa said, "You're right. When Marcus asked me to marry him, I was crying and bouncing around like a cartoon character. And Indigo did kind of rush him off the stage."

Ericka spoke up, "I hope he kept the receipt for that obnoxious blood diamond."

With the excitement at its peak, Dubois told them to give Yaba a round of applause.

The women applauded the ring; the men praised the Laker.

Everyone in the audience who had working legs stood up, gave Dubois a standing ovation. He looked toward Destiny's table as he took his bows, looked at her and nodded.

Then he winked. That wink felt like an insult, and his subtle grin stole part of her sanity.

He had the nerve to wink at her.

She shuddered. Destiny's jaw tightened as she closed her eyes and held her breath for a moment. She tried to make that old fire go away. But the anger didn't subside. The fire bloomed. Destiny Jones stood up, barked out Dubois's name, and hurried toward the stage.

Chapter 71

Dubois halted his exit, and the applause gradually died. Destiny walked up the five stairs to the stage, to where Dubois was standing, confused, no longer in comedian mode.

All attitude, she stopped in his face, and asked, "You really want to take me out?"

"Yeah, DJ. I really do."

"Prove it. Prove it here. Prove it now."

"How am I supposed to do that?"

"Figure it out. If you're afraid of what your mother will think, stop bugging me. Don't wink at me. Don't call my friends asking for me. Don't give me tickets and buy me drinks."

"Happy birthday. Thanks for the tickets, Dubois. Why, you're welcome, Miss Jones. Thank you for sending my girls and me eight expensive-ass drinks. Why, you're welcome."

"And don't tell me happy birthday. I don't want you to remember my stinkin' birthday."

"Is that what you want?"

"That's what I want. Don't stalk me."

"DJ."

"*What?*"

Dubois reached for her. He reached for her and she looked at him like he had lost his mind. Then she gradually gave him her hand. She let him touch her.

She let him pull her closer.

She said, "You didn't call me for ten years, then I run into you in a parking lot and you're smiling and flirting with all of my friends."

"I'm sorry. And I was not flirting."

"Liar. I was standing right there."

"I was being friendly. Sisters are so unaccustomed to a brother having manners that when a brother is just being nice, sisters think they're being hit on. You need to get over yourself."

"Ten years. That really hurt. I never want to see you again. That's all I have to say."

"I'm sorry."

"Let me go."

"I have missed you."

"Are you just being friendly now?"

"No, I'm flirting."

"Whatever."

"I've thought about you more than you'll ever know."

"Is that your Morehouse mack? Is that what you use on the hood rats at Greenbriar Mall?"

"I'm going to kiss you now."

"No, you're not. Mess around and get smacked."

"If you don't want me to kiss you, now is a good time to walk away."

"Your girlfriend won't like that."

"I don't have a girlfriend."

"All these women in here, you can pick and choose a thot without thinking."

"What if I choose you because you are in my every thought?"

"I'm not a thot, and if that's what you think, you need to think another thought."

"But you're all I think about, so I choose you."

"You un-chose me ten years ago and now I am un-choosing you back."

She stared at Dubois and the rumbling from the crowd was unheard by her ears.

He put his hands on her waist, pulled her closer.

She did something she swore she would never do again; she capitulated.

She put her arms around his neck, and as he tilted his head, she tilted her head.

They kissed. They kissed for a second before she closed her eyes.

She kissed the first boy she had ever really cared about, in the style of the French.

And she liked it. He hadn't kissed like that ten years ago.

Destiny Jones kissed her first romantic love like she was still in middle school.

Again the room applauded, and she found it hard to pull away from the kiss.

But she did. She looked out at the crowd.

Somewhere in the far reaches of the room, she heard someone say her birth name, heard someone say the name of Destiny Jones, heard a pejorative about crazy Jamaicans, about crazy Jamaican bitches shooting dicks, about bleach, about slashing someone's face, and again a coldness ran up her spine, the memories returned, the bad memories flooded her, and her soul went into fight or flight.

Fight or flight.

She wanted to do like she had always done. She wanted to pull her hair loose, let it become her cocoon, and hide. She wanted to kick off her heels and run out a side door. If she had been alone, she would have hurried through the curtains and found the first exit. Destiny looked toward the Blackbirds, toward her place of friendship and comfort.

They had heard someone call out Destiny Jones as well.

Ericka and Kwanzaa were rising to their feet, ready to protect their warrior. Indigo was behind the stage, ready to rush back out before a riot began.

Destiny looked out at the crowd, then she turned and faced Dubois.

She faced the boy who had been her first heartbreak one more time, eased away from him, then walked to the microphone. She tapped it twice, made sure it was still on. She looked out at this swatch of the world, at this mini universe, the one in which she lived.

With perfect diction, in private school mode, the voice that many on this side of town used to mock and laugh because to their untraveled ears she sounded white, she said, "I heard someone out there ask if I was

Destiny Jones. Well, guess what? My name . . . is Destiny Jones. My name is *Destiny Jones*. I am Destiny Jones. *Destiny Jones*."

It took a moment.

First there was an acute silence, and for some, profound confusion.

Destiny saw the shock and fear in the faces of Kwanzaa and Ericka.

Destiny repeated, stronger, "My name is Destiny Jones. My name is Destiny Jones."

Then whispers. Then more recognition and explanations. Then waves of judgment.

Phones appeared and the room became a legion of freelance photographers trying to get shots of a celebrity. They shook up Instagram. Periscope. Twitter. Facebook.

The ignorant, the evil were always the first to speak, the first to text, the first to blog.

She hardened, ready to fight the room.

She said, "If you know me, and you don't like me, *I don't give a damn.* I don't care if you are blessed with melanin or dammed with recessive genes, don't care if you're tall, short, male or female, like the late great Bernie Mac said, *I ain't scared of you muh'fuckers*. That's straight off the muh'fucking press. One at a time or as a collective, *I ain't scared of you muh'fuckers*."

Destiny mocked Bernie Mac, and stared the room down, dared any one to vilipend her like she was a second-class citizen. Boldness. No fear. Unapologetic. That was all it took to make an army of bullies take ten steps in retreat.

Mocking the late great Rick James, she emphasized, "I'm Destiny Jones, *bitch*."

The room erupted in laughter, and many in the crowd repeated that like a mantra.

"You don't understand. Make sure you tell a friend to tell a friend to tell a friend. The real Destiny Jones came to tell everybody who hates her, *I ain't scared of you muh'fucking mitches and bitches*."

To some, Jamaica was the land of guns and corruption, of rebels, of drugs. To others it was the land of music and Bob Marley, a man who wanted peace and fairness.

Which part of her mother's Jamaica they woke up in her, it was up
to the crowd. The vulgar *fuck all y'all* speech she had said when she was
at Catalina with the Blackbirds, she repeated it word for word, looked
down on the room of would-be oppressors, looked down on a room that
had people who would give a pass to a murderer, pedophile, or rapist if
he could catch a ball, sing, or tell jokes, and instead of running, she
stood her ground, and communicated with them on the level she despised, in the language of Hoosegow, used the same unkind vocabulary
that had been directed at her since she was fifteen.

No one challenged her. The bullies had retreated back into their
caves.

Destiny raised the mic high, paused, let it drop.

Done.

The room once again exploded in applause.

Destiny Jones owned her universe. She felt like she owned her life.

She looked up at the ceiling as if she could see the stars, as if she
could see the universe. She heard them. Out there across the galaxy,
every version of Destiny applauded her as if she were their leader. That
was how she felt at that moment, as she looked at her table and saw
Ericka and Kwanzaa on their feet, as she looked behind her and saw
Indigo standing next to Yaba the Laker, both of them applauding.

Destiny Jones exhaled what she had held in for so long.

Destiny felt like every version of her ever created across the multi-
verses had her back.

Dubois said, "Happy birthday, Honey Rider."

"Stop calling me that."

"You sho' know how to upstage a brother."

"Dubois, dude, stop trying to sound hood-rific."

"What'cha talking 'bout, Honey Rider?"

"First and foremost, Dubois, you're a private school nerd, just like
me."

"*Muh'fucking?* Which one of us is really trying to sound *hood-rific* up
in here?"

"Your mother would slap the taste out of your mouth if she heard
you talk like that."

"My mother is here. She came to watch the show."

"You kissed me in front of your mother?"

"I kissed you in front of my mom, my uncle Tyrone, my aunt Shelby, my cousin Bobby, his wife, Alexandria, ten cousins, and about twenty more of my friends from around L.A."

"Too late for me to be embarrassed."

"Yeah. A little too late. You might as well wave at her. She's over there."

"You cursed in front of your mother?"

"So did you. Your cursing made my cursing sound like a Maya Angelou poem."

"Oh, Jesus."

"She will spank me later, I'm sure. She'll hit me with a few Bible verses too. I'm sure she will come looking for you too."

"Well, I guess I need to gather the Blackbirds and exit the building in a hurry."

"Wait, DJ?"

"What, DJ?"

"So, are you ever going to let me take you out or what?"

"Of course not."

"Are you serious? After all this?"

Destiny said, "You are my enemy."

"Serious?"

"You were my first enemy."

"You were my first."

"I was your first enemy too?"

"No, my first. I was a virgin. I know I said I had been with other girls, but I had lied."

"I was your first?"

"I was scared after that. I was too scared to call you. I didn't know what to say. I thought you could tell I didn't know what I was doing and you were going to tell everybody how bad I was in bed."

"Are you serious?"

"Give me an apology date. So we can talk and put this behind us."

"That will happen when they start drug-testing members of Congress, or when Mexicans build a wall to keep Americans out of Mexico."

"For closure. A short meeting."

Destiny paused. "Sure. To get you off my freakin' jock. So I can tell you how I really feel, how I hate you, and you will wish our paths had *never* crossed again."

"When are you available for this said meeting so you can verbalize your hate?"

"Right now. I'm available right now."

Chapter 72

Ericka Stockwell showered.

Skin still damp, she sat on her bedroom floor covered in a red house-coat.

She felt exhausted. She had barely made it through the day.

Diving at Catalina had taken too much of her energy, but she had pressed on. She had made it and no one had noticed anything different about her.

She had not disrupted anyone's joy.

Destiny had been bold tonight. She had been so *muh'fucking* bold.

Destiny Jones had confronted her past in front of many hardcore naysayers.

When Ericka had looked around that comedy club, she had seen the faces of men, but had focused on the faces of the women. Many had been assaulted during their short existences on this planet. Many had been assaulted and never said a word. What Destiny had done had been akin to a preacher striking a chord during a sermon, one that brought the shamed to their feet, one that made spirits rise, one that made many do the Holy Ghost dance. Women had shaken off their disgrace, then stood and applauded Destiny Jones like they had found a new leader.

Destiny had taken to the stage and faced the world. She had become, as they said years ago back in the '60s, free, white, and twenty-one. She was beholden to no one. When Destiny had left the stage with Dubois, practically every woman in the club had run to her to try to get a selfie.

It had been quite a night.

Quite a night.

Now back to her reality. Back to her truth.

Ericka looked over papers from Kaiser, messages from her doctor, test results, the request for her to contact her doctor again, and then laid them aside.

She opened a journal. On each page was a list of the things she owned.

Next to each item she had written one of the Blackbirds' names.

Next to a few things she had written Mr. Jones's name.

She picked up the four chapters that had been given to her by Dr. Debra Dubois.

After reading what Dr. Debra Dubois had revealed in her memoirs, after sharing all with the Blackbirds, Ericka had still been unable to confront that part of her past in front of one person.

Ericka's past was Mrs. Stockwell's past as much as it was her own.

Ericka read the four chapters written by Dr. Debra Dubois again and again, read how she and her mother had been perceived two decades earlier, read truth as recalled by someone else. That old pain percolated, rose to the surface, became bubbling magma.

Ericka waxed lachrymose, walked around in the dark, wiped away tears, and then sipped half a glass of wine before she dressed in gray joggers, a green hoodie, and yellow running shoes. Fashion was not on her mind. She stopped, stared at herself in the mirror.

She stared at her short mane, at her fresh baldness. She put moisturizer on her face, and then put on lip gloss and a pair of big silver earrings. She didn't want to look totally busted.

Pages that accurately reflected her life at the age of thirteen at her side, she went down the concrete stairs, passed by the doors to the apartments of the other Blackbirds, and went to her convertible, the car acquired after her divorce, another symbol of part of her life gone wrong.

She sent Destiny a text. Destiny was at a hot club on Sunset, dancing with Dubois.

She told Destiny she was leaving.

Destiny told Ericka to tell her dad hello, and thanked her for the heads-up.

Ericka let the top down; pushed the remote that opened the gate to Little Lagos. She was the only Blackbird in her nest tonight. She was glad. Some things had to be confronted alone.

Ericka Stockwell looked at the apartments, waved as if her best friends were there standing in their windows. This was the start of her good-bye to her sisters by other mommas, her confidants in most things, her gym partners, her motivators. She waved at the vacant nests of the Blackbirds, then turned her phone off and the music up, then drove away, took to Crenshaw Boulevard. Mr. Jones was on Ericka's mind. She had finally found the love of her life.

That had been the most important thing on her bucket list.

She whispered, "This isn't fair. This just isn't fair."

She wanted to take her issue to him, seek counsel from him. She didn't. She wouldn't. She drove with those chapters on her mind, and scenes pulled her back into her past and left her in anger, in sadness, in a trance, and she didn't become fully aware again until she was halfway to her destination. She came up on the Urban League and Happy's Pizza, where View Park kissed Leimert Park. She was at the section by the beauty college, the streets like the roads in the islands, as uneven and harsh as her thoughts, rugged due to metro construction. A gigantic billboard proclaiming STRAIGHT OUTTA CONDOMS spied down on her from overhead. Ericka stared at the billboard and wondered if she was being shamed.

She wondered if after she was gone, she would be allowed to keep her memories.

Soon Ericka slowed. Traffic had halted because people had been injured in a shooting, and that shooting had caused a car crash that ended up on the curb at Krispy Kreme. Ghetto birds flew over Los Angeles in two-hour shifts, and at that moment, like it had been when they protested, it seemed like all the LAPD's helicopters were over her head. The bright light was a sign and it was as if the skies had opened and heaven was calling her home. She wondered if there was life after death.

Maybe it had been calling her all along. Maybe Y-H-W-H was calling.

Maybe she was as strong as she would ever be, as beautiful as she would ever be, and all the good things that would happen to her, including her health, were now in the past.

Maybe nothing was left but suffering.

Not yet.

Not yet.

Ericka crept by police cars, moved by the flashing lights of several ambulances, moved around the homeless using bus stop benches and storefronts as their overnight bedrooms. After dark, the homeless owned every park.

Ericka whipped around traffic and looky-loos, sped north, broke the speed limit, changed lanes like a race car driver, didn't slow down for two miles, not until she had crossed the Rosa Parks section of the 10 freeway, and the reason she slowed was because she was trapped at the light at Washington Boulevard, a light she had considered running, but cars were in front of her and in both the right lane and the left turning lane. She was going to back up and whip around them, break the light, but someone pulled up behind her. She was boxed in. She grinded her teeth, felt road rage in her blood.

The universe had let her get this close, then blocked her way and laughed.

She felt like she was thirteen again. She felt young, unwise, and defenseless. She had never felt white, free, and twenty-one. She had never lived without burden.

Anxiety grew.

She was but one red light away from the narrow street named St. Charles Place, the unassuming, hidden-in-plain-sight road just beyond Sojourner Truth Industrial Club, one red light away from her own truth, and all she needed to do was let the universe allow her to turn down the avenue that had signs both warning and boasting there were no other entrances or exits.

St. Charles Place offered the only outlet into historic Lafayette Square. With Ericka's thoughts, there was no other outlet either. And tonight there was no other out for Mrs. Stockwell.

Ericka took deep breaths, clenched the steering wheel, her music loud, but not loud enough to drown her thoughts. The light at Washington changed, then Ericka was caught at the light at St. Charles Place. She beat her steering wheel, then scowled to her right and saw an Asian man looking at her like she had lost her mind. He looked away, then eased his car up a few inches. The last seconds before the big moment were taking forever to arrive.

She wasn't turning around. If the light took two days to change, she would be waiting. After what felt like forever, the universe surrendered, gave her the green light.

Ericka entered the affluent community where W. C. Fields, Fatty Arbuckle, and boxer Joe Louis had once lived. She inhaled, expected the air to smell like private schools and money that could afford summers in Barbados and weekends in the Hamptons, but it was just as stale as the air on her end of Crenshaw Boulevard, only without the noise to spice it up.

Ericka cruised the smooth, pimple-free roads, passed a few homes with the natural desert xeriscaping in the front. She parked on Virginia Road, across from her mother's two-level Mediterranean-style home. Ericka turned her car off, but left her convertible top down, this area blanketed with the illusion of safety. She had arrived. Now she was too scared to leave her car.

She looked at the chapters, her tears dried on the paper, on the power of words.

She stared at her mother's magnificent home. There was a concrete and lighted driveway that led down the side of the property and ended at the rear of the well-maintained mansion. A three-car garage was in the far reaches, and off to its left a smaller home was situated on a large lot. Halfway down the driveway was a car. Ericka shook her head. She guessed that since she had seen her mother last, she'd been blessed tenfold and had bought herself a new luxury ride.

But her thoughts were bigger than new cars and castles hidden off urban tracks.

She eased out and walked down the long driveway, toward her mother's new car.

Ericka did a double take as she passed the luxury car in the driveway, and she paused, then stopped, backed up, evaluated the car, shook her head in disgust, and cursed.

It wasn't her mother's car. Ericka stood in shock, but that only lasted a moment. Ericka went back to her roadster, pulled it into the driveway, parked behind her mother's guest.

Ericka made sure that car wouldn't be able to leave during the bewitching hours.

It felt strange because the three or four times she had been to this home, the place her mother moved after living in Windsor Hills, Ericka had never parked in that driveway.

She had always parked at the curb, on the streets, like an unwanted solicitor.

The last time she had been here, her mother had told her God wanted her to have cancer. Ericka had sworn to never set foot in Mrs. Stockwell's pristine home again.

In the distance, she imagined God was laughing.

She would see Him soon.

She would ask Him to explain the joke.

Chapter 73

After Ericka rang the doorbell a dozen times, lights came on upstairs. Ericka rang again and again and again. The porch light came on, blinded her, and made her cover her eyes. Soon lights came on over the grand stairway that led to the foyer. The front door was wood and glass, and the glass allowed strangers to look inside and see the glory of success. Mrs. Stockwell came down the stairs like she was the belle of the ball, the fluid movements of a ballerina long past her prime, but still limber. Instead of carrying her Bible, she carried a gun.

Mrs. Stockwell opened the heavy wooden door, her hair down across her shoulders, feet bare, her body wrapped in a red kimono that stopped above her knees. She had a wardrobe malfunction that created a Nipplegate moment.

Ericka took a deep breath. Her mother was in Jayne Mansfield mode, was trying to be more Marilyn Monroe than Marilyn Monroe ever was. Her mother smelled of a soft perfume. Her lipstick had been kissed away. Or she had lost it when she was on her knees giving head. Her mother held the gun at her side. Ericka was not surprised. Her mother slept nude, "man ready" Ericka called it, and kept a gun on top of her Bible. Mrs. Stockwell had bought her .38 after her estranged husband had slapped her one time too many. Despite all the long dresses her mother wore, at home Mrs. Stockwell was practically a nudist, and the woman would pull a gun on a trespasser like she was Nina Simone having a bad day.

Mrs. Stockwell asked, "Is there something wrong with your mind, Ericka?"

"You should be ashamed of yourself, Mrs. Stockwell. But we know that is not possible."

"And what did you do with your hair? That's the only reprehensible thing I see."

"Don't worry about my hair."

"Why are you bald? That ugly hairstyle you had, it was better than being bald."

"Worry about getting yours pulled out of your head by the handful."

Ericka motioned at the vehicle parked in the driveway, the one that would not be able to go anywhere unless it sprouted wings. Ericka was sure that her mother's company had already spied out the window, and if he had thought he could sneak away, he had another think coming.

Ericka said, "The hood of his hot car is stone cold. He's been here supplicating awhile."

"This is my home, my life, and what goes on between these walls is not your concern."

"Have the decency to have your *guest* park in *the* garage before you allow him to park inside *your* garage, Mrs. Stockwell. When you screw a married man, he should hide his ride, or at least be smart enough to park two blocks away, in case his wife drives by. My ex-husband never parked in front of his mistresses' homes. You have to learn to play the cheater's game. That's why you're at the door with a gun. In case his wife and daughter were here with me too."

"Are you here to castigate consenting adults?"

"You deserve severe castigation and a scarlet letter for both adultery and hypocrisy. Women have been turned to stone for less. Women have been *stoned* for what you've done."

"Are you going to leave now, run back and tell all of your friends?"

"I'm not going to be the one who breaks up her family. That man's wife and daughter would go Dark Continent on you and beat you down, leave you on the floor naked and crying while they waved your panties in the air like their flag of victory, but you don't have any panties on, so they would pull your precious hair from your head by the roots and wave that instead."

"Why are you here at this ungodly hour?"

"The chapters from Debra's memoir. I have the four chapters she wrote about us."

"You are at my door ringing my bell like you've gone mad because of her?"

"It's time for us to face these words, at the hour when God is on Benadryl."

"You know I have company, yet you come to my door, ring my bell like a madwoman."

"I can make one phone call and this night will only be the beginning for both of you."

"You wouldn't."

"Her mother is more of a mother to me than you have ever been, *Mrs.* Stockwell, and I barely know the woman. But I am not here because of that. I am here because of us."

"Whatever you have, I don't want to deal with that mess from yesteryear at this moment."

"You think I give a damn what you feel like dealing with? Do you think I feel like dealing with this? Do you? I am dealing with this now because I am forced to deal with this now."

"I want you to leave my property, Ericka."

"I want you to invite me inside of your home."

"*You're not welcome here.* How dare you invite me to *leave* where you stay, and then have the audacity to show up on my front porch and expect entrance into my blessed home?"

"Invite me in, or I will drag you out and be loud enough to wake your neighbors."

"Ericka, don't do this. Don't make an ass of yourself."

"I'm not the ass. He needs to be ashamed of himself."

"Lower your voice."

"*You need to be twice as ashamed.*"

"Don't force me to call the police."

"I'll call them for you, right after I call Mount Olympus and tell his wife he's here putting some African inside of your American. You make a call and I'll make a call, and we'll wait on his family."

Mrs. Stockwell stepped aside, held the heavy door, and surrendered her space.

Ericka entered her mother's version of heaven on Earth.

To her, it was just another beautiful, well-decorated hell.

Those who had the worst behavior seemed to garner the highest rewards.

"Why tonight of all nights did you have to appear at my front door?"

"Ask God."

"I'm asking you."

"Put the gun down, pick a Bible up, fall on your knees, and ask God to forgive you for being on your back with a married man, shower, then meet me in your lovely dining room."

Chapter 74

From Chapter 16 of the Memoirs of Dr. Debra Dubois

Faith said, "Put your boxing gloves on, Debra."

I said, "What's up?"

"Mrs. Stockwell is here."

"For what?"

"Annual checkup."

"Great. I am always so happy to see that woman."

"Oh, the sarcasm."

"Well-deserved."

"Straighten up and fly right. I've got a couple more here for prenatal, so take Mrs. Stockwell to room one."

My lips moved and formed a very nasty word, but it wasn't heard.

I said, "Is Ericka with her?"

Faith said, "Yeah. That poor child is at her side."

My attitude softened. Some. I did a breathing exercise, stalled another minute just to make her wait a little longer. A moment later I was in the lobby waiting for Mrs. Stockwell to hand Ericka her purse and keys for safekeeping. Mrs. Stockwell was a shrewd bitch of a woman. My concentration went from her to her daughter. Ericka's flesh was pale, almost the color of bone, all except for her cheeks. It looked like blood had risen to the surface due to sudden pain. Under her puffy eyes I saw a weary child with flaking hair and skin that was about to turn pimply.

Ericka put her textbooks and paper down long enough to try to smile when she said, "Good morning, Miss Mitchell."

I smiled. "Good morning, Ericka."

"I like your uniform."

"Thank you."

"I didn't know nurses could wear pink uniforms."

"We can wear any color uniform we want."

"Miss Mitchell, how long did it take you to become a nurse?"

Mrs. Stockwell interrupted, "Ericka. Please. Hush."

There was a pregnant pause between us. Ericka's eyes went to her mother, then back to me. I wasn't in the mood to be controlled.

I moved closer to Ericka and said, "Studying?"

"Uh-huh."

Her mother made a sound of disapproval.

Ericka corrected herself, said, "I mean yes."

I asked, "How are you feeling today?"

"Scared."

"Why?"

"I keep throwing up."

"That's not good."

"I've been eating too much Mexican food and it's making me run for the border."

I laughed a little. So did Ericka.

Mrs. Stockwell made a grunting sound. Ericka's eyes went to her mother.

My eyes went the same way.

Mrs. Stockwell and I stood face-to-face. No words were shared between us.

I led Mrs. Stockwell down the hallway, but my mind was with her pregnant daughter. Ericka Stockwell was thirteen. I wondered how Ericka had done the deed, how many times, with whom she had done it, and how many boys there were. I wondered what words had led this innocent child down the road of surrender. I wanted to know what kind of pleasure she could have gotten out of an act she didn't understand, something her body wasn't ready to receive. But pleasure had nothing to do with pregnancy.

I kept my true feelings in check, masked my mixed emotions with an air of nonchalance, and worked with a soft adept tone and expressionless face as I took Mrs. Stockwell's weight. Measured her height. Next would be temperature and blood pressure. I reviewed her medical history and did my best to put my mind in many places, refused to let my anger and disgust for the heartless woman sitting in my face reveal itself, refused to give her any victory by letting my feelings show. I thought about the comedian, thought about Leonard Dubois, the man I had just started dating, the man who would eventually become my husband, and he was the only thing, the only person I could think of to keep me anywhere near a smile. I wrapped myself around the memory of our first kiss, of the memory of his tongue waltzing with mine and tried to create a pillow-soft cloud to float on.

On the back of the door, at eyesight level, was a chart detailing STDs and their symptoms. Staring at that chart got Leonard off my mind real quick.

When I put the blood pressure cuff on Mrs. Stockwell's arm, she asked, "Do you have the recommendations I requested?"

I pretended that I didn't know what she was talking about. I had hoped she wouldn't bring it up, but she had.

"What recommendations would those be?"

She lowered her voice. "For an abortionist. Time is of the essence."

"You will need to confer with Faith regarding that issue."

"I see."

"So, Ericka is with you. Is it an in-service day?"

"She is out of school on a few days' sabbatical so we can handle this family emergency. The sooner the better. Soon she will start to show, and we can't have that. Rumors will spread. Then this will become more than it really is."

I said, "Please remove your clothing. Put on a gown with the opening in the front. Faith will be with you in a moment."

Without acknowledging her with any real eye contact, I handed her a hospital gown, then I walked toward the waiting room and took another patient to another room. I began taking the next patient's stats. Minutes later, I was back in Mrs. Stockwell's room with Faith. Mrs.

Stockwell's clothes were neatly hung on yellow plastic hangers she had brought with her. Faith was getting ready to inspect Mrs. Stockwell's grotto, the place Mr. Stockwell had released his pleasures.

Faith went into the routine. "Scoot down. Feet in stirrups. Relax your knees."

I handed her gel and tongs.

Faith said, "You're going to feel a little pressure."

Mrs. Stockwell *humphed*, then glued her eyes on the ceiling and said a bitchy, "Until your teenage child becomes pregnant, you don't know what pressure is."

When we finished, Mrs. Stockwell raised the issue of the abortionist again.

Without making a comment, Faith reached into her smock and pulled out a sheet of paper and several numbers. Mrs. Stockwell didn't bother with a thank-you.

Faith took a short breath, then said, "With Ericka in her second trimester, it won't be a one-day, two-hour thing. It's going to be a complicated procedure."

Bottom lip trembling, Mrs. Stockwell barked, "And you think having a problem child is not complicated? You think being a parent is a one-day, two-hour thing?"

"That's not what I was implying."

"What were you implying? Just say it to my face."

"They will have to prep her on day one, then induce labor on day two. That's all."

Mrs. Stockwell said, "After you ladies leave, will one of you have Ericka come here so that I may speak with my child about our predicament while I am getting dressed."

I volunteered to go get her.

Shaken, emotional, Faith went across the hall to another examination room. But by the time her fingers touched the doorknob, her professional face had returned. Those two moments of empathy were twice as much as I was used to seeing. I headed toward the lobby. Each step down the gray-carpeted hallway felt like I was going to get a pubescent prisoner and escort her to death row. It didn't feel natural. Nothing about the situation was natural. But it happened. This was the reality for many. Ericka's body had the physiology and capabilities of a woman, but she was nowhere near being an adult mentally. In theory, she shouldn't be going through this. But theory wasn't reality.

There was another patient in the lobby, a woman who was bringing her sixteen-year-old daughter for a simple checkup and a recommendation for birth control, but no Ericka.

I said, "Did you see the girl who was sitting right there?"

They hadn't.

In one of the mauve-gray seats were schoolbooks and a purse, all in a disarrayed stack, like they had been dropped or thrown to the floor in anger. Mrs. Stockwell's purse and King James Version were dropped on top of it all. The handbag was sideways and wide open. Heart racing, panic in my every motion, my first thought was that if her mother's purse had been left unguarded, Ericka couldn't be far. That was what I hoped.

I checked outside to see if Ericka had stepped out to get some fresh air, didn't see her, then came back inside and checked the bathrooms, the lounge, went back outside and walked around the back of the building, double-checked the parking lot to see if she was resting inside her mother's car. I didn't see Ericka. I told Mrs. Stockwell and she fell into silence and anger while she fought to get her clothes on as fast as she could, but she made sure everything was proper and in place before she went into a room filled with other people. Image was priority. Mrs. Stockwell checked her purse when she got into the lobby. Everything was there, except six hundred dollars in cash. That was the money Mrs. Stockwell had withdrawn to pay for Ericka's procedure. Mrs. Stockwell had planned on getting the procedure done under an anonymous name. She didn't want it on Ericka's charts. Mrs. Stockwell clutched her Bible, went outside and screamed her daughter's name, over and over, like she was a woman gone mad. She screamed Ericka's name like her anger was the magnet to bring her daughter back home to her. The woman screamed until her throat turned raw.

She marched from the Marshalls, still screaming, to the Wyndam Bel Age Hotel, still screaming, to the Fox Hills Mall, still screaming. She drove her car and checked from Sepulveda to La Cienega, and there was no sign of Ericka Stockwell. When Mrs. Stockwell came back, her voice was almost gone. She dabbed sweat from her forehead with a white handkerchief and asked if Ericka had returned. I told her no. Without asking, she brushed by me and went into Faith's private office. Mrs. Stockwell phoned everyone she could think of, including the middle school Ericka attended.

I said, "The boy."

Mrs. Stockwell snapped, "What?"

"The boy she is pregnant by, would she have gone to him?"

"She refuses to say who the bastard's father is. She's living with her legs open and her mouth closed. If she has, at least she can't get pregnant again."

"Mrs. Stockwell?"

"Why are you asking questions? Can't you see I'm in the middle of a crisis? Help or be gone. I've already taken a day of work—without pay—and now this . . . this . . . this *shit*."

A curse word was at the tip of my tongue.

I was about to ask her if she cared about what her daughter was going through, but I didn't. I would have gone nuclear. I let my words hang in the air like a kite on a windy day. Her fingers were busy dialing more numbers. That lasted another hour. Faith and I were busy with other patients, doing prenatal and postnatal, trying to keep the trouble of the morning covert and the air as serene as the jazz playing over the building PA system. After her anger changed to worry and nervous words, Mrs. Stockwell called the police.

Within minutes, three squad cars were at Faith's office.

Chapter 75

*From Chapter 19 of the
Memoirs of Dr. Debra Dubois*

"Ericka?"

"Yes, ma'am."

I choked. It was the same voice that had called me in the middle of the night and hung up on me. I wanted to freak out, but I had to stay calm and figure out where she was.

I said, "Ericka? Where are you?"

"I can't tell you."

"Are you back with your parents?"

"No, ma'am."

"Why can't you say where you are?"

"Just can't."

"Everybody is worried sick over you. Have you called your mother?"

"No, ma'am. I'm not calling my mother."

"Why not? Your parents are very concerned about you."

"She don't, I mean doesn't, want me to keep my baby."

"I know, Ericka. But you need to contact your mother."

"She doesn't care about me."

"She's worried."

"Will you tell me the truth about something?"

"If I can. If I know the answer, I will be honest as I can be."

"If I stay gone a little while longer, then she can't stop me from having the baby, right? She can't make me take the gin-in-side stuff and kill my baby, right?"

My fingers massaged the bridge of my nose. I wanted to shout and say she was only thirteen, that her mother was wrong and right, and right and wrong, that Ericka didn't have any business being pregnant in the first place, and her mother should value life. I had prayed for her every second she'd been gone, but I had to be professional.

I said, "You're pregnant and you need to be looked after."

"I'm fine."

"You're not fine. Me and you, we need to make sure you're healthy."

"I know."

"Have you been eating?"

"Yes, ma'am."

"What have you eaten, Ericka?"

"McDonald's."

"That's not healthy."

"I'm not eating enough to get fat like the other customers."

"That food is not recommended. Not enough nutrition for a well person, let alone for a pregnant woman . . . I mean child. I hope you have had more than fast food."

"I went to Sizzler and ate a steak too."

"I'm not big on red meat either, but it's better than fast food, I suppose."

"What do you eat?"

"Ericka—" I almost snapped, damn near lost my patience. "Ericka, you're the only teenager I've seen come through the clinic who wanted to keep her baby."

"For real?"

"Can I ask you a question?"

"Yes, ma'am."

"Are you pregnant by—did someone in your family—Ericka, who are you pregnant by?"

"I can't say."

"Do you know?"

"Yes, ma'am. I'm not a slut. I'm not a whore."

"That's not what I was saying."

"I'm not a slut, Miss Mitchell. Momma says I am, but I'm not."

I swallowed, tried to think of what to do. "Why do you want to keep your baby?"

"So I'll have somebody to love me. So I'll have somebody to love."

"Oh, God."

"What?"

"Nothing. Nothing. Wait, how did you get my home number?"

"I called 4-1-1 and asked them if they had it. I heard the doctor call you Debra, and my mother called you Miss Mitchell, so I figured your name must be Debra Mitchell."

"Why did you call me? We hardly know each other."

"I like you. If I had a big sister, I'd like her to be you."

"Ericka, there are certain responsibilities that come along with my job. I have a responsibility to the community, to both you and your mother. You understand responsibilities, don't you?"

"Yes, ma'am. It means you have to do things, even if you don't want to."

"So, there is something I don't want to do, but must. I am going to have to tell your mother and the police that you called me. They need to know that you're okay. Are you?"

"Yes, ma'am. I'm just scared."

"How do you feel?"

"Tired. Like I've got the flu or something."

"Tell me where you are. I'm scared for you too. Very scared. Let me see you."

"You'll make me go back home."

"I won't make you go back home."

"Promise?"

"My word is bond. I need to know for myself that you're okay. I need to see you with my own eyes."

"I don't want to go home."

"If you go home, everything will work out fine."

She paused for a moment, then said, "Will you do me a favor, Miss Mitchell? Please. It's important. It's urgent. It's the reason I had to call you. It's very important. Time is of the essence in this."

She almost made me laugh. She was definitely her mother's child.

I said, "Will you please come home?"

"I don't mean to be disrespectful, but, uh, no, ma'am."

"Will you at least call one of your relatives?"

"I need you to do something for me." She was almost in tears. Maybe she was in tears, but didn't want me to hear her cry. Whatever she wanted sounded like a matter of life and death. She said a stuff-nosed, "Miss Mitchell, please?"

"Ericka—"

"Ma'am?"

"Stop saying *ma'am*. I'm not that old."

"Okay. Will you help me, Miss Mitchell?"

"Depends on what it is. If it's for your own good, yes."

She wanted me to pick something up.

Something she was leaving in the lobby at the Bonaventure Hotel.

"You're in downtown Los Angeles?"

"Yes, ma'am."

"Oh, God."

"What?"

"Ericka, I'm an adult and I don't go downtown by myself."

I thought of the strong urine and feces smells that wafted through the streets. Certain sections where Skid Row looked like Tijuana, and others like Chinatown. But mostly I thought about the time I rode through there at 3:00 A.M., one night after Shelby and I had finished partying at Little J's with whomever we were dating at the time, and tattered people were all over the streets, moving aimlessly like the walking dead.

I snapped, "There are all kinds of germs and homeless people, and drug addicts, and perverts and everything you can think of walking around downtown."

"I know."

"What are you thinking? Has anybody touched you?"

"No, ma'am."

"How much money do you have left?"

"Most of it."

"Where is it?"

"In my backpack."

"Take it out of your backpack and put it in your underwear. Find something and pin it to the front of your panties."

"Why?"

"Just do it. Don't let anybody see you do it. You understand?"

"Okay."

"Do you have food and shelter?"

"Yes, ma'am. I took care of that first."

"If you can't come home, call your parents. Please?"

"I'll make you a deal."

"A deal?"

"If you come get this, I will call my daddy at work. He might not be home. He never is."

I paused. Something about the way she said what she said made me wonder.

I asked, "Do you live with your daddy?"

"No, ma'am. He used to live with us, but my mother made him move and now he lives by himself. But he comes over and spends the night sometimes. I like it when he does because Momma is in a better mood. But she cries after he leaves."

"I didn't know. I thought . . . I assumed . . . never mind."

I tried to keep her talking. Part of me was listening to see if I could figure out where she was at that moment, the way people in the movies heard a church bell or a fog horn and knew where to go to find whomever they were searching for. That kind of luck only happened in the movies. There was too much static to pick up anything.

"Ericka?"

"Ma'am?"

"Call me Debra."

"Okay. Miss Debra."

"No, just Debra. I'm your friend, okay?"

"Okay, Debra."

"You said that I was the big sister you would want, right?"

"Yes, ma'am."

"Debra."

"I mean, yes, Debra."

"Thank you."

"You're welcome."

"Is this how you would treat your big sister? Would you make your sister who loved you worry like this? If something happened to you, I'd feel responsible. Forever. And nothing could make that go away. I want you to think about that."

We hung up.

I wiped my eyes and dialed 4-1-1 to get Mrs. Stockwell's number in Windsor Hills.

It was unlisted.

I called Dr. Faith.

She wasn't home.

No one answered at the clinic. In fact the messages were rolling over to the service. I called my best friend, Shelby, thought maybe I could get her to come down and get me so I wouldn't have to get Leonard involved, but she had flown the coop.

I was alone in crisis.

I closed my eyes and said a silent prayer for Ericka.

Then I called Leonard.

I called the man I would one day marry.

Chapter 76

From Chapter 22 of the
Memoirs of Dr. Debra Dubois

When Leonard Dubois and I stepped from the pandemonium on Figueroa and stood in the massive, peaceful lobby of the Bonaventure, we rushed to the concierge.

The package was waiting.

I opened the manila folder that Ericka had left for me at the concierge desk. Homework was inside. Pages of homework. She had made sure she kept up to date with all her homework. Ericka had completed an English paper that was due, a report on *The Outsiders*. Her note in purple ink said that it was due tomorrow for full credit. Time is of the essence. All of her advanced math on figuring out perimeter and area, social studies on the American Revolution, Spanish assignment on stem verbs, everything neatly done, to perfection.

I stopped being amazed and asked, "How would she know what to do if she hadn't been to school?"

"Homework hotline."

"What?"

"They have homework hotlines in most of the schools. All she had to do was call and get the assignments from a recording."

Leonard and I stood side by side, shoulder to shoulder, watched multi-ethnic people with upper-class attitudes check in while others lounged near the classical piano player with drinks in hand. We watched peaceful people indulge themselves.

I said, "Maybe I should call the police now."

"If you were scared, would you rather see a friendly face, or badges and guns?"

I agreed in silence.

On the verge of tears, I decided I would give her a few more minutes before I called the police. The city was huge and she could have gone anywhere by foot, bus, or by taxi.

I said, "I prayed she would be here."

We searched around again.

Leonard asked the concierge which way Ericka had gone after she dropped off the package. He wasn't sure, wasn't paying attention, but he pointed toward the glass elevators. From what I could tell, she had dropped the package off before she called me. We rode the exterior elevators, the glass carriages that overlooked the city and faced Figueroa and the 110 freeway, up to the revolving bar. Ericka wasn't old enough to be up there, but I had to make sure. We peeped on every floor.

We went back to the ground and walked into every shop in the lobby. There was no sign of Ericka.

Leonard asked me again, "What does she look like?"

"Me. She has my complexion. She's taller. Looks fragile."

Leonard put his hands on my shoulders. Turned me around.

He said, "Is that her?"

Ericka was standing near the shops. She stepped from behind some plants. She waved. I waved. She looked like she wanted to run in the other direction. I held my arms out to her. I let her take the first step toward me.

We walked toward each other. The walk turned into a jog.

We hugged. She trembled and cried. I exhaled.

I said, "Well, if it's not my little fugitive."

"Hi."

"What you did was—"

"Stupid."

"Not stupid."

"Momma said I was stupid."

"You've talked to her?"

"No. She just always calls me stupid. Especially now."

"Never stupid. You made a mistake."

"A big mistake."

"Yes. Big. I can't have a stupid little sister, can I?"

She said, "Are you mad at me?"

"No. Yes. Ask me after I calm down."

Leonard was a few feet way. I nodded at him. He did the same. He shifted, ran his hand over his hair, looked relieved, but not relaxed. He was giving us space. My fingers intertwined with Ericka's and I led her to the chairs near the bar. I touched her face.

I said, "Are you okay?"

She nodded. "Are you going to make me go home?"

"When you're ready."

"I'm not. I don't think anybody's proud of me right about now. Don't know if I'll ever be ready."

"Not until then. You're going to have to go, but it's going to have to be your decision. You have things you need to face."

"Figured you would say something like that."

"But I'm not making you. I'm encouraging you to do what's right." I felt her head, looked at her tongue, took her pulse. Inside I wished I had the wisdom of Chinese healers.

I said, "My word is bond."

"Debra?"

"Yes?"

"What does that mean? Your word is bond. Is that like James Bond or something?"

"No." I laughed a little. "It means I keep my word. I do what I promise. I try to anyway. I am glued to whatever I promise."

She said, "I'm glad you came."

I kissed the side of her face. "I'm not going to leave you. You have to call your mother and let her know you're okay. Tell her you called me and now I'm with you."

"She'll be mad at you."

"Let that be my problem."

Ericka told me she had been hiding at one of her classmates' house in Windsor Hills, around the corner from her own home. She had slipped through a bedroom window and hid out. Her friend had her own room and privacy. While her friend's parents were asleep, she showered and ate food the girl had brought her. Then early this morning, Ericka slipped out of the girl's window, walked right through her neighborhood, caught a bus, and came downtown. She figured she could blend in down here and nobody would notice. The way children walked the streets all day and all night like strays, she was right.

She had done well for a child.

"Debra?"

"Uh-huh."

"I need to get my homework to my teachers. I want to keep my A's. I could've gotten perfect attendance again this year, but you know, this happened." She asked, "Is that man your husband?"

"A friend of mine. His name is Leonard."

"Does he know?"

"He knows. Don't worry. He's cool."

"Is he your boyfriend?"

I smiled. "Just a friend."

"Wasn't he on TV? On *Moesha* or something?"

"I don't know. I don't watch much television. I only watch *60 Minutes* and *20/20* and stuff like that."

Her face was pale. She might've been queasy.

I said, "How did you get pregnant?"

"Stupid sex."

"We know that. Who's the father?"

"I don't want to get him in trouble."

"He's gotten you in trouble. He knows, right?"

She nodded. "I mailed him a letter."

"Is he out of town?"

"He lives here."

"How old is he?"

"He's old. Almost sixteen. He's going to get his driver's permit this year."

"So, he's in high school."

She nodded.

"Is he black?"

She nodded. "Why did you ask me that?"

I shrugged.

Ericka told me the boy who impregnated her was a dancer, and that the boy said if she told his mother, she wouldn't let him dance. His situation was damn insignificant, but the fear in her voice told me she thought inconveniencing his life was more important than the life spawning inside her thirteen-year-old womb. Her logic didn't make sense to me, but then again, it wasn't adult logic.

She said, "If his mother finds out, then she might make him stop dancing, then his career would be over, and he won't get discovered and make millions of dollars. That would be money he would have for me and the baby, when he came back for us."

"Who told you that?"

"He did."

"Really."

"He can dance better than MC Hammer. He can rap. He did a Dr. Dre song and won the talent show at Inglewood High."

I said, "An entertainer."

She nodded. Smiled a little.

I didn't say anything.

She said, "One time."

"What?"

"I only did it one time. So I didn't really know, you know, how I got like this. You're not supposed to get, you know, just from one time."

"It only takes one time."

"We only did it a minute."

"That was a minute too long."

"It hurt."

"No doubt. More ways than one."

"But I didn't take all of my clothes off and I was standing up and the yucky stuff ran back out."

"Sweetheart, that doesn't work. Once it's in you, it's in you. Why did you do it in the first place?"

Ericka gripped my hand with hers, ran her thumb up and down my skin.

She said, "He told me if I wanted to be his girlfriend, and if I wanted him to *really* be my boyfriend, then we were supposed to do what boyfriends and girlfriends do. And there was this dance that this girl was giving. It was a birthday party, and he said he would take me if, you know, if we became boyfriend and girlfriend."

"Did he take you to the dance?"

"No."

"Didn't think so."

"Why not?"

"Been there, done that."

"I heard he went with this girl from his school."

"What does that tell you?"

"His word wasn't bond."

"If his word isn't bond, and he makes a million dollars, do you think he's going to come back for you and your baby?"

She shrugged. "Maybe."

"Maybe?"

"Probably not."

"What did he say when you told him you were pregnant?"

"I haven't really talked to him since. I mean, I told him, but he hasn't really talked to me since, you know, since that day I met him behind the bleachers."

My cry of anguish oozed out. "Oh, God."

"What?"

"You had sex with him behind the bleachers?"

She lowered her eyes and nodded.

I put my hand on her chin, brought her eyes to mine.

I said, "At school?"

She nodded.

"And he hasn't talked to you since then?"

"Just that one time when he told me not to tell anybody."

"Ericka, it's been almost four months."

She nodded again, now with tears falling across her cheeks.

I said, "Are you sure you want to have this baby?"

She shrugged. "I get tired of Momma making me do stuff. She never asks me what I want to do."

"You ever think that some of it might be for your own good?"

She chewed her lips and held her thoughts hostage.

I massaged her arm and allowed her to think for a while. I hoped I was doing the right thing. Hoped I had done the right thing when I didn't call the police. Regret was all over her face. She had the same expression, the feeling I'd had after my own mistakes. I stayed calm to keep her calm. I wanted her to keep talking. Let her go through her own thought process and come to her own decision, whatever was right for her.

I'd never seen a child look so confused in my life.

What we were doing was delaying.

The inevitable could be set aside for only so long.

Ericka's breathing, her eyes, her tears told me she knew that she had to face her mother. She had to go back where she didn't want to go.

Ericka took my left hand and stood.

I had never seen a child so terrified.

As men could father a child and never be considered a daddy, many women could have children, but that did not make them mothers.

But there was nothing I could do. Not a damn thing I could do to save Ericka.

I didn't even know what saving her would look like.

Ericka sighed. "Are you taking me home now?"

"Are you ready to go?"

"I want to get this over with."

We headed toward the payphone, walked by tourists, hand in hand, like sisters.

Chapter 77

From Chapter 25 of the Memoirs of Dr. Debra Dubois

"Excuse me for being late, Mrs. Stockwell."

"I understand," she said. "Your duties take precedence."

I didn't say anything else.

Her arms were folded in front of her cream suit. Her shoes were blue, just like her silk blouse. This was as contemporary as I'd ever seen her. But she still had her Bible in her purse.

Ericka wasn't with her.

My watch said 12:45 P.M. and my watch was ten minutes fast.

I decided I would donate fifteen minutes to her. Twenty at most.

"Miss Mitchell, thanks for taking time away from your day and meeting me."

"You're not working today?"

"We had a shortened day. The school let out at noon."

"That explains all the kids hanging out at the mall."

Mrs. Stockwell and I were upstairs in the clamor of the food court in the Fox Hills Mall, standing near the rail that faced Macy's. One side of the mall was two levels; the side with the food court had three levels. The mall was near my job, but I drove due to the heat, then spent more time and energy searching for a parking space than if I had walked the two hundred yards. That was what we did in California. Driving was in vogue. People who walked looked broke and homeless. Mrs. Stockwell had called my job first thing this morning and asked me to meet her for lunch.

She asked, "Would you like something to eat?"

"Thank you, no. I've eaten. And I only have a few minutes."

"Then I won't delay."

We moved to the food court and sat in the blue metal chairs. She sat straight-backed, formal in a casual world, kept her purse in her lap. I waited for her to talk. Another glance at my watch was my not-subtle hint for her to get the show on the road.

Mrs. Stockwell started, "I don't want you to think badly of me."

"What do you mean?"

"My behavior has not been the best. Do you agree?"

I agreed with a simple, definite nod.

She tapped her Bible. "I've never behaved in such a way."

I didn't agree or disagree.

"I want you to understand, this isn't easy for me. Or Ericka. As you know, I can't bear any more children."

"I know. I'm aware."

"So the child in her womb means the world to me. It is not just her child. It's my first grandchild, my mother's first great-grandchild. She is the seed of my seed."

"Without a doubt."

"Either way, I'll carry a burden. If I allowed her to go on with this, well . . ." She closed her eyes tight, like she was trying to squeeze a vision out of her head, then opened her eyes and looked beyond me and continued. "You know what this would do to her life. She's a smart girl."

"In some ways."

"And she has a long life ahead of her."

"Without a doubt."

"So it wouldn't just be Ericka getting an . . ." She cleared her throat, then let me fill in the *A*-word in my mind. ". . . It would be all of us. Her, me, my mother, my mother's mother, and their mothers."

"I don't understand."

"What do you need clarification on, Miss Mitchell?"

"Why are you telling me this?"

She shrugged. "Guilt. I have to tell someone. I have lost too much sleep."

"Why?"

"I've been questioning my parenting." She patted her Bible, soft and unsure. "Questioning a lot of things. I have asked for answers, but there are only more questions."

I sighed, almost reached over and patted her hand, but I didn't.

I remembered who I was. More like, who I wasn't. I wasn't her friend.

She said, "Ericka sees you as a role model. I've been her mother all of her life, and she's hardly known you a day, but she'll listen to you before she listens to me. What I say has no value. She'll do what I say, but takes your words as the brand-new gospel."

"Have you always struck her?"

She shifted in her seat and moved her eyes from me. "I discipline my child. Spare the rod and you'll end up with a gang member staring at you from the other side of Plexiglas. I need her on the right path. It worked for my mother. You understand?"

"Yes. You discipline with disdain."

Mrs. Stockwell twitched. "Not disdain. I'd give my life for her. She had lied to me about the whole thing. Looked at me like I was crazy, then swore on the Bible she wasn't having sex. You think she's all sweet, but she's slick and not to be trusted."

"Children gravitate toward whom they can trust."

"If I hadn't been counting her pads, if I hadn't seen that none had been used for two months, then she would've kept dressing in those baggy clothes and the next thing I would've known she would've had a bellyache and had the baby at the dinner table."

"You don't have to strike her. We don't have to imitate slave masters."

She shook her head. "I pray you never find yourself in my position."

"How is she?"

"She asked that I give you this."

She took a card out of her purse. It was a handmade card decorated with smiley faces and glitter and ribbons. Inside was a school picture of Ericka. She had ponytails and wore a peach, sleeveless mock turtleneck. Ericka had sent me a thank-you note.

The envelope had already been ripped open, the message already read.

My eyes went to Mrs. Stockwell.

She said, "I had to open it."

"Invasion of privacy."

"A child has no privacy, not when I have the responsibility for all she does."

My lips tightened when I looked at her. I shook my head a little.

She said, "It says you're her big sister."

I read it and then put it in my purse. "That it does."

"Did she tell you who the boy is?"

"No." A moment passed. I said. "You made your decision?"

"Yes. I've made her an appointment. Time is of the essence."

I wanted to know where, but I didn't ask.

I glanced at my watch again.

Mrs. Stockwell said, "I need to know something from you."

I nodded.

She asked me to explain the two-day procedure to her.

I did. I told her everything in detail, in clinical terms.

She said, "It's going to be a rough couple of days for us all."

"And she will need a lot of healing after that. A lot of physical and psychological healing will follow."

She let a moment go by, then exhaled unsure air.

She said, "As a nurse, what do you think I should do?"

"It's not for me to decide. I can only tell you what to expect."

"Now I am asking you your opinion, as a woman; what do you think I should do?"

"Do what you think is best for your child. She is young with life growing inside her. You are a woman of faith. So am I. You have to convene with God. I have no answers."

"I don't want to kill my grandchild. I can't . . . have my child go through that. But I can't allow her to be a mother when she barely knows how to wipe her own ass."

"Maybe you should have this conversation with someone else."

"I have no friends. There is no one else to talk to about this."

"I'm sorry. But I can't advise you."

She shrugged. "I don't think I'll ever be the same."

"No doubt."

"I guess I called you because I wanted to say thank you."

"For?"

"Thanks for getting my child back home safely to me."

"Will I be able to see her anytime soon?"

"I am thinking about letting her go live with my sister in Oklahoma. This is giving me a breakdown. Maybe she needs to be away from me, and maybe I need to be away from her. At least until the next school term. Her father agrees that would be wise."

"Oh. So he has been informed."

"A few people know. I think we should let the rumors and shame die down."

Mrs. Stockwell stood to leave. I did the same.

She wore two-inch heels. I wore running shoes.

She said, "Well, I won't be seeing you for a while."

We said simple, shallow good-byes and walked in opposite directions. Left like we didn't know each other. She headed toward JCPenney. I put on my shades, moved across the tile, held on to my purse and went in the direction of the stairwell located in the middle of the food court vendors, the one that went up to the open asphalt parking lot.

I saw a pay phone and had the urge to call my mother and father in Montana and thank them for everything I could think of. I wanted to thank them for life. Thank them for staying together. I wanted to thank my mother for disciplining me, but doing it with love. I wanted to thank my father for always being involved in my life.

We were all Ericka, lambs in the world, but some of us had had love and guidance.

We didn't feel like we had to procreate to feel loved.

I had to get back to the clinic, but I was more in the mood to listen to some sad music, something sadder than *Beaches* and *Terms of Endearment* combined, or just walk until my legs gave out or the anguish went away. Maybe when I got off work I'd skip the gym and go down to the Santa Monica Pier and walk the sands and give my thoughts to the sunset. Maybe ride the roller coaster over and over by myself and eat cotton candy until my stomach ached.

I had almost made it to my car when I turned around and sprinted back into the mall. I raced past security and headed toward JCPenney, peeping inside every store along the way. When I made it to the far end of the mall, Mrs. Stockwell was on the escalator, going down. In a panic, I called her name. Yelled it over the rail. Did one of the ill-mannered things I used to get on my best friend, Shelby, about doing. I shocked Mrs. Stockwell. She waited at the bottom. When I got to her, I stopped in my tracks. Tears were quietly rolling from her eyes.

She spoke in a whisper, "Yes, Miss Mitchell?"

I said, "I'll take her to her appointment. I can go with her when she has it done. If you like, if it's too much for you, if you don't think you'd be comfortable, I will go with her."

She chewed her lip. "I'm her mother. This is my cross to bear. This is our cross."

I said, "It's up to you, but if you need me, please call me."

Tension was in her neck. So much pain in her face, in her eyes. When I started to move away, she reached out and touched my shoulders. She was trying to say something.

Her words barely got out, "The boy. Some boy did this. Some damn boy."

I nodded.

She said, "She will not tell me who he is. I don't want her to go through this alone. That boy should be there. He should hold her hand through this. But I know he won't. When this happens to a woman, a girl, the man, the boy moves on. The boy will bear no scars. The boy will forget what Ericka will always remember."

I nodded again.

She said, "I am no saint. I have fallen short and I am trying to stay on the right path. It happened to me. The cycle repeated. I failed."

"I'm sorry to hear that, Mrs. Stockwell. It wasn't on your records."

"And now it has happened again. To my daughter. At the same age I was."

"I just wanted to offer my help, my professional advice."

"God is showing me that he has not forgotten my sins. This is my test from above."

"What will you do?"

"I will pray. I will ask God to show me what He wants me to do."

I was back on the escalator going up before Mrs. Stockwell could close her purse. Wiping the tears from my own eyes, never knowing that after that day I'd never hear from Ericka Stockwell again. Her mother never called me, and I never interfered.

But not a day has gone by when I didn't wonder where Ericka was, how she was, if she had had the baby, and if so, how she was doing, how her baby was doing.

I imagined her with her child, past the drama, happily married, out of college with a PhD, in a great relationship with her mother, reconnected with her father, flourishing.

Chapter 78

Ericka sat at the formal dining table, uncomfortable, shifting, facing Mrs. Stockwell.

Mrs. Stockwell had refused to change from her kimono into regular clothing, refused to get dressed as she granted Ericka an audience, was being arrogant, haughty, defiant, self-righteous, defensive. She was being herself. She was being her hypocritical, damaged self.

Ericka watched Mrs. Stockwell put on her glasses, watched her mother read each page, watched her mother read another woman's words and take that same trip down Memory Lane, down the rabbit hole, watched her mother become outraged line by line, paragraph by paragraph, page by page. Ericka watched her mother, made sure the woman who had birthed her read every word. The first time, Mrs. Stockwell read those pages as if she felt violated, then Ericka watched her read those pages again, slower the second time, swallowing, restless, bouncing her leg, rubbing her neck, in pain, breathing deeply, trying to keep her back straight, trying to fight the tightness in her throat, trying not to admit what had been done two decades before.

The next time Mrs. Stockwell read the pages of memories, there were many tears.

Ericka stood up from the table, grabbed her mother's gun, marched toward the living room, then went up the stairs, took each step one at a time, moved down the hallway to the master bedroom, and pushed the door open. Indigo's father was sitting on Mrs. Stockwell's bed.

It was pointless trying to hide. His car was in the driveway. He had made a major error.

Mr. Abdulrahaman was there.

Indigo's father stood up in slow motion, so slow his knees popped. He stood in the dim light, nervous. He had been waiting for Mrs. Stockwell to return, maybe had hoped she could control and resolve this, and maybe that was what she had told him she would be able to do, especially when she had left with a gun in her hand.

He was now surprised to see Ericka with the gun.

Enraged, tears in her eyes, Ericka looked at him without blinking, the gun pointed at him.

He didn't look like a man who was jovial, a man who hugged and kissed his wife as if she were all that mattered in his life, no longer looked like a powerful businessman, no longer like a respectable father, looked only like a man of flesh and blood, a man foolish enough to sacrifice the empire he had built to scratch an itch with a woman who was so lost she would never be found. Ericka despised that woman, but she was still Ericka's mother.

Even in familial hate, there was an unbreakable bond.

And that man's daughter was one of Ericka's closest friends, a woman Ericka loved. Indigo was her sister, not by birth, but by choice. The message had been delivered, and it had been clear. The look of regret and terror on Indigo's father's face told Ericka that she had communicated effectively. He saw his own shame. He saw his own death. He saw a brokenhearted wife and a distraught daughter who would never forgive him for being so weak. He didn't challenge Ericka. He didn't make excuses. He knew he was wrong.

She didn't say a word, but disgust was etched on her face, carved in her expression.

Bit by bit, Ericka lowered the gun, held the weapon at her side pointing at the floor. Indigo's father reached to the side of the bed and picked up carry-on luggage.

He was here and he had packed to be here more than one night, if he hadn't already been here more than one night. He grabbed a second bag, one that Ericka assumed had his laptop and electronic devices.

He looked at Ericka, his body language asking for permission to leave. Ericka's expression told him that he didn't have to go home, but he had to get the hell out of Mrs. Stockwell's zip code. Indigo's father walked by her, his head down, and hurried down the stairs.

He rushed out the front door without so much as a glance toward Mrs. Stockwell.

He was concerned for his own safety, not her well-being.

Mrs. Stockwell was still at the dining room table, rereading the chapters again and again, trapped in an infinite loop that led only to the past. She was still crying. She was still twenty years in the past, back during when she had made the only decision she knew how to make.

Outside her door was the sound of luggage being thrown into a car's trunk.

Ericka tried to convince herself that parents were human. They became dissatisfied, cheated on each other, and made smiles for public show. They destroyed themselves and the lives of their spouses and families in one single action.

For every man who cheated, a woman was involved. Both wanted power. Some women moved from being abused to the position of power. The slave saw the master's position as powerful, then mimicked the master, became an abuser, beat and hit and slapped so he could feel as powerful as the master. When she was a child in Oklahoma, Mrs. Stockwell had been raised by a heavy hand. Her marriage to Mr. Stockwell had come with a heavy hand. A woman who had been cheated on could live in resentment and envy, could become hardened, and do to others what had been done to her.

Indigo's father waited at his vehicle, jaw tight, trapped, unable to leave.

Ericka took her time, walked past his car on the passenger's side.

She wanted to drag her keys down the side of the car.

She didn't.

She stared him down as she crossed between the hood of her roadster and the trunk of his luxury vehicle. She went to the driver's door on her car, then faced Indigo's father again.

She was not done staring.

She was not done transmitting her contempt.

She glowered at Indigo's father, at her friend's hero, and he twitched. He opened his mouth like he wanted to plead his case, to make a profound yet clichéd statement about marriage and fidelity, about the difficulties of being human, of feeling suffocated and needing to be able to breathe for a moment, and there being no real harm done to anyone because no one knew. Maybe he just wanted a woman he didn't see as a wife and the mother of his child. Maybe he desired a Half-rican American concubine he could call up at two in the morning and when the phone rang, she knew what the call was about. Maybe he wanted a woman who didn't require attachments.

Maybe, maybe, maybe, maybe, maybe.

He stood with his mouth open, face contorting with his thoughts, vacillating between fear and anger. Ericka waited to hear the excuses she had heard from her ex-husband.

But Indigo's dad said nothing. He didn't talk down to her that way a man from his generation talked down to women. An angry woman holding a gun made a man think twice about saying stupid shit.

Anything he said would not make him sound human. There was no combination of the 1,025,109 words in the English language that could make Ericka empathize with the devil.

Ericka took out her cellular.

She called Indigo. The trepidation and burden in his face quickly became a father's tears. In silence, with facial expressions and body language, he begged Ericka not to call his daughter. Ericka put the call on speaker. Gun in one hand. Phone in the other.

When Indigo answered, Ericka extended the phone toward Indigo's father. Again, in silence, practically falling to his knees, he pleaded with Ericka, and at the same time looked like he wanted to tackle her, but he didn't move from where he stood.

This was serious. He knew he wasn't good at tackling a bullet.

In a cheery voice Ericka said, "Hey, tall, dark, and sexy Blackbird. Where are you?"

Indigo said she was unhappy, having the unhappiest day of her life, and was sitting in a café in Marina del Rey with Yaba, an engagement ring on the table between them. She didn't like the surprise. Indigo didn't like surprises. She had to gently undo what had been recklessly done. People had posted pictures of them kissing, it had streamed, was blowing up online.

YABA THE LAKER GETS ENGAGED was trending on Twitter, so it was trending around the world. People had recorded from the moment Yaba had stepped on stage, and that video was now the hottest thing on Black Twitter, Facebook, this, that, and the other sites on social media.

Olamilekan had already seen it online, had seen the whole thing because dozens of people had streamed it live using Periscope, hearts flying every time they hit the LIKE button.

Ericka asked, "Do your mother and father know?"

"My mother would have a fit. I tried to call her, but she's not answering, so she's probably sleeping. She's already in bed by ten on most nights. This is not the breaking news I want her to wake up to in the morning. It will be seen all over Nigeria. Yaba has a country of fans that follow his every move, same as Olamilekan. Yaba knows I see Olamilekan, and asked me to marry him. That is insane. How can a man ask my mother's only Nigerian daughter to marry him and he has not spoken to her first, if our families have not met, if he has not followed tradition?"

Ericka took a step toward the luxury car. "What would your father say?"

"He would be glad that he could get free Lakers tickets. He'd sell me for a goat."

"Where is your dad? Have you talked to him today or tonight?"

"He's on a business trip. He called me when he was driving to LAX."

"When did he leave Los Angeles?"

"He left yesterday. He will be back tomorrow, and he will find out. Who proposes to a woman at a comedy club? That is so damn ghetto. Who listens to black racism all night, listens to black people call themselves the N-word all night, hear them be as biased toward white people as white people are racist to them, then gets on his bad knees and asks a woman to marry him?"

"You said yes."

"I had no other choice. I didn't want to get booed like I was at the Apollo. Black Americans would have booed me and started throwing things at me."

"You're Nigerian, but you're also black American, too."

"Not to them."

"Well, I had called because I thought I saw your father on Crenshaw near the 10."

"You're not home?"

"I went for a drive."

"Wasn't my dad. He's not back until tomorrow."

"Where is Yaba the Laker?"

"Signing autographs for some man who was rude enough to interrupt us as we were arguing. These people. What, am I invisible at night? I know I'm dark, but I'm not that damn dark."

"Those are the problems when you date famous men. You're invisible to the public."

"I need to talk to someone who is sensible. I'm feeling overwhelmed right now. My heart is aching and my head is in a vise grip, and Olamilekan is panicking and calling every two seconds and when I don't answer he's texting and sending messages on Facebook trying to call me on Tango and Viber. I can't talk to him now. I can't deal with Yaba and I can't deal with Olamilekan while I am dealing with Yaba."

"Are you going to be okay?"

"This has stressed me out. I'm glad you called to check on me. I was about to scream."

"Well, I called because I swear I saw your father down by Crenshaw and the 10."

"He's out of town. Houston, I think. Maybe Dallas."

Ericka paused. "See you when you get home, Indigo."

"If a light is on, or the television is on, I will come by your apartment."

"Do you really think you're coming home tonight?"

"I doubt it."

"Enjoy Yaba. Talk to him. Express your concerns. Tell him what you want, tell him what you're afraid of. Tell him the kind of man you want in your life and see if he can be that man. Let him know the kind of woman you are. Be real. No games. Write it down. Read it out loud. Be clear. Put it all on the table. Have him answer all of your questions, and if he falls short, slide the ring back across the table. In the end, it's your call, and I have your back no matter what. I'm here for you. The Blackbirds are here for you. Call back if you need me to run interference."

"If one more woman comes over to Yaba while I am here, I will scream."

"Make sure that's the type of lifestyle you can handle."

"These bitches are so damn rude."

"Don't end up waving no woman's panties in the air tonight. There are a lot of trifling women out there, women who will cheat and sleep with a man who is powerful and has money, and I know you would beat another woman down and pull her hair out by the roots."

"I am bad. But my mother is worse."

"Get back to Yaba."

"Okay."

"He loves you."

"I know."

"He told the world he loves you."

"I know."

"Olamilekan would never do that."

"You're right."

"What's wrong?"

"I have found out so much about Olamilekan."

"How?"

"I will tell you. It's too much to tell. I can show you and tell you."

"Focus on Yaba."

"He stood on a stage in front of everyone and asked me to marry him."

"Give Yaba a chance. Tell him how he has to do it based on your culture. It's his culture too. He will understand. Take your time. Be engaged a long time. Get to know him all over again."

"This is why I love you, Ericka."

"Bye, Blackbird."

"Bye, Blackbird."

Ericka ended the call. Indigo's father was in tears.

He understood the seriousness. He understood Ericka's dark side. He understood that she was a Stockwell, and the Stockwells were beautiful, but they were a cold-blooded lot.

It would take one phone call for him to wish Ericka had given him a bullet instead. She gave him her emotions, and he felt all the words she didn't have to say out loud.

But she said them anyway.

"You are *despicable*. You cheat on your wife. You lie to your daughter. I hope you rot in hell. Leave here and never look back, never come back. Whatever is missing in your life, it is not here, it is not in this bed. Never call my mother. Never speak her name. Never say a word to me ever again. I will ruin your life. I will ruin your life in ways you can't even imagine. Leave now."

Ericka eased into her car, turned on her bright lights so they would smack Indigo's father in the middle of his head. She wanted to temporarily blind him. Ericka put her roadster in reverse, but didn't actually move for a moment. She let her car idle and let him suffer another eternity.

Two minutes passed before she backed out in the wide street.

Indigo's father didn't hesitate. He backed his car out, sped away, not turning on his headlights until he left the prestigious and historical community. He turned his lights on at the last moment, as if he didn't want to be seen too close to where he had dampened his cock.

He abdicated his throne-away-from-home without saying a word.

Someone started their car and pulled away without turning their lights on. Ericka looked to see who had seen them, to see which neighbor had witnessed her with a gun on a man.

The car slowed down. It had out-of-state tags. Florida plates. A Hertz rental car. Ericka held the gun low, moved it behind her back. The car stopped and the window went down.

Ericka saw who had been watching her, and she froze.

It was Indigo's mother.

The spy was Mrs. Chimamandanata Abdulrahaman.

Chapter 79

Indigo's mother had been there the entire time. Ericka assumed she had seen it all.

Ericka walked to the rental car, took slow steps, afraid, speechless. The anger on Indigo's mother's face, her disgust, it was silent but deafening. Nothing was said for a moment.

Indigo's mother's luxurious hair was pulled back into a warrior's ponytail.

Ericka said, "I swear to you, Mrs. Abdulrahaman, I just found out about this. I came to see Mrs. Stockwell regarding another issue, a family issue, came unannounced and . . . I had no idea."

Indigo's mother looked like she had been insulted like never before, but she nodded.

Ericka said, "It's over."

Voice heavy, cracking, laced with rage, she asked, "Is it? Is it over?"

"He knows not to come back."

"He has been here many times. I can prove that."

"Whether I am here or not, he will not come back."

"Does she know not to invite him back? Does the woman inside that house know?"

"She knows."

"I saw you run him out of your mother's home. I heard you tell him to leave and never come back. But the question is, will he listen to you, or will he return if your mother calls?"

"How long have you been out here?"

"I was right behind you when you arrived. You turned left into the neighborhood seconds before I did. I recognized your car, saw your face. I slowed when I saw you in front of me."

"You saw the whole thing, you heard me, so you know where I stand."

"I almost went to the door after you had gone inside, but I turned back around, and I prayed. I am no longer a teenager in Lagos. I had to ask myself if I wanted to lose all I have built in one foolish night."

"I encouraged him to leave."

"Do not prevaricate. Do not become a sycophant. Do not tell me what you think I want to hear. I already know the truth. I know more of the truth than anyone can even imagine."

"I am not lying. I am not part of this conspiracy."

"When I return home, when he returns home, he will know that I know he was here. We will have a very intimate discussion. Now I should leave before I do something unwise. I fought for him when I was young and foolish. When you start off fighting for a man, you will always find yourself fighting to keep that man. I have had my last fight. I am done fighting."

She put the car in drive, but didn't move. She was boiling. Ericka saw her struggling with what to do, if she should drive away. God and Satan battled. Mrs. Abdulrahaman threw the car in park, pushed the door open hard, then jumped out. She wore yoga pants and a UCLA hoodie, no earrings, no makeup, no jewelry, the barebones accoutrements a woman wore when she was going to pull out hair and raise panties in victory. Gun in hand, Ericka moved out of her way, but followed Mrs. Abdulrahaman as she marched down the driveway toward Mrs. Stockwell's home, followed her as she opened the door and walked inside the home her husband had just exited.

Mrs. Abdulrahaman stood in the foyer of her rival uninvited.

Ericka pointed. "She's in the formal dining room."

"Do not interfere."

"Yes, ma'am."

Mrs. Stockwell jerked when she looked up and saw Indigo's mother, was shocked out of her moment, pulled from the past to the present, realized her state of dress, and tried to cover herself.

The bell always rang the loudest in your own home.

Eyes red and puffy, Mrs. Stockwell was as panic-stricken as Indigo's father had been.

That too had caught Mrs. Abdulrahaman off guard.

Seeing Mrs. Stockwell crying had surprised her, but it didn't stop her. It enraged her.

Ericka knew Indigo's mother assumed Mrs. Stockwell was crying over Indigo's father.

Mrs. Abdulrahaman barked, "'If a man is found lying with the wife of another man, both of them shall die, the man who lay with the woman, and the woman. So you shall purge the evil from Israel.' The same goes if a woman is found with *my* husband. Do not play with your life again."

Scared shitless, Mrs. Stockwell sat up straight, defensive and defenseless.

"You have been warned, *Caledonia* Betty Stockwell. With your daughter as my witness, you have been warned. Do not take yourself to an early grave over him."

Indigo's mother splayed her fingers and said things in Yorùbá, wicked things that did not need a translator. The expression on her face, the motions of her hands, it was pent-up rage unleashed.

Mrs. Stockwell held her kimono to cover her breasts, and she nodded once, as if nodding twice would have been an insult to the slightly younger woman who had stormed her castle.

Nostrils flared, Indigo's mother walked out of the home. She exited like a lady. She did not run. She did not flip things over. She did not look back, not even a glance. She exited not like she had been run off, but would gladly turn around if Mrs. Stockwell said one thing to challenge her. Mrs. Stockwell exhaled and knew she should be grateful. She knew that if something that was going to chop off her head only knocked off her cap, she should be grateful.

Mrs. Stockwell trembled. She had been scared straight.

Ericka followed Mrs. Abdulrahaman back outside, trailed her down the driveway and past the spot where her foolish husband had parked earlier. Mrs. Abdulrahaman eased into her rental.

Ericka stood at the door, made eye contact with Indigo's mother, didn't know what to say.

"Mrs. Stockwell should be thankful you are her daughter. I like you. You are a wonderful person. She should be very thankful I see you as a daughter. Tonight I will not destroy a village due to the imprudence of idiots. But if it is not over, I will return to see her, and I will be prepared."

"I know. If it's not over, you should return to see her."

"And Caledonia Stockwell will rue the day she ever heard my name."

"Do whatever you have to do. It will be grown folks' business from here on out."

"Tell her to remember what her God has said. 'Let marriage be held in honor among all, and let the marriage bed be undefiled, for God will judge the sexually immoral and adulterous.'"

"I will remind her."

"'But as for the cowardly, the faithless, the detestable, as for murderers, the sexually immoral, sorcerers, idolaters, and all liars, their portion will be in the lake that burns with fire and sulfur, which is the second death.' That is in the Bible your mother carries day and night."

"I will remind her of that as well."

"And even if she does not fear her God, she needs to be terrified of me."

"Okay."

"My husband thought he was so smart. He bought a second phone and kept it hidden in the trunk of his car. It was underneath the spare tire. It took time to figure that out, but I found that phone. Late the other night, I was in the garage and heard it ringing. He was sleeping, the phone I knew of on the charger in the house, yet I heard a phone ringing. He had forgotten to turn it off. I found it right before he left for his pretend business trip. That second phone was how he communicated with your mother. When I get home, he will lie, but it will be in vain because I will send his text messages to my wireless printer and show him his own words."

Ericka nodded.

She took a deep breath. "Ericka, I'm sorry you had to witness this."

"I'm sorry you have to go through this."

"But at the same time I am glad you happened to be here. They should be glad."

"I'm sorry my mother has done this to you."

"You deserve a better mother."

"She is the one God gave me."

"Do not tell my daughter. If she is to know, it must come from me."

"I won't tell her."

"*Od'aro*, Ericka. *Od'aro*."

"Good night."

Mrs. Abdulrahaman drove away, the same as Nagode Allah Abdulrahaman had done, only she didn't speed away. She didn't leave like she was afraid. She left like she was a queen.

She had also had a weapon. When Mrs. Abdulrahaman had opened her door to get out, the light had illuminated the interior, and Ericka had seen it on the rental car's passenger's seat.

She had brought a weapon and binoculars.

They sat next to two cellular phones.

Chapter 80

The streets were so quiet Ericka imagined she could hear her body turning on itself, feeding on itself. Sirens were in the distance, on the streets that bordered the enclosed community, but the zone of estates was as peaceful as the roads down in Palos Verdes.

Ericka went back inside Mrs. Stockwell's domain. She walked across the floors, back to the massive dining room. She put the gun on the dining room table, made it *clunk* on the glass.

Mrs. Stockwell looked up at her, broken down.

Indigo's mother had come and gone, as her husband had come and gone, only with Mrs. Abdulrahaman there had been a curt hurricane in this space. The moment the storm had ended, Mrs. Stockwell had gone back to reading the chapters written from Dr. Debra's memory. She had returned to her life, to her world, to her past. She had gone back to reading as if nothing else mattered. So many tears marred the pages.

Too many chickens had come home to roost. Too many at once.

Ericka lowered her head, ran her hands where there used to be hair, remembered when her hair was long, down her back, so pretty, and men gave her so much attention.

She went across the room, picked up Mrs. Stockwell's worn Bible.

It was the same Bible her mother had struck her with when she was a child.

She took it to the table where her mother sat in tears, her body quaking.

Mrs. Stockwell raised her eyes, cringed, waited to feel Ericka's wrath, lowered her head as if she expected some form of flagellation. Mrs.

Stockwell cried like a broken child. She cried like she had suffered from bad love, bad men, and a bad marriage, cried like she had tolerated a horrible daughter, cried like she had suffered PTSD after PTSD, and this was how she acted out when she was afraid, lonely, and swimming in pain so severe nothing written between the pages of the Bible could comfort her. This was how she medicated her misery. She regressed to being Caledonia.

Ericka asked, "So who's the tragic mullato now?"

Ericka put the Bible on the table in front of Mrs. Stockwell, tapped the cover three times, Father, Son, and Holy Spirit, then she backed away. Ericka took slow steps backward until she bumped into a wall, then turned and walked toward the front door. She made sure the lock was on, made sure no boogeymen or angry wife could enter without knocking, and she pulled the heavy door made of exotic wood and engraved glass closed behind her.

She knew that she would never see that house again.

She knew that she would never see Mrs. Stockwell again.

She was okay with that.

Ericka slipped inside her roadster.

Head throbbing, and as Mr. Nagode Allah Abdulrahaman had done, as Mrs. Chimamandanata Abdulrahaman had done not long after him, Ericka drove away.

Chapter 81

Ten minutes later Ericka Stockwell pulled up into Baldwin Hills, parked going uphill in front of Mr. Jones's cluster of town houses.

She sat outside in the desert air, in the drought. Wanting to go in. Wanting to be with him. Knowing it was time to leave this behind and move forward.

She loved Mr. Jones, but her life was complicated, and would be more complicated tomorrow. She was no longer sure if she wanted to drag anyone down that road with her again. Her birthday was next. It would be soon, but not soon enough. She didn't think she would be present for the occasion. She knew she wouldn't be. Cancer was back, and it was angry.

Her phone rang. She jumped, heart racing, scared. It was Destiny. Something was wrong. Ericka didn't know if Indigo's father had been busted, or if something had happened to one of the Blackbirds. Ericka answered the phone in a hurry, answered in a stiff tone of worry.

Even now she was more worried about her friends than she was herself.

Laughing, Destiny asked, "Ericka? Why are you not home, young lady?"

"You're drunk. I can tell. I'm on the way back. I'll come over and bring a barf bag."

"Sorry. No room in the inn at the moment. I have already notified Indigo and Kwanzaa."

"What's going on?"

"Dubois is over here getting on my nerves."

"Should I come by and cock block so the guy you despise will get the hint and leave?"

"We're just kicking it. We went dancing on Sunset, got sweaty, had fun, and now I guess we don't want the night to end, so I invited him to come in and chill so we can keep on talking."

"Thought you were not interested in him other than for public kissing and castration."

"His kisses keep coming at me like a drone attack in Northwest Pakistan. Only the bombs as kisses. His kisses *are the bomb*, Ericka. Every time I turn around he's trying to put his stupid tongue in my mouth."

"You like it."

"He's getting on my nerves. How many times is he going to kiss me in one night? At the comedy club, in the parking lot, in line at the Club, on the dance floor, before we had a drink, while we had drinks, while we rode back here in the Uber, on the stairs, in my living room."

"An Uber came to our area at night?"

"I know, right? I will have to borrow Indigo's Rubicon or the BMW to drop him off in the Uber zone."

"Where is your guest sleeping?"

"That Morehouse jerk is sleeping on the sofa. Away from my lips."

"Both pair."

"Away from all of my lips."

"Where are your lips sleeping?"

"They won't be on the sofa next to his lip kisser."

"He likes you and is not scared to let you know he likes you."

"We had so much fun. He took me out on a date like I was a normal girl."

"Destiny, once again, as I have told you countless times, you are normal."

"He's not ashamed of me. His mother knows who I am. She has no issue with me. She actually hugged me tonight, and her son's not embarrassed that I am sort of an ex-con."

"You're not an ex-con. You didn't go to the big girl's Hoosegow. It's not on your record."

"So if Dubois Junior plays it right and stops talking so much, he might get lucky and get an upgrade from the sofa to first class, but it will be a bumpy ride, a real bumpy ride."

"Two drinks, after you've had two drinks, you have no morals."

"It's calculated. If I hook up with him again, good or bad, I get this one-off off my record. And maybe he'll be better at it now that he's ten years older and has that ATL experience."

"So slutty of you to consider sleeping with him again so you don't seem like a slut."

"You smoke Kush, then sneak and get freak nasty with my dad."

"Your dad is the freak, not me. I started it, but he took it to another level."

"That's plain nasty. You and my dad together, that is almost like *Game of Thrones*–level incest."

"You're still a slut and don't ever mention incest when you refer to me and Mr. Jones."

"Incestuous person. No wonder you are a schoolteacher. All of you are perverts."

"Slutty birthday girl."

"It's my birthday. No woman is a slut on her birthday. A birthday is a slut-free day. As a matter of fact, no Blackbird can be considered a slut on any of the Blackbirds' birthdays. From now on we get *four* slut-free days a year. We need to have a meeting and make that a proclamation, and then we find cute dudes and give them keys to the titties. Get it? *Titties.* Like keys to the city. I think I will have to give Dubois a key to the titties tonight. Two keys. And one to the clittie. He might not need a key. I think the brother knows how to use his tongue to pick a lock. He might not be from ATL, but he's trying to go down south."

"Destiny Jones, you are wasted."

"Let me get my titties and clittie back to Dubois. I'm going to challenge him to strip Scrabble, and we might do the Hokey-Pokey."

"Don't forget to close the windows before you start riding his beard or fracking."

"Oh, wait. The reason I called. Condoms? Where do you keep your condoms?"

"I don't have any. Indigo has some. Look in her bottom drawer, left side, in a tea can."

"Why don't you have condoms? Don't you use condoms? Are you not protected?"

"Bye, Destiny. Stop slurring your words. Go turn your friend into your lover."

"You're gross. You'd better not give my dad the Kwanzaas."

"You are so tipsy right now. Go shower, get naked, and yield to temptation."

"I'm going to borrow your Scrabble board. You know, the one you borrowed from me about a year ago and never brought back, just like you did about twenty of my novels."

"I hope you wake up in your right mind and are able to study tomorrow."

"It's my birthday. I had an *unbelievable* birthday. I am so happy tonight."

"Yeah, you did. And yes, you are."

"See you in the morning. And not before the morning."

Ericka paused. "Destiny, let me tell you something."

"Why so serious?"

"Listen. You won't see me in the morning. So let me tell you how I feel."

"Okay."

"You are a powerful young woman. You are a fire. Fire scares many. They sent you away, deprived you of light and oxygen. They made it hard for you to breathe, to live, then disgraced you. Tonight you showed them all. You stopped buying what they had peddled to the public. You rejected their lies, their revisionist history, and you did it in their damn faces, not from behind a keyboard, not from behind a screen name. You are amazing. Stay amazing, okay?"

"Thanks, Ericka."

"You are a deep, spiritual, beautiful, intelligent woman. You are a true Blackbird."

"Are you about to ask me to marry you?"

"Stop being silly."

"You'll have to ask my father first. After you dump him, of course."

"Stop it."

"Hey, don't make me get emotional right now, okay?"

"Just remember, you don't have to have a pretty past to have a beautiful future."

"From private school to Hoosegow to USC. People know I'm not the best of people."

"But you're one of the best people I know, that's what matters to me. Listen to me. It's been a rough road, but you're a Blackbird, and you're with the guy who gave us that name. That's your kismet. He's your destiny. You went separate ways, and maybe now you're back on track."

"You're messing up the sexy mood."

"Now, books before babies, so don't forget the condom."

"Condoms."

Ericka laughed and shook her head. "Slut."

"Don't hate. I just hope it lasts longer than the first time we did it in his mom's bed."

"I hope it's not that messy."

"Blackbird out."

"Blackbird out."

They hung up and Ericka stared at the townhomes again. She knew Mr. Jones was sleeping. A coyote trotted toward Kenneth Hahn Park, someone's cat in its teeth. The cat was alive five minutes ago. Death had claimed its prize. Ericka was over thirty, but time had flown by, as if it had been only five minutes, and once again the coyote was coming after her.

Ericka called Kwanzaa, hoped she was home, available to sit up and talk, but Kwanzaa was downtown in the Arts District for the night. It was quality-time-with-the-new boyfriend night for her. Ericka left Kwanzaa a message and told her the same thing she had told Destiny, that she was wonderful, that she was remarkable. She called Indigo and left her a similar message.

Ericka smiled.

Her Blackbirds were something else.

They were all something special.

There was something about each one she wished was a part of her own DNA.

Knowing them had given her life.

She had gone from just being alive to living.

Ericka whispered, "I've had fun. I've sky-dived. I've snorkeled. I've protested. I've danced like it didn't matter. I didn't learn to drive a motorcycle, but I rode on the back of one every chance I could get. I have three friends who will bungee-cord jump without me and miss me, and when someone misses you, you will never die. I met the love of my life and had a chance to be with him. And for a while, I was sexy. No regrets. No regrets. There will be no funeral. No one will look down on me when there is nothing left worth seeing. I'll be cremated. No one gets to see me dead. Not the Blackbirds. Not my students. Not the other teachers. They will remember me alive. They won't forget me like Seneca Village."

Ericka wiped salty water away from her eyes, water that would never make flowers grow.

"I've traveled. I have BFFs. I've faced my biggest fears. I've lived alone. I'm independent. I made the first move on a man I wanted to be with. I've challenged myself. I've gotten fit."

At some point what nature gave, nature reclaimed, the coyote its proxy. Cancer was a coyote too. Cancer was nothing but nature's nasty proxy.

She whispered, "I don't want to die. I don't fucking want to die."

She turned the radio on. By the time Jim Croce had sung "Operator," her storm had passed. Ericka pulled it together and drove away, decided not to see Mr. Jones ever again.

A happy ending was determined by when a story ended. Any tale that went on too long took the risk of undoing happiness. A happy ending was all about timing. About knowing when to leave the stage.

Leave while they were applauding.

Leave them wanting more.

Leaving now would be as close to a happy ending as the journey would become.

She would go to her apartment, collect Hemingway and drive away, far away. She would drive through the night, and then see the sun come alive one more time.

Chapter 82

Ericka made it halfway home.

She was turning on Crenshaw, this night being her last, when her cellular rang.

She was about to reject the call, but she took a breath and answered, prepared for negativity, for words that would come as a fit, as an attack, almost like a recurrence of the disease that lived between them. Their silence after the hurricane had been their remission and now that period was over. They had their own cancer, and it had spread over the years, had spread while they had been birling like lumberjacks, each hoping the other fell first.

Ericka anticipated a paroxysm of anger.

But the voice on the other end of the phone was surprisingly soft and kind.

Mrs. Stockwell said, "I'm sorry. I'm sorry. I'm sorry. I'm sorry."

Ericka pulled over.

Seven letters crippled her.

Two simple words being repeated over and over made her break down. Two words. Words she had wanted to hear from her mother for decades.

Now it felt like too much, too little, too late.

Ericka said, "I'm sorry, too."

"You were a child. I was not a very competent mother."

"You did as you were taught to do."

"I should have done better."

"I'm sorry for not being the perfect daughter. I'm sorry I wasn't a better daughter."

"If only your father had been part of your life."

"I'm sorry for putting you in that position."

"What would you have done?"

"I don't know."

"I did what your father told me to do."

"I know."

"It has burned inside of me every day."

"You told Dr. Debra things I didn't know."

"These words Dr. Debra has written, these memories, they have given me so much pain."

"That is part of our truth."

"Each word hurts me to read."

"Those are but a few chapters that make up many chapters."

"I may not have always liked you, but I have always loved you."

"Have you, Mrs. Stockwell?"

"Not a day has gone by when I haven't wished things were better between us."

"I don't like you either, but I love you, too."

"You don't have to say that. I know you hate me."

"You're my mother. That is undeniable. That is inescapable. I love you. Even after tonight. I'm glad that one of us didn't end up in the grave before there was some sort of an apology from the other. I was a child. I just wanted love. I've never felt loved, until now."

"Ericka."

"The cancer is back."

"No."

Ericka smiled. "It's done a boomerang and come back. Outside of Kaiser, no one knows but us, Mrs. Stockwell. I don't know why I'm telling you of all people. But it's back. It's back and it's aggressive."

"What's the plan?"

"Like you said before, maybe this is God's plan. Fighting makes no sense. My arms are too short to box with God. He doesn't fight fair. And no matter who He fights, He always wins."

"This isn't God."

"What is this, if this is not God?"

"It's a disease."

"One that has no cure. Billions in research, for what?"

"But what is your plan? Have you started treatment?"

"No. I have not."

"Why not?"

"I can't go through this again. I made it to my happy place. I finally made it all the way to happy, and I don't want to stick around until I end up back at sad. I made it far enough."

"What does that mean? What do the doctors want to do at this point?"

"I'm not going to rot on the inside while they put gallons of poison in my body again. I don't want to be cut open, and given chemotherapy and radiation. I don't want to die that way. My life is but a short story."

"Ericka."

"Bye, Mom."

"Ericka."

"I'm glad we sort of sorted this out the best we could."

"Ericka."

"What?"

"Let me take you to breakfast tomorrow."

"To breakfast?"

"Let's go to Gladstones. We can sit and try to talk. Or not talk."

"We haven't done that in decades."

"Not since you were nine or ten."

"I liked that place when I was a child."

"Let's sit by the ocean. Let's break bread. Let's figure this out."

"It's too late for that."

"Please?"

"Why are you trying to be my mother now?"

"Please? Let me try to be something to you."

"It's too late."
"It's never too late."
"For us it is."
"Ericka—"
"Bye."

Chapter 83

Ericka pulled up to the gate of their quad and sat outside Little Lagos for an eternity. She parked by the pool. Ericka left her engine humming as she went to her apartment. Inside, she stood for a moment, and looked at material things. She went to the bedroom and picked up Hemingway. Three envelopes were on the dining room table.

One for Destiny. One for Indigo. One for Kwanzaa.

Ericka whispered, "Please don't be angry with me for being the weakest Blackbird. But I am happy now. I should leave when I am happy. Not when I am dying and unhappy. I don't want to become a burden."

She headed back outside. She didn't lock her door.

Destiny's living room window was open.

Ericka heard laughter, both male and female.

Then Destiny Jones turned off her lights. She closed her windows.

It was Destiny's birthday.

She was the only Blackbird in their nest tonight.

She had never had a man over to her apartment.

She was truly being herself. She had opened up her world.

Ericka smiled.

When she got downstairs, Olamilekan was parking outside the gate.

Shotgun in hand, Ericka went to him. He had the same face Indigo's father had had not long ago. She wondered how many men around the world would wear that same face tonight.

Ericka said, "She's not here."

"She's with Yaba."

"She's going to marry him."

"I don't want her to marry him."

"You had your chance. Now, be a gentleman and bow out. Even if she doesn't marry Yaba, set her free. You're not husband material. You're not even boyfriend material, not for a girl like her. If you love her, then respect her, and if you respect her, let her go. She is young. She is learning. She deserves better than you, and you know she deserves better than you. You have offered her nothing but confusion. You've made her angry, left her perplexed, and now there is a man who at least wants a second try at being the kind of man she deserves."

He reached into his pocket and pulled out a box. "I have a ring. I bought her a better ring than the one Yaba put on her finger tonight. Look at this. Look at this ring. It is like the ring Jay-Z gave Beyoncé."

"You bought that under duress. That blood diamond is your Hail Mary."

"I bought this for her. They opened a shop after-hours so I could buy it tonight."

"This isn't a contest, Olamilekan. This isn't a game where she's the prize. She doesn't go to the highest bidder, but to the one who loves her the best. If you love her like you say you do, set her free. If she calls you, don't answer. That is the kind of love she needs from you. That is real love. If she texts you, don't return the text. De-friend her on Facebook."

He pulled at his face.

Ericka said, "She's with Yaba. She will probably be with Yaba all night, and then maybe the rest of her life. You saw the video. She accepted the ring. She's engaged. You can move on."

"I've lost her."

"I hope you have. If she loses you, then she can find herself."

"I've lost her to Yaba."

"When you make it a game, someone has to lose."

"I had her."

"You did. The problem was she never had you. You wanted all of her to yourself while you were not willing to give her all of you. That's not love, Olamilekan. For her, that was slavery. If not slavery, with all the women you were seeing, with all your side chicks, she was on your plantation *sharecocking*. She's too good to be sharing any man's cock."

He paused. "I had the most remarkable woman God ever made."

"And now you don't have her. Indigo is a true queen. She is royalty. If you don't protect the queen, you lose the queen. Lesson learned."

Olamilekan went to his car, eased in. A moment later he took off speeding. Right away, an Inglewood cop lit up his siren and pulled him over.

Ericka went to her car, put Hemmingway in the trunk, made sure she had shotgun shells, and drove away. With her antepenultimate and pen-ultimate tasks competed, a numbness did its best to cover her as she headed toward her end, toward her ultimate destination.

Even now she was more worried about Indigo than she was herself.

Ericka didn't know that Indigo's mother had cloned her husband's second phone in order to find out about his affair with Mrs. Stockwell. She didn't know that Indigo had done the same and had cloned Ola-milekan's phone and had accessed his messages and social media.

By sunrise, as Indigo rested on a sofa in Pacific Palisades with Yaba, the engagement ring on a table and not on her finger, as too many talks needed to be had and tradition would have to be followed if those talks were indeed productive, she would take a page from Victor Cruz's fian-cée's handbook and send messages to the two hundred and forty-five women Olamilekan had on standby. By noon, Tiger Woods would look like a saint. Indigo would delete every email she had written him, would purge every text, and erase every photo of herself first. If Indigo didn't know Destiny Jones, if she wasn't sensitive to what her friend had gone through, all of the porn Olamilekan had recorded between himself and so many women, she would have made it look like it had come from Olamilekan's account and posted it all over social media.

Indigo didn't want to punish the women, only let them know who they were dealing with.

She realized that Olamilekan was a hero to many, as were many ce-lebrities, but in her life he had only been a villain. If Indigo had been drowning in her own tears, he would not have thrown her a life vest, only more lies, each heavier than a blue whale.

*   *   *

Ericka Stockwell had to focus. She needed to continue with her own mission. She would silence the disease that lived within.

With her shotgun named Hemingway, she would do like the writer Hemingway had done in his final moment.

It was time to check out.

This was the promise she had made to herself.

She would leave when she was ready, not when cancer was done playing with her.

In life she had suffered enough.

No more.

The civil war inside her body, she knew that it would be too much.

It would be too much for the body.

Too much for the mind.

She would drive east on the 10 freeway, meet the sun in Arizona, and dare that ball of fire. Then she would load the shotgun and have breakfast with Hemingway. More like have Hemingway for breakfast.

She cried.

She pulled over to the side of the freeway and rubbed her hands over her head.

She had friends.

She had a man whom she loved.

Ericka turned back around, drove past homeless encampments that sprung up each night, paused as fire trucks and emergency vehicles zoomed by, then drove the speed limit with helicopters flying overhead, drove as misogynistic and misandrist music laced with creative rhymes and uncreative profanity bumped in cars all around her.

Tonight it all sounded beautiful. The world she lived in was so alive.

She drove her emotions through danger zone after danger zone, went back to Baldwin Hills, parked exactly where she had stopped before, then picked up her phone and stared at it for several minutes before she blew her nose, wiped away tears, and dialed a number stored as "Beel-Zebub."

Mrs. Stockwell answered on the first ring. "Miss Stockwell?"

"Mrs. Stockwell. I'll go to Gladstone's with you."

"We need to try to see if we can get beyond the damage that has been done."

"But not tomorrow. It's too soon. After what you did tonight, it's too soon."

"When?"

"Next week. Or the week after. Let's see where I am, both physically and mentally."

"Okay."

"Keep away from that man. His wife will kill you, and not because of him, but because of the kind of person you have become. She has seen that. You can't pray yourself out of everything. You smiled in her face and had her husband in your bed. She will kill you."

"Okay."

"I saved your life tonight. Which is ironic. There is a lot of irony in there. But I did."

"And I thank you. I mean that."

"You need Jesus."

"Pray for me, Miss Stockwell. Please, pray for me."

"Sure. Pray for me Mrs. Stockwell, and I'll pray for you."

Ericka hung up.

Chapter 84

Ericka jogged toward Mr. Jones's condo, punched in the code to the gate, then dug her heart-shaped key ring from her purse, a key ring with one key, and used that key to get in the front door. She turned the alarm off, then reset it to alert them if a door or window opened.

She called out, "Mr. Jones?"

There was no answer.

She went to the kitchen, saw dirty dishes, shook her head, rinsed those off, and put those and the dirty plates in the dishwasher. She wiped off the counter, then saw pages on the table by the sofa. Mr. Jones had printed out the twenty-four hottest restaurants in L.A. Cassia. Esters Wine Shop and Bar. Dudely Market. Belcampo Meat Company. Hopdoddy Burger Bar.

He left Ericka a note:

We should go eat at all of these places.

He had made plans for them. He wanted her around in the future.

She had been so preoccupied she had failed to notice something else. There was an African-American themed envelope and a single red rose. Ericka saw her name scribbled on the envelope. She opened it. Inside was a beautiful card. An African American man and woman caressing. She smiled at the image a moment and then opened the card.

Miss Stockwell,

I love you.

I want the world to know I love you.

Don't say anything back.

Let the universe absorb that which I feel for you.

I love you. I love you. I love you.

Mr. Jones

She put her left hand over her mouth.

Again there were tears.

She had almost missed this. She felt so stupid.

She whispered, "Fuck you, cancer. Fucking fuck you."

She headed downstairs. Ericka undressed, reached in her drawer, and pulled out a plain black T-shirt. She went to the bathroom, showered again with her soaps, dried off with her beautiful red towel, put on lotion, gargled with her mouthwash, used the dental floss they shared, then brushed her teeth with her electric toothbrush.

Ericka eased in bed with her lover, her man, with Mr. Jones, crawled in on her side of the bed, the side of the bed away from the door, eased under the covers and relaxed into the queen-size nest where she felt safe.

She gave Mr. Jones baby kisses, awakened him with soft laughs and softer words.

She rubbed his chrome dome.

He pulled her close, kissed her head a dozen times, gave her forehead kisses and told her how much he adored her. They kissed like lovers. From the start, she had always kissed him like each kiss could be the last. She made love to him each time the same way.

He asked, "Why are you crying?"

"Because I'm happy."

"You see your card?"

"It's amazing."

"It reminded me of us."

"What you wrote . . . that was beautiful."

"Wanted to say that since before Vegas."

"The rose is beautiful."

"Are you okay?"

"I'm happy and I don't want to stop being happy."

Soon she pulled off her T-shirt and he pulled off his T-shirt and boxers. She spooned against him. Skin to skin. Her love for him was strong.

He said, "Your birthday is next."

"Yeah. My birthday is next."

"What do you want to do for your birthday?"

Her love for him was worth living for. She wasn't done yet. She wasn't done loving. She wasn't done fighting. She wasn't done winning. She wasn't ready to fade away. She wasn't ready to let this universe go.

Too many people needed her.

A classroom of sixth graders needed her.

And God knew that Indigo, Kwanzaa, and Destiny needed her.

Her mother needed her. Her mother had always needed her.

Mr. Jones needed someone to take care of him.

She had to be here for him. She knew he would be here for her.

No matter how bad, she knew he would be there.

The tears wouldn't stop.

She had to sit up.

Mr. Jones sat up too.

He held her, rubbed her head, and kissed her.

"I love you."

"I love you, too."

She felt his kisses absorb her angst, fear, and pain.

This was love. This was real love.

Again he asked, "What do you want to do for your birthday?"

She smiled. "I want to live."

ERICKA'S BIRTHDAY

For Ericka

"She knew she loved him when 'home' went from being a place to a person."

—E. Leventhal

For Destiny

"I saw that you were perfect and so I loved you. Then I saw that you were not perfect and I loved you even more."

—Unknown

For Indigo

"And then my soul saw you and it kind of went 'Oh, there you are. I've been looking for you.'"

—Iain Thomas

For Kwanzaa

"I can't remember what it was like before you, and I don't even know how we got here but maybe that's exactly what I needed. Someone who could make me forget where I came from and someone who could make me love without knowing how to fall."

—R. M. Drake

For the Blackbirds

"Girls will be your friends—they'll act like it, anyway. But just remember, some come, some go. The ones that stay with you through everything—they're your true best friends. Don't let go of them."

—Marilyn Monroe

ACKNOWLEDGMENTS

Whassup everybody!

Peace and blessings from Los Angeles.

Before I ramble on and thank all the supercalifragalistic people who have helped me on this expialidocious literary journey, I have to remind you, oh ye faithful reader, if you don't already know, that Ericka, Destiny, and Kwanzaa have been part of the Dickey-verse for a while. I'm sure the hardcore readers will probably kinda-sorta remember Kwanzaa Browne as a little bitty baby and the center of conflict in *Liar's Game*, Ericka Stockwell as a terrified teen in *Friends and Lovers*, and Destiny Jones holding it down in *Chasing Destiny*. They have grown up and now are living on the other side of innocence. And by the way, mannish Hakeem Mitchell was around for a bit in *Cheaters*, doing his best to steal Chante Marie Ellis from his uncle and get her to ride on his Big Wheel. Eddie is the son of Bryce from *Friends & Lovers* and well. At least I think he is.

LOL.

The novel actually was given the name *Blackbirds* because my wonderful editor asked me the title of what I was working on, and "Blackbird" happened to be the song I was listening to at the moment. Well, I was at the end of the movie *Beyond the Lights*, and Gugu Mbatha-Raw was singing the Nina Simone tune and it stayed with me. It really worked out, listening to the song, and getting a feel for who I wanted the four women in this novel to be as a group, as friends, as sisters, then coming up with the moment they were given that marvelous name. I have to say, so far as Ericka, Destiny, Kwanzaa, and Indigo, I guess you can say this is a sequel that really isn't a sequel, because it can mos def be read as a stand-alone novel.

A few notes to the readers. Dr. Debra's memoirs were actually written circa 1995, so they are very accurate. There were mentions of pagers and using public phones in the original. Might have been a dinosaur sighting or two. LOL. Technology has changed, slang has changed, but the affairs of the heart remain the same. The Bible and the blues bemoan the same issues. Dr. Debra's personal segments were intended to be a part of the novel *Friends and Lovers*, as normal chapters, but Ericka's part and involvement was cut to keep the novel focused on Debra and Leonard. Hmm. Well, I guess you could say Leonard Jr. was in that novel as well.

Writers: Save everything. You never know when you'll find a chance to use it.

A few other things, besides ages, have been massaged to make the story work.

And, nah, I'm not telling what I had to do to make it do what it do.

I won't call out what had to be changed, or whose backstory had to be massaged a bit, but hopefully it wasn't enough to make the reader not suspend disbelief, only appreciate what we are able to do in a fictional universe. This is where I go to have fun and play What if?

To my homie, Kayode Disu, chillin' across the pond with the beans and toast eaters and waving at the queen, thanks for allowing me to pick your brain in order to create Indigo. I know only a true Nigerian can create an authentic Nigerian character, because you know the culture inside out the way I know both the south and east sides of Memphis, and I'm on the outside of your amazing culture looking in, however I hope I did an okay job bringing Indigo's world to life. You get the credit for all I did right, all I said correctly, all I spelled correctly, and I'll take the blame for any faux pas, for anything I misinterpreted or didn't fully understand. I think this is the third Nigerian character I've created. Time to get to Lagos! Yemi! Tiwa! I'm on the way! Start sangin'!

Hola to my fantabulous agent, Sara Camilli! Well, this time we've put out three novels in twelve months. Pretty cool! At this rate I'll make it to book 100 before I'm eligible to join AARP. LOL. Since before '96, you've been in my corner. Thanks for giving the kid from Kansas Street in the 901 a chance to have fun and create a few interesting stories and characters here and there.

I wonder what the character count is thus far? From Valerie to Indigo . . . how many?

Someone should also do a degrees-of-separation chart for the characters.

At this point I think most could show up at the same picnic. But if Gideon walks in, everybody better run! Well, everyone except Reaper.

Special thanks and much love to all the wonderful people back in NYC on Hudson Street!

To my amazing editor, Stephanie J. Kelly. It was great working with you on this project. Thanks for the hard work. Sorry I made you cry. ☹

Hopefully there were a few LOL moments in the mix as well.

Emily N. Brock and everyone in publicity at Dutton/Random House, thanks for being such a wonderful team. You and the crew make it happen. Hugs, kudos, and blessings to all.

And thanks to my amazing copyeditor (Mikayla Butchart). Thanks for helping me make this tale flow from the rooter to the tooter.

And to my wonderful readers, those who have been around since the start and those who have grown up with Ericka, Destiny, and Kwanzaa and have come along for the ride, thanks for the love both in the stores and on social media. Thanks for the mentions and the posts; thanks for the tweets and retweets. As I said before, thanks for posting photos of the novels as you work and play all over the world. It's really inspiring to see my work travel to other parts of the world. Now, if I can only get NASA to fly one of my novels up into space . . . that would be a photo and a half . . . Earth in the background. Hmm . . . Paging NASA.

To the Planer Group (Karl Planer and Tammee) thanks for helping this distracted writer keep his life and house in order. You rock!

In case I had tunnel vision and was distracted as I recover from having my deviated septum corrected (Oh, the pain! Even my pain has pain.), if I forgot to mention ye, trust me, it wasn't intentional. No need to flip out and lose the plot as my face throbs like it was closed in a steel door. This upcoming section is just for you and only for you. Hear ye! Hear ye!

I want to thank _____ for all s/he did/thought about doing/wanted to do in order to help a brother out while he was working day and night on creating/writing/editing/ rewriting the astounding women now known as the Blackbirds. Your help was the help of all help, and I can't help saying that.

Peace, love, and November 7, 2015, smiles from a lifetime member of A Phi A.

Yeah, I do need some ice, ice, baby.

Soon I will be able to breathe again.

☺

Latitude 33° 59' 56" N

Longitude 118° 20' 33" W

8:51 P.M. 62 degrees Fahrenheit

Gray T-shirt, blue sweat pants (University of Memphis colors!)

Okay. Time to pop a pain pill or two, then bedtime for Bonzo. Deuces!

Eric Jerome Dickey

www.ericjeromedickey.com

Follow me on Twitter @EricJDickey

When writing a novel, there are only three difficult parts: the beginning, the middle, and the ending.

ERIC JEROME DICKEY is the *New York Times* bestselling author of twenty-four novels, and is also the author of a six-issue miniseries of graphic novels for Marvel Enterprises, featuring Storm (X-Men) and the Black Panther. He also penned the original story for the film *Cappuccino* directed by Craig Ross Jr. Originally from Memphis, Tennessee, Dickey is a graduate of the University of Memphis, where he pledged Alpha Phi Alpha, and also attended UCLA. Dickey now lives on the road and rests in whatever hotel will have him.